About t.

AJ Waines is a number one international bestselling author on Kindle. She has sold over 400,000 books worldwide and topped the UK and Australian Kindle Charts two years' running with ***Girl on a Train.***

The author was a psychotherapist for fifteen years, during which time she worked with ex-offenders from high-security institutions, gaining a rare insight into abnormal psychology. She is now a full-time novelist with publishing deals in France, Germany, Norway, Hungary and USA (audiobooks).

Her fourth novel, ***No Longer Safe***, sold over 30,000 copies in the first month, in twelve countries worldwide. In 2016 and 2017, the author was ranked in the Top 10 UK Authors on Amazon KDP (Kindle Direct Publishing). AJ Waines lives in Hampshire, UK, with her husband.

Find out more at **www.ajwaines.co.uk** or follow her Blog at **www.awaines.blogspot.co.uk.** She's also on Twitter (@AJWaines), Facebook (AJWaines) and you can sign up for her Newsletter at: **http://eepurl.com/bamGuL**

Also by AJ Waines

The Evil Beneath
Girl on a Train
Dark Place to Hide
No Longer Safe
Inside the Whispers (Dr Samantha Willerby Series - Book 1)

Writing as Alison Waines

The Self-Esteem Journal
Making Relationships Work

Lost in the Lake

(Dr Samantha Willerby Series - Book 2)

A J WAINES

Lost in the Lake
A Novel

Copyright © 2017 AJ Waines.

The moral right of the author has been asserted.
All characters and events in this publication are
fictitious and any resemblance to real persons,
living or dead, is purely coincidental.
All Rights Reserved.

No part of this publication may be reproduced,
stored in a retrieval system, or transmitted, in any form
or by any means, without the prior permission
in writing of the author.

ISBN-13: 978-1543163988
ISBN-10: 154316398X

Find out more about the author and her other
books at **www.ajwaines.co.uk**

In memory of Tigsey,
my treasured companion, who was
by my side throughout the writing of this book
(1996-2017)

Prologue

Did I make you jump? Turning up like that in your own kitchen? You have to admit, it must have been a nasty shock.

I bet you thought you'd been ever so smart at covering your tracks. But, be honest, you made a complete hash of things. You made out you were one step ahead of the game all along, but once you scooped the ultimate prize you couldn't work out what to do next! Face facts, you were too ambitious for your own good and hadn't thought things through properly.

You took great delight in explaining your cunning scheme to me, even though it was bound to leave you with egg on your face. I could see you thought you'd have the last laugh. I could tell your little brain was ticking over, thinking that once you'd told me the whole story, there was no way I'd be walking out of there. But that's where you went wrong. You underestimated me. Most people do.

I could feel rage burning up my insides as you brandished that bottle of whisky like we were mates – in it together.

'Let's toast our windfall', you suggested, trying to make me smile. By then, however, my fury with what you'd done had ignited from a niggling spark into a white-hot ball of fire. Every moment I was forced to endure with you, a growing, uncontainable frenzy was building inside me.

You reached over to the draining board to find two glasses and that's when you made your fatal mistake.

You should never have turned your back.

Chapter 1

Sam

October – Four months earlier

'I was early,' she said, as I invited her inside my consulting room. 'But you know that already, don't you? You've been watching me.'

Her directness took me by surprise, but I didn't let my welcoming smile falter.

She eased past me and helped herself to the wrong seat, the one I always use that's closer to the door with a clear view of the clock. 'I've been observing people coming and going,' she went on without a beat. 'Humans are weird, don't you think?' she laughed. 'But then, you know *that* too. That's what you're interested in, isn't it?'

Rosie Chandler had barely been in the room ten seconds and already I felt like she'd spun me around. I casually pulled up the other chair, outwardly cool and unruffled. Working within the field of psychotherapy is strange; you have to be a blank screen and usher all your own feelings out of the way.

Rosie was right; I had spotted her, nearly two hours earlier. As a psychologist well practised in interpreting behaviour, I should have read the signs there and then. A young woman *not* clutching a mobile phone and with nothing better to do than sit alone amid a bank of plastic hospital chairs. It was out of the ordinary, to say the least, and I should have recognised the implications.

I took a breath ready to launch into my usual introductions, but she beat me to it.

'I knew it was a mistake,' she continued. 'None of us wanted to be there. Shall I just tell you about it?'

I'd been caught in the starting blocks.

'Yes, go on.' I reached for my notebook. She was here to tell me her story. The formalities could wait until later.

'It happened two weeks ago. I was in the back of the van, not far from Penrith in the Lake District; we were on our way to the B&B after our final rehearsal. I was looking at the curve of the road behind us as it cut into the hillside. Stephanie and Max were in the front with Richard. He was driving. The man with the van. Everyone likes a man with a van, don't they?'

Her words came tumbling out with tiny snatches of air between each sentence. Then she stopped.

'You were in the van…' I nudged.

Her cheeks flushed a little. 'Oh, right. Yeah. It was pretty clapped out; one of those small delivery vans with seats only at the front. One of the windows at the back was missing. I didn't know it then, but…well, that botched-up piece of cardboard saved my life.'

There was an unfortunate whine in her voice and she stared into the far distance with a puckered brow, as though struggling to see something.

'I'm not even sure why I ended up in the back…'

It sounded, although straws weren't mentioned, like

she was used to being the one who drew the short one.

'Do you believe in fate?' she said, staring straight at me as if she genuinely wanted to know.

'That's a big question,' I said. 'Can we come back to it later? Why don't you tell me more about what happened, first?'

'Sure,' she said cheerily.

I'm meant to be a sounding board, a flawless mirror so patients have space to explore how they genuinely feel, without interruption, opinion or judgement. The job suits introverts like me. I'm naturally private and it's second nature to me not to give anything away, but I know the downside is I can seem detached. Lacking in personality even. So much so, that most of my patients wouldn't recognise me if they saw me 'off duty'. A male patient once spotted me shaking full-blown shimmies on the dancefloor in a bar and turned away in horror. I worried for days that it might have undermined all our work together, but I'm only human. In reality, I love gossip, filthy jokes, too much champagne and wearing off-the-shoulder dresses with stilettos. Just not between nine and five.

Rosie drew her knees together.

'The road was windy and I was getting thrown about in the back without a seatbelt,' she went on. 'Did I say Richard was driving? He was going far too fast. Showing off and trying to shake us all up…'

Again, she seemed to float off into a daydream.

She had dense but patchy freckles on her face that gave her the look of an unfinished pointillist painting. She tugged at a loose ginger curl trapped under the arm of her clunky specs and as she let it go, it sprang back into a tight coil. Her hair was busy like that all over. An unkind person might have said it was the most interesting thing about her appearance.

'The van...' I said.

'Oh, yeah...the engine was revving like we were on a racetrack and Max was yelling at him to slow down. Richard tugged the wheel to take the next bend and that's when it happened. All of a sudden the view from the back shifted completely. The road disappeared and it felt like we were flying. My stomach was sucked up inside me; that lurching feeling, you know, when you go down too fast in a lift?'

She pressed her knuckles into her mouth. Her twitchy mannerisms and trilling voice reminded me of a teenager. I had to check my notes again; was she really in her mid-thirties?

'We were diving, dropping...branches and foliage scraping the paintwork. Instinct told me to duck down, wrap my head in my arms and squeeze my eyes shut. Then, with a smack, we hit something, but it wasn't the landing I was expecting. I was waiting for a metallic, bone-rattling jolt, but it was more of a dull thud like an egg dropping into flour.'

I was disconcerted. Lots of patients describe a traumatic experience in a deadpan tone, skimming over the details, as if it had happened to someone else. It's a common defence mechanism. But Rosie was the opposite. She was embellishing her 'story' as if she'd been asked to engage a bunch of school kids at morning assembly. I made a mental note to address it if our sessions continued.

'The cold made me yelp and the sounds went hollow and boomy,' she went on. 'The light was kind of silvery, then too dark. The shapes were so blurred I couldn't recognise anything anymore. There was a roaring sound, pressure on my eardrums and I couldn't work out which way was up. I lost my glasses.'

Her sultana-brown eyes glistened behind the thick lenses; alert and intense.

'Everything happened in slow motion. There was a heavy clunk and that's when we hit the bottom of the lake. I yanked at the back door handle, almost wrenched it off, but it wouldn't budge. Then I remembered the sheet of cardboard and kicked at it in a frenzy with both feet.'

Rosie suddenly looked up as if to check I was still there.

'More water gushed in and the van filled up faster and faster. In seconds I was right under. I thought I was going to die.' She tugged her lip. 'What I did next was stupid, I know, but it was pure instinct. Instead of getting straight out through the back window, I felt around and grabbed my viola. Can you imagine? What was I thinking?'

Her knees had been jiggling up and down the entire time.

'Then, somehow, I was through the broken window and out. I kicked frantically against the water, but it took forever to reach the light. Eventually, I broke the surface, gasping for dear life, the viola case floating beside me.'

She was silent for a while, breathing hard, still inside the memory of it.

'The first thing I noticed was how quiet and still everything was. It was like bursting out of a bubble of chaos into bliss. Like suddenly finding I'd gone to heaven. Then I realised there was no one else up there on the surface with me. It was the first time I'd properly considered the others. For a second I wondered about diving back down, but I didn't have enough energy left. I'm a pretty good swimmer, but not *that* good. I knew I'd die trying. Besides, my glasses had gone and everything was fuzzy. I couldn't tell one shape from another.'

Her eyebrows dipped towards each other and she dropped her gaze. 'I felt this terrible pain trying to rip open my chest, so I rolled onto my back and just floated. For a while I just let the water lap around me. I remember thinking the sky was perfect, like a thin skin of forget-me-not blue wrapped around the earth. I heard a bird squawk, clear and close by, and I knew then that I was going to be okay.'

She reached forward and gulped down a sip of water, then looked up and gave a small smile.

I pressed my hand against my chest. I wanted to stand up, walk around, take deep breaths, but I didn't want to look shaken. At this stage in our encounter it was better for me to stay in tune with Rosie's emotional response, not distract her by bringing my own reaction into the equation. Nevertheless, I needed a moment to pull myself together; I felt like I'd been down there, drowning in the lake beside her.

'I managed to get to the bank with my viola,' she said, her voice slow and barely audible. 'I was dizzy, shivering with the cold; I didn't know a body could shake so violently. It's all a bit hazy after that.'

'You must have been terrified…' My voice came out in a scratchy whisper.

'You know what? I was on autopilot when it happened. There was no time to feel anything. I was too busy fighting to stay alive.'

I nodded, not taking my eyes off her.

'You only get scared afterwards, don't you?' she said. 'When you think about what actually happened…about what it meant…about the others…'

Rosie's incomplete medical notes stated that she'd spent two days drifting in and out of consciousness in a Carlisle Hospital, before being discharged. Ultimately, she'd escaped very lightly and returned to London with only bruises, scrapes and minor respiratory problems. The extent of the psychological damage, however, remained to be seen.

'We can talk about the full impact of it when you're ready.'

'Does that mean I can come back?'

'If you think it could be helpful. The NHS will let you have six sessions, then we'll see if you need more.'

A wave of triumph seemed to envelop her and I invited her to give me more background details. She told me more about the quartet, how they'd originally got together at college fifteen years earlier.

'I was in my second year,' she told me. 'It was college policy for tutors to select players to form chamber ensembles, based on performance level and personality. To start with, I wasn't picked for anything. Then the viola player in Max's quartet dropped out and they needed someone to fill the place.' She shrugged. 'I think I was the only viola player left without a group, so they asked me.'

Before long our time was up.

'Everyone said it was one of those things,' she said as she got to her feet. 'The police put it down to a combination of driver error – the sun in Richard's eyes, driving too fast round the bend, brakes not as sharp as they should have been – and bad luck. But I know that's not how it was. That's why I'm here, really.'

'Sorry?'

'What I mean is, I don't need any support, you know, to deal with what I went through.'

'You're not here for psychotherapy?'

'Oh, no, absolutely not.'

'Psychotherapy can help you deal with the trauma, Rosie; the shock, the complex and often contradictory feelings people have after a—'

She cut me off. 'Oh, no, I'm not in a bad way or anything like that. I'm fine – you know, *emotionally*. I just need to *remember*.'

I didn't quite understand. She'd been to hell and back, but seemed to be dismissing the experience out of hand.

'So, it's your memory you're concerned about?'

'Yeah, that's why I'm here. There are so many gaps.' She took hold of the door handle, ready to leave. 'The thing is, I knew as soon as it happened…'

She turned to go.

I stood up, took a hasty step after her. 'You knew what, Rosie?'

'Oh. That it wasn't an accident. I know that for definite. Someone *meant* it to happen.'

Chapter 2

Rosie

I think it's going to be all right.

Her name sounds very grand: Dr Samantha Willerby, and I was expecting someone older, so that was a pleasant surprise. She's pretty too, with glossy hair that's nearly black and swings like a hairspray ad when she turns her head. She looks like a character from the cover of a Mills & Boon novel.

I asked if I could call her Sam and she looked a bit taken aback. She said most patients call her Dr Willerby, but that I could use whatever I felt comfortable with. Nice touch, I thought – letting me decide. I prefer 'Sam'; it makes our relationship less formal.

So here I am, sitting on the wall outside the staff entrance to the hospital. London Bridge is easy to get to in my lunch break from work and my GP says St Luke's has a good reputation. Besides, the place I go to is called a 'Mental Health Unit', which sounds so much better than 'Psychiatric Department'. I don't like labels; people get pigeonholed and then spend their whole lives being treated like nutters.

If I spot Sam popping out for her lunch I'll give her a wave. See how she responds. It would be nice to see what she's like outside her office; see how she acts when she's not being all professional and aloof. I imagine her to be the kind of person who would wave back and even come over to join me to share a bag of nuts or sweets; she looks like a Turkish Delight kind of girl to me.

The office smelt of geranium oil. I like touches like that. There were freesias in a swirly pink vase on the desk, too. Quite homely. No photos, though. Shame. I like it when people have their family in frames beside the computer; it makes them seem more real somehow, like they belong somewhere.

Sam's an expert in memory recovery as well as stress and stuff. I admit I did lay it on thick with my GP about how badly the crash had affected me. I gave him a clip from the newspaper so he could see my name in black and white. In the past, doctors have had the nerve to question what I've said – bloody cheek. That gruesome shot of the van being dragged out of the lake obviously helped though, because I got an appointment here really quickly. It usually takes months on the NHS.

I felt cagey talking to Sam at first – she's quite posh – and I don't like having to see her at the hospital. It's too clinical. She asked if she could record us next time. Therapists tend to do that and it really annoys me. I hate the idea of someone else listening in on our conversation. I agreed though. I don't want to get on the wrong side of her, although I'll need to be super careful I don't slip up and say something I shouldn't.

She asked me if I'd ever thought about suicide and I put on my shocked face that said, *Fancy asking an awful question like that?* – like no one had ever asked me it before. They have, of course, and needless to say, I lied this time. I was scared she might pass me on to a psychiatrist if she knew the truth. I just need to get to the bottom of the crash, that's all; piece all the memories together in my head. I had to tell her I've had therapy on and off since I was about sixteen, though – she'd find that out from my medical records anyway.

'I haven't seen anyone for six months,' I said. I didn't want to put her off, make her think I had too much 'baggage'.

I saw her write a note on her pad at that point. I know if something I've said is important because up goes the pen and down go her eyes for a second or two.

I hope she's as good as she looks. My memories are like strands of a broken spider's web; tiny wisps that itch just out of reach ever since that wreck of a van went off the road. I want them all back, in the right order, because just now nothing makes sense. I made it clear I didn't want proper therapy. I don't want to go into all the stomach-churning stuff. I just want to remember.

'I know from the police that Max, Stephanie and Richard are still missing,' I told her, 'and that one of Stephanie's shoes and her coat were found floating in the lake. I expect other belongings will turn up too, over time. Our purses and wallets have all gone, which is odd, don't you think? Shouldn't they have been floating in the water too?'

She didn't say anything – actually, she looked a bit ruffled. I reckon she's used to being the one who asks all the questions.

'But you rescued your viola?' she'd said eventually, leaning forward, her pen resting on her chin.

'Ah – no. I got it out of the van, but I must have

passed out on the bank once I climbed out of the water. When I came round my viola had gone. I don't know if it floated away. Maybe it got trapped in the reeds somewhere along the bank. Do you think it'll turn up?'

She opened her eyes wide like she didn't know what to say. It makes me think she's someone who likes being in control the whole time. I carried on. 'Whatever happened, it looks like none of the others will be needing their instruments anymore.'

Sam looked a bit shocked at that point and I wished I hadn't said that, at first. I don't want her to think I'm heartless, but I do need to show her I'm not going to get all drippy over what happened. They weren't my friends, after all. We played a few concerts back at college, but I never really knew them.

'The police said that dead bodies usually sink first, then reappear again a few days later,' I went on. 'Especially if the water is cold – which it was, being October. They said there are lots of reasons why some bodies don't ever surface at all; they get snagged underwater in the weed and old branches or come up during the night and don't get spotted, so they sink again. Something to do with the gases in the belly, I think.'

Sam – I like her name – it's kind of cute and tomboyish, squirmed when I said that. I was glad. That means she's sensitive and she's paying attention – not just going through the motions.

'As it stands, it looks like I'm the only one who's survived. You'd think they'd send divers down to scour the whole lake, wouldn't you? But Ullswater gets deep close to the edge and goes down to over sixty metres in places, so the police have only searched near the van. They said Donald Campbell – that guy who set world water-speed records – wasn't found in Coniston Water until over thirty years after his terrible crash. If they couldn't find him in a smaller lake, they won't find…the others, will they?'

I trailed off then. Something rubbery was stuck in my throat. Suddenly it felt weird that I might be the only one who'd made it, but I didn't want us to get sidetracked with how I was feeling. All I want are my memories back.

Sam waited – I respected her for that, she didn't press me.

'We all hated the idea of doing the concert,' I told her. 'Max in particular. He was a total pain. He kept going on about "having to play with crappy amateurs."'

'You didn't like him?' she said.

'I had a bit of a crush on him when we first met at music college – crikey, when was that? Sixteen years ago now, but nothing happened. I'm not the sort he'd take any notice of. I did an online search for everyone when we first talked about re-forming, but Max was the only one who'd come to anything. He took distinct pleasure in rubbing that in. I hadn't seen him since we graduated.'

'And Mr Hinds organised the concert?'

Sam didn't need to look down at her notes for that; she must have remembered his name from the start of the session. I had to hide a smile, but that gets a gold star from me – she's certainly listening. 'Yeah. He'd booked another group, apparently, but they'd cancelled and as we'd done a performance for him at his tenth wedding anniversary, he thought it was worth seeing if we could all come back for his twenty-fifth. I was going to say no, but, thing is – Mr Hinds was offering a cracking good fee for it.'

I stopped and listened to the sound Sam's nail made on her tights as she scratched her ankle. Her legs are slim and you can see shapely grooves alongside her calves, like she works out. I could tell she was going to ask about the others so I saved her the trouble.

'Richard was down on his luck,' I told her. 'Doing odd jobs by the sound of it – hence the crappy van. He'd given up playing professionally ages ago, but like me, he needed the money. I don't know about Stephanie; she was really quiet the whole time. I hardly had a chance to talk to her before…'

'Go on…'

I knew what Sam was doing; she must have heard something catch in my throat again. This time she was trying to find my breaking point; the furthest I could go before it all became too much for me, but I was determined not to go there.

I stuck to the facts. 'Max never let his violin out of his sight. It was a Guarneri – you heard the name before? It's a world-famous make of violin from Cremona in Italy. Richard asked about it, but you could tell he was only being polite – I'd switched off by then. It wasn't just me who didn't like Max. None of us did. He was a real big-head. Always was.'

'How did you get to the Lakes?' she asked.

'Richard offered to drive Stephanie and me up from

London the day before. Stephanie didn't say much the whole time, she just stared out of the window, but me and Richard kept talking about how scared we were at the thought of performing in public again. We talked about how Max had always got on our nerves at college and wondered what he'd be like now. I remember Richard saying, "He'll be insufferable," and he was right.

'We had two rehearsals at the Hinds' mansion on the day of the concert and things went from bad to worse. Max was tetchy. Said we were all wasting his time. I have to admit we were pretty rubbish. Stephanie hadn't played her cello in ages and her strings kept slipping out of tune and Richard's E string snapped.'

Sam took a quick look at her watch at that point, slyly, like she didn't want me to see. They're always so fussy about time these shrinks – can't they just let you finish what you have to say without worrying about squashing everything into that measly fifty minutes?

That's when I realised I was sitting in her chair, because I could see the clock inside the bookcase and she couldn't. I wanted to giggle; I'd stolen her special space in the room and she hadn't said a thing, but I didn't want to have to explain myself so I carried on.

'When we finished the afternoon rehearsal, Richard decided to take the scenic route back to our B&B to have a rest before the performance. Max complained. He was staying in a different place to us and wanted to go a more direct route. "You need to see real life for a change," Richard told him.'

'So, it was Richard who suggested you go that way – beside the lake?' Sam asked.

'Yes – I suppose it was.'

She nodded and made a note. She's sharp. I'm not going to get anything past her. I'm pleased she's on the ball. I've had some pretty dim therapists in the past. Sometimes all they seem to do is repeat exactly what you've just said, as though you haven't heard yourself say it, or something. I mean, what use is that?

When Sam said it was the end of the session, I gasped. The time had flown by. I couldn't believe it; I had to check the clock again. But I left on a high. Sam had passed the initial test as far as I was concerned and she didn't sneak in the dreaded question, *How do you feel about that?* once. That's another reason I'm going back.

I slide off the wall and make a decision. This evening, I'm going to browse a few online fashion sites and get a new outfit for our next session. Time will tell, I know, but we've made a good start. I feel like Sam could be on my wavelength. Although, of course, even if it all goes swimmingly, I won't be telling her *everything*.

Chapter 3

Sam

Hannah was waiting for me at the bar. She tapped her watch as I dropped my bag at her feet.

'Doing overtime, Willerby?'

'Sorry. My last patient was late and I didn't want to cut the session short.'

She linked her arm through mine and rested her head on my shoulder. 'So diligent...' she said.

Hannah and I had met at university, although I'd gone on to pursue clinical psychology while she'd qualified as a psychotherapist. She was my best friend, my favourite cheerleader and my own personal therapist rolled into one. Sadly, though, she wasn't always around. She hated the routine of the five-day working week and found any excuse to travel. Her latest trip had taken her to Iceland – she'd seen a documentary and wanted to experience the Northern Lights for herself.

'Usual G&T?' she said, holding out her purse. I stuck out my dry tongue by way of a reply.

Hannah ran her own private practice in Harley Street, so she could take breaks whenever she felt like it. She earned packets more than me, but it had never been an issue between us. We both offered psychotherapy – just using different models – and I preferred the community feel of an NHS hospital and the fact that I got to support patients who hadn't the money to pay. Hannah was smarter than all the therapists I knew put together, which was very handy for me when I needed a second opinion. In that respect her generosity was unflagging; in my view, she deserved to indulge her wanderlust.

'How's life at St Luke's?' she asked. 'Got any new amnesia patients now you've added memory retrieval to the mix?'

She handed me my glass and we found a table on the mezzanine overlooking the boats at St Katharine Docks. An air balloon advertising an oil company hovered dangerously close to one of the masts, before drifting off out of sight.

'It's still mostly PTSD, but it's refreshing to have more tools to help patients with memory issues.'

Hannah ran her finger along the hem of her ruched purple dress. On me it would have looked like a giant toffee-wrapper, but she had the height to carry it. 'And it's just memory loss associated with trauma – not dementia or Alzheimer's?'

'Oh no,' I flapped my hand, 'just trauma related. I couldn't bear to work on the degenerative side of things. Too depressing.'

She nodded. 'Absolutely. Digging up memories can be tough, though.'

I squashed the lemon against the side of my glass with the plastic stirrer. 'Yeah, I'm not looking forward to dealing with torture or abuse, but you know me…' I cocked an eyebrow, 'I like helping people find the missing pieces, love discovering a way to unlock their subconscious, so they can…' I trailed off. We were meant to be switching off from work and letting our hair down, but this happened every time. We were both passionate about psychology and found never-ending fascination with the subject. Although, to be fair, I was probably more obsessed than she was.

'I don't know how you do it, Sammie.' She rested her hand on my arm. Her coral lipstick was halfway between the colour of her freckles and her loose coppery hair. Sitting next to her either made me feel like I belonged to an exclusive club or that I needed to get my act together, depending on how buoyant I felt. Today it was the latter.

'I'm sticking with the "worried well" for now,' she added. 'Mostly existential issues at Harley Street this week; the meaning of life, identity, status, striving for success…' She drew the back of her hand across her brow in a demonstration of mock exhaustion. 'Oh, so demanding…'

I laughed. Hannah had never denied that she embraced the 'softer' end of therapy, whereas I'd always been a sucker for a challenge. And not just at work. At school once, my class had to set a goal in PE designed to sorely test us. Most of the girls chose to cycle 5K or jog around the school grounds. I decided to join a kayaking group and paddle twenty miles from Windsor to Teddington through all the locks on the way. It took me the whole day, but I did it. Never again, mind you.

'So, any juicy gossip?' she said, teasing me.

Confidentiality is an issue for any therapist, but as

we shared the same line of work and I trusted Hannah implicitly, I knew whatever I told her about patients would never go any further.

I took a long sip of my drink, waiting for the hit of alcohol to set my veins tingling.

'I've got an odd situation, as it happens.'

She was interested now, sitting forward so I could keep my voice down. 'In what way?'

'A new patient came to see me today – she's hard to describe – full of contradictions.' Ice rattled against my teeth as I tipped up the glass. 'She was all light and bubbly, then she said she nearly died a couple of weeks ago in a horrific car accident in a lake, up north somewhere.'

'What happened to her?' she said.

'She was trapped in the back of a van that shot off the road and sank into the water.'

'Whoa…' She snatched a breath.

'I know,' I said. 'I mean, normally, trauma patients find it painful to recount their experiences, don't they? You have to wait for them and gently coax them to reveal what happened, bit by bit.' Hannah nodded. 'But, this woman was different. It was like she relished telling me every little detail. She made it sound dramatic, like she was reading a story – it was bizarre.'

'Does she need to be the centre of attention, do you think?'

'Maybe.'

'Is she making it up?'

I shook my head. 'Don't think so. There's a copy of the press report of the crash on her file from the GP.'

'You sure it's kosher? It's not like that dreadful time last year, is it?'

'Hell, no.' My mind flashed back to the distressing episode at St Luke's she was referring to, when survivors of a Tube fire were all giving me accounts that didn't add up. I did the extra memory training straight after that experience, desperate to get a better grip on how the brain worked in that respect. Although if I'm honest, it was partly to take my mind off what happened. 'This is different. I'm convinced she's not faking it. It was more that she seemed kind of thrilled to have an audience to entertain.'

'Lonely, maybe?'

I nodded. 'Possibly.'

'Is she coming back?'

'Looks like it. Her parting words were that she didn't need therapy, she just wanted all her memories back.'

'Well, at least she knows what she wants.'

'I'm intrigued, actually. She's obviously in denial about how she feels, but there was something else…'

'Spill…' Hannah said, twisting her mouth to one side.

'I don't know…there's something tragic about her. I'm waiting for her full medical records to come through, but I get a sense there's some damaging history there. She's a bit older than us, but she's almost like a naïve little girl wrapped up in a huge tangle of sadness…'

Hannah sat back blowing out a big sigh. 'Sounds like you've got yourself a handful there.' She straightened up and wagged her finger at me. 'Be careful.'

I shrugged.

A waiter brought over a bowl of warm olives and the oily aroma made me realise how hungry I was. I stabbed a fat green one with a cocktail stick and chewed it with relish.

'Anyway, enough of that. What about you?'

She talked about her clinic, but her tone was flat and she wrinkled her nose a lot. It was obvious that she was growing tired of seeing celebrities who showed up week after week to dump their petty grievances, but had no real problems at all. 'I need a change,' she said.

She left a little pause which made me think that what she had to say next was going to be significant.

'Actually, Alan and I are thinking of moving.' She whipped her eyes away from mine. 'We're thinking of leaving London.'

Her words hung in the air and I swallowed a pang of dread – that awful feeling you get when everyone has rushed to catch a train and you're left behind on the platform.

'What? No, no way – you can't,' I said, leaving my mouth gaping open. What would I do without her?

'We want a bigger place, Sammie, with a garden and roses around the front door and a little white picket fence…' She stared out over the balcony at a soaring seagull. I wanted to tell her that her pipedream was little more than a cliché, but the wistful look on her face warned me not to.

I was close to tears. 'Won't you miss…London?' I said. '*Our* London, the centre of everything – concerts, galleries, films…' I thought about the momentous times we'd shared here, the deep discussions, the support we'd been to each other and the fun, the escapism, the riotous laughter. 'And there's always that creative sparkle in the air in London…the glamour…' I stopped. She knew all this.

She pulled a face. 'Our flat is so pokey with no privacy. Alan is sick of not being able to get a seat on the Tube in the mornings, sick of the commute altogether. We want to settle somewhere now, before we think about having a family.'

A family.

My stomach sank. Hannah deserved to be happy, of course she did, but right now all I could focus on was the stinging certainty that she was about to move on to another stage of her life without me.

She glanced up at me as if she could read my mind. 'Obviously, you and I will still be joined at the hip,' she said, squeezing my hand.

Yeah…by email, I wanted to say, but managed to hold my tongue. I forced myself to nod with a lukewarm attempt at a smile.

We ordered more drinks and a cup stacked with tall, bendy French fries.

'How's the flat-hunting? Your sister? Any gorgeous man I need to know about?' she asked, shaking salt off a long thin chip.

I cleared my throat. Was it really over three weeks since she'd come back from Iceland with the schnapps that had practically taken the skin off the back of my throat? I was embarrassed there wasn't more to tell.

'I still haven't got round to looking for somewhere better to live,' I said. I'd grown to love my do-for-now Victorian flat in Clapham Junction. It was like a snug, threadbare dressing-gown made of bricks and mortar. 'It's still tricky with Miranda – I'm treading a fine line between watching her blossom and keeping an eye on her. She's flighty and unpredictable half the time, but I love her to bits.'

'So leaving Linden Manor was a good move on her part?' Hannah knew my sister had been diagnosed with schizophrenia at the age of twenty and had been in and out of institutions. She knew my upbringing had been blighted by Miranda's wild and erratic behaviour: breaking my toys for no reason, causing uproar in public places, ruining family gatherings.

'Definitely. She paints all the time, spending most of her week at the Community Arts Project in Camden plus a few hours' waitressing in a local café. It's just right for her.'

Hannah was already in the picture about how much I wanted to support my sister – and how Miranda hated anyone trying to wrap her up in cotton wool. It was common knowledge we'd had a prickly relationship until recently – me the 'interfering busybody' and my sister the small child kicking back whenever she sensed any form of restraint. She hadn't grasped the notion of 'moderation' in any area of her life. Nevertheless, things had improved over the past year or so. During the difficult time at work Hannah referred to, I'd seen how capable and warm-hearted Miranda could be and I'd finally discovered a new bond with her. I was doing my utmost to foster it.

'And as to a man…I'd really love to meet someone…but…' I stared at the ice cubes melting at the bottom of my glass.

Hannah shuffled forward on her high stool. 'In that case, I'll have you set you up with a date,' she said, sounding smug.

Hannah put her arm around me. She knew all about Conrad, my ex. We'd split up over a year ago and he hadn't spoken to me since. I'd found him knee-quiveringly attractive at first, with his tousled black hair and exuberant spirit, and was totally blown away by his ability to hold the stage at the Young Vic. He played rogues and charming villains effortlessly in my view and when he actually showed an interest in me, I hadn't been able to resist. I was infatuated with him, felt compelled to discover the depths of his enigmatic personality, but there were signs I should have spotted sooner. He was possessive by nature, which made him aggressive at times, too. It took me months to come to my senses.

Hannah chased the last olive with her stick, stabbed it and offered it to me. 'As it happens, there's a lovely new guy who's just joined the clinic. He's a hypnotherapist – and maybe your Mr Right.'

'Mr Halfway-decent would do,' I said wistfully.

'There's a retirement do coming up soon. I'll invite you.' She fluttered her eyelids. 'How about it?'

'Sure. Go for it.' I was on my third G&T by then and would have agreed to anything.

I missed having someone special in my life. It wasn't just Con's possessiveness that drove me away; we'd never been on the same wavelength. Con liked late nights and lie-ins and I was up with the lark getting on with my to-do list. Con didn't have a to-do list, or a diary, or even a watch on his wrist most days.

Countless relationships accommodate such clashes, but our problems ran deeper than that. My strength is my ability to listen and he was distinctly lacking in that department. He assumed, he decided things for me, he speculated and never bothered to find out how I actually felt about things. It was mostly my fault, though. I'd fallen for an idea of him and gradually found out it didn't match who he really was. I'd had my head in the clouds. It wasn't the first time.

There'd been a handful of false starts since then. Not many people knew that although I was Ms Level-headed in most situations, I was hopeless in my choice of men. I couldn't help it. I'm always sucked in by charisma. I spot someone from afar and fall head over heels. (Hannah says I'm terribly superficial.) I'm especially attracted to talented men: a lecturer, TV comedian, film director, even a high-powered politician. I fling myself into a relationship only to do a U-turn once I discover they're narcissistic, arrogant, cruel or all three.

Lately I'd been trying to convince myself that being single suited me – gave me time to get on a better footing with Miranda and seriously consider where my career was heading. But I was fooling myself. The simple fact was I'd given up on finding a relationship that worked.

I dragged my coat onto my lap. 'I should go,' I said. 'I'll be dropping off during consultations, tomorrow.'

'You total wimp,' Hannah said. Her energy never seemed to dip, in fact her life seemed to be locked permanently on full steam ahead.

'I know. I'd love to stay and knock back at least another couple of these,' I wiggled my empty glass, 'but it would be just my luck to meet a patient on my way home and somehow end up making a fool of myself.'

'Ooh, you party-pooper, Willerby,' Hannah snorted, clapping her hands together. 'Bring on making fools of ourselves – it makes life just that little bit more interesting.'

Chapter 4

Sam

I'm not sure how she got past the receptionist, but at her next appointment Rosie burst into my office without waiting to be called in. She bounded towards me with a big grin on her face as if she was my best friend dropping in to wish me a Happy Birthday. Fortunately, my previous patient had already left and I was only catching up on notes. I thought of Hannah; she would have insisted on discussing boundaries with Rosie, but I let it go this once. Hannah said I was a soft touch with people; too lenient for my own good.

Nevertheless, I jumped in first this time and explained to Rosie how we'd use various techniques over the coming weeks to try to recover more of her memories about what had happened in the Lake District. She nodded eagerly. She said she had her heart set on remembering everything.

I laid my notebook on my lap, activated the voice recorder on the laptop and the session began.

Since our first session, I'd done my homework. I'd read about crashes where a vehicle had ended up in deep water. It wasn't for the faint-hearted. I'd learnt that floating time, depending on the car, ranged from a few seconds to a few minutes. The more airtight a vehicle is, the longer it floats, but you can't afford to hang around.

Experts say the doors won't open underwater; no matter how hard you push, the pressure of the water outside is too great. People waste vital seconds that way. It's only when the vehicle hits the bottom and the pressure equalises that the doors become accessible. Advice seems to be to get a window open straight away. Whatever you do, the water's going to be coming at you – fast – from the opposite direction, filling up the car, squashing out every remaining pocket of air. My stomach flipped just reading about it.

Rosie explained that her memories from immediately before and after the accident were patchy. I reassured her it was normal.

'I went back, when I got out of hospital, but I couldn't find it,' she said. 'I checked the bank and behind the rocks, but it wasn't there.'

'Find it?'

She was chewing her nail. 'My viola. I found the tyre tracks where the van left the road and the broken fence, but maybe I climbed out of the water somewhere else.'

'Your viola is very important to you,' I said.

'Will you help me find it?'

'I'll try. We'll aim to get back as many memories as we can.'

I assumed Rosie was fixating on the viola, giving it disproportionate significance, to avoid focusing on Richard, Stephanie and Max. It was early days, but Rosie hadn't talked about the others with any degree of regret so far. They were all still missing. She said she hadn't known them well, and certainly wasn't keen on Max, but I would have expected at least some level of macabre speculation about them at some stage. With every day that passed, the chances of any of them turning up alive grew more and more unlikely.

'Something was wrong,' she said, pressing the heel of her hand into her hairline. 'I need to fill in the gaps. It didn't *feel* like an accident. Sometimes you just *know*.'

She shivered, but looked away and coughed to try to cover it. No doubt she'd been putting on a brave face like this ever since the incident happened. Probably didn't want people to think she wasn't coping. She'd told me she'd gone back to work – in a music store – straight away. In my opinion it was probably too soon. Part of Rosie was still underwater trying to figure out which way was up.

'Max's violin is worth two million pounds,' she said flatly. 'You'd think I would have grabbed that, instead, wouldn't you?' She plucked at her lip, tears gathering in her eyes, and answered her own query. 'It wasn't mine, that's why. I only had one pair of hands – you always save your own child first.'

Rosie changed the subject after that, but I could tell she was talking about one thing and feeling another, trying not to reveal her emotions. Perhaps she thought if she stuck to the facts the feelings would go away. Perhaps she needed to trust me more first. I wondered about her background, whether anything had happened to make her think twice about reaching out to people. She had guts and determination – that was obvious already – against all the odds, she'd fought her way out of that sinking van. But, in therapy, being tough has its drawbacks. Patients with high defences are always the hardest to work with – they are guarded, evasive, and want to do things their way.

I'd scoured her medical records, but they were full of gaps and revealed very little about her childhood. I needed to find out more.

'There's not much information about your past in my notes,' I said, tapping my file. 'Obviously, you're not here to focus on your upbringing, but it would help me to get a sense of how to proceed with the memory work if you could give me a very brief outline.'

Delivered in her high-pitched earnest voice, Rosie's account described a childhood that started out straightforward enough, if less than ideal. Her father worked on the oil rigs and was hardly at home and when he was, Rosie kept out of his way. Her mother spent her life at a cosmetics' factory, making up for all the money he lost when he came back.

'He gambled,' she said. 'My mother was playing one long hopeless game of catch up. She was careful with money, saved it and put it in the bank, but Dad insisted on a joint account. She had to start hiding bank notes in the airing cupboard, but then Dad got wise to that and got there first. He spent every penny within days of coming home. Every time. Then he'd take it out on her…'

Rosie stared at the floor as if she was watching the rest of that image unfold. She blinked fast and I knew something awful was going on inside her head, but she stopped there.

'Do you like Christmas?' she asked suddenly.

'Um…I think it can be a difficult time for lots of people.'

'When most people picture their family Christmas,' she continued, 'they see a sitting room with worn comfy chairs and a bunch of happy people wearing party hats, opening presents. Most people, no matter how miserable they are, or how low they have sunk, can find an uplifting memory from their past.'

She looked up, her face entirely neutral.

'I don't have any memories like that. Not one. Instead, I see dark hallways I don't recognise, people asking me to leave the room while they argue about not having space for me or about it not being "their turn". Instead of the twinkling fairy lights on a Christmas tree, I see the headlamps of a taxi catching the light on the buckle of my suitcase as I look forward to another hour in the station waiting room. No one wanted me around to spoil their festivities.'

'You had nobody? Your mother and father…?'

'They died – on the same day,' she said simply. 'When I was seven years old.'

Those words jolted me like an electric shock, but Rosie didn't look as though she wanted or needed any compassion. She was just filling me in, telling me how it was, so I'd get a better idea of the sort of person she'd become. All the same, it made me crumple inside for her.

'Rosie,' I said. 'You've had such a hard time in the past. We might need to talk about that a bit more, sometime, if it feels okay.'

'It was a long time ago,' she said, her voice thin, flimsy. 'I don't think about it much. After they died, though, it felt like I was being punished. I didn't know my grandparents; Mum was an only child and Dad's brother died in a motorbike accident, so I have no proper aunts or uncles either. Doing the trawl of distant relatives and being farmed out to foster homes when they didn't want me – that was the really crap bit.'

She blew into a tissue from her sleeve. 'Can we go back to the crash?' she said.

I nodded and changed tack, but I knew at some stage I'd need to dig deeper into her shattered past. Sometimes in working to retrieve recent memories, old ones pop up to the surface unexpectedly and I needed to know what I was dealing with. Rosie appeared to be coping well, but my instinct was telling me there was something beneath the surface she wasn't yet able to let me see.

Chapter 5

Rosie

I'm sitting in my dreary flat near Streatham Station, listening to the trains from Victoria thundering past. My cheapskate landlady has just told me she won't pay for the cracked toilet seat. She says I must have done something to break it. Unbelievable! I never touched it – it must have been the cold. This dump is like an icehouse. I haven't told her the shoddy plastic base of the shower is cracked too; there's water running through it, doing all kinds of damage out of sight, no doubt. But I don't care. I don't intend to spend much time here, if everything goes to plan.

That last session with Sam was tough. She asked me about growing up. We only have six sessions and they're supposed to be about getting my memory back, so I trust that little diversion is all done and dusted. She said she has to ask, because it all has a bearing on my personality and she needs to know how I cope with things. I could have saved her the trouble by telling her I cope by blotting everything out and pretending it never happened. Only, I don't think she'd have been the least bit impressed with that.

The worst part was that I could see she was upset by what I told her and I'd hardly even started. She doesn't know the half of it! I didn't go into any of the nasty stuff about what actually happened. I want her to care, but I don't want to make her feel bad. She might not like me if I do that. I don't want her to feel too sorry for me either – she needs to see what a strong and resilient person I am, to see that I've learned to cope and done a damn good job of it. If she thinks highly of me she'll want to know me better.

Some of my therapists have turned all gooey when I've told them the heart-breaking stuff. One even burst into tears on me. I hated that – the silly cow had no control; she showed no consideration for how *I* might feel. I need someone solid. I can't be doing with a wimp who's going to go to pieces at the slightest sob story.

Sam isn't like that, though. I reckon, if she caught me off-guard and the really dark stuff came out, she'd cope really well. Obviously, I'll never tell her the stuff that has to stay safely locked away forever. She doesn't need to know those details; certain things I've done that have nothing to do with her. They would only complicate matters. As long as I bear that in mind, everything bodes well. I think we're going to get on just fine.

I wore my new dress, but I'm not sure she noticed. She didn't mention it, anyway. She probably isn't supposed to talk about things like that. I'm never quite sure what the rules are, but I think, as a therapist, she's only meant to talk about the stuff I bring up first. That's what I've learnt from my other shrinks, anyway. I know already she'll be better than the last few; she's softer and more gentle – more like a real person – so that's a brilliant start.

I've decided I don't like the room we're in. It smells

nice, but it's got sickly yellow walls and too many office things in it; the filing cabinet, a laptop open on the desk, and that angle-poise lamp that's like a giant stick-insect watching us all the time. The flowers have gone now, so there's nothing personal. I suppose it would be too much to expect the hospital to provide nice touches like a few books and ornaments on the shelves and Sam hasn't done much to make it homely. No plants or nicknacks. So bloody clinical. I hate hearing people talking outside and trolleys rolling past; it's like being at a bus station. I want more privacy. I want to feel like I've got Sam all to myself. Someone could walk in at any minute and disturb us.

I didn't mean to cry, yesterday – the tears just bubbled up. Sam must have pressed one of my buttons without me realising. I'll have to be careful. Can't afford to let things run away with me like that. But I *do* like her – I get all goose-pimply sitting on this moth-eaten bed thinking about her.

I reach down to my feet and turn up the heater. It rattles like it's about to take off. Another train roars past, shaking the windows. One day – soon – I'll be out of here for good.

When we first met, Sam gave me her business card and I take it out of my purse now and place it in my lap. I run my fingers over her printed name, then I take a pen from my bag and write 'Sam' in curly writing on the back. I go over and over it, big and bold, making a soft swelling in the card. Sam's card given to *me*, her name written by *me*, with *my* pen. All mine.

Chapter 6

Sam

I was standing outside the deli during my lunch break with a hot samosa in one hand, my mobile in the other. Miranda wasn't returning my calls. It always unnerved me when that happened. If it was anyone else, I'd just assume they were busy or having trouble with their phone.

It was different with Miranda.

Straight away I had visions of her taking off on some wild rampage. Stupid really, because the new medication she was on had transformed her in the last eighteen months – but that's the problem when someone close to you has schizophrenia – you always jump to conclusions.

A text finally arrived from her four hours later, just as I'd closed the door behind my final patient. She didn't give a reason for not responding to my zillion messages, instead she sent an invitation to an exhibition that evening at the V&A entitled *Modern Textiles as Art*. She knew I wasn't a big fan of modern art and she was probably expecting me to turn her down. I texted straight back and accepted.

I knew she'd be late; I'd never known Miranda to be on time for anything. I was half expecting she wouldn't turn up at all. I'd been standing around for twenty minutes by the entrance to the gift shop when she welcomed me with a low-key 'Hi' and a raise of her hand, before racing through the corridors to the right gallery. She didn't even make eye contact. I spent most of the exhibition trying to keep up with her. She kept striding on to the next picture before I'd managed to focus on the one in front of me.

'I'm thinking of adding hessian to my oil paintings,' she said finally, as we made our way towards the exit afterwards. Miranda was due to have another exhibition soon at the Arts Project; the centre for artists with mental health issues where she'd made so many friends.

'Great,' I said, not sure how else to respond. 'What's led to that idea?' We spun through the revolving glass doors out on to the street.

'I want more depth to my pictures. I'd like people to want to touch them.'

Miranda's pictures weren't pretty. They were macabre and sinister; big bold explosions of dark colours. It was a big enough ask, in my view, to expect people to *look* at them, never mind get their fingers dirty. I gave myself a mental kick for thinking that way. Painting was her lifeline and helped her deal with her inner demons – none of which had taken root inside her through any fault of her own. Finding positive things to say about her pictures, however, was hard – they were abstract, ugly and full of rage – and I ended up resorting to comments such as *how interesting*, in a sickly, pointless kind of way. I'd have to do better.

We went on to a wine bar in South Kensington, ordering as if we were in two separate bistros. Me, a Mediterranean tapas with vine leaves, hummus, olives and a glass of Merlot. Miranda, thick-cut chips, a bowl of peanuts and a Diet Coke.

Our relationship had always had plenty of ups and downs. We'd been on an even keel for a while now, but something had obviously happened to send us on a downward slide again, though for the life of me I couldn't work out what it was. Miranda denied there was any problem when I asked about it, which made things worse. And she'd stopped telling me things. In fact, when I was around, it felt like she was trying to keep all the important details of her life locked inside an iron vault.

Somehow I managed to keep putting my foot in it. I was 'too full on', too 'in her face' – her words.

She was frosty towards me most of the time: outspoken, hostile and downright hurtful. It was a strain, but I wasn't giving up on her. It's hard to wipe out a lifetime of misunderstandings and even harder to forget that, in spite of stabilising medication, there was always a label around Miranda's neck that read *mentally ill* in bold letters. Nevertheless, I was determined to stand by her, to hang on in there and hope she'd turn to me once in a while. We were always going to be chalk and cheese, but I wanted a better relationship as siblings. Except, maybe I wanted it more than she did.

Miranda leant over and dunked a fat chip into my hummus without looking up. Had I done something to bring about this recent logjam in our relationship? Said something? I needed to find the right time to ask her about it again – to clear the air – but I wasn't convinced now was that moment. I was tired and knew broaching the topic was likely to result in some kind of demonstrative outburst from Miranda – always best handled in private.

'I know that look,' she said. 'You punishing yourself, again?' When Miranda chose to address something, she didn't beat about the bush. 'It still gets to you doesn't it?'

She was on the wrong track, but I didn't put her straight. 'That business last Christmas,' she added, chewing with her mouth open.

That business last Christmas had nearly brought me to my knees.

'It's always going to be a big deal,' I said, with a sigh.

'What was her name, again?'

All of a sudden my head became too heavy for my neck. I rested my elbows on the table and let my hands take the weight. 'Joanne.' I held her gaze. 'Her name was Joanne. I don't really want—'

'Can't you just move on? Everyone knows it wasn't your fault – can't you just get over it?'

'Can we talk about—?'

She cut me off. 'How's work?' she said, making bubbles with her straw in the bottom of her thick glass.

'Busy.' She knew she'd chosen a dead-end subject; I wasn't able to give her any details.

'You're always worn-out and grumpy when I see you,' she said, slumping back in her seat.

I drew my head back in shock. 'I'm not grumpy…'

'You don't have feelings like other people, do you?' she said, accusingly. 'You're hard. A cold fish.'

Despite knowing I needed to take what Miranda said with a pinch of salt at times, her words burrowed deeply into me. More so, as she wasn't the only person to see me that way. The issue isn't that I don't feel, it's that I don't often *show* how I feel. I tend to scoop up my reactions and carry them away with me, so it looks like I have none. In reality, I let my emotions emerge once I'm on my own, out of reach of other people's scrutiny.

Her mouth puckered as if she'd tasted something sour. 'You're all serious and distracted.'

Diners on nearby tables had started to turn round; Miranda delivered her comments several decibels above the general hum.

An unwanted memory rushed into my mind of her leaping onto the table in a top-class restaurant and taking her knickers off. Then I remembered her weaving her way around the chairs in a waiting room with a pair of scissors snipping off people's hair. There were uglier incidents in fact, but thankfully not for a long time.

'Actually, I'm worried about you...' I said calmly.

'*Me?* What's wrong with me? I'm fine. I'm selling pictures. I'm great.'

It sounded defensive and forced.

I waited, hoping the heat around her would cool a fraction.

'Are you free tomorrow evening, perhaps?' I said, striking up a fresh tone. 'I thought we could go to the cinema.'

Her eyes took a detour over my shoulder before she answered. 'I'd love to, but I promised Amanda I'd help with her bridesmaid's dress.'

'Oh. Shame.'

Miranda looked like she was about to say something important; she seemed to be rehearsing her next sentence – but then she shrugged and folded her arms.

I glanced at my watch under the table. Two hours

spent together and she seemed as estranged from me as ever. Miranda sighed as if she was bored and pulled a biro out of her bag. She folded up her napkin and started doodling on it.

When Miranda came out of residential care for good, we were both excited about renewing our bond. She'd held up amazingly well when unspeakable details about her past had come crawling out of the woodwork and the more I understood our dysfunctional family dynamic, the more I realised I shouldn't be blaming her for making my upbringing such a bumpy ride. We'd grown closer as a result.

For a while we'd tried living together, but it soon became obvious that we both needed our own space. I'd never known Miranda as a proper older sister and I couldn't get used to the idea. She'd always felt like the 'child' in the family. Unfortunately, in attempting to establish our new sisterly roles, we'd both started mutating into different versions of our mother! One moment I'd be admonishing Miranda, the next she'd be nagging at me. It was as if Moira Willerby had joined us in the flat too; the three of us squashed into that tiny space. It was a recipe for disaster.

Miranda moved in with Con briefly when he needed a flatmate, then Dad paid for her to rent the spacious one-bedroom apartment near the Arts Project, in Camden. It meant she could have more freedom creatively than she'd had with me. I'm a carpet kind of girl, whereas Miranda needs to feel rough floorboards under her bare feet. I'm not a big fan of oil paint in the bathroom and paintbrushes in the kitchen sink either, but in her own place, she could spread herself out and have her wet canvases dripping against every skirting board, if she wanted to.

Miranda reached over and pinched one of my olives, breaking my train of thought. 'You seeing a new man, yet?' she said.

'Er, no. I'm fine on my own.'

She took up the pen again and added swirls to the doodle. 'Yeah – and I'm the Queen of Geneva,' she said, without looking up.

'It's the Queen of Sheba.'

'Whatever…' She turned her head on one side, engrossed in her drawing. It had started off as a random squiggle, but was turning into a serpent.

Chapter 7

Sam

The most memorable consultation that week was with Rosie. She burst in and bounced down onto the correct seat this time, looking like she couldn't wait to get started.

'It must be hard seeing screwed-up people all day,' she said, rolling her eyes knowingly, as if she couldn't possibly be in that category herself.

As I clicked the button to record, Rosie started speaking. 'Before we go back to my memories of the crash, can I tell you a bit about my viola?' she asked. 'It won't take long.'

Rosie told me about the role music played in her life; how she'd left school with one A level – in English; an unremarkable grade – but in her music studies she'd risen well above mediocre.

'I took up the violin at eight, then when someone else at school wanted to use the instrument I'd borrowed, I was given a viola instead. "Viola players are always in demand," my Auntie said. "You don't even have to be very good at it."'

The woman she called Auntie Doris was her guardian at the time and had instructed Rosie to practise two hours a day after school. To keep her out of her hair, I thought cynically.

'There was no television at her place and I didn't seem to click with many of the other kids at school, so I just practised all the time. I kept practising when I moved from house to house. Much to everyone's surprise I got into the Guildhall School of Music, but in the third year some idiot broke my little finger.' She held it up and wiggled it. 'The neighbour's gardener slammed a blinking garage door on it during the college vac and even after it healed I had terrible pain in the middle joint. I could still play, but by the time I finished college it was clear I'd never make much of a go of it, professionally. I had to look for something different and I'd hardly played at all before going up to the Lakes again.'

'You agreed to the concert even though you were totally out of practice?'

She grimaced. 'To be honest, the request came as a very nasty shock, until Mr Hinds said there would be a fee of £850 each. That put a different slant on it, I can tell you. I'd have learnt to hula hoop in my birthday-suit for that!'

I laughed out loud and Rosie glowed with pride, tucking her hands under her thighs. She seemed emotionally stable, buoyant even, but I couldn't let her get side-tracked with anecdotes.

'Right,' I said, changing tack. 'Are you ready for some focused memory work?'

She rubbed her hands together. 'Definitely!'

'You told me about being in the back of the van with the instruments just before the crash, but what do you remember about earlier that day?'

She slowly guided her specs up her nose. 'In the morning, we played an early Beethoven and hacked our way through the Elgar, but we had to give up. Richard kept getting lost and Stephanie couldn't manage the high notes. It was too complex for just a couple of rehearsals and I was struggling to keep up. Max said we should swap it for some early Mozart, much easier – the first violin carries it, so he was in his element.'

'Then what?'

'Lunch was weird. Cameron Hinds had put on a big spread and his second wife, Ambrosia, was there and Karl, his son. Cameron was asking us each in turn what we'd done since that first concert fifteen years before. It was a bit embarrassing. We let Max take the floor – he was the only one with anything to boast about – I think the rest of us felt like losers. After he'd bored everyone with his tremendous triumphs, he reminded us all about an incident, two incidents actually, that had happened at that first party in 2001. They'd nearly spoilt everything.'

I picked up my pen.

'I'd completely forgotten about them,' she said. 'I don't know if they're important or not, but I'll tell you anyway.' When she smiled her lashes brushed her plump cheeks.

'When we were rehearsing in the drawing room, a bloke – we thought he must have been a friend of the family – turned up. He came in through the French windows and put his finger to his lips, then stood and listened for a while. We found out later from the police, that his name was Mick Blain. "I hope you don't mind," he said, when we'd finished. "I was outside and it sounded like a CD." We were flattered, so we weren't about to kick him out.

'As we packed our gear away, he took an interest in

our instruments. Max wouldn't let him anywhere near his, but Mick said he'd never seen a viola before. I held it up for him so he could get a closer look. "I couldn't have a little go on it, could I?" he said.

'Normally, I'm very careful about anyone touching my viola, but Mick was so wide-eyed and fascinated that I let him. Max and Richard had disappeared by then as we only had about an hour to grab something to eat and get changed before the concert. Stephanie stayed in the room for a few minutes, dusting down her strings, then she left me to it.

'Mick took the viola and started trying to play. He was hopeless, scraping the bow too high over the fingerboard and making a dreadful racket. I reached over to take it back and I'm not sure what happened next. He must have caught his foot on the edge of the rug and staggered forward, almost dropping the instrument. I reached out to make a grab for it – and there was a loud crack. I thought at first someone had fired a pistol, it was so loud.'

I made a few notes, mindful however, that she seemed to have gone off on a remote tangent. She was in full flow by then and I didn't want to cut her off.

'I thought the neck had snapped, but it wasn't as bad as that. As I held up the viola, there was a rattling sound inside and the strings had all loosened. "It's okay," he said, as if he knew what he was talking about. "Something's come loose inside and that white bit on the top has fallen down. We can stick it back up again".

'I told him it wasn't as simple as that. With only fifty minutes to go before the performance, I was in real trouble. I told him you needed a special prong to get that bit of wood that was rolling around inside back in place again.' She did a little air-demonstration for me. 'It's a very tricky operation and I'd never done it before.'

She raised her eyebrows and gave a wry smile.

'My first thought was that Max would know what to do. I laid the viola on a cushion and told Mick, in no uncertain terms, not to touch *anything* as I flew out of the room. Max was doing yoga in our changing area. I went barging in and told him what had happened. To cut a long story short, Max fixed it. He put the sound-post back up inside and retuned all the strings, just in time. '

'And this was during the first visit, in 2001?' I asked, as I jotted down the sketchy details.

'Yeah.' She smiled. 'I laughed when Max handed it back to me, because he asked, jokingly, if I'd ever had it valued. "There's a label inside," he'd said, but he must have been teasing me; I knew it had been made in 1970, in a factory in Borehamwood. "Makers often put labels inside, you know," he'd told me, "hoping one day they'll be famous." Max knew from the sound, just like I did, that it was worth diddly-squat.'

Rosie placed her hands deliberately on her thighs and carried on telling the story as if she was delivering a fairy-tale to a hooked audience. 'Two hours later Mick was dead.'

My pen came to an abrupt halt. Maybe this *was* important after all.

'That second incident – when Mick came to a sticky end – happened soon after, when the concert was underway in the big hall,' Rosie went on. 'The Hinds' residence is massive, all columns and staircases. Everyone was mingling, sipping glasses of champagne and we'd just started the last piece when there was a kerfuffle. A number of guests were pushed aside and chairs toppled over. Several women screamed and a man wearing an anorak, certainly not a guest, ran through the hall and up the stairs. The four of us looked at each other mid-crescendo; we all recognised him as the interfering bloke who'd very nearly wrecked my viola that afternoon. Two policemen charged up the stairs after him. We found out later that Mick was involved in some sort of scam to do with a stolen painting or document or…I don't know what. He ended up climbing out of a bedroom window, but he fell off the drainpipe and broke his neck.'

She brushed an errant curl away from her eyelashes.

"'The police never did work out who he was working with, did they?" Max had said during the lunch.'

She stared ahead, looking as confused by the story as I was. 'Nothing untoward was found on his body when the police got to him, so it was all a bit odd. But apparently Mick Blain had had an accomplice.'

She paused, waiting for me to say something.

'And this incident with Mick was fifteen years ago?' I asked, unable to hide my scepticism. Was it seriously likely to have had anything to do with the accident in the van so many years later?

Rosie twirled a loose strand of hair around her finger and gave a puzzled shrug. 'The Hinds' didn't have much luck hiring us for their parties, did they? A man fell to his death at the first one, then when we all show up again, there's the awful crash.'

She gave a half-laugh. I waited to see if her expression dropped, but she looked up expectantly, waiting for me to speak again.

'So, on the day of the crash,' I said, 'you can remember the lunch, the afternoon – everything up until the van was in the water?'

Rosie looked at the floor for a moment, thinking. 'No…there are definitely gaps when we were on the road before the crash…and bits when we were underwater…it goes a bit sketchy after I passed out on the bank, too.'

'We'll work on trying to fill those in,' I assured her.

'Actually, something else strange happened at the lunch now I think about it. Max was entertaining everyone over raspberry pavlova with more drab little yarns, and I remember Karl Hinds looking fidgety, in a world of his own. It was almost as though Max had reminded him of something and Karl was back at the original party.' She fiddled with a button. 'Karl said something then, but I can't remember what it was. It probably doesn't mean anything. That's all really. After lunch, we had another crappy rehearsal and called it a day.'

'And what about the day you drove up to the Lake District? Any memory lapses there, do you think?'

'Yeah, absolutely. I remember getting to the B&B, but scraps are missing here and there. I don't know if any of that is important.' She stared at me as if I should know. 'I want to find out why the van crashed, but what I want more than anything is to get my viola back,' she said, her voice unsteady.

The desperation in Rosie's screwed-up eyes said it all, and given the way she'd been shunted from one home to another, taking scant belongings with her each time, I could see why the viola would be so important. It was probably about as close to 'family' as anything she'd ever had – or anyone she'd ever known.

'I don't like to think of it being lost out there, all alone,' she added, fiddling with her lip. 'It's probably ruined by the water, but I don't care. I want it back.'

Once she'd left, I leant against the edge of my desk mulling over everything Rosie had told me. I'd looked up the incident online on the North West news site shortly after our first session and I'd been keeping an eye on it every few days, in case there were any further developments. One thing certainly seemed odd to me. After nearly a month, coats, shoes, music and rucksacks had come to the surface, but none of the three bodies had been recovered. Nor had any of the instruments or wallets. Not one.

Chapter 8

Sam

It was my first afternoon off in ages, but when I got home from the hospital my flat was crying out for a tidy up. Last week's newspapers were spread out on the table, covered in dirty tea-towels and unwashed mugs. Furthermore, a tower of ironing was about to topple off the sofa. I wasn't in the habit of letting it get to this state, but it seemed as if a tide had swept over all my belongings when my back was turned, leaving a trail of random detritus behind it. I needed to pull my finger out.

I purged every room, stuffing dishes into the sink, clothes into drawers, junk mail into the bin, until the surfaces were clear. From coat pockets in the hall, I emptied old shopping lists and sweet wrappers, picked up the crusty rind of a clementine from the ledge by the front door, but left the spare set of keys where they were. I'd been meaning to do a key swap with Mrs Willow for at least a week – ever since she slipped over in her bathroom and no one could get into her flat to help her.

I should have got the vacuum out to begin the real work after that, but apathy got the better of me. Instead, in a moment of ultra-decadence, I rang my favourite spa in Chelsea. Twenty minutes later, I was on my way over for a steam and massage.

The package was pricey – but just what I needed. In the last few months I'd buried myself in my job at St Luke's and I'd had virtually no quality time to myself. Miranda might have a point – maybe it was making me worn-out and grumpy.

I got off the Tube at Sloane Square and started walking along The King's Road. I love London's incessant barrage of sounds: car horns, bicycle bells, people hailing taxis and selling newspapers. The soundtrack of this hot-blooded city at full throttle.

Leaves had already begun peeling away from the trees and were catching on the bottom of my shoes. I didn't want autumn to take hold. I hadn't made the most of summer, still hankering after the chance of an evening sitting on the warm grass with a dazzling new guy, watching the sky slowly dissolve into darkness.

In the midst of my daydream, I walked straight into a man carrying three buckets of roses. The collision sent water all over his jeans.

'Watch where you're going, you stupid bitch,' he yelled, shoving past me.

My little reverie was gone.

I got changed at the spa and left my gear in a locker, taking just my towel with me. *Aqua Dulcis* is a small place and there was no one else in the steam room for the 'women-only' session. Blissful solitude. I laid out my towel on the slatted bench and stretched out. The soft hiss of water droplets turning to steam acted like a potion from a magic lamp, letting my body float away into relaxation. As I luxuriated in the inertia, the heat eased my pores wide and cleansed me from the inside. My arms and legs flopped as I closed my eyes, feeling weightless.

My mind, however, wasn't playing the game. I wanted to drift away onto a tropical beach somewhere and have pina coladas in tall glasses brought to me by tanned hunks in floral shorts. Instead, my thoughts were straying to places I didn't want to go. Places that were dark and tragic. I might have been able to send my muscles to paradise, but my brain was pulling me in the opposite direction.

An altogether different scene was playing inside my head. A video loop without a stop button. It was all so abhorrently clear: the dressing gown on the back of the door, the door creaking as I pushed it wide, the cat oblivious to everything still curled up on the pillow.

Last Christmas.

Was it Rosie – child-like, innocent and eager to please – who had brought it all back? Did she remind me of Joanne?

No, I couldn't blame Rosie. The shadow had never gone away.

Miranda was the only person I'd told about it and even that had never been my intention. The night it happened I'd gone back to my flat in a terrible state and she'd turned up unexpectedly to return a pile of cookery books. She'd prodded and pummelled me until I opened up, then kept telling me it wasn't my fault. I didn't believe her.

I quickly scrabbled around inside my head for

something else to focus on and Con's face floated into my mind. I couldn't help but smile to myself. Although we hadn't spoken in a long while, I'd heard Con was doing well. He'd had good reviews for his part in a British film and was auditioning for a meaty role as a ship's captain in a potential Hollywood blockbuster. He'd sent a postcard to tell me about it. I only got cards when he wanted to brag; perhaps it was his way of reminding me how foolish I'd been to let him go.

As the steam enveloped me, I found myself finally drifting off to a sweet and dreamy place. But not for long. Lost in my reverie, I began to hear Rosie's voice breaking through, telling me about the crash. I found myself picturing the van before it went off the road and hit the water. The pompous Max with Stephanie beside him and Richard behind the wheel.

I saw the three of them in my imagination clawing at the door handles. I thought about how they must have fought to get the seatbelts off, ripped their nails to shreds as they clawed at the windows, launched their shoulders at the doors. At least Rosie, in the back, didn't have a seatbelt to worry about. She was the only one with a way out. The picture brought up a question about the windows I hadn't thought to ask before. Were the winders manual or electric? If they were electric, would they work underwater? Had the others ever stood a chance?

I didn't want to think what they must have gone through as they knew they were running out of breath, about to drown.

As I laid still, safe in the spa, the steamy water

hissing under me as my skin got hotter and hotter, I couldn't help wondering whether there was any realistic chance Max, Richard or Stephanie could have survived.

Rosie's voice was clear now, almost in my ear.

'…seeing you here…' she said.

I opened my eyes.

'I said, fancy seeing *you* here?!' she repeated gleefully.

I sat bolt upright, rubbing my eyes, half in and half out of my daydream. This was the real Rosie, no doubt about it – she was right there beside me. She had a yellow towel tightly coiled around her fleshy body revealing only a tiny chink of cleavage. All nicely covered up – unlike me.

I gave her a weak smile. 'Yeah, fancy that?'

I was lying in front of her completely naked. As slowly as I could, not wanting to seem prudish, I edged the towel out from under me and innocently used it to dab my face allowing it to fall across my body. Rosie seemed oblivious to my awkwardness and sat on the bench in the far corner, her hands over her belly, thrusting her feet out.

'Oh – I *so* need this,' she said. 'Afternoon off from the music store. It's in Charing Cross Road, did I tell you? CDs, DVDs, sheet music, we even sell—'

'Rosie, it's…nice to see you, but we shouldn't chat. We have a specific therapeutic relationship and chatting together confuses that.'

'Oh…does it?' She looked perplexed.

We were quiet for a while. I closed my eyes, but I had no hope of relaxing now. I felt overheated, sweaty, irritable. I was tempted to get up and leave, but I wasn't sure how she might interpret my sudden exit. Besides, I hadn't had my full thirty minutes; I wasn't going to let her impromptu appearance cut short my precious treatment.

'I wasn't going to see anyone, you know, after the crash,' she said, ignoring my earlier comment. 'But I'm glad I did.'

'Right…' I opened one eye. She was lying flat on her back now, her eyes closed.

'You're very good at your job,' she added. 'I think I'm going to get a lot out of our sessions.'

I made a noise that came out like a little yelp and cleared my throat.

She opened her eyes and held up her little finger; the one she'd told me had been damaged by the garage door. 'I was quite good on the viola once, you know.' She winced. 'It's been bothering me again in the last few days. I had such early promise and it all came to nothing.' She sniffed. 'Playing the viola was the focus of everything. I don't have any other gifts. Without that I'm nobody…'

I could sense tears bubbling away under the surface, but she battled to fend them off. I was annoyed that Rosie had put me in this awkward position, but I felt I had to say something.

'It must be hard working in a music store with other people's music around you all day.'

'You get used to it.'

'You so dearly wanted that for yourself,' I said. 'To be playing to an audience and recording your own CDs. You could so easily have been one of them.'

She gave a hollow laugh and turned to look at me. 'I'm used to being invisible.' She wriggled on to her side and made a pillow with her hands. 'Do you believe in God?' she said.

'Er…that's a big question, Rosie.' I hid a sigh.

'It makes no sense if I was the only one who survived the crash. I mean what would be the point in that? Why would God or fate or whatever bother to save the runt of the pack?'

When I got home I opened my laptop. I needed to know. Rosie had skimmed over her history during our sessions, but I wanted the details of all the bits she'd left out.

I typed a few key words into the search engine: *death*, Rosie's surname and *seven years old* to see what came up. It was all there. Big news at the time, twenty-seven years ago. Mildred and Keith Chandler lived in a tiny rundown terraced house, in Bognor Regis. Rosie was their only child.

Mildred had come home one day, ready to pack her bags. She'd had enough. She was finally leaving the man who had gambled away all their money and beaten her on and off since their wedding day. She'd told a close friend she was taking Rosie to Portsmouth then heading over to the Isle of Wight, until she worked out the next stage of her plan. Keith Chandler had other ideas, however. He'd come back unexpectedly from the pub and as soon as he realised what was going on, he locked Rosie in the garden shed, telling her to see if she could count to a hundred before he came back. Then he took his air rifle, went into the bedroom and fired fifteen shots at his wife at close range as she folded her pyjamas. Rosie climbed out of the shed window and walked in on him just after he'd stopped firing.

He'd led her to the kitchen, saying there had been a 'terrible accident' and told her to butter slices of bread for tea while he went to get help. As she ran the knife across the squares of Sunblest, he took a length of rope from the shed and hung himself from the banister on the landing.

I closed the lid of the laptop and pressed my hand over my mouth. Rosie had been seven years old. Both her parents had died within minutes of each other. Right in front of her. How does anyone ever lead a normal life after that? How can you possibly pick yourself up, dust yourself down and get on with your life after something so devastating?

Rosie said she'd been passed from one set of distant relatives to the next never getting close to any of them. They took turns to reject her and then she embarked on an endless round of foster homes.

In the three sessions we'd had she came across as terribly immature for her age: hapless, inelegant and unsophisticated. Quite possibly, a result of never having had a consistent and solid role model. It occurred to me that she'd probably not been any real trouble to anyone; her only crime being a desperation to be loved.

I drew my feet up on to the sofa and stroked the threadbare velvet cushion that had gone everywhere with me since I was a teenager. What happened to Rosie wasn't fair. It wasn't her fault. None of it. I squeezed the cushion and made a decision. I was going to help this woman. I was going to give her the best shot I possibly could.

As promised, Hannah sent me an invitation to the retirement party of a psychoanalyst at her clinic. Being Harley Street it was a lavish affair with lashings of champagne and trays of speciality nibbles; odd little creations involving caviar, king prawns and avocado. There was even a melted-chocolate fountain for marshmallow and strawberry dipping.

Hannah wasted no time in introducing me to Giovanni, the new hypnotherapist. I saw his eyes travel down my slinky black cocktail dress and dizzily high stilettos and felt sultry and a little risqué, especially as our glasses were being constantly refilled by the waiters hovering at our elbows.

Hannah had already told me that Giovanni was in his mid-thirties and from Milan. A thin, expertly clipped chinstrap beard made him look like a philosopher and the whites around his smoky brown eyes were pure, without a single red vein. He explained he'd travelled as far as Peru, loved reading the Russian Classics and was partial to dancing salsa. He listened attentively, asking pertinent questions about our shared interest in the hidden machinations of the human mind. He was smart, erudite and thought-provoking. He couldn't have been more perfect – except there was simply no spark.

After the obligatory speeches, a singer took to a small stage at the side of the room and began crooning his way through a few slow ballads. When I heard the opening sax intro to *Careless Whisper*, I stood and listened, my neck tingling as the melody surged around the room. The singer caught my eye and from then on he seemed to be directing the words straight at me, holding his microphone suggestively, his voice seductive and intense.

Guilty feet…should've known better…

He was breathtakingly good-looking – and very young.

'You're *not* serious?' exclaimed Hannah, when she spotted me ogling him. 'Melissa, over there, has just told me he's *twenty-two*, for goodness sake – and lives in Leeds.' She put her hand up to my eyes to block my view of him. 'He's totally unsuitable – don't even think about it.'

'But…he's gorgeous…'

She tugged my arm and pulled me to one side. 'Sam, listen to me. Your relationships are always the same; fabulous sex at the start, then weeks when you're scratching your head trying to work out what on earth you're doing with the guy.' She discreetly checked over her shoulder. 'What about Giovanni? I thought you two were getting on really well.'

'We were,' I avoided her eyes, 'but there's no umph.'

'Don't give up so fast!' she hissed. 'Can't you try being friends first – give it time and see if the magic happens later? Do you at least like the guy?'

'Yeah. He's…' I struggled to find something remarkable to say, 'interesting…'

She tutted at me. 'Interesting is one of those *bland* words, Sam. Try a bit harder.'

'The problem is I've met loads of guys like Giovanni who seem, on paper, like they're a perfect match, but it rarely seems—'

'You're hopeless,' she groaned, but didn't walk away.

'You're spot on,' I conceded. 'I'm supposed to be an expert in psychology, paid to counsel others on affairs of the heart amongst other things, yet I'm a complete fraud when it comes to my own love life.'

She nodded with enthusiasm. 'Yes, you are, Willerby…yes, you are.'

I leant against her, the alcohol causing havoc with my ability to stand upright in high heels. 'One of these days I'll get myself into therapy again – get someone to sort me out.'

'That's the best idea you've had in ages, Sammie,' she said, putting her arm around me. 'You're still bloody gorgeous and I'm truly blessed you're my best mate.'

I felt myself flush and my thoughts led me back to Con. I fell so hard for him at the start. The sex had been brilliant and I'd loved feeling desired; just being in his presence seemed to heighten all my senses, but the rest of our relationship had been out of kilter. As well as his possessiveness, he didn't really 'get' me as a person. I'd tried to understand and respect him, but it felt like a one-way street.

Things came to a head between us when I got close to someone special at St Luke's, although I never stepped over the line while I was seeing Con. I'm loyal like that. Nonetheless, it was enough to show me how much emotional intimacy was missing between Con and me, and after that it was hard to make the relationship work. It was a shame and I missed him. The world had felt different when we were together; brighter, fuller, more alive and exciting, trembling with possibilities.

'Why is love such a minefield?' I said, with a sigh. 'I know "companionship" and "compatibility" are essential qualities for a lasting relationship, but in the heat of the moment, the chemistry takes over with me. My brain wants one thing, my body wants another.'

'Because there are so many kinds of love,' Hannah said gently. 'It gets mixed up with attraction and sex and family patterns…'

'You see, I know all that. If a patient came to me in my situation – you know, lust obliterating common sense every single time – I'd conclude they were damaged in some way.' I looked into her face. 'Am I damaged?' I tottered slightly and she kept her arm around me.

'We're all damaged, if you want to use that word,' she replied.

'What word would you use?'

She shrugged. 'I'd say we're all still learning.'

I thought about it and smiled. 'That's a much better way of looking at it.' I grabbed her hand. 'I'm going to miss you like crazy when you go,' I added.

At that point, Hannah was swept away by a colleague with an album of wedding photos, so I helped myself to the buffet.

Shortly afterwards, the singer took a break from his set and I watched him weave his way around the room, stopping to chat to people, nodding and smiling, hands in his pockets. His messy hair fell in long blond layers over his forehead – it probably took him ages to create that unkempt look. His skin was immaculate, so smooth that perhaps he hadn't even started shaving yet. Inwardly I cringed. Sonny (that was his stage name) was way too young.

He saw me and I felt my cheeks prickle. A raw desire ignited inside me, but after my brief chat with Hannah I was determined not to act on it. If he'd been interested I could easily see myself jumping into bed with him, but I knew it wouldn't lead anywhere and I'd regret it the next morning. He'd have left by first light, back to Leeds, anyway, without so much as a *nice knowing you*.

Instead, I slunk back to Hannah and tried to look interested in the wedding album. Would I ever manage to sort my own love-life out?

Sonny was beside the fondue fountain by then, talking to a woman around my age wearing tight leather trousers. When I looked up again, they'd gone.

Chapter 9

Sam

Rosie came hurtling in to her next session, her hair in a cartoon frizz as though she'd been plugged into an electric socket, her eyes panda-black with smudged mascara.

'I can't come any more,' she gasped between sobs. 'Work won't let me. They won't give me any more time off. I can't believe it. It was all going so well. What am I going to do?'

'Hold on. Slow down. What's happened exactly?'

She flopped into the chair. 'My boss thought I was only going to need a couple of appointments, like physiotherapy or something. I thought they understood!' She dropped her face into her hands. 'I can't see you anymore. It's a *disaster.*'

Knowing Rosie's fractured background, I could see how this could, indeed, feel like a catastrophe to her.

'You don't work weekends…or after hours, do you?' she asked looking up, her face suddenly hopeful.

'I'm afraid not.'

Her shoulders sank. 'What am I going to do?' she repeated, she had a finger in her mouth and began chewing from nail to nail. 'I don't know how I'm going to cope…' She put her head to one side. 'You don't work in another clinic, do you? Or privately?'

I hesitated. No, I didn't, but there was, in fact, no reason why I couldn't work from home. I'd thought about it many times. All I needed to do was set up the insurance.

I was about to explain this to Rosie when I stopped myself. I could almost hear the blare of a loudhailer in my head shouting, *Don't do it!* I knew exactly why. I'd come across clingy patients before. Was Rosie likely to be one of them? Would I regret inviting her into my own personal space? She'd already turned up 'coincidentally' at the spa. Did I want her knowing where I lived?

'Listen, I'll give our sessions some thought. I'll contact you – but I can't promise anything, okay?'

'Okay…' she whispered, with an undertone of defeat. Her cheeks puffed out into a pout as she dropped her eyes to the floor.

I waited.

'Are you ready to try a memory exercise?' I asked softly.

'Er…yeah,' she said, shuffling in the seat, as if she'd forgotten why she was there.

I invited her to lie down and get comfortable on the low chaise longue I use specially for this kind of therapy. I unfolded a blanket, laid it over her and pulled it up to her chin.

'I'd like you to close your eyes and visualise exactly where you were before the crash. Choose a moment when you were in the van, before it left the road. Can you do that?'

'Mmmm,' she muttered, her eyelids fluttering.

'Now keep that image in your mind and really imagine that you're there. Step into the scene as if it's happening now. Notice the temperature, the quality of light and what you can feel under your hands...' She stayed still. 'Try to recall the taste in your mouth, what you can smell, whether anything is touching you and what's going through your mind. Can you do that now?'

She dipped her chin a fraction, without a sound.

'Try to keep all your senses alive as we proceed.'

She made a little sighing noise and held out her hand. 'I want to keep part of me here in the room with you,' she murmured, her eyes screwed firmly shut.

I took it, allowing her fingers to wrap tightly around mine. It wasn't unheard of for patients to reach out for support as they sent their minds into the darkest recesses of their past.

'Tell me where you are,' I said.

Rosie wriggled for a moment, then settled. 'I'm sitting hunched on the wheel hump...' she muttered. 'It's dusty and I can feel a layer of grit under my hands...'

'Good...' She had tuned into the exercise straight away. 'What else?'

'The windows aren't open. Why not?' she mumbled, squirming. 'It's stuffy inside the van. I'm sure Richard had his window down when we came up from London.'

'Okay, stay with it. Focus on what you can see out of the back of the van...the road...how fast you're going...'

I stayed quiet, watching her face as she began

reliving the horror of what happened next.

'I tip to one side as we go round a bend, then we seem to be going really fast all of a sudden. I'm getting thrown around and I'm trying to stop the instruments from getting bashed about.'

She winced. 'There's a rough jolt.' She squeezed her eyes tighter, scrunching up her face, gritting her teeth. 'We're falling forward and the instruments are sliding towards the front seats. Whoa…I can hear a splintering sound…we've broken through a fence. There's another thud...' She squirmed, her hand sticky now, holding on for dear life. 'Oh, God, it's coming in. The water. Really fast. It's covering the floor, swooshing over my legs…' She tried to sit up, her eyes still shut, but I gently eased her back down again.

'It's okay, Rosie, you're safe,' I said. 'Try to stay with it. What else can you see?'

'I don't know…f-figures in the front seat.' She snatched a breath and her skin whitened a shade. 'Stephanie's throwing herself across Max, hammering at the door. She's yelping like a dog. Max is swearing. He's shouting out something about the seatbelt. They're both wrenching at the straps and the plastic sockets. I can't remember Richard. The water's getting higher. Hurgh…'

She sounded like she was about to be sick and reared up, opening her eyes. 'I've got to get OUT…'

'It's okay – you're at the hospital. Let the pictures fade for now and take some deep breaths.' I peeled my hand away from hers and held out a glass of water.

We left the exercise there. I was astonished: Rosie was a natural. Most patients took weeks before they could relax sufficiently to relive a traumatic incident like this.

I brought her fully out of the trance state and she sat with her knees pulled in towards her chest, still under the blanket. Revisiting a shocking event brings its own level of trauma, so I gave her a few moments to establish that she was back in my office and out of danger. She returned to her original seat soon after and we discussed what she'd remembered.

She looked grave. 'I think there was a problem with the seatbelts. I don't think Max or Steph could unfasten them. They were trapped.' She sat up holding her throat and I thought she might be about to heave again. I ran for the waste bin.

'I'm okay,' she said, patting her chest.

'When you travelled up from London were you in the front of the van?'

'Yes.'

'Did you have any problems with the seatbelts, then?'

'They were a bit stiff...'

'Did the windows have winders or were they electronic?' I'd been meaning to ask this question for a while.

'There were buttons. I remember fiddling with them on the motorway and Richard told me off.'

In reading up about the crash, I'd come across reports of similar accidents where the central locking had gone haywire underwater. One driver, having escaped from a submerged car, had gone back down inside it to find his wallet. Without warning, the windows and doors had locked – the system jammed shut – trapping him inside.

'You think someone messed with the controls so we couldn't get out?'

'It's more likely that the central locking system shut down underwater. I've read that can happen.'

'But what if someone wanted us trapped down there so they could get their hands on Max's violin? I mean that's the obvious motive, isn't it?'

'I really don't know, Rosie. It's probably best not to jump to conclusions.'

'Max certainly wasn't shy about telling everyone how much it was worth.' She stroked her earlobe absently. 'Such a terrible risk, though – deliberately sending the violin into the water…it doesn't make sense.'

I shrugged. 'I don't know much about musical instruments, but if anyone did try to sell it, wouldn't it be recognised straightaway?'

'Well… it would be pretty impossible to pass it on through traditional routes, but I've heard of high-profile instruments going underground through the black market.' She fiddled with the buckle on her belt. 'It could end up stashed away in a dealer's vault or in a villa on the Cayman Islands. I can send you links to articles about that kind of thing, if you like?'

'Well…I'm not sure that's necessary, just now.'

She rubbed her eye, then picked at a scab on her hand, constantly fidgeting.

'I forgot to say,' she went on. 'The girl who lives in the flat above mine works at Rothman's Auction House in Wigmore Street. I find out a lot of stuff from her. Dawn mails out catalogues to customers and gets listings for all the big auction houses in the UK.'

'Go on...'

'After the crash, I asked if she'd keep her eyes open for any musical instruments that came up for auction and she added me to the mailing list. I mean...as I spoke to her, I knew it was a long shot...but I thought I'd keep checking, anyway. Like you say, no one in their right mind would try to sell a stolen instrument as distinctive as Max's Guarneri on the open market. It would be spotted a mile off. For one thing, it's so distinctive – the tail-piece is inlaid with mother of pearl and the pegs have little sapphires in the ends.'

'Still, it was a smart thing to do.'

'Thanks!' Rosie's face melted into a smile, then tightened into a frown. 'Maybe there was another motive I don't know about,' she said slowly.

'Let's stick with what we know, shall we?' I didn't want her to get side-tracked speculating.

In our remaining five minutes, I asked about Rosie's friends, to find out who was looking out for her. She was vague and unforthcoming. It seemed she had 'acquaintances' at work and a few regulars who said hello at the local library, but no real friends or family. No one had been to see her when she was in hospital after the crash.

'I send Christmas and birthday cards to a few people – Auntie Doris, and another lady who took me in for a year when I was thirteen – but I don't get many back. No one seems to remember my birthday. I think it's one of those difficult dates...you know?'

I waited for her to explain.

'It's in a few weeks' time, actually, on November

30th, but everyone's already thinking about Christmas by then, aren't they?'

I gave a faint nod. This was the justification she'd used to convince herself over the years.

'So, I'll see you again, outside office hours somewhere, next week – you'll text me?' she said when our time was up.

'I didn't say that exactly. Something *might* be possible,' I said, laying heavy emphasis on the 'might'. 'But I can't give you any guarantees right now…I'll let you know.'

'You'll try your best, though?' she pleaded, rubbing the door handle as if it was the hand of someone she couldn't bear to be parted from.

After she'd gone, I stood for a while with my back against the door. The same raw sadness I'd felt when I first met her sucked at my stomach. I let it tug for a while, then jotted down a few notes:

Rosie's initial response to the memory techniques is very positive and we've started to recover lost fragments from the traumatic event. She believes there's a lot about the accident that remains unexplained and is very keen to unravel the mystery. My view, ultimately, is that she won't gain a sense of control and stability until she can piece together more about what happened…

I stopped writing. If the best way forward for Rosie was to find answers, then continuing our memory therapy was crucial.

As I put down my pen, a vision of Joanne came to

mind, falling as a heavy shadow across my shoulders. Her pale young face scrunched up with desperation, her voice fighting back tears. It made me wince, bringing with it an abrupt reminder of what can happen when a patient hands over their trust and a professional fails to follow through when it mattered most.

Was I going to deny Rosie my support because she might be a handful? Rosie was vulnerable after the accident. Wouldn't *I* be in a similar state if I'd had such a close brush with death? And wasn't dealing with loneliness and isolation part of my job? Surely, I was experienced and professional enough to handle this kind of situation. Only a few days earlier I'd taken a private oath to do all I could to support her.

In the last few moments before my next patient was due, I scribbled a note in my diary reminding me to fix up indemnity insurance. I didn't have an option; it was my duty to carry on seeing Rosie and the only way we could do that was if she saw me privately.

I scanned the impersonal space I used as my office, with its built-in alarm system and team of professionals an arm's length away. The next time I saw Rosie she'd be stepping across the threshold of my flat. Into my home.

I focused on the positives: she was keen to work hard, she was fully engaged with the process and was making headway. Hot on the heels of that thought came another: one I didn't want to hear that sent an icy shiver down the back of my neck.

Chapter 10

Rosie

I can't believe it! She's just sent me a text; I can have appointments at her house! It's going to be so brilliant, seeing where she lives and spending time in her own personal space. Touching things she's touched. Breathing the same air. I thought she was going to give up on me, when I said I wouldn't be able to come to the hospital any more, but she's come through with flying colours. I knew she would. She's got a heart of gold. She knows we've got something special already. This is only the beginning. I'm so happy!

I put my phone down and kick off my slippers. I'm too excited to stay in on my own. It's time to celebrate; I haven't had a good night out in months. The last time was at a leaving party for one of the girls at work, but it wasn't much fun in the end. Turned out I was only invited so I could help clear up afterwards.

So, I'm sitting in The Great Boar (which would have lived up to its name with a different spelling) and I've dolled myself up a bit with a mini-skirt, a low-cut top and one off those push-up bras. My cleavage looks like two cream buns stuffed together on a tray, but I don't care. I feel like a pot of honey: attracting the city bees who've had too much to drink – the ones who have cold and empty homes to go to. It's done the trick before.

Even for a dowdy carrot-top, like me. Only, I'm not looking for a quickie in a back alley; I'm not bothered about the sex at all, really. I'd rather have the touching, kissing, holding. I want to connect with someone, to gaze into someone's eyes, to flirt and be treated like a lady. Is that too much to ask?

As I look for a free table, a woman in the far corner gets up from her chair, laughing. She reminds me for a moment of Sam, although her dark shoulder-length hair isn't as glossy. She isn't as elegant or as slim as Sam either. As she walks towards me in the direction of the bar, I notice she actually looks quite tarty. Too much make-up and her lipstick is bleeding on to her teeth. Sam wouldn't be seen dead looking like that – or in a dive like this, for that matter.

I sit in a corner I'd like to describe as cosy, but in fact it's just gloomy. I hope I'm not going to make a fool of myself. I just want to feel special and wanted, that's all, to find someone who's interested in me. I know I'm going to see Sam again soon, but I'm aching for attention *now*. To cuddle up with someone and be close – do what couples do.

My hopes are high to start with. I look up, try to plaster a light-hearted expression on my face, to pout my lips a tad so people might see me as a temptress. A man begins heading my way, but he reaches behind me for a stack of business cards on the window ledge. I'm certain the next one is going to catch my eye. He gets as far as my small table then grunts when he discovers it isn't vacant.

I sit there for over half an hour and not once does

anyone, male or female, acknowledge me – worse than that – no one seems to *see* me at all. It's like I'm invisible. I half expect someone to walk right through me. Is this how my life is always going to be? Forever screaming from inside a soundproofed glass tomb where I can see out, but no one can see in?

In the next half hour, I sip two more rum and blacks, one after the other, as slowly as I can. Then, something happens, my luck is in. A group of men saunter over from the bar and one of them comes right up to speak to me. He asks if the seats beside me are free. I nod with a big smile and the four of them join me at the table, or rather take possession of it. After that, not one of them speaks to me again or even looks in my direction. They just wanted the table.

It becomes embarrassing. As a group, they gradually seem to expand, like cake mix swelling in the oven and I'm pushed further and further back, trapped in the corner. I pretend to check my texts, scan my diary. I'm tempted to pull out my paperback, but the light is too faint to read. Eventually, I get up, squeeze through crowds of people laughing and joking and go to the bar. This is a better spot. No one can ignore me here. I perch on a stool and offer punters peanuts, but no one exchanges more than a sentence with me.

The door swings open and a group of rowdy West Ham fans crowd in and elbow me out of the way as they order their pints. One of them turns to me and actually makes eye contact. An unruly football supporter with caterpillar eyebrows and too much nasal hair, wearing a T-shirt that fails to cover his muffin-top. He isn't exactly what I was hoping for, but I'm prepared to lower my standards just this once. He looks like he's about to give me an oafish chat-up line, but then he calls me a fat slag and guffaws with his mates. It isn't the kind of human contact I had in mind. I've had enough by now, so I get up and leave.

When I get home a pang of nostalgia hits me hard. It's that time of year, with my birthday coming up. I pull my box of memorabilia out from under the bed. It sounds grand, but there isn't much in it. I take out the only photos I've got and lay them on the tatty candlewick cover like playing cards.

I pretend I'm showing them to Sam, make-believe she's here in the room with me, sipping a late-night cocoa before bedtime.

A woman I called Auntie Joyce took me in first, after Mum and Dad died. I've got one photo of the two of us in Trafalgar Square one winter in the snow. We're wrapped up in scarves, gloves and hats, bulked out like snowmen. We aren't smiling at the camera or holding hands or anything, just standing next to each other like we're in a bus queue. I wasn't with her long; she was a friend of my mum's when they worked in the cosmetics' factory. Then it was Mrs Laine for a couple of months and after that it was Auntie Doris – that's when I got my viola – but I don't have any photos of her.

I only have two pictures of Mum and one of Dad in the whole world. None of them together. They're tatty from years of fingering and flattening down. If my eyes were lasers, the photos would be bleached white by now,

I've looked at them so often. I try to find more in them each time. I keep hoping for a dog or a bicycle to materialise in the background to bring a fresh memory to light, but there's never anything there. The only one of Dad shows him wearing an RAF uniform. He looks preposterous in the jacket. He'd borrowed it and it was two sizes too big. I know for a fact he never flew a plane or went anywhere near an airbase. The picture has been folded across his face, so I can't tell whether he's smiling. Probably not.

It's Christmas in a month. Already the shops are full of it. I told Sam I had no joyful memories of family Christmases. When I think of it again now, I can only bring to mind Dad flying off the handle, because the apple sauce was too sour or the parsnips were burnt – he had a ballistic temper.

Christmas Day was no different from any other day in our house. Plates would be routinely thrown, chairs got broken, a grandfather clock was pushed over once on Boxing Day, sent crashing to the floor with a discordant clang. Mum bore it all. She never fought back, except with words under her breath. There were only ever two states at home when Dad was there: incessant shouting or a trembling silence. The silence was the worst of the two, because you always knew something was brewing. Even when he didn't say a word, I could tell the threats and foul language were flying around inside his skull.

When I think of my dad, I only see a shadow. He was away from home a lot when I was small, but then, when I was about five, there was a massive explosion on his oil rig that sent the whole platform up into the sky. It scattered pieces on the water the size of Mars bars. Dad survived, but he was in hospital for weeks. He came home with a limp and never worked again. He spent his days going to the pub and the bookies – I thought that was some kind of library. I asked to go too, but he shook me off saying it was only for grown-ups.

It's hard to lose someone who has never really been there in the first place. Would Sam understand that I grieve most over what might have been when I think of my dad? Without the photograph I have no memory of his face, his voice, or the smell of his jacket. That thought makes me feel more isolated than ever.

I suppose if Sam wants to know all this stuff, it won't do any harm to share it; it's just that I've gone over it so many times on my own and with other therapists, that I don't see the point. Recounting it never gets me anywhere.

I pick up the most recent photo of my mother and try to imagine being next to her. I do remember her. She was pretty. Her hair was a shade closer to blonde than mine and she had petite features, like a bird. When I look back, I can see that men liked her because she looked vulnerable, not in a weak way, but as if she needed protection, like expensive cut glass.

I remember Dad once saying he didn't like the way men ogled her, one bit. I didn't know what it meant then, but it made him so livid that he'd sometimes pull out the wire to the phone and lock me and Mum in the house. I notice keys now; I tend to spot them if they're lying around because I know how important they are.

Mum missed important tests at the hospital one time, because we were trapped inside. I guess he was possessive and that's one of the reasons Mum wanted to get away.

There are plenty of unpleasant incidents I could tell Sam about, if I had to. Like the time he'd come back from the bookies one afternoon and demanded a fruit pie with a decent crust on it. Two hours later, Mum proudly carried a lemon cheesecake into the room. Dad got to his feet and at first I thought he was pleased, but his voice didn't sound right. *Cheesecake is NOT a pie,* he said. *Cheesecake is a CAKE!* And he smashed his walking stick into the centre of it.

Unbelievable! When I explained this to my last therapist, Erica, she said he sounded like a character out of Dickens.

'Even in the 1980's,' she'd said, 'your mother shouldn't have had to put up with that.'

But everything got worse. No one seemed overly surprised about what happened on that horrible day when they both abandoned me forever. Neighbours nodded knowingly when the police cars came and the two of them were lifted into the ambulance inside long thin bags. Some said they saw it coming, others that it had only been a matter of time. I remember that half-filled suitcase on the bed – Mum and me were supposed to be going away together. Instead, they both left without me.

Chapter 11

Rosie

As my shoes crunch up the gravel drive of Sam's Victorian house, I'm disappointed. There's a board with buzzers and nameplates by the front door, which means it's been divided into flats. I was expecting Sam to live in a detached property all by herself or at least somewhere smarter than this. Once inside, I can't see much of the flat. She's closed most of the internal doors, but I swear it only has one bedroom.

The decor isn't what I was expecting either. It's a bit odd. Quirky. A hotchpotch of battered old and shiny new belongings. An overused velvet settee – but a stylish gold-framed mirror above the fireplace. A trendy light-fitting that's like a gnarled tree branch suspended from the ceiling and a coffee table from a huge slab of tree trunk on a Persian rug. Bookshelves made with bricks. I want to stop to take it all in properly, I want to work out what it says about her. While she picks up her notes from a small table, I move closer to an unusual painting on the wall.

'Did you do this?' I say. It's loud and colourful, but I'm not sure what it's meant to be.

I get a measly one-word answer. 'No.'

She isn't going any further than that, but I'm one step ahead of her, having spotted a signature in the bottom right-hand corner. Another Willerby. Sam's mother?

'A relative?' I say.

'Mmm,' is all I get back.

I take a chance. 'Your sister?'

'Yes.' Neutral. No, she's actually verging on being annoyed. What's the big deal?

'Must be nice having a sister,' I say, but she says we're not here to talk about her.

I'm dying to ask if she's married or has a boyfriend, or any kids, if there are any other brothers or sisters lurking in the wings, but I'm going to have to work everything out for myself. She's not wearing a wedding ring and she uses the same name as her sister, so that's a start.

There are no photos of her or any family groups about the place. Instead, just a few pale grey outlines on the wall where several frames have been removed. Is that for my benefit? Something inside my chest shrinks. Why does she have to hide things from me? I'm letting her right inside my head after all. It's not fair.

I don't need to go, but in the middle of our session I ask to use the bathroom. You can tell a lot about a person from their bathroom. Sam has put out a tiny guest towel, so far unused, and there's expensive oil on the side of the bath and only one toothbrush. Only one dressing-gown hangs on the back of the door, too. While I'm in there, I take a quick peek inside the mirrored cabinet above the basin. Wax treatment, nail varnish, creams, hair mousse. Nothing to indicate a second person. I'm rather relieved at that.

There's no sign of any pets in the place, either. A thought about Erica catapults into my head. She had a scruffy little dog who sat in during our first couple of sessions and seemed to listen to what I said. After that, he lost interest (the story of my life) and stayed in his basket in the hall. I wonder where Rupert is now. Erica always used to offer me a cup of tea when I arrived and she'd sit with her stocking feet resting on a footstool. Now I come to think of it, she was more relaxed, more informal than Sam, who's wearing the same trademark pale silk blouse and black skirt that she wears at the hospital. I thought she'd be more laid-back at her home; hoped she'd be a bit more chatty.

Our chairs in the sitting room are spread out, so we're not even within touching distance, and there's the statutory box of tissues and two glasses of water, making the place look business-like. There are two clocks in the room, so we can each see how much time is left and vases and plants, but few personal items. I can see gaps in the bookcase as well as the walls, as if she's removed certain books and ornaments. A tiny nugget of hurt hardens in my throat when I think she might have also done that because I've turned up.

All in all, the place feels stripped bare, not personal or cosy in the least. Just another room where Sam works. It's sterile and soulless. Not like a home at all.

I'm miserable and depressed for most of the session and, from the questions she asks, Sam assumes it's about the accident. I don't enlighten her. I can hardly tell her I want her place to feel more homely. That I want to feel like she's properly invited me in.

Towards the end, Sam explains we'll have another session to complete our first block, then a further three to six sessions to see how I'm getting on. I'm pulled up short by that and a bubble of anger explodes inside my chest.

Now she's seeing me privately, isn't it open-ended like it was with Erica? Can't I come for as long as I like? Bloody hell, I didn't think there was going to be a time limit. You can't rush this sort of thing. Doesn't Sam realise that? I could be cast aside after just ten or twelve weeks, kicked out, like all the other times I've had to move on. Then I'll be forgotten as usual. *Rosie who?* I can picture Sam's therapy notes now: *The frumpy ginger one who nearly drowned.*

As I leave, I notice there's some post lying on the tufted front mat. Being helpful I pick it up for her. I can't help noticing a postcard on the top, writing side up. I quickly scan the text. It's from someone called Con, but there are no kisses at the end and there's no sign of serious affection. A brother, a friend or an ex? I hand the pile to Sam and wait for her to open the front door.

As she flicks down the latch, I spot a small bundle on the ledge. In a flash, my dismal visit doesn't seem so fruitless after all. I scoop it up when she isn't looking and hold it tightly in my hand – all the way home.

Chapter 12

Rosie

The following day, someone deliberately sets the fire alarm off at work and a couple of kids scarper with two trolley loads of DVDs. They aren't on special offer, so this probably means our pay-rise will be put back a few months, if we get one at all this year. Sid, the manager, is insisting he needs to recover the cost of the increase in insurance premiums through our wages, because we aren't vigilant enough. The whole business reminds me of Max's violin. I wonder where it is. Caught up in the weeds at the bottom of the lake, or sitting safe and sound in someone's sitting room? I've been checking the catalogues that Dawn emails every week — it's stupid really. Sam's right, no one would dare try to sell that kind of instrument on the open market.

Back at Streatham after work, my basement flat hits me as dark, dingy and damp. The three 'Ds'. A combination of rotting fish and cat's pee bleeds through the carpets, even though, in the three years I've been here, no cat has ever set foot in the place. Sam's place is airy, aromatic and artistic. I want three 'As' instead of three 'Ds'. Story of my life — again. I want my sister's paintings on the wall and Chanel bath oil on my flannel, but I have neither a sister, nor a bath. There are so many black holes in my life. Family, luxury and love being key gaps I can single out straight away.

I'm keeping what I took from Sam's flat warm all night under my pillow and at the bottom of my bag during the day, just in case. I'm thinking about when to put them to use when I notice my answerphone is flashing with a new message.

It's the Cumbria Constabulary; they must have found something. I ring straight back, but my hopes are raised unnecessarily. DS Eric Fischer, the person I'm supposed to liaise with, says they've found a cello smashed up by the bank of the lake, about a hundred yards from where the van entered the water. A little boy was fishing nearby and thought it was a boat. The case was floating under a wooden jetty nearby.

'We've also got the detailed results back from the van,' DS Fischer tells me. He has an irritating lisp on every 's'. 'The steering wasn't stable and there was a slow puncture in the front left tyre, but there's nothing to suggest it was anything other than wear and tear.'

'Anything else?' I ask.

'The brakes were locked at the time of the crash – it looks like the vehicle could have done with a decent service.'

'And the other passengers?'

'I'm sorry. Max, Stephanie and Richard are still missing.'

I replace the receiver and sit on the edge of my threadbare settee staring into the empty blackened fireplace. Just the cello then. Three more instruments and three bodies to go. Are the police going to get in touch every time something new breaks the surface?

In our last session, the first one at the flat, I told Sam more about the other three players. Not that I know a great deal; I hadn't followed their lives at all since we graduated and barely knew them at college outside rehearsals.

'Like I said before, sorting out groups at college was pretty random really, it was down to the tutors, but Richard was the one I saw the most,' I said. 'He was a bit of a laugh. He liked to take risks and muck about; too easily distracted from his studies. You have to be pretty obsessed to make it as a serious musician and Richard spent more time on the football pitch or at a snooker table than in a practice room. He scraped by, an instinctive player, winging performances on a couple of rehearsals, and he was an exceptional sight-reader. But he didn't have enough dedication to get to grips with the technique…you know, to make it professionally.'

Sam asked if I liked him.

'I didn't fancy him, if that's what you mean. I'm not sure I knew him well enough to feel anything either way. He was always joking about and I never knew whether to take him seriously or not, so I was cautious with him. But he seemed sweet enough. I wasn't exactly in his circle. But then I wasn't in anyone's circle.'

Sam asked me what had happened to him after college, but there wasn't much to tell.

'I got the impression he'd been an odd-job man for longer than he liked to admit. He did everything from pulling down sheds to putting up old ladies' net curtains. Personally, I think it was a waste of his talents. He would have made a great school teacher. I can see him getting a bunch of kids excited playing songs from *West Side Story* on recorders or something.'

She asked about the others and I said I'd told her everything I knew about Max. 'Stephanie was the quiet one,' I continued. 'I remember her in the college orchestra at the front of the cellos. She was pretty good, I think, but she let it go after she left college. Married a Japanese bloke and had kids. Her career never even got started.'

Sam asked if we could do the trance exercise again, to access memories that were lurking beneath the surface. I know it's useful, but the whole process does get me flustered. What if I accidentally give away something I'm not ready to tell her? I don't want her to know, for example, about my recent trip to the pub in search of a willing guy. I don't think that will go down too well, although there's something far worse I can't afford to reveal.

She let me hold her hand again. She seemed hesitant at first, but I suppose she shouldn't make it obvious that she's starting to feel something deeper for me. From the way our sessions ended at the hospital, I reckon I'm the first patient to see her privately in her flat, so that must mean something. She's certainly made an extra effort for me, but she's got protocol to follow, I'm sure. Erica was always banging on about that when I was seeing her. She was always keeping her distance, saying we weren't meant to have hugs or contact, even if I was upset; all kinds of rubbish like that. I'm hoping things will be different with Sam, given a bit of time.

Sam led me through the usual trance thing. As it happened, something new did come up, about the lunch with the Hinds' family, the day of the accident.

'It's something Karl said after Max reminded us all about Mick coming to a sticky end at that first party. Karl asked if we were still playing the same instruments we'd played fifteen years ago. Thinking about it now, it seems an odd question to ask, don't you think? Why would he be interested? He wasn't even a musician. He worked for his father in property and investments. Anyway – we went round the table and everyone said yes, "except Max of course," Richard butted in, "who's upgraded his old box to a two-million-quid deluxe model."'

'That conversation seems significant to you,' Sam had said, narrowing her eyes.

'Yes, but there's something else, I'm sure of it.'

Chapter 13

Sam

As soon as I opened it, I felt my scalp prickle. It was sitting on the mat when I got home from St Luke's. My first thought was that someone had sent me an early Christmas card. It was pretty; a real dried rosebud, with the words *Thank you* in silver letters on the front and a handwritten message inside:

> *I'm so glad you've agreed to see me 'out of hours'. I feel you're someone who truly understands. I've never had that before.*
> *Rosie XX*

The kisses were larger than any of the other letters. *Big* kisses.

I slipped the card back into the envelope and dropped it into my briefcase. I'd take it to work and leave it with my other work correspondence.

I wondered again if seeing Rosie in my own home was such a good idea. It made our connection less clinical, more personal. I'd need to be careful from now on; I mustn't confuse her in any way or do anything to give her the wrong impression. She had to understand she was my patient and nothing else – not my friend, not even an acquaintance – a patient on a purely professional basis.

I threw my heavy briefcase onto the sofa, then ran a

deep bath. I sank down into the soothing water and dropped the soap. The sound of the splash made me think again of Rosie's accident. I pictured the van sinking like a stone into the lake and Rosie searching for her viola as water came gushing in. It would have been dark, suddenly so cold; a massive shock to the system.

There's no way I'd have reached out for any possessions in that situation, no matter how valuable. Rosie had told me her viola wasn't worth anything, so I couldn't quite get my head round the fact that she chose that case deliberately, and not the violin. I needed to fully grasp the tremendous *sentimental* value Rosie's viola held for her. It was her one and only long-term friend.

I dried myself off and returned to my briefcase on the sofa. A ridiculous new directive had been introduced at work; from now on we had tons of forms to fill in with boxes, graphs and charts to show weekly levels of improvement with each patient. Ugh!

I was rescued by the trill from my landline; a local number I didn't recognise. I lifted the receiver. 'Hello...?'

'Dr Willerby?'

'Who is this?'

'It's Bruce Lennox, Dr Willerby. I'm sorry to disturb you, only I wondered if you'd had time to think about the question I asked you in our final session.'

Bruce was a recent patient; forty-three, short and schoolboy thin, with two hedgerows of bushy hair that didn't meet up on the top of his head. Awkward and unforthcoming, I'd got the impression he'd spent most of his life stooping under a low cloud of inadequacy.

He'd had some memory issues after being attacked in a bar. I'd brought our sessions to a close last Friday so he shouldn't have been calling me.

'Bruce…er…how did you get this number?'

'Er…I think it was on your website.' I knew for a fact it wasn't. I was also ex-directory.

Three minutes before the end of our last appointment, Bruce had asked me out on a date.

'I'm really sorry, Bruce. I'm flattered, of course,' I'd told him, 'but there's a clear directive that means someone in my profession can't date their patients.'

'Why not?' He'd been indignant, hurt.

'Because we've had a very different relationship so far and changing the dynamic between us could interfere with all the good work we've done.'

'I'm prepared to take that risk.' He'd moved a little too close to my chair, so I got up and eased my way past him to get to the door. Before I could reach it, he was right behind me, breathing into my neck, his hot hands on my waist.

'Bruce – this isn't a good idea. I don't want to have to call security.' I hadn't told him my alarm button was a million miles away under the rim of my desk, but he let go and stood back.

'Just think about it,' he said. 'It doesn't have to be over. You've been so kind, so supportive. I can't believe you don't have any of the same feelings I feel…but, I know you can't say otherwise, not here…I don't want to cause you any problems with your job…'

He'd held out his sweaty little hand and I'd taken it reluctantly.

After that, thankfully, he'd left.

But, clearly, it wasn't over.

'Dr Willerby?' his voice grated again in my ear.

'I'm in a rush, Bruce,' I said, my only thought being to end the call as soon as I could. 'But my answer's still the same, I'm afraid. I could lose my job for meeting patients or even ex-patients socially.'

'I won't say if you won't...' his voice oozed conspiratorially down the line.

'That's not the point.' I sighed. 'I'm sorry, it's not appropriate.'

'If the rules were different, might you be interested?'

I scrabbled around in my mind trying to find a rejection that wouldn't sting too much. 'Sorry, Bruce – we had a professional relationship, there's nothing else to say.'

'But you might think about it?'

He simply wasn't getting it. 'Listen – the contract between us has ended,' I growled, in a steely militant tone usually reserved for persistent cold-callers. 'There is nothing more. Please don't contact me again.'

On Saturday, Miranda wasn't answering her phone again, so I decided to drop round to her flat. I wanted to make sure she was looking after herself. The last time I'd been there I'd been horrified by the number of pizza boxes that were littering her living-room-cum-studio. Evidence of too many take-aways, when she knew good nutrition was a key factor her specialist insisted on to keep her on an even keel.

According to Miranda, several friends had turned up

with 'spicy pepperonis' one night. But I know my sister too well. When she scratches behind her ear, or turns away as she begins a sentence, I can tell she's lying.

It started to pour down as soon as I got to pavement level at Camden Underground. I jogged for several blocks, having not thought to bring an umbrella.

'Why didn't you call?' she snapped as she opened the door. She sounded put out rather than surprised. She stood in bare feet, one on top of the other, wearing nothing but an oversized T-shirt. Her bleached blonde hair stood up in spikes so she looked like she'd just got out of bed even though it was lunchtime.

'I've *been* calling. You're not answering.'

I tried to push past her out of the rain.

She thrust her elbows out. 'No – let's get some fresh air.'

'But it's raining…and you're not dressed.'

'I'll get changed.' She started closing the door on me.

'You're not leaving me out here!' I raised my voice, storming past her. She dropped back with a huff, and let me inside. 'What's going on, Miranda?'

'What do you mean?'

'You're not returning my calls, you're distant with me. Secretive. You didn't even want to let me in.'

'Let's go out for a coffee,' she said. 'I'm going dizzy with paint fumes. There's that really nice place down the road. I'll only be a moment.'

She disappeared up the spiral staircase, leaving me to breathe in the sickly smell of linseed oil. I wandered into the kitchen and took a look in her fridge. Pots of yoghurt within their sell-by date, cheese triangles, a bunch of celery, half a tin of baked beans, half a loaf of bread. It wasn't brilliant, but it wouldn't kill her. I sniffed the milk. That was okay, too.

I heard Miranda hurriedly shutting drawers and cupboards upstairs. Why was she so keen to get me out of there? I retraced my steps and sat on the arm of the only chair in the room that didn't have tins or dirty rags on it. As I scooped my coat under me to avoid wet paint from nearby fresh canvases, my foot caught the edge of something tucked under the seat. I slid it out. Another pizza box. It wasn't shut, so I took a quick look to check there was no mouldy pizza inside it. Instead, there was a palette knife and a roll of oily cloth.

The sound of Miranda slamming a door upstairs startled me and in my rush to hide the box, the contents tipped out onto the floor. The last thing I wanted was for Miranda to know I'd been snooping, so I dived down to put everything back where it was. As I grabbed the bundle of cloth, something slipped out onto the bare floorboards. I froze, unable to take my eyes off it.

This was not good. This was not good at all and I had no idea how to deal with it.

The next moment, I heard her footsteps rattling down the iron staircase. I thrust the box under the chair and folded my arms.

Miranda gave me a prim smile and grabbed her keys from the kitchen table. I didn't move. I was in two minds about confronting her there and then, but I decided it would be better to deal with the situation once we were outside. Then at least she wouldn't be able to bundle me out and lock the door on me.

As soon as we were on the high street, I opened my mouth to speak. But she beat me to it.

'Someone is interested in one of my pictures,' she said. Miranda's canvases had been selling steadily since her last exhibition at the gallery. 'She works at Battersea Dogs and Cats Home…Denise someone.'

'That's great. Is she paying enough for it?'

'I don't need any handouts, if that's what you mean.'

'No. It wasn't. Never mind. I'm glad.'

Would it ever be possible to have a conversation with Miranda without her getting defensive?

There was a steady reggae beat thumping away in the background at the Urban Shack Café. A warm-faced Rastafarian with dreadlocks down to his waist, and an attitude so relaxed I was surprised he was still standing, asked what we'd like.

Miranda ordered a chocolate milkshake and I had a latte. We sat on high stools by the window.

'It's nice here,' I said, looking over at the waiter.

She'd pulled the folded napkin from under her tall glass and had started scribbling on it. 'Dezzie is really sweet. He plays his guitar in here, sometimes.' She bopped around to the beat, rattling the pen between her teeth. 'You seeing anyone yet?'

I ignored her. Why did she keep asking me this? 'I haven't seen enough of *you*, lately,' I said pointedly.

'I get preoccupied with my painting.' The doodle she'd begun started to evolve into a dragonfly. She stopped and looked solemnly into my eyes. 'I'm sorry.'

She gave the words considerable weight.

'You're sorry about what, exactly?'

She let a silence hang. 'We're just different, that's all,' she said.

That seemed to be my sister's answer to all our problems. I was too sensible and straight-laced in her eyes; she was reckless and irresponsible, in mine. Poles apart.

There was a moment of awkwardness, then I bit the bullet. 'I know I shouldn't have looked, but—'

'You've been spying on me,' said Miranda indignantly. She scrunched up the napkin and stuffed it under the edge of her saucer.

'My foot got caught on—'

She shoved her glass towards the window. 'Yeah, yeah, come on, spit it out.'

I took in her entire face. 'I found it, Miranda. I found a syringe in the pizza box.'

She tutted and flapped her hand at me. 'Oh, that. I use it for paint. To get the right mix of oil base, otherwise the white, in particular, goes all lumpy.'

I was on full alert waiting for the scratch behind her ear, a turning away, but there was nothing. Maybe I was losing my touch, or maybe Miranda had wised up to it. Whichever way, I didn't believe her. It all added up; her distant behaviour, sleeping in late and now I was seeing her in daylight, the orange rings around her eyes and her brittle hair. Were her pupils dilated? Was she sweating more than usual? I'd have to pay more attention.

'Are you sure?' I said. I'd come across plenty of schizophrenics self-medicating with heroin before.

She reached for her bag. 'If you don't trust me, that's *your* problem.'

I didn't know what to do. Should I go straight to her case worker? Should I try to squeeze the truth out of Miranda first? Had I got it entirely wrong? I pulled at her wrist. 'Don't go, Miranda. Please.'

She plonked herself back onto the stool and sat in sufferance, playing with her top lip. I chose another option. I'd drop it for now, give her the benefit of the doubt, and go to the Project where she worked to speak to her tutor and friends. I'd be tactful. I'd ask if they knew about her painting practices. Check if white paint was a particularly difficult one to work with. I was determined to find out for certain, one way or the other.

A couple came in who recognised Miranda. Her face instantly shifted out of the shadows into blazing sunlight and she gave them a cheery wave. 'I'm glad you've made friends,' I said.

'That's Sponge and Kora – they work at the gallery.' Miranda extended her smile to me. She seemed to have completely forgotten about my accusations. Good timing, I thought. Now I knew who to ask. It was obvious she wanted to join them, so I left her to it.

Later that evening, as I was getting ready for bed, my landline rang. It was Rosie.

'I know I'm seeing you soon, but I thought you'd like to know they found Max's violin case…'

I felt unexpectedly vulnerable hearing her voice as I stood barefoot on the cold kitchen floor in my pyjamas.

'Rosie – okay, but this isn't—'

'It turned up in a cove. The police said it probably broke open, but there was nothing inside. I thought you'd be interested. They also found Stephanie's cello a few days ago. It was all smashed up in the lake. They think the violin is probably ruined, too – but they haven't found it yet.'

'Rosie, this is all very interesting, but you do know we agreed that you'd only phone if you needed to cancel a session?'

Silence.

'Rosie? You remember that sheet I gave you last week? Have a look at it again – it does say that we—'

'I thought you'd want to know, that's all.' Her voice was clipped, sharp.

I softened. 'I know this is stirring things up for you, but our contract doesn't involve you ringing me outside our session times. I thought you understood that.'

'I did. I do, but I'm all on edge about it. I want to know what really happened. Did someone go back for it? Did it float into the cove on its own? Did a complete stranger find it? It had a special Xenara case. They're really expensive and they're supposed to protect a violin under extreme circumstances. Do you—?'

'We can't go into this now,' I said firmly. 'Why don't you write down your questions and we'll talk about it all on Thursday? I really have to go now.'

I dropped the receiver back into its stand as though it was on fire, before she could utter another word.

After charging across London for my emotional meeting with Miranda, I'd spent the afternoon fighting the Christmas crowds trying to find suitable gifts for

Mum and Dad and I was wrecked. I'd been winding down for an early night, but now I was fully alert. And angry. How dare Rosie think she could call me whenever she felt 'on edge'?

I'm not the Samaritans…

I went into the bedroom and stood blankly in the middle of the carpet. Rosie's call had jolted me straight back to last Christmas. That *other* call. I'd thought at the time that I'd handled it well; I'd been firm, but kind.

Little did I know.

I'd made a vow then that I'd never get involved in that kind of situation again, but here I was, getting sucked in. I stared at my reflection in the wardrobe mirror, my hand over my mouth, looking like I'd woken up to find myself sleepwalking in the middle of a busy road at midnight.

I could picture the book on Joanne's bedside table, smell her perfume left suspended in the air. I shivered and wandered over to my bed in a daze.

No. Rosie was different.

Completely different.

Chapter 14

Sam

Dr Minette Heron was an inspirational psychologist I'd heard speak many times before. She was one of the warmest people I'd ever come across, with a surprisingly raunchy sense of humour. I did my best to get to all her London lectures and we'd often squeeze in lunch if neither of us had to rush off somewhere.

Cutting it fine, I bolted out of St Luke's before lunch and hailed a cab to get me to King's Hospital near Brixton. For once, I was delighted that the driver was a maniac, weaving around buses, dodging a red light and even mounting the pavement at one point to keep us moving. I arrived with two minutes to spare.

Minette had a penchant for the colour orange and sure enough, she lit up the stage, her jacket, scarf and shoes in a blinding shade of tangerine.

In her presentation that day, she was making the case for matching the right style of therapy to each individual, especially in cases of low self-image. Her arguments were always fascinating and I liked the way she included recorded extracts of sessions. Most of these came from the psychotherapy teams she supervised, though of course she used pseudonyms to preserve patient anonymity.

She was getting towards the end of her presentation

and I was finally starting to flag, when she introduced a recording of a patient she called 'Kitty'.

'I won't go into Kitty's history,' she said, 'but suffice to say she'd had years of rejection to cope with. A childhood bereft of love. In her mid-thirties, and after a string of therapists, she believed she was being respected and heard for the first time in her life. This was a person-centred, client-led approach and Kitty felt in control.'

Minette stopped and scanned the faces in the hall. 'But some therapists didn't work so well for her – those using more analytical or cognitive approaches, for example. She felt they were replicating authority figures from her past who had instructed her, questioned her, made demands on her. For Kitty, *acceptance* in a relationship was crucial.'

I jotted down a few notes. My NHS role required a cognitive approach, and with all the CBT forms we now had to complete, straying into other methods held less appeal. Minette's words were a reminder, however, that the patient's needs should come first. She was right.

A hand went up in the auditorium. 'Are you suggesting we should contact patients' previous therapists to find out which approach worked best? That could take months…'

'No, I'm not proposing that,' came Minette's response. 'I'm advocating a couple of simple questions at the start of your first session – you'll find these on the handout; page three.' She glanced down at her notes. 'It saves time. It gets results. It saves *money*.' She gestured towards the chief executive of the NHS commissioning board, sitting at the front. 'Anyway, enough of me, let's hear what Kitty had to say.'

The recording had barely started before my pen slipped from my hand. I knew that chirpy voice. She was telling her therapist months ago that she was so pleased she'd found someone who seemed to truly understand her.

'You really seem to get me,' came the voice. 'It's such a relief. I've never had that before.'

I felt a spine-tingling chill of déjà-vu. Almost the exact same words were written in the card Rosie had sent me: *I feel you're someone who truly understands. I've never had that before.*

The recording went on, but I didn't hear any more after that; my head was filled with questions that drowned out any outside noise. Who was Rosie's psychotherapist? How long had they been working together? How had she coped with Rosie's emotional neediness?

I missed the end of the talk altogether and suddenly everyone around me was getting up to leave. I got to my feet and swayed, staring blankly ahead as the auditorium broke into geometric patterns. I started to walk down the steps and the next moment, everything in my path turned orange. I was face to face with Minette and she was smiling, waiting for me to say something.

My mouth felt like it was full of glue.

'Hey – are you okay, Sam?' she said.

'Yeah…sorry. I wanted to say it…your lecture…very enlightening, as usual. Really useful, interesting.' Most people had drifted into the corridor by now.

'Thanks – I'm glad it came across as more than just a cost-cutting exercise.' She glanced down at her watch. 'I'd love to chat, but I've got a flipping board meeting.' She gathered her papers against her chest. 'We must do lunch again soon.'

'Yes…sure.'

I must have looked gormless, barely able to string two words together.

'Just one question before you go,' I managed. 'The woman Kitty was working with – who is she? I'm not sure if you said.'

Her face clouded over. 'Erica Mandale, a dear friend of mine. Over at Guy's.' She shook her head. 'Died suddenly earlier this year. Such a shock.'

Chapter 15

Sam

I had no time to dwell on Rosie and her previous therapist; I had to use the return journey to St Luke's to bolt down a sandwich and prepare for my remaining patients. At the end of the day, I was about to lock my consulting room when I heard hurried footsteps coming up behind me in the corridor.

'Sam…sorry, Dr Willerby…' It was Rosie, out of breath. 'I'm glad I've caught you. I'm so sorry to bother you here, but I've just been for a lung check-up and—' A paramedic swung around the corner with an ambulance trolley and we were forced to back against the wall before she finished. 'Sorry,' she said again. 'I need a form for work – to prove I attended the sessions we had here.'

Standard procedure. Form D1.11. I told her to wait in the corridor and went round to the main office.

It took longer than I'd expected to get my hands on the right form and when I returned, Rosie wasn't there. I turned full circle and went back into my office only to find she'd made herself at home in my room, sitting in my chair, swinging it from side to side.

'Great,' she said, smiling as I came in. She had no idea that she was overstepping the mark. Rosie didn't seem to grasp established social protocol.

I hesitated, torn about what to say. 'Rosie, I asked you to wait outside. This room is private.'

'Oh,' she said, getting up, a flicker of confusion crossing her face. 'Oh, well…see you Thursday at your place,' she added merrily as she left.

As Rosie disappeared down the corridor, Debbie, who managed several units on my floor, appeared at the door.

'You've made someone happy,' she said. 'Are you handing out special pills or is it just your innate charm?'

Debbie was tiny in size, but big on warmth and generosity. We'd been best buddies ever since I joined St Luke's over eight years ago. She was the one person at work who could be counted on to offer two rare comforts: a sympathetic ear and decent biscuits.

'You finished now?' she asked, tapping the face of her watch.

'Totally finished,' I said, my shoulders sagging.

She beckoned me with a curled finger. 'My office, Willerby. Now. Tea and Hobnobs.'

I followed her like a new puppy.

'Doing anything exciting tonight?' she asked, handing me my steaming tea in a mug decorated with the words, *I may be short, but I'm in charge*.

'Er. One word. No,' I said with a shrug. 'I've got a spin class on the way home.'

'And how many eligible guys in the class?'

'Um. One word, again,' I replied with a giggle. 'Zero.'

She'd been nagging me for weeks about ditching spinning and taking up Spanish or boxing instead. 'You need an activity with more *men* in it, Sam,' she sighed.

I waved her words away. 'I want a relationship that "unfolds naturally", you know, where I just turn a corner in the supermarket or bump into someone gorgeous at a friend's wedding.'

'Well, good luck with that one,' she said and we both laughed.

I'd tried online dating, but only because Debbie and Hannah had goaded me into it; I'd been half-hearted from the start and hadn't bothered responding to the 'likes' I'd got.

'I'll be fine,' I said. 'Relationships are overrated.' I thought of Con as I said it, feeling something of a fraud, because I still found myself wishing we'd had another chance.

Debbie, on the other hand, had every right to be cynical about things that were meant to 'unfold naturally'. She and her husband had been on IVF treatments for months and she was starting to give up hope. Numerous times after work we'd stopped off for a drink on the way home and she'd dissolved into tears. Every time, she apologised.

'Oh, Sam, here I go again,' she'd blubbed only last week. 'As if you don't have enough of people's problems at work…'

That's one drawback about working in my profession; friends always assume you're inwardly cringing the moment they start talking about themselves. 'Don't be silly,' I'd said, pulling her close. 'You must *never* think that. This is a huge deal, Deb. I can't bear that you're suffering and there's nothing I can do to help.'

'But you *do* help. You let me drivel on,' she'd said, crushing a tissue into a tight ball. 'I'd go mad if I didn't have you.'

Miranda had told me she was going to Eastbourne for the day, so I took the opportunity to head over to the Arts Project. I was looking for the couple Miranda had said hi to in the café the other day: Sponge and Kora.

I found Kora wiping up mugs in the kitchen.

'I'm Miranda's sister,' I said, as I picked up the tea towel she'd dropped.

'Oh – she's not here today.'

'I know. It's you I came to speak to actually, and Sponge if he's around.'

'You're a doctor, aren't you?'

'Sort of. Psychologist.'

She grimaced. 'Even worse,' she said. 'Don't tell Sponge. He doesn't like shrinks. He's in the back yard. Someone smashed a pile of bottles over the wall, last night.'

She waited. I wasn't sure where to start. 'Miranda seems to be doing well with her paintings.'

'Yes – she's selling at a steady rate. It's a good spot for us here.'

'You paint too?'

'Mixed media – sculpture mostly. I'll show you.'

She led me through to a studio that was out of bounds to the public. The strong smell of glue made my eyes water. A handful of people were working; one using his fingers to pummel clay, another bending a long coil of wire into a shape that looked like a bicycle frame.

She showed me a row of shiny limes and lemons made of melted wax on copper mesh. 'These are nearly finished. I've sold two "still lifes" in the last month.'

'Wow, they're good enough to eat,' I said, in genuine awe.

'Everyone says that,' she laughed, looking pleased. She leant against the bench waiting for me to explain the real reason I'd turned up.

I caught her cagey stare and cleared my throat. 'I wanted to ask how Miranda was getting on. How she's been lately.'

She folded her arms. 'Checking up on her.'

'Yes, I suppose so. She doesn't tell me much at all these days. I want to make sure she's okay.'

She looked me steadily in the eye. 'To be honest, she seems to have had a new lease of life lately. I've known her since she started here and she's the happiest I've seen her.'

'That's…good.'

'She's had a real surge in her painting. She's been trying new techniques. Mac, her tutor, is very pleased with her.'

I decided it was best to come clean.

'This is going to sound like a terrible betrayal, but I found a syringe in Miranda's flat…she said she uses it for painting…'

Her expression didn't change. She looked like she was used to prying family members trying to rock the boat.

'Don't jump to conclusions,' she said. 'Believe it or not, some artists do use clean syringes. It's not something we do here, with ex-users around, but I know artists in other studios who use them to soften oil paint, especially white.' She lifted an oily rag to wipe her fingers. 'For some reason white gets lumpy and dries out quickly and you can easily control the consistency on the palette with a syringe.'

'Wouldn't a bottle with a rubber dropper work better?'

'Oil rots the rubber.' Kora raised her eyebrows. 'Perhaps if you'd looked closer you'd have seen paint on the syringe.'

I nodded with a wince.

'I'm so paranoid about what Miranda might be up to next that I didn't stop to look properly.'

She twisted her mouth into an expression of contempt. 'Miranda's newfound enthusiasm for life has nothing to do with drugs…' She hesitated. A brief acknowledgment of confidentiality. 'I'm not sure I should tell you.'

I gave her a look which said she'd gone too far to backtrack.

'I might be wrong – but I'm pretty sure she's got a new man in her life.'

My eyes widened. 'Someone from here?'

'I've no idea. You'll have to ask her.' She began walking away. 'That's all I can tell you.'

I managed to find both Sponge, Kora's boyfriend, and Mac, Miranda's tutor, and both were adamant that Miranda wasn't using.

'According to her medical records, she's never been into drugs,' said Mac. 'I thought you'd know that.'

'I did. I do…it's just…' My sentence fizzled out into a sigh.

It made sense. Miranda had started taking medication for schizophrenia when she was twenty and hated it. It was years before her doctors got the dose just right and she'd always loathed taking the stuff. The idea that she'd play around with her dosage or mix her prescribed drugs with any illicit substances was entirely out of character. I should have realised.

I thanked him and came away with a weight lifted from my shoulders. One less thing to worry about. I was intrigued, however, by the new boyfriend. Why hadn't she told me?

Chapter 16

Sam

By the time Rosie arrived for her next session, I was feeling a bizarre mixture of confusion and compassion. Rosie had claimed that I was the 'only person to ever understand her', but in the recording at the lecture, she'd made exactly the same claim about her previous therapist. Presumably, she made desperate bids to ingratiate herself with anyone who would listen. Maybe she was even more fragile and damaged than I'd thought.

I didn't want to bombard Rosie with questions about it, but I did want to know how Erica's death had affected her. It must have been a nasty shock to lose someone she trusted.

But before she sat down, Rosie launched straight in with an update on the crash. She was clearly obsessed with Max's empty violin case showing up and had been trying to work out what it meant. I'd already assumed that musical instruments and water didn't mix, but I'd done a little research of my own and discovered that all the joints in a stringed instrument are water soluble, so even busking in the rain is risky. If a violin is immersed in water, the damage can range from discoloration, to the whole instrument coming apart at the seams, beyond repair.

Rosie hitched her seat a few inches closer to mine. 'Something doesn't add up,' she said defiantly. 'It's about the case.'

'Go on.'

'I mentioned when I rang you that Max's violin case came from a company in Naples called Xenara,' she explained. 'They claim to be the best in the business. Typical. Nothing but the finest for wonder-boy.' She tutted. 'The company have run tests by sending a violin inside one of their cases into the Gulf of Naples.' She rolled her eyes. 'Can you believe it? It stayed afloat for hours and because of the waterproof coating, neither the inside of the case nor the violin got wet.'

I raised my eyebrows, taking it in.

'There's something else – even more significant. There's a pull-down lock system on this type of case that makes it watertight. The makers say it's "almost impossible" for it to be opened accidentally.' She paused, bit her lip. 'I'm sure the case was shut properly when we got in the van. Max always made a point of locking it, too, even if he only had a short trip to make. Habit, I suppose.'

That *was* interesting.

She carried on. 'It makes me think it couldn't have broken open accidentally. What do you reckon?'

I blinked fast. 'I really don't know, Rosie. I think we should try to stay focused on what you can remember. We'll have to let the police sort out the rest.'

'Can you take me back again? I'd like to try to catch more of the lost pieces. My memories are like dandelion clocks. I'm trying to snatch at them, but most of the time I'm not quick enough and they float away.'

I smiled at the image she portrayed. 'The way you describe things...' I said, as I invited her to lie down, 'it's striking. I'm not saying you're deliberately trying to keep me entertained, but if you are, you really don't need to. I'm listening, no matter what.'

Her cheeks flared up into a sharp pink colour. 'I didn't realise...' She sounded chuffed rather than embarrassed.

She closed her eyes as I pulled the blanket up to her chin. I gently led her back to those scenes in the Lake District, starting a little earlier on, when the quartet were packing up the van.

'Was it just the four of you or did any of Hinds' people help you with the instruments?'

'It was just us. Max wouldn't let anyone touch his violin. He wanted to keep it in the front beside him, but there wasn't room. He even suggested Stephanie give up her seat for it and she went in the back with me, but Richard wasn't having that.'

'Richard stuck up for Stephanie?'

'Yeah. The others took their seats and there was only one place I could go.' She blew out a long breath. 'Like I said before, being in the back saved my life.'

'I'd like to try something, Rosie. Do you drive?'

'Me?'

'Yes. Have you passed your test?'

'No. I had some driving lessons when I left college, but...I wasn't... I never...'

'That's okay. You know how a car works, that's the main thing.'

'Yeah. Sort of.'

She tried to extend her hand towards mine, but I tucked the blanket around her in a measured and firm stroke, keeping her arms inside. The whole 'holding hands' business had started to become a habit and I wanted to break it.

'Can we run the incident from the time you got into the van, but can you describe it as if you were in the front, in the driver's seat?'

'From Richard's position?' She cleared her throat. 'I'll try.'

I helped set the scene. 'So you're getting into the driver's side, sliding on to the seat. Are Max and Stephanie already in? Is Rosie in the back with the instruments?'

'Er, yeah. Max is just clicking his seatbelt,' her voice became a slow monotone as she began to relive the events. 'Stephanie is wriggling about, because it's a tight fit in the front…I'm behind her…' She ground to a halt and opened her eyes. 'Sorry…'

'It's okay. Try to stay with Richard's point of view from now on. I know it's weird, but tell me everything from *his* perspective. You're Richard, behind the wheel. Feel your feet on the pedals, touch the handbrake, check the rear-view mirror…can you carry on?'

'I'm Richard…I'm…behind the wheel. I put the key in the ignition and the engine groans. It's slow to get started. I try again. Then we're off. We pull out of the Hinds' gravel drive and head down the track towards the lane that leads to the lakeside road.'

'As Richard, what do you see, how do you feel?'

'I'm quite hot, I've got my sleeves rolled up. Stephanie hands me a bottle of water, but I don't want it. She hands it to...Rosie in the back...no, hang on, that's later...'

All of a sudden, she stopped and shot upright as if she'd been stung by an insect.

'I can remember something,' she said, dragging the blanket into her mouth, her eyes wide. 'It was Richard. Before the crash. We were in the pub – it must have been the night we got there.

'"Wouldn't you love to see the look on his face?" he'd said. "It would be worth it just for that."'

Memory recall is like that at times. Things jump around, come back in the wrong order. I went with it.

'Was it just you and Richard in the pub, or was anyone else with you?'

'No, it was just me...and Richard.'

I waited. She sank back down again, closed her eyes.

'He was talking about Max's violin.' I watched her eyelids flutter. I imagined the pictures inside her head coming to life, like photographs emerging in a developing tray. 'He put his hand over mine and then he asked me.'

She waited, as if she was listening for his words.

'He said, "Are you in?"'

'Are you in?' I repeated neutrally.

'And I said, "How? What do you mean?"'

'"We steal it," Richard said. "Are you in?"'

She made a little snoring sound followed by a sigh. I was aching to prompt her. I didn't want her to lose the thread, but I didn't want to distract her, either.

She sat up, alert, and pulled out of the trance. 'It's gone. I can't remember what I said. But it would have been no, of course.' She rubbed her eyes. 'He can't have been serious anyway. He would have known, like we said before, that there was no way it could be sold on. Unless…' She stopped, seeming to think about it. 'Could Richard have set up other avenues for fencing it, do you think?'

We tried revisiting the memories several more times, but got no further.

'Why would Richard run the van off the road deliberately and risk killing *himself*?' she pondered out loud. 'He'd have had plenty of other opportunities to make Max's violin disappear, wouldn't he?'

She took a sip of water and waited for me to say something.

'I'm afraid we'll have to wait and see if you get any answers to that.'

I'd been itching to ask her a question, and with a few moments left I finally managed it.

'When we first met, you said you hadn't had any therapy for about six months, is that right?'

'Yeah, that's right.'

'Is it okay to ask how long you'd been seeing your previous therapist?'

'Yeah, sure. About…' she appeared to count in her head, 'eighteen months.'

'That's quite some time. And…you decided to end the sessions?' I felt a twitch of guilt for putting her to the test.

Her eyes dodged across the room. 'No. She died.'

'Wow – that must have been really hard for you. You didn't say…'

'I didn't know you at first. I was too upset to talk about it. I would have told you eventually. Bit of a shock, actually. You get to depend on someone always being there. Then, out of the blue, they're gone.'

It was hard to imagine what impact Erica's death must have had on Rosie, given her unstable background and lack of formative attachments.

'Did you…did you get on well with her?'

She sniffed. I could see she was aiming at nonchalance. 'Yeah. Not bad.' She glanced up at the clock. 'My time's finished now. I'd better go.' She got up and left before I could pry any further.

Chapter 17

Rosie

She thinks I'm special. Okay – to be honest, she didn't actually use that word, but she seems to like the way I describe things. She thinks it's unusual. It's probably about as close to feeling special as I'm going to get.

She's asking a lot of questions about the accident, so I know she's intrigued by the mystery of it. We pass ideas back and forth; sometimes, it's like sharing gossip with a proper friend.

She's even done some research herself. I'm impressed by that – really chuffed. Erica would never have gone that far. She only ever asked me how I felt about things, how I was coping. Sam seems to want to be involved. It's as if we're a team, trying to solve the mystery together. And that's exactly how I want it to be.

She was really sensitive around Erica when I told her she'd died. I bet she was wondering whether I liked Erica better than her.

I couldn't see the *thank you* card I sent anywhere – I was disappointed about that. Maybe it's by her bed or amongst her private things, so that no one else can see it. Yes, that would explain it.

It's quite relaxing lying there on her special couch, only I didn't get to hold her hand this time. I don't *need* to hold her hand, of course – maybe just that first time, but it's wonderful when it happens. I think she'd have liked to, this time, only we had work to do and she seemed to respect that. I'm hoping we'll get the balance right soon and we can show affection for each other without her feeling so awkward. It must be hard for her when she's used to seeing me at the hospital.

It's brilliant to have her hanging on my every word when she uses the memory trick that helps me access my subconscious. It makes me feel all warm inside. And I don't have to tell her everything I remember either. In fact, for all she knows, I could be making it all up. She's only got my word for it.

The following week sank into a pointless, grey wasteland until I got to see her again. As soon as Thursday came around the world was worth being a part of once more.

Sam and I did the trance thing again, but this time it wasn't so comforting. Quite scary, to be honest.

I was lying down under the blanket, away with the fairies, talking through who did what – and I'm not sure what happened next. One minute I was listening to Sam's voice guiding me along the road beside the lake, the next I was gasping for breath, with great swelling sobs jerking my body like jolts from a defibrillator. All of a sudden the horror of it overwhelmed me. Richard trying to take evasive action even though we were already airborne. Stephanie wailing in the brief moment before we hit the water. Max frantically trying to wriggle out of his seatbelt.

I shot up on the couch, my hands clawing the air, my nose running, and I couldn't see a thing. My eyes were pumping out tears like a burst water main. Sam held me. I couldn't believe it. It was like being lifted up to heaven with my angel of deliverance. She wrapped her arms around me and stayed still. Like that was okay. Nothing out of the ordinary. Like I deserved it. I had to practically peel her arms away from me; she didn't want to let me go.

'I can see blurred images of their terrified faces.' My voice came in short bursts, between ugly snorts. 'But I couldn't have seen them…I was behind them…I could only have seen the backs of their heads.'

'It's your imagination playing tricks on you,' Sam reassured me. She gave my arms a rub and finally let go.

'Why is my brain trying to give me nightmares?' I cried.

'It wants to fill in the gaps. It's trying to create its own video of the event. It's what our brains do.'

Sam retreated to her chair and I pulled my knees in to my chest, shivering under the blanket. My tears had left damp patches on the pillow and the side table. I felt stupid, a bit like I'd wet myself.

'Why am I crying when I was the one who came out alive?'

'I've been expecting this,' Sam said calmly. 'It's a perfectly normal reaction. It's partly the shock; you're still trying to process what happened and why.'

'It's over nine weeks since we went down, since they went missing. Why now?'

'Take your time,' she said, waiting for more.

'I keep going through the normal routine of my life, then remembering that Richard won't ever down a pint of real ale again, Max won't ever play the Tchaikovsky or tune up his beloved violin. Stephanie won't see her kids going up a shoe size. I want them to have those things again. It's like I'm trying to live their lives for them inside my head, because they can't.'

'It's partly survivor's guilt,' Sam reassured me. 'You might feel a range of strange feelings and reactions as part of that. I'd like you to know that you can talk about all of those confusing feelings here.'

'Am I having a breakdown?'

'I don't think so. It's completely normal after what you've been through.'

Sam soothed me, talked to me, listened. She waited as I tried to finish my sentences, gave me space to say what I needed to say in my own messy way. She didn't patronise or belittle me; she took everything I said seriously. I felt embarrassed about my little outburst. I thought I was more in control of myself than that. I'm used to showing people what I want them to see, not letting it all spill over like a pile of dirty washing. Sam didn't seem the least bit perturbed, so I found myself bringing up stuff I'd hardly ever talked about with anyone.

You'd think having had therapy on and off since I was sixteen, I'd have gone back and forth over my childhood, like a seamstress pressing creases out of crumpled linen. But I haven't. I've covered the ground, of course. Done it to death. But only in terms of what happened. The facts. I've never felt able to open up sufficiently to tell someone how I *felt* about it. How it affected me. I've wandered into that territory on my own many times, but never taken anyone with me. Now it felt like Sam might be the one to go alongside me.

'I have yucky black thoughts when I look back over my childhood. They're not even as clear as thoughts,' I told her. 'They're more like gloomy smudges that spoil anything good that ever happens. It's hard to pin down what I feel – I try my best not to feel at all, really.'

'We could try to pin it down now, if you feel ready?'

'I'm not here for that though, am I?'

'Well, you know our original agreement was for memory retrieval after the crash, not for more general therapy, but it doesn't mean we can't explore your past in more detail. You've told me some of what happened and we can develop that. In fact, it might be useful. Your past has made you who you are and it will directly influence how you react to significant events.'

'Can I tell you the most vivid memories from my childhood?'

Sam nodded, earnest and concerned.

'One is of my mother – seeing her on the floor in the bedroom with a red pool spreading beneath her, across the carpet. I didn't see the rifle straight away; I thought the bangs I'd heard were doors slamming or something. And the other one is of my father swinging from the banister; the rifle must have been too big for him to turn on himself.' I felt my mouth twist to one side. 'It can't have been a quick death. I remember his tongue turning black, a wet stain seeping down his trousers. Those two events happened in the space of about half an hour.'

Sam looked distressed. She put her notes down and

I thought she might have to leave the room. I pursed my lips and heard them make a strange popping noise. I didn't want to cry any more.

'Sorry,' I said. 'I didn't mean to upset you.'

'Rosie, don't apologise. It's so terribly sad. Such devastating memories to have to live with.' She looked genuinely appalled.

'Oh, I'm used to it. The worst part is that after my dad died, a policewoman or social worker, I can't remember now, told me he'd left a note. It said he'd planned to take me with him, but then he'd changed his mind.'

I couldn't stop the tears this time. There was a backlog going back decades.

'Even in death you see, my dad *didn't want* me.'

Those words, I'd never said them out loud before, they'd been rotting inside my heart for over twenty-seven years.

It was good to tell her. I cried on and on, but Sam didn't seem to mind.

After about twenty minutes, I started to feel better and put the tissues she'd given me onto the side table in a soggy bundle. 'I don't have anyone close any more; no sister like you do,' I reminded her. 'Sometimes women like us need a shoulder to cry on, don't we?'

Her mouth did the funny twisty thing it does sometimes when she doesn't quite know what to say. I cleared my throat and asked to go back into the trance. Ironically, it was a bit of relief to go back to the crash after my little detour talking about my family. And I did remember something new, as it happens. From when I got out of the water.

'I was sopping wet and the ambulance had arrived to take me away,' I told her, lying under the blanket. 'There was a shape in the bushes. A thin board sticking out. A number plate.'

'When you say number plate, was it lying there discarded or was it attached to a vehicle?'

'Attached,' I said. 'I can't see anything else, though.'

'Can you remember any of it?'

In my mind I tried to look, but it was a mush of letters and numbers. I shook my head.

'And was it on your left or your right as you came out of the water?'

'On my left.'

'So, it was a vehicle that had come *past* the crash site – unless it was there beforehand…'

Sam was thinking aloud then. She does that sometimes when I'm in my trance. I don't think she expects any answers; she's working it through for herself. I love the way she's so interested in the puzzle of it all. She wants to get to the truth almost as much as I do.

We were interrupted at that point, by the intercom buzzer. Someone wanted to come up. So irritating. I thought she'd have some way of switching it off while I was there.

I sat up, coming out of the memory with a huff so she'd know I was put out. I was expecting her to ignore it, after all, we were right in the middle of things, but she said she'd better see who it was. What a cheek! I'm paying for her time.

She got to her feet, slipped out of the room and, to be fair, she wasn't long. In a jiffy, she was back saying it was nothing. She apologised, at least that was something, but by then our time was over.

In spite of the disappointing ending, I couldn't keep the smile off my face as I walked down the street. Sam didn't know, but when she rushed out to the intercom, I made the most of being left alone and took a quick look at her appointment diary – it was open on the table beside her. I wanted to find out what she does when she's not 'on duty'.

My name was scribbled in for that night and there was only one other entry all week. It was for Saturday night and there was one word: *Wyndham's*.

Ah-ha – this was my chance. I was going to get beneath the skin of the real Sam, for a change.

Chapter 18

Rosie

It's Saturday morning and I've put on my dusty old trainers and taken to the streets. I know there's no point in breaking into a jog – I'd only get as far as the first bus stop – so I take big strides and swing my arms and huff and puff around the block.

Why on earth am I doing this? Well, last night I had a nasty shock. Normally, I cover my bedroom mirror with scarves and bags so I can't see myself, but when I got undressed, I pulled everything off it and took a good look at myself, stark naked. I didn't recognise what I saw. It was as if someone had run amok with my body when I wasn't looking and slapped great chunks of lard over my belly and hips. My thighs looked like they belonged to a rhinoceros. I'm never going to be properly loved looking like that. I have to *do* something.

Being out of breath like this reminds me of another time after Mum and Dad had gone. I must have been around ten. There was a gang at school who never let me join in; kids in my class, who I thought were edgy and cool at the time. They went everywhere on bikes and they'd ride towards me in a group, scaring the shit out of me. They'd snatch my school bag and toss it into the beck, grab hold of my jacket as they spun past and rip the sleeves, the lapels, the pockets off.

I didn't have a bike. But I wanted to be like them. Be one of them.

Then, one day, they said they'd consider letting me join their gang if I gave them half my dinner money. They said if I did it for a week, I was in. I was over the moon. I stopped having a main meal at lunchtime and ate a bit of fruit instead. They were true to their word and invited me to meet at Picket's Wood, at the back of our local supermarket.

They got off their bikes and pushed them along the muddy tracks into the thickest part of the wood. It was getting dark and the undergrowth grew thicker as we got deeper into the tangled mass, but I wasn't scared. I was with my gang now.

Ralph suggested hide and seek. His dad was a policeman. He whispered something to Neil. They said because I was new, I could go first. Ralph and Julie wrapped a woollen scarf tightly over my eyes. Miles and Kelly spun me round, then put my hand against the trunk of a tree and told me to say the Lord's Prayer out loud three times. I was excited, so I kept having to start again. When I finally got to the third 'Amen', I took off the blindfold and started looking.

At first, I thought it was fun. Then all of a sudden, it wasn't fun anymore. The sun had slipped away and I could barely see what was on the ground in front of me. I tripped over a branch and fell into some nettles. Everywhere looked the same. I didn't even know which direction we'd come from. I stumbled over a tree stump, narrowly missing a coil of barbed wire and stopped to listen. Looking up, I could hear the rustle of leaves high above me in the treetops, and nothing else. I called out. Nothing.

I wanted to go home. It was cold and I didn't know which way to go. The light had almost gone completely, there was only the moon flickering between the branches.

Then I knew what the whispering had been about. It was a trick. They'd never intended for me to join their little gang at all, they just wanted to make fun of me.

'I want to go home now,' I called out. 'I don't want to play anymore...'

I started to sob, standing there, helplessly, making little circles. Then it was as though a bomb inside me exploded. It came from nowhere. A fiery, scalding ball of flames that sent energy to my legs. I know now that it was anger; a surging, roaring rage that I'd never felt before, not even when Mum and Dad died. I wasn't having this. I was going to show them – the snotty, shitty bastards. They weren't going to get away with what they'd done. I was going to get home for tea and somehow I'd pay them back.

I began striding out fast, tripping and falling every few steps, but plunging onwards with darting eyes and determination. I didn't care that my knees were shredded with thorns and broken branches. That my jumper was torn and I could smell dog poo on my shoes. I kept going. I knew if I walked through the wood for long enough in the same direction I'd come out the other side. The air around me was boot-polish black by then. I staggered on, humming to keep myself company and then I saw a sprinkling of white dots. I was near enough to the edge of the wood to see the car headlights. I started to run towards them, breaking out of the undergrowth into a car park.

I'm back at my flat by now, exhilarated after my walk and ready for a shower. I haven't reached the end of that particular story, but I want to put my mind to my next task. I can savour the way it turned out another time.

I dry off and dress in my usual gear. A tunic top that hides my stomach, leggings to cover my dumpy legs, my purple Doc Martens, because they're comfy.

I was never introduced to make-up when I was growing up. My various 'aunts' were too old to bother with it and younger foster carers didn't take the trouble to show me. I wasn't allowed in their bedrooms. Everything 'ladies did' was behind closed doors and I've had to learn about it from magazines.

No one warned me about periods either. I screamed when I went to the toilet and found the mess. Thank goodness I wasn't at school when it happened. Mrs Lillie tore an old bed sheet into small squares and told me to pin one to my knickers with safety pins. I felt like a leper.

I'm sitting on the grubby settee in my dingy flat, feeling lonely. I'm hungry, but I'm not going to eat. I think about having sex. It's not something I've done very often. I haven't fancied anyone in ages and there's no one at the music store. Jack is a laugh, but he's always falling in with the wrong people and getting involved with dodgy deals. The store attracts those kinds of people. There's an underground element; drug users, fraudsters, people out to make a quick buck. Lee is more 'sane' than the rest of them. He smokes weed, is vegetarian and goes on animal rights' demos. Swears by fennel tea for constipation and something chewy called tofu. He's a bit too downbeat for me.

Lee and Jack know various 'low-lifes' who lurk outside the back exit now and again. It's designated for smokers, but I often hang out with them and they don't seem to mind. They think I'm dim and gullible and haven't a clue they're smoking pot half the time.

Anyway, finding romance at work is a non-starter, but I'm not bothering about it for now. I'm going to throw all my efforts in a different direction, and to do that, I'll need to make myself more presentable. I should maybe pluck my eyebrows and polish my nails for a start. What else do women do to spruce themselves up? I'll have to get along to Boots and buy some spot cover and lipstick.

I grab the newspaper and check the TV listings. There's a programme on that afternoon called *Style Diva*. I'll watch it and get some tips.

Sam's going to get one heck of a shock!

Chapter 19

Rosie

I'm ironing when the phone rings. It's DS Fischer with an update on the crash. My heartbeat shoots off like a greyhound bursting out of the starting box. What have they found this time? A body? My viola?

'Nothing like that I'm afraid,' he says, clearing his throat. 'Do you remember anyone wearing a green Barbour jacket before the accident?'

I can picture it straight away, almost smell it. 'Yes. Max had one.'

'Just Max?'

'Yeah. Richard wore a kind of baggy brown hoodie.'

There's a silence.

'You found it?' I say, my mouth dry.

'Can you remember if Max was wearing it when he got in the van?'

I recall the crackly sound it made when he put it on and the waxy look of it, but the images are from Hinds' place, not from driving around the lake.

'I don't know,' I tell him.

'Okay. It was found this morning in the water, about seventy metres from the place where the van went down.'

'After all this time?'

'Let me know if you remember anything about him

wearing it, will you?'

'Sure.' I can see what he's thinking. When did Max and the jacket part company? That's his real question. In the water? In the van? Did Max shake it off in the lake in an effort to swim to safety? Did he manage to escape? Is he still alive?

His voice breaks through my chain of silent questions. 'We've also had a call from Richard White's sister. She'd like to get in touch with you about what happened. We don't usually give out numbers, so I wanted to check if you felt comfortable speaking to her.'

'Oh,' I don't try to hide my disappointment. 'That's fine, I suppose. You can give her my number.'

'You sure? You don't have to.'

'It's okay.'

I don't mind talking about it with people, even if they are ringing about their loved ones and not really interested in me. I might even be able to find out some background information that could be useful in explaining the crash.

The call comes through that same day. Lucy White lives in Kent and hadn't seen Richard since a couple of months before the accident.

'I don't really know why I'm ringing,' she says. 'I suppose I needed to speak to you, because you were the last person to see Richard...' There's a gap. She can't bring herself to add the final two syllables.

'What have the police told you?' I ask.

Lucy runs through what she knows: why Richard was in the Lakes, how we drove up from London together, that for some reason his van left the road.

'They don't even seem to know if it was an accident or not,' she says. Her voice is light and thin, like pink chiffon. 'They said the steering wasn't right and there'd been a puncture in one of the front tyres, but they didn't know if that was wear and tear or signs of…'

'I know,' I commiserate. 'I can't add much, I'm afraid. I remember we swerved and left the road. I don't know why.'

I don't tell her that the police have worked out that the brakes were jammed at the time of the accident. It meant Richard wouldn't have stood a chance.

'I suppose what I really want to know is – do you think he suffered?'

God, what a question. Has anyone ever drowned and not suffered? I'd only had a flavour of it: the water scorching my nostrils, the pain as it burst into my lungs, the terrifying panic when I realised I couldn't breathe. But I'd got out before the worst part set in. Surely, drowning couldn't be anything other than a frenzied, frantic agony.

'It would have been quick,' I say with assurance, leaving it at that.

I don't remember any glimpses of Richard after we hit the water and I'm trying not to allow invented images of him, fighting to get his seatbelt off, his door or window open, to flood into my mind.

'Did he seem happy?' she says hopefully. 'I know he'd been struggling with money lately. He'd fallen out badly with Dad and he'd had terrible fights with his brother. Greg's always been a liability. He stole from Richard a couple of times.'

Richard hadn't told me any of this. But then, why would he?

I scrabble around for something positive to say. 'He was chatty in the van on the journey up north. He thought the whole idea of us playing together again was a lark and he seemed to...be enjoying himself.' That wasn't strictly true. Wasn't true at all, in fact. Richard hated the whole idea as much as I did, but he was there for the generous fee, like the rest of us.

'Did he tell you about the first time, when you all did that original concert, years ago?'

'What about it?'

'Apparently Richard slept with the wife of the guy who organised it, the night before the celebrations.'

Shit! This is news to me. I wonder if Cameron Hinds knows about it. I try to think back. Had he seemed hostile to Richard at any point? Had there been a bad atmosphere or was he completely in the dark about it, like me?

'Did you tell the police?' I ask.

'Yeah.' I can hear her fingernails tapping on the edge of the phone. 'Do you think Mr Hinds might have got you back up there after all this time under false pretences?' Lucy says. 'Did he find out about his wife's infidelity and decide to punish Richard?'

She's way ahead of me. She's obviously spent time working all this out.

'Hold on,' I say, flopping back onto my settee. 'Mr Hinds didn't get us all together on a whim, it was for his twenty-fifth wedding anniversary.'

'Yeah, but what if her infidelity just came out while

you were there, somehow…maybe they were talking about that first time and his wife let something slip…'

'You think Cameron Hinds messed with Richard's van? You think he felt angry enough to *kill* him?'

'Why not?'

'But Mr Hinds knew Richard was ferrying us all around. Are you saying he didn't care if he murdered *all* of us?'

She goes quiet.

'Cameron Hinds doesn't come across as the mass-murdering type,' I conclude.

'Maybe you're right. I just, you know, need someone to blame.' She starts to cry.

I hold the phone away from my ear. Even though I've had plenty of therapy I still don't really know what to do when someone else is upset. In any case, I'm not sure I'm up for offering full-blown counselling, so I apologise and tell her I'm going to the theatre.

I take my seat early and watch everyone file in. It's years since I've been to see a play. It isn't really my thing. But, I couldn't miss this opportunity to see Sam 'out of hours'. Good job she put 'Wyndham's' in her diary, and not just 'theatre' – I wouldn't have known where to start. Not that I intend to bump into her. I'm wearing a beret to hide my flaming hair and I've experimented with a bit of make-up to make me look different. Even so, I slide down low in my seat.

It isn't until we're halfway through the first act that I spot Sam through my little binoculars, towards the front of the stalls. Expensive seats. I watch her for a while to see if she's made any contact with the people sitting on either side of her, but she doesn't seem to know them. On her own, then. I'm surprised she isn't with friends. I watch her as the play unfolds. During certain scenes she sits upright and during others she slumps a little and appears to be delving into a packet of sweets. She seems to be most interested whenever 'Frank' comes on. When he has a short scene to himself, she sits there, completely transfixed – you might say she is ogling him. Then I twig why she's here.

According to the programme, the actor playing Frank is a guy called Conrad Noble. I remember the name 'Con' from the postcard I read at her flat. She has every reason to be interested, too. The black and white photo of him in the programme barely does him justice; he's gorgeous.

Is this love in its early stages, or love gone wrong?

As the final curtain comes down, I feel a wave of extraordinary excitement as if I'm the one in love with him. I watch him take his bows, clapping wildly.

It's okay, Sam. This is going to be our little secret.

Chapter 20

Sam

I poked the hot crumpet out of the toaster with a fork and smothered it in butter, watching as it slithered into the holes. My mind was on Rosie; our last session had been a tough one.

There was so much I still didn't know, not just about the accident at the Lakes, but about Rosie's background. I couldn't imagine how she coped with those chilling memories of the day her parents died, nor could I get those shattering words out of my mind: *Even in death, my dad didn't want me.*

She'd reached out and I'd let her hug me. What else could I do? She'd have slumped to the floor if I hadn't caught her. Then I'd had to peel her fingers away to make her let go of me. It was getting decidedly tricky working with her; such a fine line to tread between wanting to help and creating a situation where she was starting to become dependent on me.

I barely tasted the crumpet and put another in the slot, mechanically. She'd told me her childhood carers had ranged from brusque, no-nonsense types, who'd shown sporadic kindness, to zealous religious types intent on saving her soul from the sins of her father. Was there really no one she was close to?

As I took another bite, the phone rang. I answered it absent-mindedly, with butter oozing down my chin.

'Hello?'

There was no reply.

'Sam Willerby – hello?'

More silence. I sank my weight onto one hip. 'Bruce? Is that you?'

One long background hiss. I put down the phone.

Wrong number, that's all. I swallowed hard, my tongue inexplicably gritty as if I'd taken in a mouthful of eggshell.

I leant against the sofa and recalled how Rosie hadn't batted an eyelid when she'd told me about finding her mother in a pool of blood. She must have developed such thick skin over the years.

I was still intrigued to know what had happened during the eighteen months of therapy she'd had with Erica Mandale. Losing a surrogate parent figure when she died must have brought back all the pain. And yet, Rosie *seemed* unscathed by it.

I dearly wanted to know how Rosie had coped at the age of seven, watching her mother and father die so gruesomely within minutes of each other. How had she dealt with it? How had the loss and shock affected her as an adult?

She'd clearly learnt the knack of detaching herself and switching off, but what about all those horrifying images locked up inside her head? Had she ever really opened up to anyone? I was seeing more and more sides to Rosie as the weeks went by and yet I felt I wasn't seeing the real Rosie at all.

It was Sunday, my diary was blank and I was still in my dressing gown. I texted Hannah to arrange to meet up, but she sent a message back saying she and Alan were driving around Kent, taking a look at various properties. I didn't want to know. There were other friends I could try. Five minutes later, I'd left three messages on different voicemails and still had no plan for the day.

I felt like a pale, miserable shadow of myself, especially when I thought back to the theatre last night. Watching Con from a distance I suddenly felt like his stalker. I didn't even want to be with him. I'd only gone because I wanted to remember that feeling when we were first together: the excitement, the anticipation, the intense sexual charge between us. I hadn't realised ending it with him was going to leave such a jagged hole in its wake.

My friends were right, I needed to meet someone new, to move on. It had been over a year, after all. I opened my laptop and started to browse through online dating sites – and closed it again pretty swiftly. The whole scene made me wince. It was all bad teeth, receding hairlines and the ubiquitous *good sense of humour*. There had to be a better way.

The phone rang again and I checked the incoming caller: 'withheld'.

I picked up the receiver, but didn't say anything. I refused to be intimidated. Silence again. I waited. Nothing. I put it down.

Right, that was it. I was getting myself a whistle to keep by the phone. No, two whistles; one for my mobile when I was out and one for home.

Unable to settle, I threw on my jogging gear and

took to the streets, hoping the exercise might lift my mood. Outside, it was crisp and slippery and my breath made wispy clouds as I built up speed, but after about twenty paces I got a stitch; I was running too soon after breakfast. I slowed to a brisk walk instead and turned round to look down the hill at the line of trees. Most of the branches were threadbare and unremarkable, hanging inert, as if they'd given up any hope of coming back to life. It left me feeling worse. I turned and broke into a run again.

Feeling invigorated as I took the last corner, I stopped at the payphone to call Miranda. I knew if I rang from home, my number would come up on her caller ID and she might not answer. She picked up after three rings, sounding bright and breezy.

'Oh, it's you,' she said, enthusiasm swiftly draining from her voice.

'Just wondered how you were; how your day in Eastbourne went?'

'That was ages ago. Fine on both counts, thank you.'

'Any chance of a coffee? You busy?'

'Can't just now.' She didn't elucidate. 'I've got to go to the laundrette later though, how about then?'

It didn't sound like much fun, but if that was all there was, I'd take it.

'Okay. What time?' I said.

She sighed. 'About five o'clock?'

Back home, there was a small package for me at the main entrance; a CD pushed through the door with a note saying, *Just a little something for all your hard work.* I recognised the handwriting from the thank you card.

Rosie must have looked at my shelves and seen I had a couple of other Adele albums. Patients occasionally bought me gifts, but typically at the end of a productive series of sessions. I usually responded with genuine gratitude, but this only made me feel awkward. It needed handling carefully. I took it upstairs and left it on the kitchen table.

I was going to have be more vigilant with Rosie from now on. She seemed desperate to please me, hungry for the most meagre scrap of affection in return. She seemed to be trying to force open a door that, in therapy, had to remain closed. I needed to emphasise that my care for her was purely professional; I wanted her to recover her memories – that was all. But she was so vulnerable. How could I tell her the cards and gifts had to stop, without hurting her feelings?

Miranda looked fresher than she had last time we'd met; she'd had chance to prepare for my visit. We hauled two laundry bags along to the launderette and as she set the machine running, I went out for take-away drinks. When I got back, she was reading a paper, humming to herself.

'Kora rang me,' she said, stuffing the paper down beside her on the bench.

'I thought she might.'

'Everything's all right, you know.'

I patted her hand. 'I know. I just worry. That's what sisters do.'

She laughed. 'I've sold another picture and someone else is interested in a couple I haven't finished yet.' She said defensively, as though to remind me that she was not only capable, but successful too.

I nodded and sipped my hot chocolate, wondering how to turn the conversation round.

The washing machine clunked into spin. 'Kora says you're seeing someone.' It was out.

She shuddered. 'Ugh. Why can't anyone keep secrets?'

I pulled back sharply. 'Why keep it a secret from me?'

'Because I know you'll get all protective and nosey. *Who is he? What's his background? How trustworthy is he? Is he going to take advantage?*' She was spot on, of course. 'Anyway,' she continued, 'it's nothing serious.'

'Someone from the Project?'

'No. I met him at the library.'

Since when did Miranda borrow books? She gave the spot behind her ear a quick scratch. I let it go.

The wash ended and we dumped the damp clothes into two separate dryers and set them running. Once the rhythmical thudding came to a halt, she started pulling items out. I offered to help.

She elbowed me away. 'It's okay, I can manage.'

'It'll take half the time, with two of us folding,' I insisted.

I dragged out pillow cases, towels, a blouse, jeans, pairs of knickers and a bra.

'I've finally ordered a washing machine of my own,' she said. 'I'm sick of all this.'

It was then that I came across a handful of unexpected items. A pair of men's socks. Then two pairs of boxer shorts. I held them up.

'Not serious, eh?'

'No,' she said, snatching them from me. 'Not really.'

I knew I wasn't going to get any further.

Chapter 21

Rosie

Big changes are happening! I've been to the hairdresser and had my hair straightened. Coloured as well. I've taken it down a few shades to chestnut brown instead of screaming ginger. Cost a fortune, mind you – and I'll have to keep going back to make sure it stays like this. In fact, I'm going to go even darker next time, because it's not quite what I want.

When I check in the mirror, I have to say, I look terrific. A new me. I'm wearing a pair of those tight magic pants that squash in your stomach and, in my lunch-hour, I had an appointment for eyebrow threading. I'd never even heard of it. I thought it meant you get them plaited, but turns out they pluck out the stray hairs to give them a defined arch. Blinkin' painful, I can tell you. Like a rabid hamster nipping at my skin, but at least it was quick. And cheap.

Tess, at work, did a double take as soon she saw me.

'OMG,' she said, 'have you got a bloke or something? You look amazing.'

I did a twirl for her on the spot, my hair fanning out in a soft curve with no crazy spirals in sight. 'Just thought I'd treat myself,' I told her.

I didn't mention it was my birthday last week. When Jack turned twenty-five, we all went along to The

George for a few drinks and we gave him the bumps, but I knew no one would have suggested that for me.

On Tuesday, I had a massive scare on my way home from work. I was trotting along Oxford Street minding my own business when I looked up and saw him. I was sure it was Max – heading in the same direction on the other side of the road. I crossed over to get a closer look, but it was hard to be sure it was him from behind. He had the same tightly curled black hair, albeit a bit shorter, the same kind of Barbour jacket he'd worn in October. But hadn't the police found that in the lake?

I didn't know what to do. If I called out his name, he might run for it and I'd lose him. Had he lost his memory or assumed a new identity? All kinds of crazy possibilities raced through my mind. He seemed to be speeding up and I was finding it hard to keep up without breaking into a run. There were hordes of people around as usual; tourists stopping to consult their maps, groups dawdling outside shops getting in the way. I tripped on the heel of someone's shoe and ended up on my knees. A woman helped me up and I barely thanked her, I was desperate not to lose sight of Max.

I dodged through the next dense crush and saw him disappear down a side street, but as soon as I got to the corner, I'd lost him. There were a handful of people on Poland Street, but none of them were Max. Had he seen me and legged it? Had he gone into one of the businesses? There was a modelling agency on the left, a recruitment agency opposite. I walked further down the street: a Chinese restaurant, a lingerie shop, a fish bar, a printing company. I looked inside the window of each one, but he'd given me the slip, intentionally or not.

I wandered back to Oxford Street. Was it really him? Could Max have got out of the lake alive? Or had my brain turned a complete stranger into his double, because I can't take my mind off the crash? I stood on the corner for twenty minutes, watching and waiting, but it was a waste of time.

Thankful that another day at the music store is behind me, I open my French windows and stand in the dark of the overgrown garden. It isn't the least bit windy; just cold in a solid, rooted-in kind of way. Like walking into a tall fridge. I can see a sprinkling of stars, which is rare in London. It must be a clear evening. As I look up, I think of Sam. I'll be heading over there in a few minutes; she's the highlight of my week.

I try to imagine what it would have been like to get a birthday card from her. Would it have had sunflowers on the front? Or an arty photo of a woman holding a fan? I would've traced my finger over the words she wrote inside; nothing gushing, just a simple, formal greeting like, *With all good wishes, Sam Willerby*. Impersonal or not, it would have meant the world to me. It would have meant she'd spent time in a shop thinking about me, browsing the shelves to choose that card just for me. I'd have treasured it like it was made of solid gold. I'd have framed it.

I come out in goosebumps just thinking about it. I hurry back inside, lock the doors and get ready to go.

I love that feeling when I get off the bus and walk along to the end of her road. I turn the corner and see her gate, then look up to the first floor. One light goes off, this time, but another one, further inside, goes on, sending out a faint glow. She's getting ready for me. The house pulsates with her presence.

My chest starts to burn inside as I get nearer. I check my watch, but I'm early, so I have to sit on the wall and wait. No one ever seems to come out, so I'm starting to think she doesn't have any other patients before me on a Thursday. Maybe she doesn't have any other patients at home *at all*. Maybe I'm the only one she's allowed into her sacred space. The chosen one. The thought makes me tingle and I get to my feet. I walk to the end of the road to kill the last five minutes before approaching the house again.

There's a noise inside and the communal front door shudders when I give it an exploratory shove. I find it's already open. Nevertheless, it seems polite to ring the doorbell first and I wait for Sam to press the buzzer to let me in. I climb the stairs and she's waiting for me, holding her flat door open. Inside, there's a floral aroma, like bath oil, wafting into the hall, but I can't smell food. I know she'd turn me down if I suggested we go for a bite to eat somewhere after our session. It wouldn't be allowed, though personally I can't see what harm it would do.

She waits until I sit down before she admires my hair and new outfit. Does she really like it or does she mention it because she can see I've made an effort? I hate not knowing what she's really thinking. After that, she rather spoils things by asking me not to buy her any more gifts. I tell her the CD was a freebie from the music store, that's all, but she still isn't happy. I just want to show my appreciation for what she's doing for me. She says it's her job and I'm already paying her a fee. Spoilsport.

I don't know whether to tell Sam about my 'sighting' of Max or not. She might think I'm losing it, that it's wishful thinking. It's no use calling the police either, not without a photograph or concrete identification. But thinking I've seen him like that has given me nightmares. In my dreams I keep following him and in the end I turn a corner and find him, but when I pull on his sleeve to turn him towards me, his face is grey and slimy from being underwater for weeks. His eyes are sucked out by the fish. I suppose I could tell Sam about that, but there's not much point. I ask about her family instead and that doesn't go down too well either.

'We're here to talk about you,' is all she says, as usual.

'I want to know what a *normal* family is like,' I tell her, but I really want to know more about *her*. She never gives anything away, always keeps herself out of reach. It's so annoying. Therapy is terribly one-sided. She's allowed to hide behind an iron door and I can't ask her anything.

'Okay, here's something about me,' she says, as if she can read my mind. 'About what's going on inside my head right now.' She blinks twice. 'I'm wondering what you expect from me. Whether you want me to help you recover your memories or whether you want something more from me?'

That shakes me. I try to stay centred.

'Sounds complicated,' I say, not looking at her.

Suddenly I'm not sure if I want to know what she's thinking any more. The comfort of not knowing might be a safer place to be. In my case, the truth always hurts. Still, it's nice to feel real contact for a change; sometimes I feel as though I'm in the middle of a game, one with stupid rules, like I'm playing chess with a waxwork at Madame Tussauds.

'I want to remember what happened, that's all,' I add, hoping that will end the matter.

For some reason, my mind floats towards Richard. I'm putting together what his sister told me, about him having money problems, with the conversation we'd had in the pub that first night. Had he really been sounding me out, not just joking, about stealing Max's Guarneri?

I make myself picture the van as it's filling up with water. Where was Richard? Did he manage to get out and take Max's violin with him? Had he planned it from the start?

'As we work with your memories, what would you most like to resolve?' Sam asks, leaning forward, noticing I've drifted off.

'Lots of things. I want to know if the crash was deliberate or not, for a start. I want to know whether someone was trying to kill one of us. Or all of us. Or if it was about the violin. But most of all, I want to know where my viola is.'

We do some focused trance work after that and something incredible happens. Part of a phone call I overheard after one of the rehearsals in the big house comes back to me. It was the day of the accident and

I'm convinced it's significant. It's only a few words, drifting up the staircase from the hall: *It's worth a fortune and it's under the bridge.* That's all.

'I've no idea whose voice it was or what they were talking about,' I say.

'A man's voice or a woman's, do you think?' Sam asks.

'A man's.'

'And you're sure it was at the Hinds' place? Could it have been at the B&B?'

'No. It was during a break in rehearsals at the mansion,' I say. 'Max told us all to take five, while he made some "important calls to his agent". He went onto the veranda with his mobile and I wandered on to the landing to stretch my legs. That's when I heard it.'

'So, it wasn't anyone in the quartet?'

'No. It was someone already using the phone downstairs in the hall.'

'Someone from the house?'

I shrug.

Neither of us have a clue what it means. There are hundreds of bridges in the Lake District.

My phone rings straight after that. I forgot to switch it off. I think it might be the police so I answer it, even though Sam's frown says she disapproves. But it isn't the police – it's Max's mother.

I can't hide the tremble in my voice. Why is she ringing *me*? DS Fischer must have dished out my number to all-comers, given how easy-going I was about taking Lucy's call.

Feeling bold, knowing Sam is right by my side, I put

the phone on speaker so we can both hear what she says. Her questions are similar to the ones Lucy had asked about Richard.

'I hadn't seen Max for six months,' she says, her voice breathy and strained. 'I wanted to know…can you tell me what happened? Did he seem happy? Did he suffer?'

Big questions. I stare at Sam for guidance, but she's sitting back avoiding my eyes, waiting.

'He seemed in really good spirits,' I say, making my voice sound bright. 'Didn't the police tell you what happened?'

I don't want to have to trawl through it all again.

'Yes… of course, but you were there…you…'

A sick feeling takes over my stomach. *You got out, you escaped, you were the lucky one…*

'I can't remember much,' I tell her. 'I'm having memory therapy to try to bring it back…but I'm sure whatever happened, it was quick…'

It sounds like a cop-out to me, but it seems to satisfy her.

'To be honest, I'm surprised he accepted the job,' she tells me, shifting into a business-like tone.

We all were. It seemed beneath him following his meteoric success.

'Especially as he'd had a bit of a run-in with the organiser's son,' she adds, 'during that first visit, years ago.'

'I didn't know about that,' I say, turning to Sam with my eyes wide. Funny how grief seems to encourage people to reveal all kinds of personal details probably best kept hidden.

'Karl Hinds threatened him,' she explains. 'He accused

my son of stealing something from the house.'

I keep my eyes on Sam to see her reaction. She looks annoyed that I'm allowing this intrusion to hijack our session, but she can't hide the fact that she's a teeny bit intrigued, too.

'What did Karl say he stole?' I say into the phone.

'I've no idea. Max said it was all a silly misunderstanding and couldn't wait to get out of there.'

'Perhaps he wanted to go back to clear his name?' I suggest.

'Max always was an honourable boy. And so talented. He was over the moon when he was granted long-term loan of the Guarneri.'

Loan.

So, he didn't own the violin at all; it was only on loan. He didn't mention that!

Perhaps his high-flying concert tours weren't as lucrative as he liked to make out. With Mr Hinds offering such an inflated fee, no wonder he accepted the gig.

I catch Sam's eye and bring the call to an end after that. 'I thought it would save time,' I tell Sam. 'I'd have had to explain it all to you in our next session anyway.'

She shrugs. 'It's *your* time,' she says, her eyes betraying reproach.

Yes it is. And choosing how to use it is about the only way I get to gain any kind of control. I sit back and glare at her. Some of these rules are really starting to piss me off.

My mobile rings again just as we are finishing. I recognise the number; it *is* the Cumbrian police this time. I take the call, intending to be brief.

'Okay,' I say. 'Thank you for letting me know.'

'They've found a body,' I say, closing the phone. 'In the lake.'

Sam can't stop her eyebrows from shooting up.

'They need to check the dental records, but it looks like it's Stephanie.'

Chapter 22

Sam

I was on my way back from a spin class when I heard my landline ringing from the landing. My heart rate shot up, as though someone had sprung out at me from the shadows. Following two more silent calls on my mobile in the last couple of days, I was starting to get jittery. Unfortunately, I'd been on public transport both times and hadn't been able to use my whistle; blasting the phone with a loud screech wouldn't have exactly endeared me to my fellow commuters.

As soon as I let myself in, I darted over to the handset to check the caller ID. It was an outer London number I didn't recognise. I got my whistle ready and slowly lifted the receiver.

'Is Miranda there?' came the voice. I let my shoulders drop. It was Stella, a friend of my sister's from the care home she'd stayed at.

'No, she hasn't lived here for a while. I'm Sam, her sister.'

'Oh, sorry Sam. I must have got mixed up and rung an old number.'

'She's in Camden now.'

'Of course. I'll try her mobile. I know it's early days but you must all be so excited.'

'Excited?'

Stella fought to backpedal without success. 'Sorry. No. I shouldn't have said anything…I'm sorry I disturbed—'

'Excited about what?' Miranda selling more paintings? Miranda's new boyfriend?

'Oh Lord, my stupid mouth.' A strained silence. 'I thought she would have said something by now. It's gone twelve weeks and…'

I didn't notice the handset slide to the carpet.

A cruel December freeze was already clawing its way over every watery surface as I hurried to the nearest bus stop. It filled the cracks between the paving stones, sent stiff veins into the puddles in the gutter. On the bus, I took the warmest seat at the back and pulled my hood over my woolly hat, hoping to shrink into a cosy oblivion. Stella's words had hit me like an almighty punch in my stomach. She must have made a mistake. I'd speak to Miranda and find out it was all a misunderstanding. We'd laugh about it. I'd be on the bus back home in forty-five minutes.

The streets were a blur as I backtracked to my last session with Rosie. She'd remembered hearing part of a conversation in the Hinds' residence while they were rehearsing and was all fired up about it. She'd latched onto the idea of something hidden under a bridge that was 'worth a fortune'. I felt she was clutching at straws. Surely, just a random snippet of chitchat, but Rosie was desperate to make things fit, like a child forcing jigsaw pieces into the wrong place.

The bus took forever, the ice making the driver

cautious. Without warning, my mind drifted back to last Christmas. It would be Joanne's anniversary in three weeks' time. I didn't want to go there. *No – leave it alone.*

I pressed the bell for the next stop. Once on the pavement, the wind caught me unawares. It snatched off my hood and whipped my hat away down the street before I had time to react. I caught up with it lying by a grate, soaking wet. I squeezed it out and squashed it into my pocket.

I fought another savage gust of wind and hurried round to Miranda's front door. I kept telling myself not to barge in all guns blazing – she might slam the door in my face, but I hadn't concocted an alternative reason for turning up unannounced. I spent my final steps scrabbling around for one. It would be the first thing Miranda would ask.

Her face was aghast when she saw me.

'It's Dad's birthday next week,' I said with enforced calm. 'We need to think of something to get him.'

'You've come all this way…you could have emailed.' She looked up at the sleet spattering down on my hood and reluctantly opened the door.

'You never reply,' I said as I wiped my feet. 'It would have taken ages. I want to get it sorted, what with Christmas around the corner.'

'I'm busy.' Miranda was wearing a long T-shirt with smudges of oil paint down the front. I couldn't help checking to see if there was any hint of a bump underneath it, but it was too baggy to tell. A canvas stood on an easel in the centre of the room and jars and tubes lay around it on the floor. Miranda was barefoot and she'd brought a trail of yellow toe-prints to the front door with her.

'Bugger!' she said, following my eyes and spotting them. She hopped back on one leg, grabbed a rag and tipped white spirit onto it.

'You can't paint in this light,' I said. A bare bulb, an old sixty-watt at best, hung down from the ceiling. 'It's not good for your eyes.'

'Yes, *Mum*,' she said, clicking her tongue as she rubbed first her toes, then the wooden floorboards.

Bad start. Would I ever learn? I peeled off my wet coat and perched on the edge of the sofa.

'I was thinking perhaps cufflinks or a new tie…' I said helpfully.

'Whatever. You get yours on your own. I'll think of something later.'

'Okay.' I slapped my hands together, hiding my disappointment that she wanted to go it alone.

'You want a hot drink?' she said grudgingly. I accepted with exaggerated enthusiasm – at least she was making an effort. I asked her about the art gallery, the sale of her paintings, about Kora, Sponge and Dezzie in an attempt to generate conversation.

'Dezzie is thinking of buying one of my latest ones,' she said. 'He wants it for the café. A bright one to liven the place up a bit.'

'Show me.'

'It's at the gallery.' She handed me the hot mug, but didn't offer to clear any of the papers and rags that had made their home on every seat.

I picked up a flyer from the arm of the sofa.

'I'm going to a gig later in the week,' she said. 'An Indie band at The Dublin Castle – you'd hate it.'

Her last words effectively cut off any chance of an invitation.

I perched on the arm and she walked up and down in front of the easel, sipping her drink without looking at me. I wondered how I was going to find a way to tell her the real reason I'd bolted over there.

'Nice and warm in here,' I said. 'I've found a damp patch in my bedroom. I think—'

'Get it fixed.' She swung the empty mug loosely by her side. 'Is that it? About Dad's present? I've got stuff to do.'

Miranda's words hit me like tiny cigarette burns on my skin. Would we ever get to a stage where I could chat to her without bracing myself for the backlash? I would have loved to have a sister I could confide in, have fun with, but I had to accept that our relationship would never be like that.

I didn't have much more to lose. 'When will I get to meet this man of yours?' I said, dipping my toe in the water.

'Not yet.' She made a move towards the hall, ready to show me out.

'What's his name? Surely I'm allowed to know that.'

She stopped and looked around as if she was trying to remember his name. I was starting to lose my cool.

'When? When will be the right time?'

'Not yet, okay? It's too soon. It's not serious. I told you.'

'Not serious?' I glared at her. 'So, you'll tell me his

name when the baby's born, will you?'

Her eyes widened. 'What are you talking about?'

I exhaled with a huff, casting caution to the wind.

'I had a call from Stella. She said you're having a baby. Tell me she's got it wrong.'

I took a step towards her, but she backed away, putting her mug down as if I might be about to smash it.

I couldn't hold it in any longer. 'You've told people at Linden Manor before you've TOLD ME?' I screeched.

'Told you what?'

'That you're pregnant for Christ's sake!'

'I'm not!'

I stood pressing my fingers into my forehead. 'You're not?'

'There *is* no baby.'

I bit my lip, confused. 'Listen…Stella…'

'I *lost* the baby.'

I gasped.

'It doesn't matter now,' she said, walking away from me into the kitchen. I darted after her, grabbed her arm.

'Miranda! I'm so sorry. Why didn't you…? I could have…' I pulled her limp body towards mine and squashed her against me. She hung there like a rag doll, floppy and unresponsive. I let go of her and took a step back. 'Why didn't you tell me?'

'Like I say – it doesn't matter now.'

'Yes it does! It's a massive **thing** to have gone through.'

She nipped her lips together and looked past me towards my coat.

'I'm not going yet. I'm *really upset!*' I cried, tears

coursing down my cheeks. 'I'm upset that you didn't tell me *anything*. Nothing at all. You have a boyfriend, you got pregnant and you lost the baby. And I didn't know one single bloody scrap of it!'

'It's over now,' she said, leaning against the door frame, her arms folded. 'In any case, I don't have to tell you everything. I've had boyfriends before…plenty you don't know about it. Why is it so important?'

'I'm your sister!' I wailed pathetically.

'Yeah. I'm still getting used to that.'

I'm not sure what happened next. One minute I was bawling at her, the next I was getting on the bus, going home. I stumbled up the stairs to my flat, a terrible emptiness swallowing up my insides. Only a year ago, Miranda and I had discovered a new understanding, a profound closeness I never thought we'd achieve. Rock-solid at last. But in recently months, I felt like she'd broken away from the mainland and my precious relationship with her was shifting further and further out to sea.

It was after 11pm, but I was wide awake. I wanted nothing more than to switch everything off and go to sleep, but I knew as soon as my head hit the pillow my brain would start tormenting me. I couldn't seem to relax any more.

I kicked my boots off in the hall, then dropped my bag on the sofa. On top of it, I flung my travel card, scarf, gloves and coat, feeling too rattled to bother about tidying up after myself. Again. I flopped into a heap alongside the bundle, then straightened up sharply. Everything about my sitting room looked spic-and-span.

Every book in place, cushions plumped up, magazines out of sight. I crossed the hall. All spotless in the kitchen, too. No crumbs on the work surface, no papers left on the table. I was sure I hadn't left it looking like this. I needed to get a grip. I was spending too much of my life on automatic pilot these days.

As I approached the bedroom, scenes from another flat flashed into my mind. Trust those harrowing snapshots to hit me when I was already down. As I reached for the door handle, I was instantly transported back to that other bedroom door – *her* bedroom door. To the stain on the rug behind it and the curly pink letters on her dressing gown: *Joanne*.

She'd cried out to me and I'd ignored her. I couldn't forgive myself for that and I'd been trying for nearly twelve months. *Stick to the boundaries* – that's what my supervisor had said. *You don't go running to them every time they say they can't cope. You must teach them to look after themselves.* He was trying to make out I wasn't to blame, but I knew the truth. I'd practically left her to die all on her own. She'd reached out to the one person she trusted and I'd failed her. How could I ever be forgiven for that?

I could never, ever let that happen again.

I plumped up my pillows and set my phone to play a soothing Chopin nocturne next to my bed. I closed my eyes and tried to let the tinkling piano melodies sweep away my perpetual guilt over Joanne, my blistering row with Miranda, my singular ability to mess everything up.

Before the music could work its magic, my landline rang. Grudgingly, I dragged myself out of bed in search of the handset. I could see from the little screen that it was a London number, but sure enough when I answered there was nothing but silence. I reached for the whistle I'd left on the coffee table and couldn't find it. *Bloody hell!* I slammed the receiver down, kicked the door of my bedroom shut and flung myself onto the bed. I gave my pillow a thorough beating, and between clenched teeth, yelled to my four walls, 'Leave me alone!'

Chapter 23

Sam

After my last patient of the afternoon at St Luke's, I felt that surge of triumph and relief that always comes with a job well done, forgetting that my day wasn't over. Rosie was due at my flat in two hours' time. I groaned inwardly at the thought.

I finished my second cup of tea and headed over to the bike shed. I'd been waiting for the rain to stop, but it looked like it was getting worse; one of the perils of being a cyclist in winter. It was generally too dark, too cold, too wet, but at least the bike got me from A to B without traffic jams or signal failures.

I remembered Rosie telling me she'd never had a bike as a child.

'It was on every Christmas list I ever made,' she'd said, 'but Santa never came good.'

I'd never met anyone like Rosie before. I found my feelings for her hard to describe, mainly because I didn't feel I knew her at all. She seemed to switch from one emotion to another in the blink of an eye; disconsolate one second, on cloud nine, the next. She was like a tiny fruit fly that, just as you think you've caught it, dodges out of your grasp and floats away.

Now that I was seeing Rosie in my personal space, I was constantly having to keep her focused. She was forever trying to turn our sessions into chats about the books I liked, the TV programmes I watched, the food I cooked. Or she'd get up and wander around, pick up my belongings, always asking questions. It was flattering, in a way, but she wasn't paying me to be her friend.

Rosie turned up on time clutching a DVD. Visions of her pulling a bag of crisps from her pocket and suggesting we catch up on an episode of *Scott & Bailey* flashed into my mind. As it turned out, she'd brought something far more relevant to her therapy. She'd been in touch with the Hinds' family and managed to get hold of footage of the original party, from fifteen years ago. Smart thinking.

'We can do this, can't we? It's in the rules?'

I nodded, hiding a smile.

'The party was originally on video, but Mr Hinds transferred it to a disc when I told him I was seeing you – so we can see if it jogs anything.'

'That was thoughtful of him,' I said.

It seemed somewhat unorthodox to spend our session watching TV, but she was right, something on the DVD could trigger memory recall. I set it up and we sat side by side on the sofa, with Rosie taking charge of the remote.

The footage was wobbly and jumped around; from a grand hall to stairs, corridors, various parlours and drawing rooms. There was no editing to link up the sections and no sound.

'This is the ballroom where we played,' she said as the camera settled in one spot. It was steadier now, perhaps fixed on a tripod.

'Is this before the guy who'd messed up your viola fell

to his death?'

'Yeah…Mick Blain,' she said pensively.

The camera panned out to reveal sweeping stairs and a balcony. It was certainly a majestic setting, with bone-white columns reminiscent of a fancy wedding cake. Guests in morning suits and ball gowns were mingling, while others attempted to waltz across the polished floor to music we couldn't hear.

'Posh, isn't it?' she said, her voice brightening up. Rosie's quartet was positioned in a corner surrounded by sprawling parlour palms. I spotted Max straight away from his posture. Dressed in black tie, he was brandishing his violin bow like a sword. While the others had their heads buried in the music, Max was looking around him, casting his trills and arpeggios into the audience with the panache of a bullfighter.

The camera settled on the quartet for a while and I watched each player in turn. Richard, playing second violin, his blonde fringe so long and heavy I didn't know how he could see the music. Stephanie was on the cello; her long, slim legs curling around the instrument while her fingers leapt about the fingerboard as if it was red hot. She was the only one we knew for sure was dead.

Rosie looked completely different then. The flesh under her arm wobbled as she slid the bow across the strings and she didn't look comfortable in the sequined dress, which was too low at the neck and too short at the hem. She was far plumper and her bright red hair was completely untamed. It made me realise how much she'd changed, not only since her old college days, but since she'd first starting seeing me. She was slimmer, darker haired and much more attractive now; like a different person.

As we watched, Rosie pointed out Cameron Hinds, pristine and regal, greeting guests with his second wife, Ambrosia. She wore a shimmering evening dress that exposed her bony shoulder blades, with matching tiara.

'Look, she's the one Richard had a thing with,' Rosie said, with a chuckle. Ambrosia looked at least twenty years younger than Cameron; step-mother to his children, but closer to their ages.

Karl Hinds was looking furtive; he wore his tuxedo like a hired conjuror. He was talking grimly to his father, before walking away to find a waiter and knocking back two glasses of champagne, one after the other. He looked about him, wiping his mouth with the back of his hand, seemingly unaware of the camera.

'Who shot the film?' I asked.

'Don't know. That's Jennifer, Karl's girlfriend, and there's Columbine, his sister…she looks older than fifteen doesn't she?' She pointed to a man in a navy blue suit. 'And there's Greg, Richard's older brother. I'd forgotten about him until Richard's sister mentioned his name on the phone, recently. He came along for the ride.'

We kept our eyes on the screen as Greg stood with his hands in his pockets, rocking from one foot to the other. He didn't seem to have anyone to talk to. 'And that's Ambrosia's sister. I can't remember her name.'

The picture popped and fluttered for a second. Rosie straightened up. 'I've been through it twice already, trying to see if there was anything going on between Richard and Ambrosia. What do you think?'

I'd been looking out for that too, but from what we'd seen, Richard had clearly been preoccupied with getting the notes out in the right order. It was hard to tell if any meaningful glances had been exchanged between them.

'Karl is looking rather grave and edgy, don't you think?' she said, putting the film on pause. 'Do you think he knew more about Mick than he let on? He does seem nervous, he keeps looking at his watch...'

'And knocking back far more champagne than anyone else...'

'As far as I can remember, it was just after this that all hell broke loose, you know, when Mick charged up the stairs?'

'The film doesn't show that?'

'No – it stops a few minutes before Mick appeared.'

I pointed to a man and woman standing near the quartet. 'Who are these two?' I asked.

'No idea.'

'And the bloke standing at the bottom of the stairs?'

'Nope – don't know.'

'Does this bring anything back that you think is important?'

'Obviously, it was fifteen years before the crash, but I know – I just *know* – it's connected in some way. I'm just not seeing it.'

'Do the police have a copy of this?'

'I asked Cameron about that, but he said the police had looked at it during the investigation over Mick's death, but didn't think it was relevant to our crash. I think they're just assuming the crash was an accident and waiting for all the bodies to turn up before they close the case.'

We ran the footage through another time, but other than her conviction that there had to be a link between their first visit and the second, Rosie didn't pick up on anything else.

She clapped her hands together. 'Shall we take stock?'

I ejected the disc and handed it to her.

'According to the victim's relatives, Cameron could have had a grudge against Richard and Karl might also have had it in for Max,' she began. 'Let's say both Richard and Max were guilty. Do you think father and son might have got together and arranged the accident, without caring who else got caught up in it?'

'It's possible, but pure speculation, Rosie. And why would they wait so long after it happened?'

'Unless they'd only found out recently?'

'What? Just happened to find out that not only did Max steal something, but Richard had a one-night stand with Ambrosia Hinds?'

'I know…' she admitted. 'It's too weird. And they'd hardly decide to tie in some sort of payback with the anniversary bash, would they?'

'Do you know what happened once the Hinds found out about the crash?'

'They cancelled the party as far as I know.'

At the end of the session, true to form, Rosie's phone rang.

'It's the Cumbrian police,' she said, holding it out to

me as if asking permission to take the call.

'Go on – take it,' I said, sitting back.

She had a brief conversation and slipped the phone into her pocket before she stood up, looking pale and shaken. 'The police have found the van,' she said, watching my face for a reaction.

My eyes were wide in anticipation.

'It was empty – well, apart from music stands and stuff.'

'No…body there?'

She pressed her lips together, not registering my words. 'They did find something, though,' she went on. 'Tiny scraps of cardboard and a glue-like substance inside the three seatbelt mechanisms in the front of the van.'

'Cardboard?'

'They think it was some kind of crude attempt to jam the seatbelts.' Her chin began to quiver. 'You know what that means don't you?'

My hand went to my throat.

'It wasn't an accident,' she whispered, reaching out to hold the door frame. 'I knew it…I knew it…' Her breathing was noisy, irregular, running away with her.

'Are you okay?' I said, worried about sending her out into the night with that earth-shattering piece of news. Selfishly, my first thought was that this was another drawback of working from home. If a patient was ill or distraught, there was no nurse on hand to take over and offer cups of sweet tea. I quickly discounted the inconvenience and turned my attention back to Rosie.

'I think I need a hug,' she whispered, nipping her lips together.

I hesitated. With anyone else it would have been the most natural thing to offer, but with Rosie? It would be too easy for her, deprived of affection as she was, to read more into it. Nevertheless, to hold back at a moment like this would have been cruel. She'd just had a very nasty shock. I opened my arms and let her come to me, giving her a gentle squeeze, as though she was a child who'd fallen and scuffed her knees. When, after a second or two, she showed no sign of letting go, I took hold of her arms and gently stood her upright in front of me.

'Do you have anyone you can talk to, Rosie?' Surely there had to be someone. 'What about Dawn, where you live?'

'No. There's no one. I thought I'd told you that.'

A muscle twitched on the back of my neck. I didn't like the way this felt; she was far too attached to me for her own good.

'We will need to talk about the impact this has had on you, next time,' I said. 'In the meantime, perhaps you could write down some of your thoughts. Could you try that?'

'All right,' she sniffed, wiping her nose on her hand, trying to hide her tears.

'Do you need me to call you a taxi?'

'No. I'm fine, thanks. I knew, really. I knew it wasn't an accident. I'm just in shock now there's actual proof of it.' She headed towards the door. 'The police will have to turn it into a murder hunt now.'

Despite her distress, I couldn't help noticing a touch of triumph in her voice.

After Rosie left, I sat in the kitchen, staring blankly at the grain of the wood on the table top, swirling into a pattern like wind-rippled sand. I traced the lines, following the smooth tracks that always ended in a knot.

A murder enquiry.

Rosie had been involved in an accident until now, yet all along there'd been something ominous about it. Rosie's intuition had been right. She must be wondering who the target had been. I certainly was.

The police were saying all three seatbelts at the front had been sabotaged, so they'd take longer to unclip. It meant any one of them could have been the target. Perhaps they all were. It appeared to be sheer luck that Rosie had been in the back – it hadn't been planned that way. Or had it?

It seemed to me that only the Hinds had obvious motives, but the reasons were weak to say the least. Would you wreak that level of havoc if you found out your wife had been involved in a one-night stand fifteen years ago? Or if one of the musicians had stolen something? It seemed too extreme.

Did the business with Mick at that first party have any relevance? What was it that Mick had stolen, and did he have some secret accomplice? Had Max and Mick been in something together?'

Going over and over the possibilities in my mind wasn't getting me anywhere. I didn't have any answers.

But maybe Rosie did.

Perhaps the answers were right there, locked inside her head. Maybe all I had to do was ask the right question or find the right trigger and there they would be.

Chapter 24

Rosie

Sam's been amazing. And she has feelings for me, she really does. I'm sure now. I was thunderstruck when I got the call from DS Fischer about the seatbelts. I'm so relieved he rang before I left Sam's flat. It meant we could both experience the drama together.

I'm not sure how I feel, now the crash has been turned into a murder hunt. I suppose the police will take everything more seriously. They might even find my viola. On the other hand, it means there was malice involved. Someone planned it, with a motive and everything. Having that thought in my head is like carrying around a festering wound, not knowing if it's going to heal or poison my blood and finish me off. The big question is, if I was one of the targets, won't they try again?

Piles of other questions tumble into my mind. Were they after one of us, or was it just the violin? Is the violin in the lake or is the killer richer already – two million pounds richer?

I *knew* the crash wasn't an accident and I'm actually quite pleased to know the truth, because it makes everything that bit more urgent. And, best of all, Sam knows I was right!

Without any prompting from me she gave me a

huge cuddle at the end of our last session. It took me completely by surprise, but I loved every second of it. I was the one who had to pull away in the end, she didn't want to let me go! I know she's not supposed to show any kind of favouritism, but it's obvious. She gives herself away all the time now. The way she looks at me – those big grey-flecked eyes. She's my rock. My soul-sister. Despite the shocking news, I'm just so happy, I barely know what to do with myself.

Portia, at work, said that therapists can afford to look like they're interested in you, because they only have to keep it up for an hour at a time and then they get shot of you. Plus, they get paid for being nice. I don't agree. I *know* Sam has a soft spot for me. I can tell. She's probably really confused about how things should go between us from now on. She wants to help me, but she also wants us to have a proper friendship and that can't be easy for her.

There are too many rules and regulations in therapy. You're not supposed to step over the line into your therapist's personal life. But I must be patient. My first task is to make sure I can get more sessions with her. I won't be ready to pack up when we've only had twelve. After that, who knows?

The thing is, I want to find a way to show her she can depend on me, too. Call on me if she ever needs help. Anything. Anytime. I'll need to be careful though; I don't want her thinking I'm one of those sickly eager-to-please types. I've got to be prepared to play the long game.

I left the music store after lunch, because on the

spur of the moment, I decided to take the afternoon off. I knew Sid wouldn't be bothered. The run up to Christmas isn't as busy as it should be and I always have bags of annual leave, because I never go away. Trips aren't much fun on your own.

I take the Tube from London Bridge to Waterloo and walk along the Thames, but it's too cold to enjoy it. I consider going back to Oxford Street in the unlikely chance of spotting Max again, but I can't face the Christmas crowds. I've always hated the entire festive season. Goodwill, generosity, luxury and presents – I had none of that. I did the soup kitchen last year, but ended up catching a nasty stomach bug – from the food or one of the clients, I'm not sure which. I don't fancy it this year.

I've been wondering what Sam will be doing on Christmas Day. Having a cosy family gathering no doubt: a real tree brushing the ceiling, cascades of expensive baubles, holly branches draped over the picture frames arranged by an adoring mother, gifts glittering with bows and ribbons from a doting father. It makes my heart shrivel up; I don't want to think about it.

Instead, I think about what's been under my pillow for the last few weeks and hop on a bus at Waterloo to make another visit to my special sanctuary. Sam doesn't know I snatched them from her flat that first session, from the ledge by her front door. Or that I put them back in her bag that time I made myself at home in her office when she rushed off for a form. She doesn't know I got duplicates made.

So that's where I'm spending this afternoon. She'll be at the hospital, so I've got the whole place to myself. What a treat!

Chapter 25

Rosie

It's Wednesday and Sam isn't answering her phone, so I call the Mental Health Unit and tell them it's an emergency and finally someone puts me through to her. I tell her I've found something, but she tries to stop me halfway through. It's the same old 'you mustn't call me' plea, but I know she doesn't really mean it. If I can't ring her at home and I can't call her at work, how am I supposed to get in touch with her? This can't wait. It's urgent.

I tell her I have no one else and we have to act on it. Dawn has sent me the latest round-up of items for auction this week and whilst there were no musical instruments, something else caught my eye. I don't know why I was even looking in the accessories section, except I like Sam's bracelet and I was thinking of getting one the same. A Christmas present to myself.

And there it was – on page seven. Listed as: '*a gentleman's platinum automatic chronometer Rolex wristwatch with a blue dial and raised Roman numerals*'. I recognised it straight away; it belonged to Max. He'd bragged about it, of course, and we'd all been obliged to take a good look at it. The entry in the e-catalogue said there was a reserve price of £15,000 on it.

'This is a matter for the police, Rosie. Won't the

auction house have procedures for this kind of thing?' Sam says, but I know I'm sparking her interest.

'It's too late for that; the auction is today at two-fifteen. And besides, Dawn says we need more concrete evidence it's stolen before they call in the police. It might not be his.' I take a chance. 'Will you come?'

'Come with you? No, I can't. Listen, Rosie…'

Here we go – another one of her *issues* with boundaries. 'I can't be a health professional one minute and your companion, the next,' she goes on. 'It corrupts the relationship if we get the roles mixed up. It means I can't help you properly.'

What rubbish! *Can't help you properly* – what's she on about? It sounds like a threat.

'You've decided I'm too much trouble…'

'It's not that. I'm a psychologist, not a private detective.'

'Can't you help me in both ways; with getting my memories back *and* helping unravel the mystery? It's all part of the same thing, after all. It's all about getting to the truth. I'll pay you for your time.'

'It's not about the money, Rosie.'

'Can't therapists step outside the box, sometimes? I can't do this without you.' I know I'm starting to sound a bit pathetic, but I don't know how else to plead with her. 'You're not going to abandon me, are you?'

'If I helped you *outside* our sessions then our work together would have to end.'

It *is* a threat.

'You know what this means don't you?' I tell her. 'It means that someone was *there* at the crash. Someone who sabotaged the seatbelts and tried to kill us all. This same person might have my viola. Or even Max's violin. Don't you want to know?'

'Rosie. I'm sorry. You'll have to ask someone else. I've got a patient now. We can talk about this in our next session.'

Then she's gone. I can't believe it. After all we've been through. I can't describe how gutted I am.

But I don't have much time to dwell on it. I call Dawn and arrange to meet her at the front entrance of Rothman's at 1.30pm. She says the watch can be removed from sale if I recognise something conclusive that shows it belongs to Max, but I'm not interested in that part; I want to know who's trying to sell it.

'I need to see the records about it,' I tell her.

'I can't take you behind the scenes,' she says, 'it's against the regulations.'

'But if I'm right and you don't act on it, your manager will go bonkers.'

Reluctantly, she takes me to the dusty office in the basement where she works. She shows me the date and time the watch was received and valued, on her computer. The seller is a man called Teddy Spense.

His name doesn't mean anything to me.

I ask Dawn if we can look at CCTV footage from the day he brought it in and she leads me back to the foyer, then disappears to chat up Nick, the security guy. My phone buzzes as I hover by the lift, and she invites me upstairs to pore over footage that shows the watch-seller entering the building minutes before the watch was logged in. But, there's not enough to go on: he's nondescript – tallish, mostly dressed in black, with skinny legs, wearing a beanie that covers his hair.

At five past two, I'm loitering in the foyer again looking out for someone who fits his vague description and Dawn is at the back waiting for the item before his to be called. We make a good team, but not as good as me and Sam would have been.

Seconds later I text Dawn to get her back into the foyer.

'The security guard is talking to a guy who's the same height and build as the one caught on camera,' I whisper to her. 'He's wearing the same style of black bomber jacket, gloves and beanie too.'

I watch from a distance to see if he seems familiar, but he has his back to me, so I can't see his face. He hitches his foot up nervously and keeps putting his hands in and out of his pockets, stooping awkwardly to hear what the security guy is saying. From his body language, it's clearly no one from the quartet and no one I've seen with the Hinds' family or their entourage. They all walk tall with airs and graces.

There are only a few minutes left before the item is due to come up for sale. Dawn approaches him, pointing to sections in the catalogue and gives me a discrete nod. It looks like he's our man. He shakes his head, puts his hands up in a gesture that indicates he doesn't want any trouble, turns and starts walking briskly towards the exit.

The security guys are on him in seconds, tugging his arms behind his back. The man in black looks defeated and compliant.

Dawn is saying something to the guards, then she rushes towards me.

'Quick!' she urges, her eyelashes dancing around. 'It's him – Teddy Spense. I told him someone was going to talk to him.'

'Someone?'

'Yeah – *you*! Go and find out what he's up to, fast, before my manager arrives. I've told security you're coming over – Nick and Rocky, they'll hold him tight. He can't hurt you.'

She speaks into her walkie-talkie, no doubt telling her manager that there's an issue with Lot 27. She jerks her head as she speaks, instructing me to go over to him.

'No – y*ou* talk to him, Dawn.'

She lowers her handset.

'What if he recognises me?' I say. 'He could come after me. He might have killed people. He might not know I got out alive…'

My body is rocked by its own mini-earthquake at the thought that this man might have ripped the Rolex from Max's dead corpse, and has quite probably done far worse.

Dawn flicks her tongue around and finally agrees. I think she quite likes the idea. I've given her enough information about the crash for her to ask the right questions. I loiter within earshot, but take cover behind a noticeboard, just in case.

Dawn is impressive. It won't be long, no doubt, before her manager takes him somewhere secure to wait for the police, so she fires questions at him, accusing him right away of stealing the watch from the scene of the accident at Ullswater. A squeaky male voice begs her not to take matters further.

'I'll withdraw it,' he says.

'That's already happening,' says Dawn. 'You were in the Lake District when the crash happened, weren't you?'

I take the chance to move a few steps closer; I want to know how he answers this question. The guy is startled, his eyes jumping all over the place, looking for an escape no doubt. I get my phone out and switch it to video, keeping him in the frame. He tries to pull free, but Nick and Rocky hold him tight. A cluster of rubberneckers are gathering around the commotion.

'Did you plan it? Did you make the van go off the road?' says Dawn.

He looks about my age and wriggles frantically. 'What? No, man – no way! I didn't see nuffin',' he says. 'I heard a crash, then I saw the busted fence and stopped.'

Dawn asks him exactly how he came by the watch. She sounds like a real detective.

'One minute the van was ahead of me, the next it had disappeared. I left my motorbike in the bushes and went to the edge of the water, but the van was in way too deep to reach. I'd never have been able to get down and back up again in one breath.'

'So how did you get the watch?'

He sniffs. 'A coin pouch came up to the surface and it was in there,' he says.

'It just floated up, did it?' she snorts.

What he's saying could be true, as it happens. Max

always took his watch off in rehearsals and he could have forgotten to put it back on again.

'Then I saw a woman break the surface, further in and I scarpered.'

That must have been me.

'You didn't stop to help her?' Dawn asks.

'She got out, she was okay.'

The little shit...! I'm tempted to storm over and give his face a hard slap, but I mustn't let my emotions get the better of me. I need to keep myself in check and tune in to his voice. I need to listen meticulously to everything he's saying. His accent is lazy East End and vaguely familiar, but I can't place him and I can't see enough of his face, either.

'Did you call the police?' Dawn asks. 'Do they know you were there?' He splutters a reply towards his trainers that means *fat chance* and shifts to the other foot. The security guys still hold him firm. I'm expecting Dawn to be shoved aside by her superior any moment. 'What else did you salvage?'

'A handbag and a woman's shoe floated up. That's all,' he says.

'What about the others?' she persists.

'There was no one else there. I was too late. There was no one to save or I would have done somefin'.'

'You checked the van?'

'What? No. It was down too deep. I told you. I didn't hang around.'

A man in a suit is heading purposefully towards them. Dawn manages to ask her final questions before her manager takes over. 'Did you see anything else?

Musical instruments in cases?'

'Na. Nuffin'. Can I go now?'

'I'm afraid not...' She's sounding smug. 'The police will be here any second.'

The man in the suit steps in front of her. 'Thanks, Ms Fletcher, I'll take it from here.'

Teddy drops his head and the manager has a quick word with him, before he and the guards lead him across the foyer for a private grilling.

Something isn't quite right. It was all a little too easy. Teddy has just admitted his wrongdoing to Dawn without any pressure whatsoever, nor is he putting up any kind of fight. Then it becomes clear.

As they approach an office, several things happen at once. There is a loud pop and Nick falls to the floor. Rocky loses his balance as he tries to take a step backwards, the manager gets out of the way and Teddy Spense is free, making a bolt for the door. The manager kneels down by Nick's side and people are screaming. Several bystanders and staff members are darting around; half of them run towards the man on the floor, the other half get in the way, as I try to rush outside after Teddy.

By the time I get to the pavement, he's completely disappeared.

I run back in, expecting to see a pool of blood on the floor beside Nick, but he's sitting upright, straightening his hair.

I grab Dawn by the arm. 'He's gone! What the hell happened?'

At that moment two police officers come striding in.

'He kneed Nick in the balls and legged it,' says Dawn, wide-eyed.

'But, what was that bang? I thought it was a gunshot.'

'So did everyone else.' She shakes her head.

Both policemen are hovering over what looks like a scrap of foil on the floor. '"Fun snaps",' one of them calls out. 'You throw them hard at the ground and they made a loud bang.' He glances around. 'Nice diversion tactic. It's all marble in here, so I guess it echoed...'

'Didn't the security guys search him?' I groan in disbelief.

I stare at Rocky as he helps his colleague to his feet. 'We thought they were sweets...'

We troop off to the police station after that to give statements. I tell them that the stolen watch is linked to the crash in the Lake District, but they only seem interested in what happened today.

Later that evening, I check the phone footage I took, but there's no clear shot of the man-in-black's face. As I eat leftover spaghetti, I run 'Teddy Spense' through various social networking sites. I try different spellings, but can't find anyone who fits his description under Teddy, Ted, Ned, Edward, Eddie or Ed in the UK.

I tap on the door to Dawn's flat, upstairs. I want to thank her for today. We go into her kitchen, but she doesn't offer me a drink or even invite me to sit down. I stand awkwardly holding the back of a wooden chair.

'What about CCTV of him when he was in the foyer, today?' I ask. 'Can I come in tomorrow to take a look at it?

'You can if you want, but there's no point, the police said it was too fuzzy for a decent identification. I did a photofit for them, but it could be anyone,' she picks up her keys from a dish. 'They don't hold out much hope of finding him.'

'Bugger...' I say. 'I didn't get a good look at his face.'

'We should have made him take his hat off.' Dawn looks sympathetic but she's edging me towards the door. She must be about to go out.

'Yeah,' I say, 'To be honest, it did look a bit familiar...it's really annoying.' I drag my fingers through my hair. 'I can't think who, though...'

'He looks a bit like that actor on Coronation Street,' she says.

'Oh, yeah...the one with the funny eyebrows...?'

Is that who I'm thinking of?

She checks her watch. 'And Teddy Spense probably isn't his real name,' she says, her hand on the doorknob. 'His address didn't check out.'

'Ah. Oh, well. You did a great job, by the way. Do you fancy going out for a drink later?'

Her face drops. 'Sorry, my dad's sick, in hospital, I've got to go over and see him.'

'Oh, I hope he's okay. Another time, maybe?'

'Yeah, maybe.' She presses the door shut behind me and I go back to my flat.

Later, before I go to bed, I shut the kitchen window and spot Dawn hurrying in through the front gate. She's wearing a short skirt and stilettos, not exactly hospital visiting clothes. Ah. I get it. She lied; she didn't want me cramping her style on her night out.

Well, see if I care – I've got bigger fish to fry.

As I lie in bed, I think of Sam. She doesn't know she had a visitor late this afternoon. Once I'd finished with the police I didn't feel like going straight home, so I went over to Clapham again.

I knew she'd still be at work, so once I'd made sure there was no one else around on the landing, I let myself in. If she won't tell me anything about herself, I'm going to have to get to know her in a different way.

I hung my coat over one of hers in the hall and went into the bathroom. She'd left the basin in a bit of a mess, so I gave it a quick once round with the cloth on the edge of the bath and folded her towels. Then I went into her bedroom and opened her wardrobe.

I recognised a few of her suits and jackets, then slid out a folded chunky jumper she'd worn last week and held it against me. Sam is thinner than me, but I wasn't going to let that stop me. I eased it over my head and tugged the arms to make them reach my wrists. When I paraded in front of the mirror I could almost feel her wrapped around me, all soft and cosy. As I draped one of her silk scarves around my neck, a burst of her perfume gave me goosebumps and I buried my face in it. I tied it in a loose knot just the way she does.

I kicked off my trainers and tried on a pair of brown boots I've often seen her wear. They were too small, but with a bit of a shove, I managed to squash my feet into them. I stripped off and tried on a blouse and jacket but they were too small, so I unzipped the boots and laid down under the duvet, my head on her pillow.

I ran my fingers over the patterned paper behind the bed, wondering if she did this too, if my fingers were following the same fern design as hers. I could have stayed like that for hours, taking in the oily floral smell of her hair ingrained in the cotton pillowcase, knowing she spends so much time in this very same spot. The thought made my scalp tingle. I tried to see her face, think her thoughts, experience her feelings.

But there was something in the way as I lay there. I couldn't get into the mood properly this time, so I got up and started idly opening more drawers, flicking through knickers and socks, having a jolly good snoop.

In one of the cupboards I found folders and documents: mortgage and insurance papers, financial records, old birthday cards, notes and letters. I read some of them; a few were from her sister and there were smoochy ones from Con, dated over a year ago, and a postcard from someone called Hannah. My card wasn't there, I noticed.

My thoughts kept turning sour. No matter how much I wanted to feel good about things with Sam, she wasn't there when I needed her. She let me down over the auction house and it's spoilt something between us. It's broken our trust and hurt me badly. I'm not sure our relationship can be the same now.

I came home after that.

As I lie on my own lumpy mattress there's a question niggling in my mind. Does Sam know what it's like to suffer? Does she know what it's like to feel the ground crumble under her feet?

Chapter 26

Sam

I started our final session before Christmas by telling Rosie we'd be taking a break from therapy over the holiday. Her face fell.

'Then we'll have two final appointments in the new year to try to cover all the loose ends,' I added. I needed to get it flagged up, loud and clear, so there were no misunderstandings. I wanted her to be ready for our work together to end. Not to feel abandoned.

'Final?' She stared blankly. 'Only two. Is that all?'

'That's what we agreed. It will be twelve sessions in all, six more than you'd normally get on the NHS.'

Rosie was on her feet, trembling. 'But, we haven't finished. I haven't found my viola…'

'We can do a lot in that time.'

'I thought we could keep going…'

'This was always meant to be short term. I thought I'd made that clear.' *Had I? Had I made it clear enough?*

'I don't know what I'll do without these appointments.' She was still on her feet, pacing about. 'I've been feeling so much better, but, if we stop…'

'When we end our sessions, you can always see someone who works longer term, if you—'

She stood by the sofa, holding on to it. 'I thought you *liked* me.' Her face crumpled like a three year old's.

'I do...'

What else could I say? *I do...but you're complicated, clingy, trying to push me all the time and I want the privacy of my flat back?*

'The kind of therapy I do is designed to work in small blocks. Just dealing with one specific memory issue.'

She stood sucking her fingers. 'But, now we're not at the hospital, I thought it would be different.'

'I never said it would be. It's the same method, just as before. We're only here because you couldn't get to the hospital in the daytime, anymore.'

The next moment she was back in her seat again. Suddenly her distress seemed to dissipate. 'Shit – I'd better get on with it, then, I'm wasting valuable time.'

It reminded me of Miranda – the way she could blow hot and cold in the same breath. It made me wonder if Rosie was masking some deeper mental illness.

She went on to tell me about the auction house and how she hadn't got a clear enough view of the man who'd tried to sell Max's watch.

'I caught a few minutes of footage of him on my phone, when he was in the foyer,' she said. She pressed a button and handed it to me. 'Do *you* recognise him? From the video of the party?'

I watched the few seconds of shaky footage. There wasn't much to see. The skinny man in black looked nervous, lifting one foot up and rubbing it against his other leg, fiddling with his pockets. I couldn't see his face clearly.

'I can't really tell...' I said. 'The party footage you

showed me was fifteen years ago, remember…?'

Rosie looked disappointed. 'I know. He probably looked totally different back then.'

'And he may not even have been there. Why do you think he was?'

'Dunno,' she huffed. 'There's just something telling me that what happened then is connected with us all going back the second time, that's all. But you're right. It's stupid to try to link everything up. He was probably just passing the scene of the crash, like he said.'

I leant back. 'How did you feel when I said I couldn't come with you to Rothmans?'

She tossed her hand in the air. 'Oh, no problem. Dawn was brilliant.'

'You weren't angry with me?'

'Angry? No, it would have been nice, but I understand.' She gave me a plastic smile. 'Oh, and, by the way,' she said, examining her nails, 'I met a really nice guy the other day. In a café.' Her smile softened into more of a real one. 'You know when you really click with someone?'

'Yes, I do.'

I was pleased for her, but also relieved. If she was forming new attachments, she wouldn't need to rely on me so much. 'Do you want to talk any more about that?'

'No. Not now. I want to go back to the crash. Can we use your trance thingy to see if anything new is ready to come up?'

She knew the drill by now and settled into a receptive state with little prompting. She was convinced there was an important piece missing in connection with the phone call she'd overheard between rehearsals before the crash. I took her through the steps leading up to that point; how she was worried about the concert, because they were all out of practice – all except Max, who was showing them all up. Rosie had gone out onto the landing to be on her own for a while.

'You can hear a voice,' I said. 'A lone voice, a man's voice, coming up from the hallway.'

'He's on the phone,' she said in a flat tone. 'Yes, I know all this. He's saying, "It's under the bridge…it's worth a—"' She shot into a sitting position like a corpse coming to life. 'Shit…'

I held my breath.

'It was about me!' She jammed the heel of her hand into her hairline. 'He used my name, I'm sure of it, in connection with the bit about it being *worth a fortune*. He said, *Rosie*.'

I waited for her to say more, but that was it.

'You still don't know who said it?'

She shook her head vigorously.

'What does it mean?' I ventured.

'Don't you see? Whatever it is – it's connected to *me*.'

'Okay…' I must have looked like someone who hadn't got the punchline. I asked the obvious question. 'Which bridge?'

'What?'

'Well, which bridge is this "fortune" under? The Lake District is crammed full of bridges.'

She had the forlorn look of a child who's just found out that Father Christmas doesn't exist.

'Which bridge? I don't know.' She gripped the

blanket and squeezed it hard as if it was sodden with water. 'There must be another memory. There has to be more.'

I led her through recollections of being outside in the open; a walk she and Richard had taken down to Ullswater shortly after they arrived, a scurry to the local Post Office with Stephanie during a break in rehearsals – but no particular bridges seemed to jump out at her. We trawled back over the same scenes again and again, but Rosie kept shaking her head.

She left once her time was up, dragging her limbs, wishing me a half-hearted Merry Christmas.

I held open the door and watched her go down the stairs, waiting as I always did for the front latch to click so that I'd know she'd gone.

An hour or so later, I was halfway through a plateful of ratatouille when the phone rang. I picked it up before remembering that my whistle had disappeared. Sure enough, I heard the unnerving silence again, so I put down the receiver straight away.

I couldn't face the rest of my meal after that. Instead I spoke to my phone provider and reported the mystery calls. Although on several occasions the numbers had been withheld, when they'd shown up I'd made a note of them, so I had a list to reel off. All had the London area code. The man I spoke to said they could have come from public phone boxes. Great – it could be anyone.

I didn't want to change my number, nor did I want to block all withheld callers. Calls from Miranda's Project were often withheld and I didn't want to prevent those getting through. If I felt it was harassment or malicious, I should contact the police, the guy said, but as someone who dealt with the fallout from *real* traumas every day, I felt like I'd be wasting their time. I decided to wait and see.

I picked up the payment of forty-five pounds Rosie had left me on the ledge inside my front door. It was stuffed inside a plastic bag; a bundle of five-pound notes and pound coins, with two pounds' worth in loose change. It looked pitiful, like she'd raided her money box to pay for her time with me.

Something made me think of the talk at King's I'd been to several weeks ago. I remembered 'Kitty's' voice and almost without thinking, I found myself calling Minette's number.

'I hope it's okay to call after hours,' I said.

Minette chuckled and said she could hardly tell what out of hours meant any more. 'I hope you're calling to fix up a lunch date,' she said.

'I'd love to...although actually, I'm calling about something else.' My fingers tightened around the phone. 'After your talk, I didn't mention that I recognised a patient in one of the recordings: someone you called "Kitty".'

'I see.'

'In fact, I'm working with her at the moment.'

'Quite a handful, I'd imagine,' she said, 'if I'm thinking of the right patient.'

I cleared my throat. 'You could say that.' I chewed my lip. 'You said she'd been seeing a therapist called Erica Mandale, who'd died suddenly?'

'Yeah...that's right.'

'And "Kitty" was seeing Erica through the NHS, not privately, is that right?'

'Hold on, let me find my lecture notes.' There was the clomp of footsteps followed by tapping at a keyboard. 'Here it is,' she said, 'I've only got sketchy notes about her. Let me see…the sessions were at Guy's, for around eighteen months…no wait a minute,' she took a breath. 'The last five appointments were at Erica's home in Chelsea.'

I swallowed hard. 'Do you know why they were moved from the hospital to her house?'

'I'm not sure. I can't check, I'm afraid. Erica's full records are logged in the hospital system.'

'"Kitty" is a very intense patient showing symptoms of a histrionic personality disorder,' I said.

'Ooh – tricky,' she said. 'Anxious about being ignored and needing to be the centre of attention, no doubt.'

'Exactly. She comes across as demanding, pushing the boundaries. I've been seeing her for ten weeks now and I wondered what sort of progress Erica had made with her in a year and a half. Do you know how much of her childhood was covered?'

'I don't know, really. I only had a few recordings from their work together. You'd have to get access to her original records.'

'I was hoping her experience with Erica could enlighten me. I'm stumbling around in the dark with her to be honest. Something doesn't feel quite right. She's had a tragic life and I want to do the best I can for her, but I've felt uneasy right from the start.'

'Sounds like an issue for supervision, Sam.'

'Mmm...' I muttered.

I hated supervision. Dr Rosen had been allocated to me over a year ago and we didn't suit each other one bit. He was all sharp angles and corners, keen to play everything by the book, whereas I wanted to bend the rules when it was in the best interests of the patient. I'd put in a request for a replacement, but no one else was available for the time being. As things stood, I turned up to as few meetings with him as I could get away with.

I thanked her and we had a brief chat about plans for Christmas, before fixing a date for lunch in the New Year.

'By the way,' I said, just before I rang off. 'How would I go about getting hold of Erica's notes?'

'You'd need the go-ahead from the senior psychiatrist at Guy's, Professor Radley Dean. I can give you his details, but he's in America at the moment.'

'And Erica died, you said?'

'Yes, a heart attack, just like that – out of the blue. Her husband found her at the bottom of the stairs. Such a terrible tragedy.'

Chapter 27

Sam

The two weeks of demob-happy days over Christmas came and went. I took a stroll through a frosty Hyde Park with my uni friend, Ronnie, discussing the latest TV adaptation of a bestselling psychological thriller. I told him the scenes with the therapist were all wrong.

'She'd get struck off for going out for dinner with her patient,' I'd told him. 'She's asking for trouble.'

'Only if she gets found out,' he'd said.

I shared chip butties in Covent Garden with Gemma, an old school pal from Kent, saw a film at Leicester Square, visited Tate Modern...

I even managed to drag Hannah away from online properties searches for cocktails at a posh hotel bar in Covent Garden.

We took seats on the velvet sofa in front of the open fire, crackling with glittery pine cones that had been thrown into the flames. Sparkling fairy lights coiled around the edges of a broad antique mirror on the mantelpiece and sunken candles dribbled wax on to the hearth. It was a perfect festive setting: I always love the coziness of winter.

'This will be my last Christmas in London,' Hannah said, flattening my mood in an instant, as she draped her coat over the arm of a passing waiter. 'I can hardly believe it.'

In spite of the flames spitting in the hearth, a deep

chill swept through me. 'Well, you should be thoroughly ashamed of yourself,' I said, only half-joking. 'Leaving your best mate all alone.'

A day later, I met up with Debbie and Bernie from St Luke's and we went ice-skating in Bayswater.

I knew something was different about Debbie as soon as she joined us at the boot-hire desk.

'Can't skate,' she said.

'Tell me something new,' I smirked.

'No, I mean I *can't* skate. I'll sit and watch.'

I looked her up and down with concern. 'Are you injured?'

'No.' She bit her lip looking sheepish. 'I didn't want to say anything until I was sure, but…'

'You're not..?' I whispered, open-mouthed.

She pressed her hand on her belly. 'I didn't know if I was feeling nauseous because of the drugs, but we did a test and—' She burst into tears. 'Oh…sorry, I'm all mushy and hormonal.'

I wrapped her in my arms almost smothering her with my thick scarf. 'That's amazing. Brilliant. I'm so pleased.'

'I'm probably being overcautious by staying off the ice,' she sniffed, 'but I know I'll fall over and I'm not taking any risks.'

'Of course,' I assured her. I knew how much this meant to her.

She unzipped her anorak, looking hot and overwhelmed. 'Don't tell anyone yet,' she whispered as Bernie came back from the men's desk swinging his skates.

I was delighted for her, but I couldn't help feeling a

little sorry for myself. People closest to me were taking life-changing steps and I was being left behind. For a brief moment I thought about Rosie. Her entire life consisted of people walking away from her, one after the other.

I called Miranda to try to make peace and find out what she was doing on Christmas Day. True to form, she was vague, but it looked like she wouldn't be joining Dad and me in Kent this year.

'I'm going to Eastbourne,' she said. 'Some friends are having a big bash.' I waited, but there was no invitation for me to tag along. Maybe she'd be with her nameless boyfriend. I wished her well and said I'd put her present in the post.

I went to see Mrs Willow in the adjacent flat on Christmas Eve. She'd invited me, and I knew she wouldn't have many visitors over the holidays. I remembered from an earlier Christmas that her husband had died on Boxing Day, in the 1990's. We shared vinegary wine, pulled a limp cracker and I gave her what was possibly her only Christmas present – an enamel pill box I'd bought from Miranda's Arts Project. She insisted on opening it there and then, held it to her bosom, and almost wept with gratitude.

On the twenty-fifth itself, I went over to Dad's, played Scrabble and watched him fall asleep in front of the Queen's speech. Before he'd retired, Dad had been a first-rate barrister. I'd seen him in action in court and he was formidable. He was so sure of himself when it came to the law, but with Mum he'd always been hopeless:

tentative and passive. It was hard to believe those two sides could belong to one person.

At least spending Christmas with Mum wasn't an option anymore. My parents had been drifting apart for years: Mum always so demanding and Dad going out of his way to try to please her. When she retired as a professor of architecture, they were forced to spend too much time together and their relationship went through what Dad called a 'bad patch' and Mum called 'the end of the line'. Then, last year, Miranda's terrible revelation blew the family apart and Moira Willerby was out of our lives forever.

But I didn't want to think about that now; it was part of another chapter in my life altogether. Suffice to say that Dad swiftly moved out of their beautiful detached house into a pokey flat on the outskirts of Canterbury. As far as I know, Mum is still in the house on her own. We left her to it. None of us wanted to go back to that place now its history had been sullied. I hadn't seen my mother since – she knew the kind of reception she'd get if she ever rang my doorbell. Not that I would ever have invited her to my place for Christmas previously – we'd never had that kind of relationship.

Towards the end of the festive season came the day I'd been dreading. I'd been doing well until then, but I knew the anniversary of Joanne's suicide was going to be tough. When it came, I blundered my way through it by arranging lunch and dinner with different sets of close friends. I'd coped with suicides before, of course – in my line of work it comes with the territory – but it had never felt like this before. There'd been a dreadful spate of suicides at St Luke's eighteen months ago, when I was dragged into a harrowing situation involving the London Underground. But Joanne's suicide came months after that and it was different – it had been my fault.

On the morning of December 28th, I had another silent call and after repeatedly demanding that the caller reveal themselves, I blew the whistle I kept in my bag as hard as I could and put down the phone. I half expected Mrs Willow to come hammering on my door to see what was going on, but nothing happened.

It was then that I began to wonder whether it really was Bruce who was pestering me. Maybe it was someone with a connection to Joanne. Except, why wait so long after her death? Maybe the anniversary had triggered it. It could be a family member intent on punishing me for what happened. Except, they didn't need to as I was making a mighty fine job of punishing myself. Barely a day went past when I didn't think of her or taunt myself about the way I'd let her down.

I'd thought about sending a card to Joanne's parents, but what could I write inside? *Sorry, again, that I didn't respond to your daughter's cry for help. Sorry, I failed you all and ruined your lives forever.* In the end, I decided that a message from me was probably the last thing Mr and Mrs Bellings would want.

That evening, alone after cramming the day full of other people's laughter, the tears finally came. I stood in front of the bathroom mirror with my toothbrush and dredged it all up, every sickening moment of it. I'd followed the correct procedure, done everything by the book, taken all the correct steps. But I'd failed in one simple way. I hadn't done the one thing Joanne had asked me, no – begged me – to do.

I knew the worst as soon as she didn't turn up for her session the next morning. Her landlady let me into her room and there she was, her limp body hanging from the hook on the back of the door, her face still wet with tears. There was a note on the floor with my name on it.

When I bent down to pick it up, Joanne's toe twitched, I was convinced of it. I helped the terrified landlady lay her body down on the carpet, desperately hoping she was still alive, but all the signs of death were already there. I took her pulse with trembling fingers, knowing she was too cold and finally, I let her hand go.

Of course, everyone at work told me it wasn't my fault. *Suicides happen in psychotherapy. You did the right thing. She would have found a way, eventually. She was ill.* But I didn't believe them. In my view, Joanne could have recovered and moved on, if I'd just been there for her.

I closed my eyes and saw again the three piercing words she'd left for me in the note. A simple accusation in a sea of white paper. *You didn't listen.*

You're right, Joanne. I didn't listen. You had no one else and I didn't respond. And I should have done.

I climbed into bed feeling just as wretched as I had the moment I found her. I didn't even try to stop the cascade of images flooding into my mind. I let them come one after another, partly to honour her memory, partly to castigate myself. Joanne's bare toes swinging only inches away from the rug. Her slippers on the floor where they'd flopped off and the shiny green noose of washing line cutting into her throat. As I lay there, her presence felt so close I could almost reach out and touch her.

Chapter 28

Sam

A raucous party on New Year's Eve gave me a hangover with the magnitude of a head-on collision on a motorway. After that, the New Year limped in with a whimper. I spent most of the time under my duvet reading historical novels, emerging only to eat and take a shower. It was exactly what I needed. By the time I went back to work I was ready to face the world again.

When Miranda invited me out for supper on my first day back at work, I jumped at the chance. Perhaps her New Year's resolution was *be kinder to Sam*.

I dashed home from St Luke's to change first, so she'd know I was making an effort for her. I was behind with my laundry, but convinced I had a fresh bra in my underwear drawer. A special one, red with lace edging. I couldn't find it anywhere. I searched through the dirty laundry basket and checked I hadn't left it in the washing machine, but it had gone AWOL. I wore a tight-fitting camisole instead.

My comb also seemed to have disappeared since I'd last washed my hair. I checked the bathroom cabinet, my handbag, my dressing table and down the edge of the sofa and couldn't find that either. It was starting to feel like I was losing my marbles.

As I pulled on my coat, the phone rang. I let it ring, chilling the space around me, and left.

Miranda had booked a Greek place in Camden she'd raved about recently. The music and boisterous warmth of *Dimitris'* immediately felt like another world. Apart from the low swinging lanterns that nearly took my eye out when I walked in, I loved the décor.

Dimitri himself gave us a showy welcome, leading us to a table with a red-checked cloth and a prime view of a lobster tank. On further inspection, I found that more unnerving than appetising.

'Don't be so wet,' said Miranda, finally agreeing to swap places so I had my back to it. I could still hear intermittent scratching and gurgling sounds and wasn't sure if that was worse than being able to see what was going on.

I ordered vegetarian to be on the safe side – a traditional feta cheese salad, while Miranda had squid with various seafood delicacies I didn't attempt to identify.

'Good Christmas?' she asked.

'I saw Dad. We managed to burn the stuffing and the pudding boiled dry,' I told her, 'but apart from that you could call it a success.'

'He rang and said he'd had a lovely time with you,' she said, taking small sips of mineral water. 'He brought up that time I was eleven and you must have been nine, d'you remember? We did that terrible carol concert for the neighbours.'

'You played the recorder – very badly,' I added.

'And you were on the tambourine, trying to sing,'

she sniggered. 'Mr Snape's little kid…Boris, was he called?...threw mince pies at us.'

It was so good to hear her laugh. She hadn't been so relaxed with me in a long time.

'Dad said he liked the cufflinks,' she said. 'He said something about setting fire to his paper hat after lunch…'

'Those Cuban cigars were a complete liability,' I said, throwing my eyes up. 'I don't know who thought they'd be a good idea.'

She dropped her eyes. 'I only got a few to tide him over…'

I groaned inwardly, but the moment passed without her getting cranky with me.

She raised her glass for a toast. 'To selling lots more paintings this year and the perfect man for you,' she said. I tapped my glass against hers, willing the perfect man to put in an appearance before cobwebs finally smothered my heart.

She rubbed her stomach, and admitted defeat with the squid.

'I'm sorry…about last time,' I said. I knew I had to bring it up at some point.

'Forget it,' she said without looking up. 'It's over. I don't want to talk about it.'

'Okay.'

We were safely through round one, at least.

In fact, we managed to get through the rest of our main courses, desserts and coffees without a single crossed word. At one point she even reached over and grabbed my hand. At last! This was the carefree, kind-hearted Miranda I wanted in my life.

'I've missed you,' I said.

She gave me a sorrowful smile. 'I know. I'm sorry. I've not been very nice lately, have I?'

'Sssh.' I patted her hand. 'I want you to know I love you, that's all.'

'Me too,' she said, her voice quivering.

'Here's to a great relationship between us from now on,' I said, tipping my glass towards hers again.

The waiter came with the bill.

'By the way,' she said, as she lifted her bag on to the table. 'You must have left this behind at my flat.'

She held up a copy of *Enduring Love* by Ian McEwan.

In an instant, it felt as though the door had been flung open and an Arctic wind was blowing in.

'I didn't leave it there,' I said, my voice barely audible.

'It's got your name in the front.' She folded back the cover to show me.

'It's got my name in it, but I gave it to Con,' I said. 'I left it at his place.'

'Oh…' she said, shifting in her seat. Her cheeks flushed a deep crimson and she looked down.

Con.

Suddenly it all became clear. How had I been so stupid? All that crap about wanting to keep 'the boyfriend' secret. That's why she'd been playing down the whole situation.

'Oh, my God,' I said, my chair screeching as I stood up. 'Was it Con's baby? Was *he* the father?'

Miranda's face had turned from red to white in seconds.

'It isn't serious…' she said, playing the same card she'd tried on me before.

As if…

Even in my stunned stupor I noticed she hadn't actually answered my question.

Suddenly the noise of the restaurant, music twanging through large speakers and clashing dishes in the kitchen, turned from exuberance to an intolerable racket inside my head. I had to get out. I dodged my way around chair legs, handbags and those annoying lanterns and burst out into the night air.

Once on the street, I ran. Blindly, with no sense of where I was going. A post box, a litter bin, cracks in the pavement, a manhole cover, Con's face; everything overlapped into one surreal mosaic. I leapt on the first bus that came along. I didn't care where it was heading as long as it took me away from Miranda.

It was just after midnight when I got back home. I don't know how I managed to keep the feta and vine leaves down for so long, but as soon as I got in, my time ran out. I made it to the bathroom and threw up all the goodwill and false hope Miranda had offered me. I held on to my indignation, refusing to give in to the finger of guilt that reminded me I'd left Miranda to pay the bill.

I half hoped I'd find a message from her on my answering machine, something to show that she recognised the impact of the bombshell she'd dropped. Anything. It didn't even have to be coherent – just an acknowledgement. I pressed the button on the machine twice, but there was nothing there.

Chapter 29

Sam

Rosie was holding an envelope when she arrived for her session that week. She sat down with it on her lap waiting for me to ask what was inside.

'They're photos,' she said. 'From when I was little. I know it's not about the crash, but you said you wanted to know more about Mum and Dad. I thought just this once.'

Even though I was sure Rosie's tragic history would reveal a great deal, I was aware that we had only one more session left after this one. It was all coming a bit late; we couldn't afford to delve too deeply.

'Of course. Let's take a look at them,' I said. 'Then we'd better get back to the crash.'

She took a measly three snapshots out of the envelope and spread them on her lap. Rosie's entire childhood.

'It's taken me a lot of courage to bring them…' she said, with more than a trace of indignation. 'I thought you'd be interested.'

'I am.'

A flash of mistrust darted across my mind. Was this a ploy to open up a can of worms that were too fat and entangled to be stuffed back in again, during the limited consultations we had left?

I lifted a side table and placed it between us, keeping my suspicions to myself. I'd see where she went with it.

'Mum was scared of Dad,' she said.

I leaned forward to look closely at the first picture, not wanting to touch it without permission. 'She's pretty,' I said.

'A neighbour, Mrs Dunbar, told me years later that Dad was jealous of any contact Mum had with other blokes. He used to follow her, apparently.' She raised her eyebrows. 'Mum told the neighbour that she always knew he was there, lurking in the bushes or hiding in the next aisle in the supermarket. she could feel his eyes on her, but not in a nice way.'

'How did that affect you, do you think?'

'He must have had his reasons, I suppose. He used to hit her when things got really bad. I never knew what she was supposed to have done – I think it was all inside his head.'

'Did he ever hit you?'

She laughed. 'He never noticed me enough to bother. I didn't register on his radar at all – and he wasn't around much during the years he was on the oil rigs. After the explosion, he came back, but while his body was with us, his mind was somewhere else. He gambled and drank, came home late.'

She made a sucking sound like someone stepping inside from the cold.

No wonder her mother had packed her bags that fateful day. I couldn't imagine why she'd left it so long.

'I learnt how to climb out of windows and down the drainpipe when I was small, after Dad started locking us in the house. Mum was terrified for me at first, but then she realised it was our only saving grace. At least she knew I'd be able to get out if there was a fire.'

'Your mum cared a lot about you,' I said, stressing every word.

'Yeah, I suppose she did.' She said it in a lacklustre tone, as though her mother's feelings for her didn't count for a great deal.

'I think the van going in the water brought all that back to me – the clambering in and out of small windows. I know I could do with losing a few pounds, but I'm more agile than most people think.'

'Except you've lost weight recently.'

She grinned. 'I have, haven't I? I'm a lot prettier now without my glasses, don't you think?' I'd noticed in our last two sessions that the clunky specs weren't dominating her face anymore. 'I decided they make me look geeky. I'm using contact lenses now.'

'You're a smart, attractive lady,' I said. It was hard to think of her as a woman. Even though she was in her thirties, I could only ever think of her as a child. 'Do you want to say more about your mum?'

'My memories of her are hazy. Mrs Dunbar told me that when he was on the rigs, Dad made her do late shifts at the cosmetics' factory, so she wouldn't have her evenings free, but she'd often swap with her workmates to spend time with me. Thing is, I can't remember much of it.

'Do you remember any special times with your mum?'

Rosie picked up the photograph and stroked it. 'I

don't remember her ever saying she loved me, but I think she did. She got angry with me for climbing out of the window, I can remember that, but it was only because she was frightened I'd hurt myself. That's a kind of love, isn't it?'

She looked up. 'Sometimes you have to work things out like that, don't you?' she said. 'You have to work out from what people do or say, what they really mean.'

As she spoke my heart was turning to putty. Part of me wanted to scoop her up in my arms and hold her, rock her, reassure her. No child should have to go through what she'd suffered. It wasn't only that both her parents had died so horribly when she was young – and that she'd had to witness it – but she'd also had a complete lack of affection from her father and a distracted, tentative love from her downtrodden mother.

As I feared, Rosie's past took over the whole session. There was enough material spilling out for months and months of therapy. By the end my heartstrings were tugged into shreds. Rosie even asked if I was okay at one point. My face must have given me away.

'I really like you,' she said, as she put the pictures back in the envelope.

There was a lump in my throat the size of a tennis ball.

She looked up. 'Please can we have more sessions? Can't you see how this is starting to work now?'

Ah. My heart sank.

'We said we'd have only one more – you agreed to that.'

'No, *you* decided it,' she said, a prickly edge to her tone.

I didn't rise to it.

She sank back, her voice softening. 'The more I see you, the more I realise how much it's helping.'

This was the moment of truth. I had to lay it on the line once and for all.

'Your history has been really tough, anyone can see that,' I said, 'and therapy could really help you. But our arrangement was for you to recover your memories of the crash, as far as possible. To explore your past you'd need to work long term with someone else; using different techniques. It can't be with me.'

'Can't be with you?' Her bottom lip quivered. 'Are you saying you *can't do* the kind of therapy I need? Are you saying you've never worked with someone who had a messed up childhood?'

I drew a deep fluttery breath. Of course, I had. I couldn't lie.

I was about to speak when she shot to her feet. She glared at me. 'You don't care, do you? Not really.'

She grabbed her bag and ran for the door without another word.

I stood in the hall, listening to her footsteps stomping down the stairs, trying to work out what I should do.

I had a decision to make.

In theory, there was nothing preventing us from carrying on. We could change tack and cover Rosie's hurt and pain from the past, but it would be a long haul. We didn't have any hospital bureaucracy instructing us about when we had to finish. It was her will against mine. And Rosie knew it.

The problem was I wanted my flat back; I no longer wanted to be seeing patients after hours. I'd realised after our first consultation here that I'd made a mistake; I should never have suggested it.

But that wasn't the real issue.

If I offered Rosie another block of sessions, would it be enough? Would it *ever* be enough? She'd been working for eighteen months with her previous therapist and they would probably still be going strong if it hadn't been for Erica's untimely death.

I shuddered at the thought of spending so much time with Rosie. Week after week. Month after month. I'd started to hate Thursdays, especially that crushing blow to the stomach I felt when I thought my day was nearly over, then I remembered she'd be coming over.

I really felt for her, but she pushed and pushed all the time, needing more than I could give. Every time we met, I had to be on my guard, making sure I didn't say or do anything to allow her to think our connection was anything beyond a professional arrangement. It was wearing to say the least.

I had to face the fact that Rosie seemed attached to me, infatuated even. But it was like a seven-year-old's crush; regressive and tiresome, yet throwing up material we could work on productively in therapy. If we had more time.

Should I keep working with her, or let her go?

My gut was saying *No way*, but the professional side of me was prodding me, exhorting me to follow through.

Knowing Erica died out of the blue didn't help. I'd contacted Professor Dean to see if I could get hold of Erica's notes from her sessions with Rosie, but he hadn't got back to me. Erica's death must have stirred up considerable loss and abandonment for Rosie and it wasn't that long ago. I was reluctant to replicate that in any way.

I went to the bathroom and splashed cold water on my face. The bottom line was I had a responsibility of care towards Rosie; I'd taken that on when I'd started seeing her, privately, at home.

I stared at my dripping reflection. *Come on* – it wasn't such a big deal. I'd offer her six further sessions, making it clear that we were preparing for an ending. I wanted a clean ending that left Rosie fortified and hopeful about her future. I'd give her details of private therapists she could work with longer term and we'd get it all set up with a smooth transition. There were plenty of psychotherapists who were happy working from home.

I let out a deep sigh and buried my face in the towel. I *had* to get this right. I'd failed to respond to a patient in crisis once before and look how that had ended up.

I slept fitfully that night, close to the surface; I couldn't get scenes of Miranda and Con out of my head. They'd lived together as flatmates for a while, over a year ago, but Miranda had moved out in a shot when Dad offered to pay for a flat of her own with studio space. It had never occurred to me that something might have been going on between them.

At what point did she and Con turn their casual friendship into a more intimate one? I tried to find memories of the two of them together to recall how they'd acted around each other. Should I have seen it coming? How many times had they slept together? Did he say the same things to her as he'd said to me? Did he hold her, kiss her in the same way he'd kissed me?

Stop...

I woke up in a sweat and squashed an earbud into my ear to make the radio block out my thoughts.

Soon after, patchy dreams took over. Rosie was playing with the quartet and I could hear them, floating on a tiny island in the middle of a lake. I saw edited highlights from the DVD we'd watched together and then suddenly I was awake. It was as though two wires in my brain had connected and made a spark, but like a scout's campfire, I couldn't get the spark to catch.

I got out of bed, put the kettle on and tried to step back into the dream. The image of a man standing, kept flashing into my mind. I had to see Rosie's footage of the party again. There was something there I'd missed. Something that was trying to get through to me.

I paced around the flat in my pyjamas, making a little circuit of the bedroom, sitting room and kitchen. The ironing was folded on a chair. *When had I done that?* The dishes were cleared from the draining board. I stood in the kitchen biting my thumbnail, trying to recall when I'd stacked everything away. I put it down to overwork.

In the light of my dream, the next morning I made a decision and picked up the phone. Rosie sounded both surprised and overjoyed to hear from me.

'I know we don't normally have contact between sessions,' I said, 'but I wondered if you could bring the disc of the Hinds' party again on Thursday.'

'Why? What's happened?'

'I'd like to see it again. I'm not a hundred per cent sure,' I said, 'but I think there's something there that could be useful.'

I heard a tiny hiccup on the other end of the line. 'Thursday – that's our last session…' She dropped the words like rocks.

I put her out of her misery. 'Okay. I've been thinking. We could have another six sessions if—'

'Really?'

Her eagerness made me want to weep. 'Just six, mind. This is more than I usually offer, but—'

'Oh, *yes* – yes, please!' she squealed. It was as if I'd given her a million pounds.

'We'll talk about it on Thursday. I'm sorry to bother you.'

'It's no trouble at all. Thank you for…you know…'

I pressed *end call* and got ready to pop out. I needed, among other things, more Hula Hoops. They may be junk food, but they were an absolute staple in my diet and I only had a few crumbs left in the last packet. I must have worked my way through it in my sleep!

On the way back from the corner shop, I had a creepy feeling that I was being followed. Was it Bruce? I really didn't have the energy to cope with this now.

I stopped abruptly and shot round, but there was no one there. I picked up my pace and dragged my hood over my head against the sleet that was slicing the chilled air. I was being ridiculous. My imagination was running riot. Nevertheless, at the last corner I broke into a run and scrabbled around with numb fingers at the main door trying to get it unlocked. I raced up the stairs and as soon as I got inside my flat, snapped the bolt across.

I huffed and puffed like a fox getting down its burrow just in time.

Chapter 30

Rosie

I can't tell you how relieved I am! Sam told me we could have six more appointments. I nearly fell to my knees. I was so scared she was going to end it. I was getting desperate, but now everything is going to be all right.

She even rang between sessions, which I thought we weren't supposed to do! Of course, I'd speak to her every day if I could. I kind of do in my head anyway, but it's not the same. She's so caring – the look in her eyes when I showed her my family photos. I thought she was going to burst into tears…for me!

I've forgiven her for letting me down over the auction house, because she's starting to feel like, well, family. Finally, for the first time in my life, someone warm, funny, caring and incredible really cares about me. I'm so excited. I've got such plans for the two of us.

At the music store, Sid seems happy for me to take the odd afternoon off. It works perfectly for me. It's only a twenty-minute journey from Charing Cross to Clapham. I wonder if Sam has discovered any of my little liberties by now. I haven't taken much and I do plenty of good things in return, so there's no harm done. It's lucky we're about the same height, and now I'm losing weight I could probably squeeze into most of her clothes if I wanted to.

I tried on her velvet dress last time and the new pyjamas straight out of the packet. Maybe she got them for Christmas, who knows? The boots are tight, but I couldn't resist them. I've polished them up and I'll wear them at the weekend. The belt is cool, too. She had lots of others curled up in her drawer, so she probably won't notice that one is missing. I have my eye on one of her towels and a scarf for next time – the pale blue one I've seen her wearing, but I'm careful not to take too many things at once. I watched a DVD while I was there and cleaned the windows. I haven't done anything *terribly* bad – not really.

I told Sam I'd met someone really nice recently, but I didn't go into details. I don't want Sam to think I'm a total saddo who doesn't have a life – and it was only half a lie. I did meet someone a few months back and we had a cool chat, but it wasn't a man. I didn't tell Sam that, because I don't want her getting the wrong end of the stick. I've always fancied guys and I'm not into women 'like that', but I'm definitely going to see my new friend again.

The stuff about the crash doesn't go away and as I lie on my bed reflecting, I keep coming back to the question of my viola. Why is finding it so important? Would it matter if I never saw it again? Could I let it go and stop these annoying half-memories from plaguing me? I'm not sure how much progress Sam and I are making on that front.

In my dreams I keep hearing that phone call – the one that drifted up the stairs before the crash. Sam and I have gone over that scene time and time again, but I'm not getting any idea who the voice belongs to, or how it might be connected to me.

Maybe the crash *was* about me, but I can't think why. I may have been insignificant all my life, but this is hardly the sort of attention I've been craving.

Bottom line is, I can't give up; the compulsion to know what happened is too strong. Even if the crash wasn't about me, I seem to be the one left with the aftershock. I've been wondering why some memories seem locked away and thinking maybe my brain is trying to protect me. When we crashed into the lake, when the van started filling up with water, did awful things happen that my mind can't cope with?

'Sometimes the brain is too terrified to let the memories come out,' Sam explained, when I asked her about it. 'Sometimes the real truth *never* emerges.'

That was *not* what I wanted to hear. How awful would that be? To live with a huge question mark hanging around my neck every single day for the rest of my life?

If I'm really honest, I'm worried that *I* might have done something bad when we were all fighting to get out. Why can't I remember Richard after we went under water? Did he escape? Is Max still alive – was it really him I saw on Oxford Street – or is his body going to surface in the lake, like Stephanie's? I'm doing my nut with so many questions.

Oh, Richard, I wish you were here, so I could ask you in person. Get it all out in the open, once and for all. I'm never going to get anywhere like this.

*

It's Saturday, so I take a Tube up to the Urban Shack Café. I've been going there to eat lately. I want to be with chatty, up-beat people and switch off from the constant muddle over the crash.

The couple who work there are obviously high on cannabis, you can smell it when you walk in. Dezzie, the guy making coffees has a pinafore around his waist with a red London bus on it and a fat crocheted cap on his head in red, yellow and green. His girlfriend, Shontal, has a little tot who often sits in his pushchair by the till. And there's a yappy dog, that has to be shut away if the health inspector shows up.

Dezzie shouts at people as they step inside: 'Come an' join da pardie!'

He seems to recognise me or maybe he's just friendly with everyone. Trade is good around here and it's always busy. There are four people huddled around a table playing cards at the back and a woman is breastfeeding her baby just inside the door.

There's an old tune – *Funky Town* – blaring through the speakers. The music is always loud, heavy on the bass, so the windows rattle. It's not the place to come for peace and quiet.

I find a seat by the window and Shontal comes over to ask what I want. She never has a notepad. People order from a menu that covers three blackboards, another good selling point, and she always seems to get it right. You can have bangers and mash, risotto, bagels, jam and scones, paninis, curried goat, mushy peas or a weird sort of dried fish – they're not fussy about sticking to one culinary style.

By the time I've finish my toasted teacake, a nice-looking man on his own has joined my table. He smiles back when I look up; a broad lasting smile that makes his eyes twinkle. Forget the Great Boar, this is a much better place to meet people. I've always relied on guys needing a few beers to blur the edges when they look me up and down, but now I've changed my image, perhaps I don't need my edges blurred any more.

I glance down at my lovely boots. My feet are not only a bit bigger than Sam's, they must be a slightly different shape as well, because I'm working new creases into them. I'm sure she won't mind.

The nice-looking man orders a falafel burger and ginger beer and I ask if he lives around here. He tells me he's been playing five-a-side in the park nearby and has worked up an appetite. He looks like he's about to ask me something, but as soon as an empty table becomes free at the back, he gets up and leaves me on my own.

It's so easy to misread people. I wish there was some kind of rulebook we all had to live by, so it was easy to know whether someone was interested or not. It would save a lot of time.

I look at my watch. It doesn't look like my new friend is coming in for lunch, today. Shame. Never mind, I can easily see her another time and I don't want her thinking I'm deliberately trying to bump into her.

I don't know what to do with myself when I get home. I'd quite like to go for a swim, but since the crash, I haven't been able to bring myself to step into the pool. To kill half-an-hour I run the shower. I close my eyes and, as whorls of steam suck the air out of the room, something comes back to me.

It was when we were in the van just after we'd left Hinds' place. Stephanie had definitely wanted the window open. There were button controls on the armrest beside Max, but when he tried them they were locked, so she asked Richard, who had the master controls on his side.

'They're not working, I'm afraid,' he'd said. 'Problem with the electrics. We can't open the windows, but it isn't far.'

Max had said, 'Bloody piece of junk,' under his breath, but I don't think Richard heard him. That would explain why the windows weren't open when we went down, why the others couldn't get out.

But it raised another question.

Was Richard telling the truth? Had he made sure the others wouldn't have a chance of getting out so he could get his hands on Max's violin?

Chapter 31

Rosie

I finally cracked on Sunday afternoon. I was sick of huddling over my useless electric heater watching rubbish on television, so I blocked my number and rang Sam's flat. After five rings it clicked to the answering machine. Was she there, not picking up, or had she gone out?

I couldn't stop thinking about her. The way things were between us now, it felt so much better than it ever had with Erica. We've got a bond that can't be broken. Sam just needs to see it, that's all.

I had a yearning then to be surrounded by her stuff, to touch the things she owned. I decided to take a chance – even though I usually only go when I know she's at work – and headed over there.

All is quiet as I pad silently up the stairs. I wait outside her door, then press my ear against it. Not a thing. I ease my key in the lock and dart inside. I stand on the mat for a few seconds, just to make sure. Her coat has gone from the hall rack and there's an empty space in the middle of a row of shoes. I let myself exhale.

Now I'm here I feel so much better. I won't stay long. I go to the kitchen first, leaving the door ajar so I can hear if she comes back, and make myself at home. I help myself to a chocolate biscuit. Just one. I fold the packet just as she left it and put it back in the cupboard. She has some swish crockery; big white dining plates edged in silver. I lift up one of the glasses – it feels light in my hand. I flick my nail against it and it sings. I imagine Sam drinking from it and press my lips against the rim.

I hastily put it back and go into the bedroom. This is what I've really come here for. I peel back the duvet, kick off my trainers and climb in. I'm tempted to take off all my clothes, but I don't know how long I've got. I curl into a foetal position and close my eyes. I'm snug and safe and happier than I've been in ages. So close to her.

I must have been nearly asleep, when I hear a key rattling in the lock. I jerk upright. I wasn't expecting her to be so quiet. She's inside before I know what's happening.

I throw myself off the bed as I hear her footsteps in the hall, then she clomps across the lino in the kitchen. For some reason, I decide hiding under the bed isn't a smart idea, so I creep out of the bedroom and into the sitting room, crouching down behind the settee.

She comes in and I peek round the edge to see what she's doing. She keeps stopping every few steps to listen, as if she knows someone is there, then she starts opening doors and checking cupboards – the one in the hall first, like she's searching for an intruder.

Her face is serious when she comes back into the sitting room. There are no cupboards in here. I squeeze my fists and will her to go into another room, but she's so close, almost within reach. I snatch a gulp of air as she approaches the sofa, barely two feet from where I'm squatting.

I'm lucky. Her mind seems distracted by the long billowing curtains. She creeps towards them, not looking my way. As she ruffles the fabric at arms' length, I dodge behind the comfy chair by the door, hoping she doesn't hear my feet scuff the carpet. She lifts the second curtain and then draws them both, before heading for the bedroom. I daren't let out a breath. She's checking every room.

She's huffing to herself as I hear the click of the wardrobe opening. I glide behind the sitting room door, watching her every move through the crack. And then – I was right – she ducks down and looks under the bed, all the while with her phone in her hand like it's a weapon. *My trainers are still beside the bed. Will she see them?*

I could run for it now, but I know she'd hear me and it would all be over. She wouldn't understand, she'd be shocked and furious and I'd lose her forever. So I stay still and wait.

Instinctively, my hand goes to my phone in my pocket. Did I switch it off? I pull it out gingerly and press the button. I think about what else I brought in with me. My jacket – I hung it under Sam's dressing gown on the back of the bedroom door. She can't have seen it. Not yet, anyway. That would give the game away for sure; I know she'd recognise it. She's a stickler for details.

Suddenly she's in the sitting room again. She's like a

wound-up toy spinning all over the place. Why can't she calm down? I want her to change into comfortable clothes and put some music on. I want her to come and join me, sit down, so I can watch her closely. I'm getting fed up with all this dashing around. *Let's have some downtime, Sam.*

I'm terrified she'll find me, yet part of me is thrilled to be this near to her. This is what it's like to be with the *real* Sam: no professional front to hide behind, no airs and graces, no pretending.

But she's obviously disturbed. She's in the kitchen now and keeps sighing loudly as if something has upset her. I'm tempted – oh, so tempted – to break cover, to reach out and hold her. To comfort her and let her know I'm there for her. But before I get the chance to move, she's got her coat on again. I'm disappointed. She's leaving me. *Don't go. Please stay, Sam.* I hear the click of the front door. She's gone. I feel cheated. I'm all on my own again.

I go into the kitchen. Sam has boiled the kettle but not used the water, so I fill up the mug beside it and make the cup of tea she was going to have. That cheers me up a bit. It feels like we're sharing something. Then a thought occurs to me and I shiver with delight. I'm going on a treasure hunt!

I've snooped before, of course, but this time I'm looking for something specific. Would she hide it away in her own flat? She certainly wouldn't leave it in plain view in the sitting room; she knows I look at her bookshelves when we have our weekly session and she wouldn't risk leaving it there.

I go through every room with a fine toothcomb. I check top shelves, the backs of drawers, between folded sheets, under the mattress. All I come across is a couple of adverts for dating agencies torn from magazines and an out-of-date packet of condoms in a drawer. So that tells me something, I suppose. Not quite got the perfect life, then?

I'm about to leave empty-handed when I come across something. It's not her personal journal, but a ring binder with my initials, 'RC – confidential' inside her briefcase. Could it be a special file just for me?!

I slide it out. She doesn't use my full name, but it's about me, all right; on the front page she's written details of the crash and a few lines about my past. It's not as good as her diary, but it's still enough to set my heart racing.

It will be almost as good as having Sam here herself. Her words, her thoughts. I only get to see her for one hour each entire week; so that means a hundred and sixty-seven hours a week *without* her. How am I supposed to survive on that? Reading her notes will be like climbing inside her head and taking a good look around.

In my excitement I nearly drop the file and it falls open at the last page. I start reading, but within seconds I feel all queasy and churned up inside. I don't like what I see. She's written all kinds of awful things about me – saying I'm clingy and attention seeking.

'*...shows tendencies to manipulate...*'

What? I can't believe it! I thought she liked me. I read on and...what the f—! It says here she's been trying to end our sessions, *for ages*. She's had enough of me. It sounds like she *hates* me. What's going on?

I slam the file down; it's dirty, evil.

I want to rip out all the pages, but I make myself shove it back where I found it. I should go. If I stick around I might do something rash and ruin everything.

I slip on my trainers and pluck my jacket from under her dressing gown. I bury my face in the fluffy pink fabric to comfort myself for a moment and before I know it, angry tears have made their way onto the collar. I let them linger there as a gift.

Chapter 32

Sam

On Sunday, I took my bike on the train over to Richmond Park so I could pedal like a maniac into the wind and pretend I was in open countryside. As I wheeled it back to the station, I felt myself being spooked by the sound of footsteps gathering speed behind me, then by a car slowing down at the kerb. The silent calls were doing this to me. Turning me into someone who listens too hard and peers over their shoulder far too often. When I got home, I couldn't shake off that jittery feeling and for some reason my flat didn't feel as comforting as usual.

I was convinced there was a new smell in the air; some sort of floral perfume. Cleaning fluid? Air freshener?

My skin prickled. Was someone else here? How could they possibly have got in? The windows were all locked. I went into the hall and checked my front door; there was no sign it had been forced and there were mortice locks in addition to the Yale.

I had to set my mind at rest, so I started in the hall and began checking all the cupboards. I tugged at the thick curtains in the sitting room, squashing them against the wall before closing them. I checked the shower cubicle, then in the wardrobe and under the bed.

I started to feel ridiculous. If someone had got in they'd have taken things of value; the television, iPad, laptop, camera – but nothing seemed out of place. I opened my jewellery case, but nothing appeared to have gone.

Finally, I gave up and went into the kitchen. I switched on the radio so I couldn't hear the day-to-day creaks of the flat and misinterpret them. I did a few jobs to keep myself on the move; re-arranged books on the bookshelf, emptied the waste bin from my bedroom into the swing bin in the kitchen, but in truth there wasn't much to do. The bath looked shiny and clean, the shelves weren't dusty. I was about to put last week's dead roses in the bin when I realised I'd already done it. The vase was empty and upside down on the draining board.

I was still uptight and couldn't settle, so I decided to head out again. I wanted to wear my comfy brown boots, but couldn't find them anywhere. This was getting weird. Maybe Miranda had borrowed them without telling me – except she hadn't been to the flat in ages.

It was too cold to stroll around the common, so I drifted mindlessly in and out of shops on St John's Road, trying to lose myself in the wafts of freshly baked bread, the rainbow colours of thick winter woollies with twenty percent off. I held mohair scarves up to my cheeks, ran my fingers through the coarse oily fibres of Icelandic jumpers, trying to capture some of the comfort and get rid of my uptight feeling.

A display with a running model train in a window caught my eye and I stood to watch the locomotive stop at the station, then carry on into a tunnel. I was about to turn away when a shape in the reflection made me shudder. A man was standing still, conspicuous because everyone else was on the move, heading somewhere. I turned slowly, but by the time I was facing the pavement, he'd moved.

He must have had a trim; the bald patch between the two tufts was more pronounced, but it was definitely Bruce. He was carrying two plastic carrier bags and was looking away from me, marching purposefully up the road. Did he live around here? Had he been following me? Was this just a coincidence?

I didn't want to risk bumping into him, so I swiftly retraced my steps and jumped on the first bus to Camden. I found myself walking into the Urban Shack Café, where I'd been with Miranda, and ordering a coffee with a cheese and onion pasty. The people here seemed like Miranda's kind of people – colourful, exuberant and spontaneous. With the familiar bustle and lively music, it felt safe. I half expected her to walk in – half hoped she would, but I was unlucky.

I dipped the last of my pasty in the tomato sauce and decided to see if Miranda was at the gallery. I wanted nothing more than to make contact, feel connected, feel attached to the one person I hoped would be a cornerstone in my life. Finding out that she and Con had been…well, it was devastating and had hurt me more than I could ever have imagined. But, my relationship with Con had been over for months and I had to find a way to cope with it.

I walked into the main display area, the café and

workshop in turn, but Miranda wasn't around so I approached someone in the foyer.

'Miranda's not in, today. She works at home a lot. Shall I tell her you came by?'

'No, it's okay…'

I wandered out like a lost dog unable to find its owner.

Unwilling to go back now without at least seeing my sister, I crossed the road, passed a line of cars and turned into the street where she lived.

What was the point of this? If she was painting she wouldn't want to be disturbed and she could easily be out somewhere. Besides, she might not be alone. *He* might be there. Then what would I do? But still, my footsteps carried me onwards.

I was only a few houses away, when I saw her front door open. My first thought was to hide, so I dived behind a wheelie bin at the roadside as if I was tying my shoelace.

Miranda stepped out and turned to stretch a hand towards the person behind her. Sure enough, Con took it and locked the door behind them, like it was second nature. I cursed myself; I shouldn't have come unannounced like this.

They were heading towards me. I pulled up my hood and turned straight through someone's gateway, hoping no one was home. Standing on tiptoe to see over the high hedge, I watched them walk hand in hand up the road. A scorching pain flared under my ribcage. I hurried back to the pavement and strode out in their direction, staying on the opposite side of the road, watching them. They swung their arms like children and Miranda nuzzled into his neck. *Not serious, eh?*

They reached the end of the road and turned in the opposite direction from the gallery, heading along the high street. I half jogged to get a bit closer; with more people around it would be easy to lose them. What was I doing? What was I hoping to gain? I knew the answer straight away. I wanted to see how they *were* with each other. I wanted to see what their relationship was like for myself, not hear a watered down version of it from Miranda.

They went into a fashion boutique and I feigned interest in a shop window opposite, trying to find them in the reflection. I heard Con laugh as they moved on and took off after them, staying on the other side of the street.

I remembered the last time I'd been alone with Con. I'd left him sitting on a bench at a National Trust property with only a bottle of whisky for company. We hadn't spoken since. I'd had a few measly postcards from him telling me when his next film was coming out, that's all.

When had it started with my sister? Had they talked about me, about how they would keep it a secret? I was quite prepared for Con to let me down, but not Miranda. That felt like one twist of the knife too far. Except, could I really call it betrayal, when I was the one who had ended it?

I kept a steady distance until they reached the park. At times they hugged, walked arm in arm or had their arms wrapped tightly around one another, always in contact. It was difficult to watch, yet I was transfixed. I kept wondering how often we'd done that, Con and I. Not often. That had probably been my fault. He'd always criticised me for not throwing myself into the relationship.

Miranda skipped along beside him until they found a bench under a sprawling horse chestnut. They huddled together, Miranda reaching inside his coat to bury her face in the crook of his shoulder.

From time to time they exchanged words and looked at each other and kissed. Miranda gave him a playful punch at one point. Then they kissed for a long time.

Why did I let him go?

I had to pull myself up short. Hold on. *Be realistic.* This wasn't the full picture. Con had been moody and aggressive whenever other men came on the scene. I'd only had to mention a name and he'd bristled. It happened time and time again. That wasn't what I wanted. Perhaps he was different with Miranda. In any case, I didn't need to be concerned. She wouldn't put up with any nonsense. She was never one to hold back if something was cramping her style.

For a while, I hovered at the edge of the grass, watching, stepping from side to side to keep warm. I checked my watch a few times, so I'd look like I was waiting for someone. Pathetic. What had I been reduced to?

I was exposed now and it was difficult to stay close without being seen. I began to worry that one of them would look up and recognise me so I turned, head down, and hurried back to the bus stop.

When I got home, I blocked my number and called Con's mobile. As it rang, I pictured him still sitting where I'd left them. Wrapped around each other, oblivious to the cold.

'Yup…' came his chocolately actor's baritone.

'It's Samantha – er, sorry to bother you.'

'Sam…' He sounded surprised.

'It's okay, by the way – I know about you and Miranda and I'm…fine with it…honestly. I know that Miranda lost the baby, too.' My voice cracked. 'You can tell me to mind my own business, but I need to know…one thing.'

I heard a roar of traffic. They were still outside.

He was going to put the phone down, I just knew it. I gripped the receiver, as if by holding tightly enough I wouldn't lose him.

He cleared his voice. 'Didn't you ask Mirrie?' he said.

'*Mirrie?* Who's M—'

There was so much I wasn't party to. He sounded like a total stranger and he was turning my sister into one too.

'You and I haven't seen each other for over a year, right?' he said coldly.

'Yes.'

'Haven't I the right to move on?'

'Yes, of course. It's just—'

Why was I so desperate to know whether he was the father of her child or not? Couldn't I let it go?

'Is that everything?' he said. He was enjoying

exerting this power over me.

'No…no, it's not...are you going to brush this away without..?' I could hear my voice splintering and felt a tear roll down my cheek.

'Mirrie wants a word,' he said. There was a crackle and my sister came on the line.

'I wanted to ask you something,' she said chirpily. There was a tiny hesitation. 'We'd like you…to…you know…come and have lunch or something, sometime.'

I admired her bravery in attempting to smooth things over, but I wanted answers. Was I overreacting? Would any normal person think that I had no right to know the whole story, that this was none of my business?

'That would be…lovely,' I said.

I could think of nothing worse. My feelings of betrayal cut too deeply to move on so quickly. How could I sit there, helping myself to another fondant fancy, carrying on a merry conversation with this hanging over us? It wasn't so much that she and Con had been to bed together, it was the fact that Miranda had been with Con in a *relationship*, had got pregnant and *never told me*. It made me feel shut out, totally disregarded, trampled on. 'Got to go – someone at the door,' I muttered.

I put down the receiver and sank down onto the sofa, burying my face in the stale cushions.

Chapter 33

Sam

Rosie was due any minute, but I was weary after a hectic day at the hospital and had a churning stomach ache. I should have been reading through the notes I'd made last week, but my mind was meandering all over the place. It had leapt to a different time altogether. How it had all started – last Christmas. Scenes began playing out inside my head.

It began with a call from Joanne on my mobile, late one evening. She sounded like she had been running, was out of breath and babbling something about not feeling safe in a whispery voice.

'Can you come over, please, just this once,' she'd rasped at the other end. 'I'm not feeling right at all.'

Joanne was only seventeen and had been seeing me for three months at the hospital for severe anxiety following the stabbing of a fellow student at college. She'd mentioned having suicidal thoughts during our early sessions, but we seemed to be making progress and I judged her to be no longer at risk.

'You know I can't do that,' I said. 'You know I'm not able to see you outside of hospital hours, but you can get help in lots of other ways.' I'd given her the numbers of 24-hour helplines so many times that she knew them off by heart, but I ran through them again and explained that I'd contact her GP the next day, if she wanted me to. All the usual steps.

'I don't want to speak to a stranger,' she'd pleaded.

'I only want to speak to you. Please come.'

Joanne wasn't living with her parents, because they'd had a terrible row about her boyfriend. Her father had more or less kicked her out, though her mother wasn't happy about it. As a result, Joanne lived with a bunch of rowdy students in a house due to be demolished – not the best environment for her in my view.

'I can spend a few minutes on the phone with you now,' I told her, 'But that's all. You're due to see me tomorrow morning at nine o'clock. We can talk again then.' I'd already had a telling off from my supervisor for giving her my mobile number to use 'in an emergency'.

Joanne had sounded desperate and started to cry, but it wasn't *me* she needed – just someone who would listen, be with her and calm her down. There were plenty of trained and willing volunteers out there who could do that job just as well as I could.

That's what I thought, anyway.

'Can't we bring our session forward to tonight, instead, at my bedsit?' she sobbed.

It had been drilled into me, during my training, to watch out for patients who tried to manipulate situations. Dr Rosen would have said Joanne was using classic techniques to test me. He'd already warned me that turning up to 'rescue' her would only feed into her early childhood fantasies and ruin all our work together.

I knew it made sense, but nevertheless I'd always felt there had to be exceptions. *She was only seventeen – she was allowed to need rescuing at seventeen, wasn't she?*

But I didn't step in.

I should have acted on my instincts. Joanne was vulnerable and felt like my responsibility. I should have been there for her.

'I'm sorry, that won't be possible,' I'd told her. 'It's nearly ten o'clock and it's not the way this works. You managed to call me. You need to call one of the other numbers I gave you…'

Even as I said it, I knew at the back of my mind that I was wrong.

Her morning session came and went and that's when I bolted over to her house. But I was too late.

Her parents came to St Luke's every day for five days after I found Joanne's body, to point the finger at me for letting her die. There was nothing I could say or do to ease their pain. I'd let Joanne down. I'd failed her because I'd stuck to the rules.

The intercom buzzed and I let Rosie in.

She walked brusquely past me towards her chair and started talking before she sat down, obviously agitated and upset.

'…so I want to know why you don't like me,' she said, glaring at me.

'What? What's happened? What makes you say that?' I said, hurrying to catch up with her.

'You don't, do you? You want to get rid of me.'

Where had this sudden outburst come from? 'That's not true,' I said. 'I want to do my very best to help you.'

'That's not the same,' she retorted, eyeballing me. 'It's always like this. People never like me and I don't know why.'

I swallowed back a weighty sigh. We were in for a long haul.

'I was bullied at school for being fat and weird,' she went on, 'and an orphan – let's not forget that.' She gave a spluttery laugh. 'Everyone thought that was a *terrific* reason to poke fun at me. When I grew up, people avoided me. Men only take any interest if they want sex and women aren't proper friends at all. When I try to get to know them better, they make excuses. Like Dawn, from upstairs. I don't know *why*. If I knew why, I'd fix it.' She clapped her hands. 'There you are – that's Rosie Chandler, Miss Personality of the Year, in a nutshell.'

I let my eyes settle on hers. 'Shall I tell you what I think?' I said.

'That's the idea,' she huffed.

I was too tired to beat about the bush. 'I think you've never been part of a healthy family. You've never seen proper love for yourself. Your father wasn't a good role model and your mother was too busy keeping your father at bay to give you the attention you deserved.'

Her eyes started to well up, but she didn't direct them away from me. 'You've been pushed from pillar to post growing up,' I went on, 'one foster family to the next, neglected and overlooked.'

The trickle of tears turned into full, body-shaking sobs.

'You don't really know how to have deep relationships,' I told her, 'you don't really know what love is all about.'

'You see, that's why I come here,' she whimpered.

'Because you understand.' She wiped her nose on the back of her hand. 'How come you "get" it, when other people don't? They don't give me a chance.'

I held the tissue box out for her. She wrapped her arms around herself and rocked back and forth, glancing up at me as if hoping I'd offer her a hug. I was determined not to, this time. It was too easy for Rosie to misinterpret those responses. She'd initiated several embraces before, 'accidentally' touched me on a few occasions; brushed her hand against mine or patted my arm as she'd left. I needed to keep my distance. Finally she sat back and the tears dried up.

'Did you cover this kind of issue with your last therapist?' I said, without taking my eyes off her.

'Not really. She was older, for a start.' She began tracing a pattern on the chair arm with her finger. 'She wasn't as smart as you.'

I'd finally heard from Professor Dean earlier in the week to say that half of Erica's notes were missing. He didn't want to hand over an incomplete record, so he was checking with Guy's Hospital and Erica's husband, to see if she'd kept any at home. He said he'd get back to me.

Rosie wiped her cheek with the cuff of her blouse and sighed several times. Then she changed the subject.

'I've brought the DVD of the party like you asked me to.' She placed it on the table in front of her, sounding flat, disinterested.

We watched it from the beginning, in silence. Several scenes in, I pressed pause.

'There…' I said, staring at a figure near a parlour

palm, twitching in the freeze-frame. I shifted forward and pointed. 'Him. The tall, thin guy, standing on his own behind Karl Hinds?'

'Yeah?' She looked nonplussed.

'Didn't you say last time that you knew him? I can't remember his name.'

'Him?' Her finger hovered over the shape. 'Oh…no, I don't think so. I only knew a few people – mostly the Hinds' family.'

'Let's rewind and see it again. Watch his jerky mannerisms,' I said.

She peered at the screen as it ran again and shook her head. 'No – I don't know who that is.'

'I think it could be the guy from the auction house who tried to sell the watch,' I said. 'You remember that bit of phone footage you showed me?'

'You mean Teddy Spense?'

'Yes, that was his name. Look at his posture.'

'But, this was fifteen years ago,' she said. 'Surely he'd have changed a lot by now?'

'Look at the way he's shifting from one leg to the other, playing with his hair, fiddling with his pockets. Have you got your phone handy?'

She looked unconvinced, but reached for her mobile. She played me the few seconds of blurred footage.

'See? The way he tips his head to one side, the hunch of his shoulders?' I reiterated. There was definitely more than a similarity. It's part of my job to tune in to people's body language; something I can't help but pay attention to.

'If I'm right, you'll need to take it to the police,' I said. 'It looks like this "Teddy" bloke was there in 2001 *and* at the roadside just after the crash collecting his pickings. Bit of a coincidence, don't you think?'

She was shaking her head. 'Sorry, Sam. It's not ringing any bells for me. I don't think it's the same person.'

'Wouldn't Cameron Hinds know who this guy is?' I said, pointing to the TV screen. Her expression didn't change. 'It's worth a try, isn't it?'

'I can contact him, I suppose, see what he says. I want to get to the bottom of this more than anyone, but that's not the guy who tried to sell the watch. I'm certain.'

Pity. It was the one tenuous thread we had linking the party to the crash, the one single overlap, but perhaps she was right; the images were fuzzy and lots of people shared similar mannerisms.

Was I trying to find a link where there wasn't one? Was I engineering a breakthrough so Rosie could find closure and our sessions could end?

'We're still stuck,' she said despondently, as if she'd heard my thoughts.

She had a point. There was so little to go on. Nothing concrete pointing to where her viola was, who had sabotaged the seatbelts, why someone had wanted the van to go into the lake.

'But we've got six more sessions left,' I said, trying to sound buoyant, but also reminding her of our agreement. 'We can make a lot more headway in that time.' I cleared my throat to make sure I had her attention. 'I'll give you a list of people I can recommend in a week or two,' I added. There was no way I was going to get caught out this time.

Rosie didn't look up, didn't react.

When our time was up, she shuffled towards the door, like a dog being sent out into the rain.

'I'll see you next week,' I said softly.

She didn't answer as she slunk off down the stairs.

Chapter 34

Rosie

I've been in the shower too long. When I look down my skin is red and inflamed; in my agitation I've rubbed it raw with a loofah.

Only six more sessions. That's nothing. The end is coming for certain this time, I can tell, and I'm anxious as hell. Sam's going to put her foot down and that will be that. She'll shut the door and I won't be able to get back in again – at least, not while she's there. I can't let her do that to me. We've come too far.

People have always let me down and I'm sick of it. Mum was the first to do it. When I turned six, she said there was going to be an open day at the factory where she worked and that she'd take me. She always smelled of soap when she came home from work and I longed to visit. She said they sometimes set aside misshapen soaps or broken boxes of talcum powder and if I was lucky, the manageress might let me have one. I was beside myself with excitement, marking off the days on my calendar. We were all set to go and then Mum said they'd changed the rules at the factory and I couldn't go.

Then she promised she'd take me to the Isle of Wight. It was the reason the bad thing happened. We were supposed to catch the ferry from Portsmouth Harbour for a trip over the water, just the two of us. It was a secret and I wasn't to tell Dad, which wasn't difficult, because I never told him anything. Mum helped me pack my suitcase. It looked, from all the pairs of pants and socks we put in, that we were going to be away for a long time, but it was school holidays, so it didn't matter. We pushed our cases under the bed when they were full, so Dad wouldn't see them.

But on the day we were meant to go, Dad got to her with his air rifle before we were ready. He came back early from the pub and must have caught her putting her final clothes into the case. She'd had her hair done and was wearing her shiny blue shoes, all set to go. We were so close to running away together.

They left me behind – both of them. From then on I learnt never to trust a promise. Mrs Tanner said she'd buy me a rabbit, Mrs Crabbe said I could get a bike. Auntie Margaret was going to buy me a better viola. None of them did what they said they would. I got all worked up and excited for nothing. Like fireworks in the rain, their words would plop down into the damp grass and fizzle out.

Now Sam is trying to get rid of me. I thought we were getting on brilliantly…I can't understand it.

I can't settle in my pokey, damp flat, so I head for the main road and hop on the first bus to Clapham Junction. It's after six when I get there and everything is dark in her flat from outside. I know from her diary that she goes to a spin class after work sometimes. If I'm quick, I might just do it.

Once I'm inside, I search for the ring binder again and find it under a book in her bedroom. Last time, I read just a bit of it and stopped when it made me angry. Now I want to read every word, check in case I've missed something important. There may not be many more chances if she stops our appointments and my notes get filed away.

I want to know everything she feels about me.

I turn to the first page and start at the beginning.

Ah…this is better. It's clear she feels my pain. She's desperately sad about what's happened to me. She says she has great sympathy and warmth for me.

A stampede of goose pimples gallop across my whole body.

After a few pages, however, her tone definitely changes. Her words turn sour shortly after I start coming for sessions at her flat. She starts banging on about me being 'clingy' and 'pushy'. Where's that coming from? What's she talking about? I don't get it.

I want to throw the file against the wall, but I need to know more. Why did she change her mind about me?

As I skim the next section, I'm surprised to come across the occasional comment about another patient. Someone Sam worked with months ago. There's no name, but it was a young woman in a bad way by the sounds of it. Sam writes about doing the 'wrong thing' as her therapist, about being slated by this woman's parents for whatever happened. About not wanting to make the same mistake with me…

What did Sam do? Did she cross the line with a patient? Was she unprofessional?

I sit on the bed and think. What if Sam daren't write down how she *really* feels about me, because it's a professional document and other people might read it? Maybe her notes about a patient got her into trouble once before. Perhaps these records are a front to hide what she actually feels.

A tingle runs up the back of my neck. What if she secretly hopes we can move on and become proper friends? Could that be why it feels like she's trying to push me away? It would explain why she's written this rubbish about me; it's all about covering her back.

I flick back a page to where she's said something nice and stroke her words. Is this how you *really* feel, Sam? Do you want to bring our consultations to an end, all above board, so that you can *change* things between us? Start afresh as really great companions – or have I got it wrong? I'm not certain at all. Do you like me or not? Which one is it? Are you my enemy or my friend?

I know which way I want it to be, but it makes me feel uptight and restless not knowing for sure, so I strip off, dropping my clothes in the hall and switch on the bath taps. I don't need a soak, but I want to feel close to her, I want to be where she's been, personal and private places. I slide into the steamy water and allow it to wrap around me; I use her soap, her nail brush, her flannel.

Just as I'm getting out, patting myself down with one of Sam's fluffy purple towels, my mobile rings. It's DS Eric Fischer calling from Cumbria. I'm practically on first name terms with him now.

'We've found another body,' he says.

I sink down onto the bathmat and hold my breath. Max or Richard, Max or Richard – which one? I want it to be Max.

'We found Max Raeger this morning,' he says. 'Under the packhorse bridge at the northern most point of the lake.' He doesn't wait for me to say anything. I let out the breath I've been holding. 'We'll let you know if there's anything more to report after the post-mortem.'

I'm barely listening. This means I didn't see Max on Oxford Street, after all. It means there's only Richard left. Is he behind it all, or is his corpse going to surface any day now, too? I shudder and pull Sam's towel tight around my shoulders.

It seems callous to ask about my viola so I give it a miss. I'm sure the DS would have mentioned it if there was any news. Once the call ends, another idea comes into my head, and it won't leave me alone. I hurriedly get changed and check round to make sure the flat looks tidy.

I lock up and go straight to the nearest library on Lavender Hill. I book half an hour on a public computer. I don't know why I didn't think of this before. Bridges have names, don't they? I've been flummoxed by that tiny snatch of conversation I overheard at the Hinds': *It's worth a fortune and under the bridge.* I'm not quite sure how they mentioned my name, but I definitely heard it. Perhaps there is a bridge, not far from where the party was held, that literally has my name on it!

I find a site with a map of the Ullswater area and zoom in. Cote Farm Bridge, Waternook Bridge, Ravenscragg Bridge – there are so many of them. It's like trying to find a contact lens in a pile of broken glass.

I try the other way around and find the search box. I

punch in 'Rosie Bridge' – nothing. Then 'Rosemary Bridge' – nothing. There is a 'Rose Bridge', but it's near Lake Windemere, much further south. I try 'Chandler Bridge', using my surname, and stagger backwards.

It comes up.

It's just south of Ullswater. My heart is racing at double speed. Then I shake my head. Did any of us go anywhere near there on foot, or in the van? It doesn't ring any bells when I think back to either visit to the Lakes, and it's at least a mile from our B&B and the Hinds' estate. But it is a bridge, with a connection to my name near Ullswater and it *could* be the bridge the caller was talking about. In any case, it's all I've got.

I know what I have to do next – and I know it's not going to go down well.

Chapter 35

Sam

It was late and I didn't hear the letter box click over the rumble of the washing machine. I wiped the suds off my hands and stood over the envelope on the mat. My name was typed on the front. Inside, there was a note printed in small letters:

> *To set your mind at rest, Conrad Noble wasn't the father. Ask Miranda where he was three and a half months before she lost the baby. He was filming, in Norway. It was the miscarriage that brought them together – it hasn't been going on long.*
> *A well-wisher.*

No signature. No stamp. I dropped the note on the window ledge by the door, suddenly wary about touching it. Someone must be leaving the communal front door unlocked so all and sundry can get inside. I snatched my keys from the ledge, let myself out and locked the door behind me, before scampering down to the front door to check. Strange – it *was* locked.

I came back upstairs on high alert, my scalp prickling, listening for the slightest noise, peering into every shadow. I picked up the note again. Who had sent it? Someone who not only knew my sister, but also my concerns about the situation. Miranda's friend, Stella? Or Kora, or Sponge from the Project? And was it true?

I picked up the phone.

'Where were you when Miranda got pregnant?'

'Sam? Is that you?'

'Can you please answer the question. Were you filming in Norway?'

'Mirrie told you...' he said, sounding disappointed.

'You weren't the father, Con. Why didn't you just come out and say it?'

There was a crackle and an awkward silence. 'To get back at you, I suppose.' He sniffed. 'Probably a bit childish. Sorry.'

I had half expected this would be his reasoning. It was entirely in line with his character. I was cheesed off, however, that Miranda had gone along with it.

'What else have you done to punish me, Con? Is it you making silent phone calls?'

'What?'

'Ringing from call-boxes or hiding your number?'

'Hey – hang on – no! That's not me.'

He sounded so convincing, but I had to remind myself that Con was a talented actor. Maybe he'd been rehearsing this particular script, knowing we'd have this conversation one day.

I hadn't a shred of proof. It was pointless pursuing it any further. 'I'm sorry...' he said and put down the phone.

I scrunched up the note and threw it in the bin. Whoever had delivered it, they could damn well go and interfere somewhere else.

A new thought occurred to me. Was someone picking through bits and pieces in my wheelie bin? Or tracking my emails, somehow? Listening into my phone calls? I was starting to feel not just watched, but hunted.

Fuck off! I screamed and ran into my bedroom. I dived onto the bed and buried myself under the duvet.

Rosie was subdued when she came for her next session.

'I'm frightened,' she said.

'Has something happened?'

'They found Max in the lake.'

'Oh. That's awful.'

'It's not just that he's dead,' she went on. 'I've got this horrible feeling I might have done something bad. When we were all under water. Why can't I remember more after we went down? I keep thinking the others must have thought about the back window too. Tried to get out the same way I did. Perhaps we clashed. Maybe I kicked them away – hurt someone, to save myself. I don't know. *I can't remember!*'

She'd been scratching at a patch of skin on the back of her hand and made it bleed. 'It's as if my mind is locked from the inside.'

She sat back, sucked at her torn wound, retreated into herself. Several minutes clicked by before she emerged from her internal space and spoke again.

'It really looks like I'm the only one left, doesn't it? Stephanie, first, then Max…I'm sure it's going to be Richard next and – I don't know – I feel like it's wrong that I'm still here.'

Stay calm. I'd been expecting this; it's a normal

response and I didn't want to overreact.

'You're not alone in feeling like this, Rosie – many survivors believe they don't deserve to be here or feel they might even have contributed to the tragedy.'

'Why should I be the one who survived?'

'Sometimes there doesn't seem to be an explanation,' I said, knowing it sounded trite as soon as the words came out. 'As humans we want to explain everything, see how it all fits together, but it doesn't always—?'

'I want to know,' she snapped, closing me down.

She sat forward watching my face for a reaction. 'Can we go back? Revisit it?' she said.

'Of course.' I got up, ready to prepare the chaise longue for the memory work.

'No,' she said. 'I mean *go back*. For real. Go back, together – you and me – to the Lake District, to find out the truth.'

I stood looking down at her and didn't know what to say.

'I have to go there in person,' she persisted, her voice gathering speed. 'It will all come back to me if I go back. I know it will. I need to find out if I did something terrible to the others. I need to find out if any of it was my fault, don't you see?'

'Look…I don't think—'

'Besides, I think I know which bridge the person on the phone was talking about…the one with the fortune underneath it. We could solve the whole mystery, all in one…'

Rosie had a broad grin on her face, pummelling

her fists into her thighs. She'd gone from distraught to exuberant in about twenty seconds.

'That's not possible, Rosie. Our sessions take place here. Remember our discussion about the auction house?'

I had to get her to see I was providing psychotherapy, nothing more.

'Blinking rules, again.' She spat the words out.

'I know, but they're there for a reason.'

'Why do I have to be punished for your decisions?'

'I'm sorry,' I said, forcing myself to sound less irked than I felt. She was like a bug hooking onto me, constantly trying to bury into my skin. 'Psychologists have guidelines and—'

She threw her eyes upwards. 'Yeah, yeah – so you keep saying.' Her bottom lip jutted out and a crestfallen expression took over her face. She hesitated and I sensed her weighing her next words very carefully.

'I haven't been feeling good...' she said. 'Lately, I've had...dark thoughts about myself.'

My vision started blurring at the edges. I gulped down a bubble of bile. 'You've been thinking about hurting yourself?'

She nodded, examining her fingernails.

Don't panic – she's not Joanne, it's not the same.

I tried to keep my voice steady. 'We need to talk about this,' I said.

She shook her head. 'I need to go back,' she said defiantly, looking up, her eyes drilling into mine.

She was boxing me into a corner.

She glanced at my phone lying on the coffee table.

'Tell me again why you record our sessions,' she said, drawing herself upright. Since that first time, I'd recorded every one of them.

'So I don't miss anything,' I said, 'so I can check we're on track with our objectives.'

'Who do you play it to?'

'Only my supervisor. You would never meet that person. All psychologists have to be accountable to someone in a higher position…you know that.'

'And is it also so the authorities can tell if you do something wrong?'

I stalled for a second. 'Yes, that too – if it ever came to it.'

'I thought so,' she said knowingly.

She gave me an odd stare, twisting her mouth into a half-smile as if we were playing a game. She cleared her throat. 'I need to go back. If we don't go back to the place where it all happened…if we don't make this last-ditch attempt to find the truth, I don't know what I might do to myself…'

Was Rosie consciously blackmailing me? Or was this the voice of that seven-year-old desperate to be heard?

Revisiting the trauma location was an entirely bona fide form of therapy: Exposure Therapy. I'd used it with a number of patients. It might give Rosie the very best chance of recovering those last threads of memory that were floating near the surface. It might even give her all the answers she needed, so I could bring our sessions to a close with a clear conscience.

The problem was that Rosie undoubtedly exhibited traits of a histrionic personality disorder. She came on too strong, constantly seeking approval, she showed limited empathy, found it hard to tolerate frustration and was like a jack-in-a-box, always jumping from one emotional state to another. It didn't mean she was dangerous, as such, but it did mean I had to be highly vigilant in setting tight and clear boundaries with her.

Going away together? How would she interpret that?! Could it do more harm than good?

On the other hand, what if I turned her down? Was I really going to take the chance after what had happened with Joanne?

As long as I made everything crystal clear and Rosie was in no doubt about the limitations, might it just be worth a try?

'If it *was* possible, and I'm not saying it is, yet, we'd then have to bring our sessions to a close.'

'Oh…' Her mouth hung open waiting for more.

'Even if your memory didn't return fully and you were still left with loose ends.'

'Ok-ay,' she murmured, her eyes narrowing, full of mistrust.

'You understand what I'm saying? We carry out the therapy at the crime scene by the book and afterwards, no matter what happens, the sessions come to an end between us.'

'Yeah. All right.'

'Right, then…this is my proposal,' I said. 'We would travel separately and find different guest houses. We wouldn't be going as friends or companions. We'll have two or three sessions while we're there, over two days, at the scene itself. Otherwise we'll be separate. It won't be a holiday. No meals together, no chatting.'

She got to her feet and clasped her hand to her heart. 'Thank you so much. You might just have saved my life.' She took a half step forward and waited, as if she was hoping for an embrace. I stayed in my chair.

'Then, after that, we will end our sessions. By then, we'll have done a lot of work together.'

'Yes. Yes. Of course. I understand.'

'Are you happy to proceed under those circumstances?'

'I am. Yes. More than happy.' She was clutching the bookcase now, wavering as if she didn't know what had hit her.

'Then we can go to the Lakes,' I said.

Her chin began to wobble and she stared at the carpet, trying to hide the fact that her eyes were filling up.

'I need to use the bathroom,' she said suddenly and rushed off. Through the closed door, I could hear her sobs muffled by a towel. When she came back her eyes looked puffy and raw.

'You okay?'

'Yeah, I'm just a bit…overwhelmed.' She gave me a half smile, trying to compose herself as she sat down again.

'When can you get time off work?' I said.

'Any time. I'm due loads.'

'Make enquiries and then leave a message for me on the hospital number, okay?'

'Sure. I'll pay for your train fare and room, of course,' she said.

'That won't be necessary.'

The idea was already forming in my mind of staying on for a few days once we'd done the Exposure Therapy and Rosie had gone back to London. I could escape my own demons for a while – the silent phone calls, Con and Miranda, renewed remorse about Joanne. I could switch off for a bit and enjoy the bracing fresh air, peace and quiet. I hadn't had a break in ages. The whole trip was starting to feel like the right thing to do.

She gave me a wink as she departed, calling out 'See ya soon', before she hurtled down the stairs – a stark reminder of what I was taking on. I squeezed my eyes shut with a shiver of dread.

Chapter 36

Sam

We agreed I'd catch the train from Euston at 12.30pm and Rosie would catch the next one. Shortly after I took my seat, I had a message from Professor Dean to say he would email over Erica's therapy notes later that afternoon. At last...although I'd only brought my phone and didn't fancy reading piles of pages on the small screen.

I got to Penrith just before 5pm and took a taxi to my guesthouse. Rosie was staying just over the hill in the same B&B they'd booked for the quartet reunion.

My room smelt of lavender and fresh linen. The single bed was high and squeaked like an old bicycle when I sat down on it, the floorboards sloped visibly from one side of the room to the other, but the place seemed comfortable enough. A radiator was gurgling to life under the sash window and the landlady had left a fan heater near the wardrobe. There was an old sampler framed on the wall and stems of fresh holly in a vase by the window. Cosy and quaint. It was a long time since I'd been this far away from London. Already the pace of life had slowed to a pleasant crawl.

I ate steak and chips on my own in the 1930's-style dining room; it seemed no one else was straying this far off the beaten track at the end of January.

'You're lucky I was open,' Mrs Waterman said when I'd rung to make the booking. 'Most of the guest houses around here close down out of season.'

I rang Miranda from the landline before I went to bed, as I couldn't get a consistent signal. It had suddenly occurred to me that she might have sent the note about Con and the baby in a roundabout way of setting my mind at rest.

The patchy connection probably also explained why no email had come through from Professor Dean.

'Hi,' I said, when Miranda answered. 'I just wanted to touch base.'

'Where are you? The hospital said you were on leave.'

'You tried to reach me?'

'Nothing urgent…' she said, her voice cool.

I filled her in on the basics and asked about her work.

'I've finished two new pieces since that exhibition we went to at the V&A. One of the tutors thinks I might be able to get an agent; he's talking to a gallery, apparently.

'That's amazing…' I was overjoyed for her, she deserved some success.

'I sold that picture, by the way. To the woman from Battersea Dogs and Cats Home. She wants to see more.'

She was animated and sounded genuinely pleased I'd called.

'We must make a date for that lunch,' she said.

'As soon as I get back,' I assured her. I didn't have the heart to bring up the note I'd received.

By morning, my hot-water bottle had found its way onto the floor, but I woke up feeling keen and alert, so I must have had a decent night's sleep. I switched the fan heater on for an extra boost of warmth around my ankles and opened the curtains.

Outside the sky was cloudless and the window ledge twinkled with frost. I could see smoke rising from a chimney beyond the brow to the place where Rosie was staying. We'd agreed to meet at her B&B at 10am and follow the route the van had taken along the edge of Ullswater. She'd assured me it was only about a mile on foot.

At breakfast, over a warm crusty roll with homemade marmalade, I asked Mrs Waterman where I could get decent wifi access.

'You need to get to the Post Office – down the lane and to the right.'

She poured coffee from a silver jug into my cup.

'I read there was a terrible accident round here last October. The van that went into the lake?' I said, hoping to pick up a local perspective.

'Very nasty affair,' she said, wiping her hands on her frilly apron. 'They weren't from this area. Something to do with the Hinds' family up at the big Matterdale Estate. Musicians, I think.'

'I saw it on the news at the time, too,' I fibbed. 'It looked like it wasn't an accident, but beyond that, no one seemed any the wiser.'

She poked the fire and a few lumps of coal crunched into the flames.

'The police came asking questions and there's been all kinds of talk about it around here, but who's to know the truth? Some reckon it was all connected to a priceless violin, others said it was a cover for a drugs' deal. The Hinds have had trouble before. Cameron's brother was sent down for money laundering a few years ago. But didn't one of the musicians escape from the van? Maybe she's got the answers.'

If only...

I nodded vaguely, picked a dried fig from a bowl with the word 'Nuts' glazed on the side and chewed on the gritty seeds.

Cameron Hinds' *brother*. Interesting. Nobody else had mentioned *him* so far.

Rosie waved as she saw me coming. She was standing outside her B&B, slapping her gloved hands together and stamping her feet. In her denim mini skirt over stripy nylon tights she was hardly dressed for the weather, but I noticed again how different she looked these days from the person I'd met a few months earlier. She was slimmer, wore tighter-fitting trendier clothes, and her frizzy red hair was straight and nearly black.

'Frickin' freezing, isn't it?' she said. 'Sorry, are we allowed to talk?'

I smiled. 'Good morning, Rosie. Good to see you.' I turned towards the sun. 'I suggest we wander along the road beside the lake and you tell me what you notice on the way. I'll record, if that's okay.' She nodded, so I pressed the record button on my phone. 'Try to set a little running commentary going of what you remember about the setting, the surroundings, anything that comes to mind about that day…'

'Okay.' We started walking, but Rosie didn't say a word. Instead, like a child, she was going out of her way to find icy puddles on the rough track, and smash them with the heel of her boot. She looked up, jubilant, at the brittle splintering sound.

'You need to focus, Rosie. Try to take yourself back.'

'Yeah, yeah – I will.' She swung her arms shaking off my rebuke.

Once we were on the road itself, she began to look around, watching and listening intently. A blackbird flew out of the hedgerow and made us both jump.

'Nothing yet,' she reported.

Rosie walked on ahead, looking lost, mystified. We turned round one bend and then another. A car passed us, followed by a small van coming in the opposite direction, then the road dropped down until we were about two metres from the edge of the water. It looked uninviting, a grey mass wrinkled with ripples beyond the prickly hedge.

'It was here,' she said. She stared at the road, across to the wide expanse of lake and back to me.

'I remember the road being bumpy – look…' She pointed to blisters and cracks in the tarmac.

She crouched down to study the surface. 'I've got something,' she called out.

She straightened up and looked one way, then the

other. 'Richard was saying something like "Bastard – what the hell is he playing at?"...'

'As you came along this stretch?'

'He was pulling at the wheel...looking in his mirror...' Her hand went to her mouth. 'Bloody hell, there was someone *behind* us...'

I asked her to look back the way we'd come and take in the whole scene. Then I suggested she closed her eyes for a second and tried to imagine herself inside the van. 'Can you look out of the back window and tell me what you see?'

She dropped her head down and shielded her eyes. She was familiar with the process by now, but standing at the exact spot where the accident had happened felt different; far more intense. She was shaking.

I helped guide her through it.

'I can't see who it is, but I can hear a revving sound, the wheels behind us are squealing.' Her voice became breathy. 'It's like someone's trying to drive us off the road...'

'A car, a motorbike, a truck, a minibus?'

'I don't know, sorry.' She shook her head, opening her eyes. 'I can't see anything.'

I kept going; '"*Bastard – what the hell is he playing at?*" What does that say to you?'

She blinked fast. Her eyes were watering with the cold, but were wide and animated. 'Oh my God – that Richard *knew* the person.'

Rosie picked up the pace and I went with her. We came to the next bend with a section of brand new fence on the left. Broken pieces from the old one were scattered underneath it.

'This is it...' she said, the wind carrying her words away.

There were several long-dead bunches of flowers strapped to a nearby telegraph post. Apart from that, there was no evidence of the incident at all. No skid marks in the road. No chunks of missing turf or ruts in the grass. Nature had healed its wounds during the intervening months.

'Hold on,' I said. She was about to climb over the fence. 'Take your time. Just spend a moment or two taking this in.' We kept close to the hedge. A red car sped past us, blasting us with cold air. Rosie looked up at the stretch of road the van never reached and back to the hedge.

'This was all thick,' she said, patting her gloved hand on the spikes. 'Turning brown.'

'Excellent. Now take a good look around.'

She paced off, on her own, her hand over her mouth, kicking aside piles of old leaves on the grass verge. Then she came to a halt.

'You remember I told you I saw a number plate in the bushes?' She was pointing into the undergrowth. 'I must have seen it afterwards...when I'd got out...'

I recalled Rosie mentioning this memory in one of our earlier sessions. I also remembered that this was as far as we'd got.

'It was L...E...'

She was remembering it!

I stayed perfectly still.

She screwed up her eyes against the sun. 'Then…54, I think,' she added.

This was all new. I could hear my pulse picking up speed; it was roaring in my ears. 'LE54…anything else?'

'That was the top line…but, I'd lost my glasses by then, so I can't be certain.'

'The top line?' I wasn't sure what she meant.

'Yeah, it must have been a motorbike. A square number plate.' She cast her eyes down. 'I can't see any more.'

'Okay. You're doing really well.'

The one lonely cloud in the sky found the sun and the temperature dropped. We clambered over the new fence and down the grassy slope that led to a stretch of pebbles at the water's edge. The ripples were lapping at the shore, almost touching our feet.

'Take your time, just let it all unfold slowly,' I instructed.

She took a juddering breath and looked out across the lake.

'It looks so tranquil,' she whispered. 'So harmless. Richard might still be out there…'

I gazed out at the flat sheet of water and tried to picture the man Rosie had described to me. The only one left. She snatched a breath and for one moment I thought she was going to call out for him. Instead, she covered her mouth with both her gloved hands and shook her head slowly.

'The van must have gone in over there, that would match the police photos I've seen.' She waved at a spot around five metres from the edge. The water looked deep and murky. I shuddered, imagining how cold it must have been. 'I want to get to the spot where I came out of the water… it must be back this way…'

She turned and began pacing along the edge of the lake. I took my gaze back to the water; so calm and restful, yet deadly and unstoppable once it finds a way in.

When Rosie squatted down, I thought she was buckling under the emotional pressure, but she was looking up and back to the water, trying to judge the view, the distances.

'I think it was about here where I came out,' she said. 'I must have put my viola down somewhere around there.' She pointed to a clump of rocks forming a small ledge under the shrubbery. She bent down to stroke the spot, transported into a private reverie.

The hedge was denser along this stretch, the gravel shoreline petering out as the lake claimed the land. She kicked at the tufts of grass, cleared away twigs, bent branches aside in a desperate and futile search for the missing instrument. Then she climbed back up to the road and turned to wait for me to do the same.

She shook her head and shrugged with a loud sigh.

It was over.

That was as much as her memory could dredge up for now. She turned away as I joined her, but I saw tears glistening on her face. Distraught, frustrated, angry tears because she'd found nothing conclusive.

We headed back along the road. Since we'd arrived, more clouds had come from the distant hills and cluttered up the sky, so the sun didn't come out again.

'You can tell the police about the motorbike number

plate.' I said, trying to inject some enthusiasm.

'It probably belonged to Teddy Spense,' she said dismissively. 'And it seems like he was just an opportunist thief.'

'But the police haven't picked him up, yet?'

'Not as far as I know.'

'So the number plate could help.'

She sounded dispirited. 'But I can't remember the rest of the number… No one can track him down from half the registration. Besides, Dawn said Teddy Spense isn't even his real name.'

'The rest might come back later…it could take a while to remember what Richard was saying…but if you think he *knew* the person who was behind him…that's a breakthrough, it might jog something.'

'It's not enough.' She shoved her hands roughly into her pockets.

To be honest, I agreed with her, but I didn't want to admit it.

Neither of us spoke again until we reached her B&B.

'By the way,' I said, as I was about to leave her for lunch. 'Did you ever meet Cameron Hinds' brother?'

She pulled a face. 'I didn't know he had one. No one mentioned him. What's his first name?'

'I don't know. It might be nothing, but the woman who runs my B&B says he was in prison a while ago for money laundering.'

'That's interesting.' She pointed towards the guest house. 'I brought the disc of the original party. I know we've watched it plenty of times already, but I thought it could be useful if anything new came up. He might be on there.'

'Good thinking,' I said. 'Let's take another look at it after we've had something to eat. I'll come back here at two.' She nodded, her energy climbing back up to all-is-not-lost levels again. She waved and watched me go.

After a round of corned-beef and pickle sandwiches care of Mrs Waterman, I joined Rosie in the sitting room of her guest house to watch the DVD again. The dying fire smouldered in the grate and there was no one else about at first, then a cleaner came in and asked what we were watching.

'I'm really sorry, it's personal,' Rosie said, before I could open my mouth. She turned to me. 'Let's go to my room instead.'

I couldn't think of an alternative so I followed her up the narrow twisty staircase to the single door at the top.

'It's a bit small,' she said, ushering me inside.

She wasn't kidding; the room was tiny. A rickety bed stood opposite a single chest of drawers with a TV and DVD player underneath. 'Apparently the bigger rooms were being decorated,' she said.

I perched awkwardly on the narrow bed as Rosie reached forward to slip in the disc. As she picked up the controls, I noticed an opened book facedown beside me on the lumpy pillow. It was called *Soulmates and Blood Sisters* and looked like a self-help book about finding meaningful relationships. I glanced at the leaflet she was using as a bookmark. It was a menu for a takeaway pizza chain in London, with a black scribbled shape filling in the logo. Rosie caught me looking.

'It's a good book,' she said. 'You can borrow it if you like.'

'It's okay, I'll pass, thanks.'

I nodded at the screen, keen to carry on where we'd left off so we could get this over with. She started the footage. 'Can you see anyone who could be Cameron's brother?' I said.

She stopped the recording, pointing at various men in dark suits. 'There are a few guys who *could* be him,' she said. 'I don't remember anyone talking about him, or ever being introduced.'

I took the remote and pressed pause on a scene that included the whole party.

'Who's that?' I asked.

'That's one of the security guys.'

'And this guy, here?'

'I think he was an Earl or Lord from the local estate.'

I watched her eyes zigzag across the screen. 'Perhaps he wasn't there.'

She stood up purposefully. 'Shall we look at it again, later?' She didn't wait for me to answer. 'I want to get to some of the bridges this afternoon,' she said. 'It's okay, I don't expect you to come. I found a "Chandler" Bridge south of here. It's the nearest one. There are others too that might be worth a look…'

'Sure, but be careful, and make sure you're back before it starts to get dark,' I said, pulling on my coat.

'I've got a map and a torch,' she said, looking pleased with herself. 'It's nice of you to worry about me.'

I pulled on my gloves. 'I'll see you tomorrow

morning at 10am for another session, before we go back to London.'

After I left Rosie, I went along to the Post Office to see if I could get a wifi connection. I wanted to take a look at the files Professor Dean had sent through.

Sure enough, there was an email from him telling me three files were attached, but when I opened it there was only one document I could download. The other two required a password.

Damn

As I read the professor's email, I realised that even if I could access all three, we still had a problem:

I'm ashamed to say there are still a number of gaps. Erica's husband said he was only able to find a few stray sheets from the notes she kept at home. I'll try to get my hands on the rest for when you return. Attached is Erica's last report summary and notes covering the first twelve months or so. Apparently, Rosie Chandler was Erica's only patient just before she died. Hope it's helpful in the meantime.

I left the Post Office, reading the first few lines of the single document I could open – the summary – as I strolled out onto the lane:

Rosie is a quiet girl – sad and secretive. Tragic and difficult upbringing. No real friends.

I wanted to read more, but it had begun to spit a sleety rain, so I pressed my phone against my coat and hurried back to my B&B. The radiator was switched off when I got to my room, so I turned on the fan heater and huddled over it until I could move my fingers again.

I read the rest of the report without taking off my coat.

Rosie had attended seventy sessions at Guy's Hospital, but for the final five Erica had been on crutches after a bunion operation, so they'd met at her house in Chelsea:

> *I told Rosie I would be taking time off from Guy's, but she was adamant that our sessions shouldn't end. I was worried about her state of mind and, given her history of abandonment and the fact that I had only just sprung this on her, I offered her sessions at my home.*
>
> *Rosie was unforthcoming during those weeks. She claimed I'd tried to use the operation as an excuse to end our arrangement. She seemed angry with me; aggressive in her tone at times. With hindsight, I think it's been a mistake to see her at my house; she's the sort of patient who needs distance.*
>
> *Eighteen months is a solid stretch of time and Rosie hasn't made any real breakthroughs in our work together. She doesn't seem to be moving on and I'm not sure I'm the best therapist for her in the long run.*
>
> *I'd conclude that Rosie is 'deeply disturbed' by her past losses and has not dealt with any of it. I also believe Rosie is suffering from extreme emotional isolation. Throughout our sessions she talks about her parents and childhood in a detached way, but never reveals her feelings about what happened. She is well-practised at bottling everything up and putting on a brave face. In spite of her reticence, Rosie claims that, with me, for the first time, she has found someone who*

genuinely understands her, listens and gives her validation. She claims this is the only time in her life when anyone has connected to her in this way. Nevertheless, I think a new approach would shake things up for Rosie and do her good. I think we've done all we can together. I'm going to suggest she sees someone else and we end our sessions.

That was Erica's last sentence, written exactly a week before she died. Lights danced before my eyes. I could have written almost every word of it myself.

Chapter 37

Sam

The phone by the bed rang and I was jolted out of my trance.

'I know our next session isn't until tomorrow, but something occurred to me.'

'Rosie…'

'It was round about now when it actually happened. Late afternoon. I know the light was probably a bit different in October, but this is the closest I can get to actually replicating the situation. Can we go back? Have tomorrow's session now, instead?'

'But, it'll be dark soon. We won't be able to—'

'The torch I've got is really bright, if we need it.'

'You want to go back to the same spot?'

'Yes. I can't bear the thought of going back to London without finding out something new. I've been over to Chandler Bridge. There's nothing there. It's just a small packhorse bridge over a brook. I climbed down, but there are only rocks and ferns underneath. I must have got it wrong. I need to know I've tried everything…'

'Okay,' I said, switching off the fan heater with my foot. 'I'll come over to you again.'

I'd already looked up Cameron Hinds' brother while I had a wifi connection at the Post Office and I'd found several reports about his conviction for money laundering, but they were several years ago. There were more recent references to him, but the dates didn't fit. He couldn't be a suspect for the van crash – he was in prison right through October. Back to square one.

It was rapidly heading towards dusk by the time I met Rosie. The torch I'd borrowed from Mrs Waterman had felt satisfyingly solid as I dropped it into my rucksack. Flecks of snow were speckling the ground and getting denser by the minute. I really wasn't convinced this was a good idea, but I wanted to give it my all; one last chance, then we really were going to call it a day.

As we turned into the lane, I kept trying to think of a way to remind Rosie that once we got back to London our association would end. I'd explained this already, of course, but I wasn't convinced it had sunk in. I wanted to say something there and then, but she was full of hope again as we made our final visit to the crash scene. I couldn't spoil that.

She stopped at a break in the hedge and pointed to a sign that said *public footpath*.

'I know a shortcut through the woods, it'll save time,' she said, tugging at my sleeve. 'The snow won't be so bad through here.'

She strode on and I followed close behind. It looked straightforward enough.

'I came this way once with Richard, did I tell you?' she called out.

A prickly branch sprung back in my face as she forged on ahead and I remembered how Erica had reported Rosie's reaction once she'd told her their sessions were finishing. *Angry…aggressive.* I'd speak to Rosie on the way back, perhaps.

My mobile was on silent in my pocket and I was surprised when I felt it vibrate, indicating that there was a signal. Knowing it was likely to be work, however, I let the call go to my voicemail. I didn't imagine it was anything that couldn't wait half an hour, or so. A few seconds later it buzzed again letting me know a text had come through. I slowed down to read it as Rosie carried on. There was just enough light, but it was rapidly closing in; the path had quickly narrowed and the undergrowth on either side had risen, swallowing us up.

'You all right?' Rosie had stopped and turned around.

I glanced down and read the words again:

Just left a message. Call me. Found out Erica's death wasn't straightforward. Minette.

'We're nearly there.' She was getting impatient.

'I need to stop for a moment,' I said, fumbling with the phone, trying to access Minette's voice message with my gloves on. 'It's the hospital. I might need to make a call.'

'What's it about?' She came right up to my shoulder, peering over to get a look at my phone. I dropped my hand.

'It's a work thing, probably not important, but I should check, just in case.' My words sounded forced.

Rosie looked put out, her top lip stiffened, her eyes narrowed – this was *her* time. She shrugged, folded her arms and watched me, offering no privacy.

As I pressed to access the message, I noticed the network connection was low and flickering. We were, after all, in the middle of nowhere.

'Sam, I don't want to worry you,' came Minette Heron's recorded voice. 'But the police have been making further enquiries into Erica's death. On the surface it looked as if she'd suffered a heart attack before she fell down the stairs, but it seems new evidence has come to light suggesting it might have been the other way around.' Her words melted away into nothing.

There was a pause and I thought she'd been cut off. Then her voice came back. She spoke slowly and distinctly. 'It's not certain yet, it might never be, but it's possible that Erica was pushed. The police are looking at the case again. I thought you should know. It's obviously very upsetting for everyone.'

My immediate impulse was to call her straight back to find out more. What exactly had the police found? What made them think Erica might have been pushed?

Rosie, however, was standing so close that our coat sleeves made a shushing sound with every tiny movement. She exhaled noisily and waited.

I slipped the phone into my pocket. I had no option. I couldn't call Minette back. There was no way I could have that kind of conversation with Rosie hanging on my every word.

'It's okay,' I said breezily, without looking at her. 'I don't need to ring anyone.'

'Let's get going then,' Rosie said, striding ahead. 'I've got a good feeling about this.'

Chapter 38

Sam

I should have been looking where I was going. I shouldn't have taken my eyes off the path. I was so busy thinking about what Minette had said, that my heel slipped on an icy patch and the next moment I was face down in the crusty mud.

Rosie rushed to my aid. 'Oh, shit, are you hurt?'

'My ankle,' I said.

I wasn't sure whether the snap I'd heard was a tree root or a bone in my foot. I felt a sharp pain, like my leg had been walloped with a baseball bat.

Rosie took my weight, lifting me under my armpits. She shuffled me a foot or so to the edge of the path, so I could lean against a tree.

I was convinced my left ankle had already doubled in size. 'I'm not sure I can walk,' I said, with a wince.

'We'll call for help,' she said confidently. She pulled out her phone, looked at it and waited. She left me hugging the trunk of the tree and wandered into a clearing, holding up the phone. She went a little further. 'No signal,' she called back. 'Don't worry. We're nearly at the lake. We can flag someone down on the road.'

'I'm not sure I can get that far,' I murmured, my teeth chattering.

We were in the middle of barely penetrable woodland and I could see no lights ahead. I reached into my pocket. No signal on my phone now, either.

I watched Rosie take in the immediate surroundings; lines of trees, layer after layer, impenetrable undergrowth, the path trailing into the distance. Where dense trees parted overhead, no longer providing cover, everything at ground level was disappearing under a layer of snow. The darkness was gathering momentum too, actively folding around us; the little daylight that was left was sliding down from the sky.

'I'm not going off on my own,' she said. 'I'm not going to leave you.'

'You're going to have to. You need to find somewhere you can get a signal.'

'Let's at least find a spot where you can sit down and rest for a minute.'

She guided me towards a grassy ridge and helped me down. Barely any snow had got through to ground level at that point, so at least it wasn't too wet.

I checked my watch. Nearly 4.30pm. It was only going to get darker and colder.

'Looks like you're stuck with me for a bit longer,' said Rosie. 'I wonder how long the batteries will last.' The bright torch beam Rosie had bragged about wasn't exactly blinding.

'I've got one, too,' I said, patting my rucksack.

She sat down beside me on the grass, then wriggled an inch or two to her right so that our arms were touching. I bent down to scratch my leg and pulled away a fraction.

'What shall we talk about?' she said. Far from

sounding daunted, Rosie seemed uplifted by the situation. She didn't wait for a response. 'I've got you all to myself.'

She swung her legs back and forth, full of energy.

'Do any of your patients ever become friends?' she went on, without looking my way.

A loaded question. Difficult territory. 'Very rarely,' I said casually. 'And only after a considerable break, usually by chance, further down the line.'

'Can we do that? Be friends in a couple of weeks?'

I let out a tiny splutter of disbelief. 'It doesn't really work like that.'

An anguished look crossed her face. 'You want our sessions to end when we get back to London. That's the idea, isn't it?'

'Yes, that's what we agreed.'

'*You* agreed,' she said quietly.

'Our relationship is unbalanced,' I said. 'It's not really like being friends. I'm helping you with something specific and you're paying me for that service. That's not being proper friends, is it?'

'But it could be – I just stop paying you and you stop trying to dig up my lost memories. *Finito.*' She smiled. 'We're not taping this – so you can tell me what you really think.'

'I...am saying what I think, Rosie.'

'No, no, no.' She shook her head with irritation. 'I can see the terrible "professional versus personal" dilemma you must have been going through, but it's okay now. We can't carry on working together as therapist and patient. I get that. You want to end the professional side of things so we can have a *proper* relationship; closer, more real, like best friends or sisters – no more barriers, that's it, isn't it? Not a physical relationship, we're not lesbians or anything – just together...'

'No, Rosie. That's not how it is at all. You've jumped to the wrong conclusion completely.'

'I know this is confusing,' she went on, regardless. 'I know something happened before with another patient that...caused problems, but this won't be like that, I promise.'

I snapped my chin back. Where the hell had she got this from?

'Rosie, I don't know what you think you know, but there's no hidden agenda or mixed message here. Our sessions will end after today and we'll have no further contact.'

She slapped her hand down onto a clump of moss. 'Can't you shake off the therapists' cloak for FIVE MINUTES?!' she fired back at me. 'Then we might be able to have a normal conversation.'

I fixed my eyes on hers, my gaze unwavering. 'I'm sorry, Rosie. Once our sessions end we can't just carry on seeing each other socially.'

'But...I thought...'

Her mood changed in a flash; a frown knotting in consternation across her forehead. 'Isn't that what you wanted?'

It was my turn to be baffled. Where was this coming from?

'Let's see if I can walk,' I said, using a tree stump to

heave myself upright. 'It's getting dark.'

The last thing I needed was to be stuck out here with Rosie and her awkward questions.

As soon as I put weight on my ankle it screamed, but I was determined to get moving. Rosie hooked her arm under my shoulder and we staggered back to the path.

'If I keep my foot off the ground, I should be okay,' I said, forced to lean into her for balance. I held the torch and we hobbled forward at a snail's pace.

'Tell me about this new man you met recently,' I said, willing the discussion towards a different direction.

'Oh, I said it was a guy so you'd think I'd been chatted up, but it was just a woman I met in a café. She's all right, but she's not very interested in me. That's why this…you…have become so important.'

My head began to swim and I felt it roll against Rosie's.

'You okay?' she said. 'You're shaking like mad?'

'I feel really sick.'

'It's probably the shock. We'll be at the road soon.'

I pulled out my phone again, but there was still no signal.

'Do you love Con?' she said out of the blue, rocking me slightly as we shuffled unsteadily onwards.

'Con?'

'Conrad Noble, you know, the one you went out with.'

How did she know about him?

'Con and I split up ages ago,' I said to satisfy her.

'But you miss him?'

'Sometimes. Feelings don't always stop, just because

you know someone isn't right for you.'

She seemed to consider my words and started to hum tunelessly.

'It's been strange coming back here,' she said, after a while. 'It hasn't got us very far has it? I still don't know where my viola is. The business about the fortune under a bridge has led to a dead end. I'm not sure what I expected, really. Bit stupid to think I'd get the right bridge. What was I hoping for? A half-buried chest of jewels or a suitcase full of bank notes? Ha – what an idiot…'

She stroked a stray strand of hair from my eyes. She was more or less holding me upright now, both arms clasping me against her body like she was dragging a heavy sack.

'Not that it matters, anyway,' she went on, 'coming back wasn't about the stupid "fortune" anyway.'

The world around me was fading in and out. I thought at first I was dipping in and out of consciousness, then I realised it was the torch.

'It's going out,' I muttered.

'We'll wait until it's gone completely. Then we can use yours.'

We struggled on in silence for a while until the beam tailed off altogether, forcing us to stop in the middle of the track. It was impossible to know how far we had to go. The stretch of wood ahead of us looked exactly the same as the one we'd just walked through; everything turning white as though it was being slowly erased from existence. We could have been going round in circles for all I knew.

Rosie pulled me closer so she could reach behind

me and open my rucksack for the other torch. She pressed her hand against my forehead. 'You're a bit feverish,' she said.

The beam from my torch was orange instead of white, not as bright as hers and already quivering when she switched it on. It lasted about twenty seconds, then went out like a dubious omen.

'What do we do now?' I mumbled, my thoughts sketchy and feeble with the combination of pain and cold.

'We'll think of something.'

Making any headway was hopeless without the torch; the air felt heavy, as if we were wading through water. When I looked up there were only tiny fragments of sky beyond the treetops and they were saturated with snow, blocking out any light from the stars.

'Who knows how this might end?' she said, her words coiling out of the gloom. She laughed. 'Our relationship, I mean.'

The message from Minette flashed into my mind and for the first time I felt a tremble of genuine fear. Had Erica really been pushed down the stairs? Had that triggered the heart attack that killed her? When, exactly, had Rosie had her last appointment? I didn't want to think about it, I couldn't afford to let my mind wander off towards what it might mean.

I could hear Rosie breathing in small snatches beside me. She was oddly unperturbed by our worsening situation. We were lost, I was on the verge of passing out, we couldn't see a thing, it was getting colder and colder and no one knew we were out here.

'You'll have to go,' I told her, standing on one leg clutching a thick branch. 'Go and find the road on your own. I'll wait here.'

It was our only chance, wasn't it? I wasn't sure. My mind wasn't working properly.

'I'm not leaving you, Sam,' she said firmly, finding my face with her icy fingers and stroking my cheek. Her breath was in my face. 'I'll never leave you.'

'You have to,' I insisted.

'Everything's going to be all right,' she whispered, nuzzling into my neck. 'Whatever happens, we'll be together.'

I wanted to pull away more than anything, but I needed her support. 'Tell me how you *really* feel about me,' she said. 'Please. The truth.'

'Rosie, I don't think—'

'Come on…tell me…I know it's been hard for you to be honest in our sessions, because there are so many things you're not supposed to do. I know you've been trying not to cross the line…'

I couldn't cope with this right now.

'Rosie, I might have a broken ankle…I'm in pain, I can't think straight…'

She put her arms around me, dragging me back towards a fallen tree trunk. I wanted to resist, but there was nowhere to go. She pulled me down and began making little cooing noises in a world of her own.

'Let's rest and huddle together for a while,' she muttered, snuggling into me, almost smothering me, rocking me and humming, like a mother with a child.

'We can stay here as long as want, can't we?' she whispered, pressing the words into my hair.

'Rosie, no…we should keep—'

I froze sharply.

'Did you hear that?' I said.

A branch snapped.

'Someone's coming,' I said, trying to stand.

'I didn't hear anything,' she muttered, her grip suddenly vicelike around my head, trying to press my mouth into her coat so I couldn't be heard.

There was a rustling sound then a spot of light popped up ahead through the thick mass of branches.

With a twist and a shove, I pulled away from her. 'HELP!' I yelled with all my might. 'We're over here. We need help…'

A dog barked and came bounding towards us, then a voice rose out of the undergrowth.

'Who's there?' It was a deep male voice. 'What are you doing out here in the dark?' He flicked his torch over our faces and we were forced to shield our eyes.

'I've hurt my leg; I can barely walk,' I told him, clinging on to a branch.

The dog barked again, snuffling at our pockets.

'She won't harm you,' he said, as the beam flickered across Rosie's forlorn face.

I mistook his meaning for a second, then almost wanted to laugh. I leant down and patted the dog's back in gratitude.

'I'm the gamekeeper – just doing my rounds. Let's get you out of here.'

Chapter 39

Sam

I'm a bit hazy on how I got back to the B&B. I remember the quality of the air changing from chilly to icy and the moon bobbing in and out of the treetops like a balloon. I remember being helped into a Land Rover and Rosie's hand gripping mine all the way back to my B&B. I didn't have the energy to pull away.

My landlady wanted to take me to hospital, but I insisted I just needed a good night's sleep. It was a sprain I was sure of it, but if anything was broken, I'd know by the morning.

Rosie helped me upstairs to my room while Mrs Waterman filled a hot-water bottle. She knew the gamekeeper and invited him in, making us all a pot of tea.

'How strange that your friend was staying in the B&B over the ridge…?' she said, leaving two steaming mugs beside my bed. She glanced over at Rosie, clearly trying to work out the dynamic between the two of us, then backed out of the door, leaving us alone.

Rosie plumped up the pillows and suggested she slept on the floor overnight to keep an eye on me.

'I'm fine,' I lied, remaining seated on the edge of the bed.

We supped our tea in silence.

'You go back to your B&B; they'll be wondering where you are,' I said, as soon as she'd finished her drink. 'Go now, so the gamekeeper can walk you over. We'll get separate trains in the morning, like we agreed. I'll catch the one at half-past nine.'

'But, what about my last session?'

'I can't walk, Rosie. You could go back along the road on your own, tomorrow, and record whatever comes up for you, but I can't go with you.'

'It wouldn't be the same,' she said. 'It wouldn't work.'

'I'm sorry, Rosie – it's over.'

Her bottom lip began to tremble. 'There are still millions of loose ends about the crash. I can't bear it. You're saying it's all over and I've got to carry on as if nothing's happened. It's too much to cope with.'

'Yes. That's why I think it would be good for you to work long term with someone else.'

She turned to me, fingers at her mouth, like a toddler. 'So this is it then?'

'Yes, it is,' I said, staying perfectly still. 'We'll say goodbye and we won't have any more sessions or any more contact when we get back to London. I think we've done a pretty good job, both of us, under the circumstances. This mystery has been a tough nut to crack and I'm really sorry it hasn't been solved. And I'm sorry your viola's gone. I know that's a big disappointment to you.' I smiled. 'You've been very kind, helping me just now, but nothing's changed.'

In fact, if anything, her overly attentive behaviour in the woods had left me decidedly uneasy and it hadn't escaped my attention that she'd been undeniably annoyed, rather than relieved, when the gamekeeper came to our rescue.

Rosie stood by the bed, waiting, no doubt hoping I'd change my mind.

'So, we're not going to see each other…meet up or anything…back in London?'

'No.'

'It's not fair,' she huffed.

I winced and shuffled back towards the pillow. 'I'm tired, Rosie. Goodbye.'

She got as far as the door and opened it, then fiddled with the latch, standing half in and half out of the room.

I cleared my throat. 'Take good care of yourself,' I said.

'Yeah…' she muttered.

She walked out and pulled the door to, disappearing on to the landing.

In an instant, I was reaching for the bedpost so I could hobble over to the door. I turned the key in the lock and rested my back against it.

Why had I let Rosie into my life? What had I done? She was like a smouldering touch paper creeping way too close to a huge pile of gunpowder. What would have happened out in the woods if the gamekeeper hadn't found us? It didn't bear thinking about.

I rang Minette as soon as Rosie's footsteps had faded away.

'You got my message?' she asked.

'Yes, and it's got me very worried,' I said. 'I've just

been with the patient you know as "Kitty", as it happens.' I briefly explained the situation, giving Rosie's real name.

'Are you all right?' she asked.

'Well, my ankle's not great, but I'm okay.' I drew a breath. 'I'm not at all comfortable with the situation here. I'm coming back first thing tomorrow. Is there anything else you can tell me about Erica's death?'

'Only that it's clear Erica scheduled her last session with "Kitty", aka Rosie Chandler, earlier that day.'

'*That day?* You mean Rosie was with her the day she died?'

'Yes, but there were witnesses who saw her leave the house and Erica was seen alive and well shortly afterwards.' She sounded in a hurry. 'I'll let you know if I hear anything else. You just be careful, okay?'

Chapter 40

Rosie

I'm in a state. Sam has seriously gone down in my estimation. We were together at last and everything was suddenly giddy and spine-tingling between us, but she didn't seem to want to talk about 'us' at all.

I went out of my way to look after her, but she hardly showed any appreciation for my help. I soothed her and comforted her and all she could say was that she wanted us to stop seeing each other. Unbelievable. Nothing about ending the sessions and moving into a close friendship. Nothing about that AT ALL. I'm gutted. She's led me on all this time, making me think I was special and that she wanted to be my friend, but it was all FAKE.

When I suggested we went to the Lakes, I laid it on a bit thick about feeling suicidal. I wanted to give her a solid justification for making the trip, so it would look better to the authorities she has to show her cases to.

The bottom line is that she doesn't seem to feel what I thought she did. I thought she was struggling with her feelings about me, because she wanted to stay professional about it. I thought once our appointments stopped everything would take off between us, but apparently not. I've given her plenty of opportunity to turn our situation into a proper friendship, but all she's done is fob me off. I can't believe it. She's just like all the others.

How do I feel about it all? Honestly, I'm not sure yet. Our sessions have ended and she doesn't want me to contact her, she's made that very clear, so it's all over from her point of view. But it *isn't* over for me. I can't stop thinking about her, I can't let her go, just like that.

Thankfully, I've had other stuff on my mind. When Sam said she recognised 'Teddy Spense', I pretended not to see it. But Sam was right. She thinks we've reached a blind alley – but I lied. I know *exactly* who he is. He *was* at that party fifteen years ago, but I had my reasons for not coming clean. I didn't tell her that I remembered the *whole* registration on the motorbike number plate either, not just part of it.

She thinks the mystery has dried up, but she doesn't know the half of it – in fact, it's alive and kicking, so at least some good came of this trip.

I'm not going to the police, though. I don't want them getting to him before I do. I didn't tell Sam either, because the next stage means breaking the law and she wouldn't approve. I'll deal with this first, then I'll sort out the situation with Sam, once and for all.

It wasn't hard to find his address. Number one in a small block of flats in Tooting Bec. It's right there beside his name in the phone book. I remembered Richard telling me, at some point, that both he and his brother had been given stupid middle names – Oakley and Yorath – so the initial in the listing gave him away.

I spot the motorbike through the wrought iron gate

at the side. The same number plate; he'd been in the Lakes all right. I keep walking, past the flats and down to the end of the road, and sit on the wall to think.

As soon as I'd put two and two together, I realised I'd actually met him a few times in passing, but was never particularly impressed. He's the kind of guy who wants you to think he's 'cool', with his finger on the pulse, doing well for himself, but I'm not sure he's smart at all. Streetwise, maybe, in a superficial kind of way, but not adept enough to work out a seamless plan and foresee the consequences. Hence the business with Max's watch. He hadn't considered that someone might recognise it. That was pathetic.

I walk up the path and press the buzzer not for number one, but number four. No reply. I wait and press again. I try flat three and there's a crackle and a woman's reedy voice.

'I'm so sorry to bother you,' I say. 'I've been ringing Mr White's bell, on the ground floor, and he doesn't seem to be answering. You haven't seen him today have you? I'm his sister.'

'Oh…erm…let me think…no, I think I saw him go out this morning.'

'His bike's still here.'

'Yeah…that's right. He was on foot. He was with someone. About ten o'clock, I think it was.'

'Not to worry, he must have forgotten.' There are four buttons on the intercom and four floors to the house. Luckily he's on the ground floor. I know what to do next. 'Thanks very much. I'll try round the back, just in case. Bye.'

The block has a small back yard with access via a narrow alleyway. I retrace my steps and count the houses along the back alley until I reach the right house. There's a wheelie bin outside a sturdy locked gate, so I climb onto it and clamber over. It's second nature. Smart move, I think, warning the tenant I'll try round the back; she won't freak out if she spots me.

As I'd hoped, one small window at the back is open a fraction. I find a barrel in the yard, upturn it in front of the window ledge and trail my fingers inside. I find the latch and lift it. The window makes a sticky click and opens freely. I pull it wide and climb through onto the draining board, trying not to knock a pile of unwashed mugs and pans onto the floor.

The kitchen is a disgrace; mouldy takeaway cartons, age-old plates with fried egg and crusty baked beans strewn over the surfaces. My first thought is *Don't touch anything*, more out of self-preservation than to avoid leaving evidence. There's no way I'm going to take my gloves off.

I take a quick look around and then creep out into the hallway. I stop and listen for sounds. The woman in flat three saw him go out, but that doesn't mean he hasn't come back in again. I can't hear anything, though.

There's a row of hooks by the front door; one with a few loose keys and one with a leather BMW logo on it. The hook nearest the door itself is empty.

The sitting room door is ajar; I slide up to the crack beside the doorframe and look for any signs of movement. Nothing. I slip inside and look around. I know what I'm looking for, I just don't know where he'd be keeping it. Surely not out in the open: under the bed maybe or beneath the floorboards, perhaps. I recoil at having to snoop – everything about the place – the dank smell, the torn wallpaper, the bare carpets – makes me think 'squalor'.

I creep reluctantly into a bedroom. It looks like someone has got here first and trashed the place: pillows on the floor, drawers left open, a guitar leaning precariously against the wardrobe, an upturned laundry basket on the mattress. I kneel down and look under the bed. It's stuffed with boxes. I pull a few out; they're filled with CDs and computer games. I check the wardrobe and a built-in cupboard. A jumble of clothes fall out. I leave them. I don't suppose he's going to notice.

I reach the box room when I hear a noise. A click. The front door. *Bugger. He's back.* The door slams and something heavy lands on the floor. He swears. I look desperately for somewhere to hide, but there's no space; there are clothes, boxes and damp washing everywhere.

I change my mind and decide on a different tack altogether. I walk openly towards him as he bends over a large box on the doormat, making no attempt to soften the sound of my footsteps.

'What the f—' he says, snapping upright like a jack-knife.

'Hi, Greg,' I say nonchalantly. 'Surprise, seeing me?'

He clears his throat and brushes past me into the kitchen. 'Nice place you've got here,' I say, on his heels. 'Could do with a cleaner.'

'How the hell did you get in?'

I point to the kitchen window. 'It wasn't rocket science. You should put security higher up your list of priorities, especially when you're hiding priceless stuff about the place.'

His eyes narrow. He can't tell whether or not I've found it yet.

'What the hell,' he says, opening his hands by way of a forced welcome, pretending to be all laid back. 'Actually, I was expecting you earlier. What took you so long?'

His comment throws me for a second. Was he really expecting me to drop by?

'Well…' I say, forcing my eyes to meet his. 'Aren't you going to fill me in?'

'Fill you in?' He looks at me oddly.

'How you did it.' I lean casually against the fridge, trying to look more confident than I feel. He might be stupid but he's bigger than me. 'You took a hell of a risk trying to sell Max's watch.'

'Yeah, well. Didn't get caught though, did I?'

'Come on, then. Tell me everything.'

'You want to know what happened?' His eyelid twitches.

'That would be nice.'

'Are you for real?' he says. He's chewing gum, trying to look mean and hard. 'You got a wire on you or somefin'?' He's inches from my face.

'What? No…'

He makes me put out my arms and pats me down like we're in airport security. He tips my bag up on the table and tosses through my belongings.

'Can't be too careful,' he says, as I stuff everything

back in. 'Okay, what do you wanna know?' He pushes his sleeves up.

'From the beginning.'

He shrugs. 'Well...we all knew dear old Rickie was in need of a buck or two...you knew that right?'

It's my turn to shrug. 'If you say so.'

'When the second gig came up, he let it slip about Max Raeger's expensive piece of kit and I suggested we go fifty-fifty.' He scratched his stubble. 'But Rickie wasn't having that. Told me to fuck off. So I followed him up to the Lakes on my bike. Once I got there I knew my way around. I'd been there that first time, hadn't I?'

'Yeah, yeah, I remember you driving us up there in 2001, before Richard had passed his test.'

Greg is leaning against the sink, playing with a piece of foil from a bottle top. 'You know all this.' He looks at me quizzically.

'Just carry on, will you?'

A frown burrows into his forehead, then he shrugs. 'While you lot were scraping away, I messed with the brakes, loosened a bolt here and there and started a slow puncture in the front tyre – nothing so radical that the police could say for certain it was deliberate.'

My knee twitches, but I force myself to stay still, refusing to react.

'Rickie's original plan was to "skid" off the road and sink into the mud on the bank of the lake. In the kafuffle, he was going to take the violin from the back, hide it in the bushes and chuck the case in the water. He wanted to make it look like the instrument had got lost in the lake. At that stage, he knew everyone's main concern would be getting out. But someone had a better idea.' He screws his eyes up, giving me a look that implies I ought to be familiar with all this.

'Go on,' I say coolly.

'If you insist,' he half laughs and carries on. 'Rickie was soft. He only meant for you all to get your feet wet. He hadn't worked out that everyone'd be straight out of the van as soon as it touched the water: Max desperate to save his violin, not letting it out of his sight. I knew it'd work far better if the van went high speed straight into the lake and down to the bottom.'

I gulp down the knot of outrage in my throat.

'I stuffed a mix of cardboard and glue in the seatbelt clips so they'd jam. It meant the three in the front seats would waste precious time and effort trying to get out, so I had time to get *my* hands on the violin.' He wraps one fist around the other and crunches his knuckles loudly.

My heartbeat shoots off the scale and every muscle in my body is telling me to run. He's talking about it like he sabotaged a cricket match, yet he wanted us all to drown. He didn't give a toss. He's a total psycho; he didn't even care if he killed his own brother.

'So it was *you* behind us. You weren't "just passing", *you* ran us off the road. It was *you* Richard saw?'

He yawns, but he's faking it. 'The van needed to go in the water at just the right spot where it was deep close to the edge, it wasn't going to work otherwise.' He's revelling in this; it makes me sick. 'You got out pretty sharpish as it happened. Bit of a Houdini, aren't you?' He rubs his hands together. 'You heard enough yet?'

Greg is prowling around the kitchen. He's picked up an empty bottle from somewhere and is slapping it rhythmically into his palm.

Richard said they'd never got on as siblings. He'd described Greg as a waster, involved in petty crime and drug peddling. Lucy said he'd sponged off Richard, even stolen from him. Once he's told his story, he isn't going to wave me a cute goodbye and let me wander back onto the street to tell everyone what he's done. I make a quick calculation. The front door is further away, but the kitchen window involves a climb. It will have to be the front.

'I need the toilet,' I say, turning towards the doorway.

'Oh, no you don't,' he says, manhandling me into a wooden chair. He kicks the door to the hall shut. 'Sit and listen. I thought that's what you wanted. You're the one person I can share the whole story with.' I squeeze my knees together. I'm going to have to be really careful not to end up trapped with him in here. 'At least take your gloves off,' he adds.

'No, it's all right, thanks. I'm cold,' I reply.

He shrugs and stays standing. 'Once the van had been under for a few minutes, stuff started floating to the surface. I took various wallets and the little coin pouch holding Max's watch, of course,' he says. 'It was too late for him. I let his body float away.'

I snatch a breath. 'You saw him? You never said that at the auction house. You could have saved him…you just let him drown?'

'He was already a gonner by then and I had a job to

do. I let you scramble out with a case, because I thought you'd got the violin, then I realised Max's case was the big rectangular one. I watched you get to the bank and then pass out. It was too deep to dive down, but there was no one else around, so I hung around and before long the violin case came up.'

'Yeah - it was super special,' I tell him, 'designed to float and keep the violin dry.'

'That was lucky, wasn't it? I grabbed your case too, and hid them both behind a pile of rocks, further along in the undergrowth.'

'You took my viola? You've got it?!' Instinctively, my hand springs to my chest. *He'd saved it!*

'I reckoned if you'd bothered to risk your neck getting it out, it must be worth somefin', too.' He tosses back his greasy fringe. 'I strapped one case to my front, one to my back and drove back to my B&B. I mean, everyone assumed it was a terrible accident, no one was lookin' for stolen instruments. Max's case was locked, so I had to bust it open, then I went back to the lake the next day and chucked it into the water at the far end, to make the police think the violin itself was down in the depths somewhere. Smart move, huh?'

As Greg is talking, I'm back there revisiting the scene from his perspective and a new memory pops up from nowhere, loud and clear. Sam was right, when you try to recall a situation from someone else's point of view, fresh memories come out of the woodwork.

There's a man on the phone in the hallway...*It's worth a fortune and it's under the bridge*, he's saying. And suddenly I know that it's Karl Hinds' voice.

That's when I realise Greg doesn't know the half of it.

Chapter 41

Rosie

Greg walks over to the bin and spits out his gum.

'Where are they?' I say. 'Where's my viola? Max's violin?'

I get up from the kitchen table, but Greg shoves me back down again. He gives me a calculating grin.

'Did you know someone else was after the violin – right behind us, that day?'

I shrug.

'When I got back up to the road who did I see, but Karl Hinds, driving off in a fast car. Richard was convinced Karl was a sly devil. He didn't know what the deal was, but he thought he was connected to the guy who fell off the drainpipe at that first party. You know who I mean?'

'Mick Blain.'

The one who'd got his hands on my viola and had very nearly broken it.

'Yeah, him.'

It's worth a fortune and it's under the bridge…

A new piece of the puzzle snaps into place. Greg's got the wrong end of the stick with this part. Karl wasn't after the violin – he wasn't stupid enough to go for something he didn't know how to sell. He was after the same thing Mick Blain had been interested in at that first party. Something under a bridge. Whatever it was.

'Where's my viola?' I snapped.

'Just hold your horses,' he says. 'The violin's the real deal here and I want the hard cash. I mean, I'm not in the know about a blinkin' Gru…Gran—'

'Guarneri,' I correct him.

'Yeah, whatever. I knew it was bloody rare – but that's where you come in.' He puts his hands on the table in front of me, stares into my face, expecting, waiting for something. 'You don't remember, do you?'

'Remember what?'

'Any of it. I've been watching you as I've been going through it all, point by point, and you don't remember a frickin' thing.' He folds his arms, a secretive expression on his face. 'You haven't got a clue about the chat we had in the pub – the pact we made in my room at the B&B…' Again, he scrutinises my face for signs.

I don't know what he's talking about.

'You were IN on it, darlin'…every step of the way.'

'What?' I let out an incredulous huff, trying to look disdainful, but I'm actually totally thrown by what he's suggesting. I make myself think. The night we arrived in the Lakes I'd spoken to *Richard* in the pub. I try to flag up that memory – the one with him teasing me about stealing the violin, but I can't find it any more. I can't see Richard's face. And now Greg is saying I had that conversation with *him*.

'We planned it together,' he persists.

He's lying.

'When?'

'The night you turned up from London. We were all

in the pub: Rickie, you, that Steph bird. Max wasn't there – he was doin' yoga or some bollocks…'

I'm trying to go back there. 'In the pub…' I'm unable to reach it. It's like I'm clawing at layers of curtains, but as I peel each one away another drops in its place. 'I don't believe you.'

'The others had gone and it was just you and me. I asked you if you were interested in the idea. It was all a bit of a laugh at first, I wanted to know what your reaction would be.'

I'm grasping to reach into the past, but there's nothing there. 'I thought that was Richard…'

'I don't know what you talked about with him, but this was with me.' He winks. 'Let me show you.' He reaches into a tall food cupboard beside the freezer and fishes about in a carrier bag.

'Here…'

It's a sketch on lined paper of the road from the Hinds' place to the lakeside, with all the road names labelled. There's a red cross at the exact spot where the van left the road. It's in my handwriting. My eyes follow the line of the pen; I can tell it belongs to me and yet it feels alien. I can't recall putting the pen on the paper.

'You were meant to grab the violin,' he says.

He scratches his head. I'm barely hearing him. Questions are firing off like canons inside my head: *Could I have been involved? Is he messing with my mind?*

'I would never have agreed to kill anyone,' I say with conviction.

He picks up a peanut from a torn bag on the table

and flips it into his mouth. 'That's not what you said at the time.'

I shake my head. 'No, I would never do that.'

I'd remember – wouldn't I?

'For someone who's so innocent, you were pretty damn quick to volunteer to sit in the back.'

I force myself to look at him. 'The seatbelts – you're saying I *knew*?'

He snorts. 'Are you kiddin' me? Hell, you suggested it!'

'No. You're making this shit up...'

He throws his hand in the air. 'Bugger it, believe what you like. I don't care. Either way, it was the only way it was going to work. You had to be in the back, so you could stay with the violin. Then you were meant to grab it and hide it on the bank. Only you botched it up big time, when you grabbed the wrong bloody case. Talk about dead wood.'

'Why would I risk my own life?' I demand. 'Why would I have put myself through that?'

'You said you were a hotshot at getting out of small spaces. And a good swimmer. You said it would be a doddle.'

He tosses another nut in the air and catches it nonchalantly in his mouth. 'So, anyway, because you cocked it up, your cut's gone down by half.' With his sing-song voice he sounds like he's taunting little kids in the playground. 'But, you're still gonna help me sell it.'

He jabs his hands into his hips.

'Hell...you've made me wait long enough. You were meant to get in contact ages ago.'

He waves a hand up and down in front of my face.

'You really don't remember any of this, do you?' His jaw thrusts towards me, snarling, nasty. *Why is he doing this? Trying to make it seem like I knew everything?* 'You banged on about how we could fence it; how we could get the violin out of the country and make a deal overseas.'

He sees my blank expression and bursts into raucous laughter. He bends down right in my face as if he's talking to someone simple. 'Shit man, you're a weird bitch!' He's so close, his spit lands on my cheek.

His snide attitude reminds me of someone else, another bully, but I can't quite work out from where. All I know is something inside me begins to smoulder.

He moves back to the cupboard in the corner and pulls out the plastic bag he opened earlier. Then the memory shuffles into place. It's Ralph he reminds me of, when I was ten, that time at Picket's Wood. The ringleader. His bony face; scathing, vindictive, pretending to include me and then casting me aside like I was a bit of dirt stuck to the bottom of his shoe. I see my chance. I tip my chair back quickly, scoop up the small chef's knife from the draining board and slip it up my sleeve, out of sight.

As Greg is fiddling with the bag, my ordeal in Picket's Wood comes tumbling back with the force of Niagara. The little gang of five. My desperation to be part of it. The trust I put in their grubby little hands. The hurt, the humiliation. Then, the way it ended. The real ending.

It was the week after I'd been abandoned in the

dark. I'd gone back to school as if nothing had happened, wearing thick tights to cover the bruises and cuts on my legs. The group who'd staged the little charade spent playtimes and lunch breaks sniggering and whispering behind my back.

Then the tables started to turn. It began when Mrs Tanner came in to see my school teacher. Neil's Nintendo had gone missing. As a result, all our bags and desks were checked. It never turned up. Shortly afterwards, Ralph left his brand new bike outside the Post Office and it must have rolled down the bank and got run over by a truck. He'd only had it three weeks. His dad went mad.

A day or so later, Kelly came to school in tears. Her pet frog, the one she kept in a jar on the window ledge in her bedroom, had escaped. Taken the lid off its own jar and hopped out, it seemed. Then, that weekend, the day after bonfire night, Miles' treehouse burnt down. One of the other kids claimed they'd seen him playing with matches. He said he was nowhere near when it went up in flames, but his parents stopped his karate lessons anyway. A few days after that, I overheard Julie's mother saying that she'd found Julie's bridesmaid's dress at the bottom of the garden. It was in the wheelbarrow, covered in mud with a huge rip down the front, like it had been caught in a car door.

All those mishaps, so unfortunate, one after the other. Funny how the sniggering and whispering stopped after that.

Greg's footsteps bring me back to the present. He is standing in front of me looking pleased with himself.

'Here's the first piece of sunken treasure…' He delves into the plastic bag, showing me just a few inches. I recognise the scroll at the top straight away.

'My viola!' I'm on my feet.

He sniggers. 'Except – you're not gonna be playin' it anytime soon!'

He slides it out, holding up a jumble of loose strings and flaps of wood. It looks like a headless puppet with all its limbs dislocated.

'What have you done?!' I cry, trying to take hold of it. 'You've smashed it to bits…'

Greg smirks. He backs away, taunting me, swinging the remains of my beautiful instrument. 'Soddin' worthless load of shite,' he snarls. 'I stamped on it once I realised just how crap it actually was. Guy at the music shop took one look at it and said it would cost more to get it valued than it was worth!'

He makes it do a grotesque dance in front of me and breaks into hysterical laughter. The parts clatter together, like a tuneless wind chime.

Greg drops it back into the bag unceremoniously, lets it fall to the floor and kicks it into the corner. Then he reaches beside the fridge and holds up a bottle of whisky.

'Fancy a slug?' he says, 'to show there's no hard feelings. Then we can talk about the big one – the violin. Want to see it?'

I shrug and he turns towards the draining board. He has his back to me for only five seconds, but it's enough. My hand is up my sleeve and around the handle before my brain tells me to do it. Years of hurt, rejection, loss and anger, mostly anger, are seething inside me. He's taken this precious part of me, my lifelong companion and crushed it to pieces, smiling all the while. It's deliberate. Malicious.

As he leans over to pick up two filthy glasses, I spot a thin stretch of white flesh under his T-shirt. I lunge forward and sink the knife into it. It slides in more easily than I expect. A wail leaves his lips and Greg turns, falls against the chair, his abdomen exposed. I sink the blade in, again and again, drawing strength from a place of dormant rage inside me I barely know exists.

I know then what Dad must have felt. Why he pulled the trigger so many times. It was hurt that got the better of him and he couldn't stop. Outrage, anger and fury all bubbled up into one big bang inside his head. Just like I'm feeling in Greg's kitchen, with my viola in splinters on the floor and the knife in my gloved hand. I didn't plan this. I didn't come here to do this. It just happened.

Greg grabs hold of the kitchen table, then clutches the holes I've made in his body. He seems perplexed by the liquid oozing over his hands. He slides to the floor, twitches a few times then lays still, his eyes fixed on the light fitting on the ceiling as if suddenly realising it isn't up to the job.

An oily film collects over his eyes almost straight away and I know what I've done.

I'm quick. I grab the plastic bag, let myself out by the back door and swan out of the rear gate. I don't bother looking for Max's violin. I'm not interested in that now. I can't believe I ever was; Greg's story was a complete lie.

On the bus home, I finally peek inside the carrier

bag. It's heart breaking to have to look at my crushed viola, but that's when I notice something else, and it brings a big smile to my lips.

The thing is, I was right all along.

It *was* worth getting my viola back, but not in the way I expected. I've got the connection now. It's been locked inside my head, but I never quite lost it.

Mick Blain messing about with my viola before our first concert and Karl's conversation on the phone fifteen years later – it all makes sense now, thanks to Greg. He triggered memories buried under the surface and set all the cogs in motion.

The thin piece of wood holding up the strings on a viola is called a 'bridge'. That's where the 'fortune' was all this time, on the inside of my viola, 'under the bridge'.

Chapter 42

Sam

I was uneasy when I got back from the Lake District, Minette's message about Rosie being at Erica's house the day she died was still lodged in my mind. So too, images of Rosie pressuring me to become her 'soul sister', then trying to stop me calling for help when we were lost in the wood.

What was she going to do now?

We'd certainly parted on a sour note; she was obviously angry with me for ending the sessions – and refusing to stay in touch. I couldn't shake off the niggling feeling that it wasn't over.

I had my ankle checked over at my local surgery and, as I'd thought, it was only a sprain. I hobbled for a day or two, but it quickly improved.

During my recovery I managed to get the password from Professor Dean to open Erica's case notes that he'd sent me. He apologised for still not being able to provide the full set. Apparently, Erica had kept handwritten notes from the final sessions in her house and these were the ones that had gone missing.

Towards the end of my first day back at work, I dropped in to Debbie's office. We'd managed a few quick chats recently and I was up-to-date on her pregnancy, but we hadn't had a proper heart-to-heart for a while.

'Fancy lunch sometime?' I asked her.

'I'd love to,' she said, 'how about that new Lebanese place near Selfridges on Saturday?'

'Perfect. Text me the address.'

She glanced at her watch. 'Sorry, there's a mix-up in human resources I need to sort out.' She hesitated as she reached for a file on her desk. 'Remember that creepy patient you had?'

I nodded, an image of Bruce immediately springing to mind.

'Poor guy ended up in intensive care two weeks ago. He was badly beaten up. Been in here with head injuries, broken ribs, a broken wrist, broken fingers, you name it, ever since.'

'For two weeks?'

I tried to remember the last time I'd had a silent phone call. There'd been at least one in the last fortnight, for sure.

'He'd started stalking one of the nurses, here,' Debbie said, clicking her tongue. 'Waited for her in the car park. The husband caught him trying to put his hands all over her.'

So it *wasn't* Bruce who'd been plaguing me. On the train home, I ran through my current list of patients in my head. Was one of them calling my home number to freak me out? Could it be Rosie?

Whoever it was, as soon as I got another dead call, I was phoning the police.

I opened my diary to distract myself and made myself focus on the week ahead: a ballet on ice with Paula, a film with Hannah, Saturday lunch with Debbie. Nice, ordinary and safe.

When I got back, I poured myself a small glass of wine and flicked on the TV to watch a film, just catching the end of the news. If I'd switched on a couple of minutes later, I would have missed it.

I stared at the screen.

A man had been murdered in his flat in Tooting and the reporter stated that his brother was missing, presumed dead, following a car crash at Ullswater in the Lake District.

I recognised the photo; I'd seen the man in the footage of the Hinds' party from 2001. I'd thought it was the same guy I'd seen on Rosie's phone, too, the one who'd tried to sell Max's watch. Only the reporter was calling him Greg White, not Teddy Spense. He was Richard's brother.

Pieces of Rosie's mystery were whirling around inside my head.

Teddy...Greg...was dead. The reporter said he'd been stabbed; a tenant had reported a bad smell through the letter box. And a priceless violin was found in his flat. Police were questioning neighbours for any leads. The voiceover implied Greg had mixed with the wrong people and had a history of misdemeanours as long as his arm.

I was almost tempted to call Rosie to see if she'd seen the report, but I had to let her go. I had to let everything about the crash go too, and while I hate unfinished business, I needed to resign myself to never knowing what really happened.

I *could* try to make headway on the other loose end, however. After a further call to Minette, she agreed to speak to Erica's husband and later that evening, she called me back to say she'd persuaded him to meet me the following morning.

I took last-minute leave for the day and the taxi dropped me off at the gate at 9am. He must have been watching me walk up the path, because the door was open before I'd taken my finger off the bell.

'Mr Mandale?'

Erica's widower was in his early sixties and dressed in a formal black suit and tie. If he hadn't been wearing slippers, I'd have said he was on his way to a funeral. His eyes seemed sunken and moist as if he'd spent entire days during the last few months in tears. I wondered how much sleep he was getting.

He invited me inside the three-storey townhouse and led me through to a large airy room he called the drawing room. He offered me tea and I half-expected him to reach over to the wall for a bell-pull to alert a maid. The kettle could have only just boiled, because he was back in the room before I'd had chance to take off my coat.

'It was so terribly sudden,' he said in pristine Queen's English. 'I still can't believe it.' My teacup made the crisp click of bone china as I stood it on the saucer. He blew into a large handkerchief and rallied a fraction. 'You used to work with Erica?'

'Not exactly. I'm a colleague of Dr Heron's...and, I'm sure you'll know all about confidentiality...I can't reveal much, except to say that Erica and I had a connection.'

'A patient in common?'

I looked down. 'I'm sorry, I can't say, but thank you for seeing me.' I swallowed. 'Is it okay to ask you a few questions about Erica? It could be important.'

He got up and walked across to look out of the broad bay window. I took a quick look around the spacious room. There was evidence of their happy years together on nearly every surface: early photographs in black and white and later ones with children. I wondered if the wardrobes were still full of Erica's clothes, whether he could still smell her perfume when he walked into their bedroom.

He pressed his hands together as if he was praying. 'What do you want to know?'

'How did she seem on the day she died?' I asked gently.

'Oh...the usual. Nothing out of the ordinary. She'd had an operation on her bunion, but it was healing up nicely. She still needed support, but she was down to a single crutch.'

'And her patients?'

'She was taking a break from Guy's, so she only had one patient, a woman, who came to the house. Erica didn't normally work from home, but she'd made an exception. She felt sorry for the woman, I think.'

'Did she ever talk about that patient?'

'No,' he turned back towards me, smiling. 'You know the drill. Even husbands can't ask questions. Erica was very good, she never let anything slip about her work.'

'Did you see Erica after she'd given her

consultation, the day she...fell?'

'No, I saw her that morning.' He dropped his gaze. 'Her patient was booked in for 2pm. I didn't get home until six. That's when I found her at the bottom of the stairs...I was too late.'

'That must have been awful...I'm so sorry.'

The delicate tick of the carriage clock on the mantelpiece filled the hollow space between us.

'I thought, at first, she must have tripped over the dog...'

My eyes instinctively swept the room searching for evidence of a pet. 'Rupert died, not long after Erica.' He swayed slightly. 'I loved that bloody mongrel.'

'I'm sorry...' I cringed inside, aware of how much my visit must have been compounding his grief. I ploughed on. 'Dr Heron said there were witnesses who saw Erica's patient leave that day?'

'Yes. A neighbour saw a woman with red curly hair leave the house. She recognised her from previous visits. She left at around three o'clock.'

'And Erica was seen after that?'

'Yes, she went to the library, as usual – they remember her there because she nearly left her crutch behind.'

'Do you have any idea what happened when she came back to the house?'

He plucked brown petals from a display of white lilies and screwed them up in his fist – the first sign I'd seen of any tension. He dropped them in a wastebasket in the corner and stood still. 'She'd tidied up the flowers at some stage. She'd opened the mail, which usually comes after lunch…done a bit of cleaning – everything was spotless. There was no sign of any visitors, no cups on the draining board and equally there was nothing to suggest a forced entry. That's why everyone assumed she died of natural causes, at first. A heart attack.'

'At first…?'

He drew himself up and folded his arms. 'What is it you want to know, exactly? I've been through all this with the police.'

'Notes are missing from Erica's records, as you probably know,' I said.

'Is that why you're here?'

'Not exactly. I suppose I'm looking for something that happened on the day itself that might help the police, something they might have missed.'

'Oh…' He looked exhausted and shuffled over to an armchair, folding into it before his legs gave way. 'The police started to question whether it was a heart attack…that's why they re-opened the case.' He paused. 'And before you ask, Erica was cremated, so the police aren't able to—'

'Right…' I murmured, glancing down at my clasped hands.

His chin quivered, but he continued. 'There was new evidence. A neighbour came back from a long trip abroad and said he remembered someone coming to the front door the afternoon Erica died. Sometime around 3.30pm.' His voice was thin and fragile. 'The neighbour was at the front window waiting for a scheduled delivery, so he was very aware of the time. He said he saw the visitor go inside, but didn't see them leave.'

'But Erica was out, then – at the library.'

'Exactly...' He blinked slowly as if his eyelids were heavy and difficult to lift. 'I think the neighbour must have been mistaken.'

'Or the visitor had a key?'

He shook his head straight away. 'No one else had a key, just the two of us.' He toyed with a loose strand of cotton on the chair arm.

'Did the neighbour give a description?'

'He said the visitor was wearing an anorak with the hood up, jeans and flat boots. He reckoned it could have been anybody, male or female – he couldn't be sure.'

'Did the police find anything else?'

'They came to re-examine the house and discovered brown marks on the skirting board at the top of the stairs. They think it's possible there was some kind of scuffle. Apparently they're trying to match samples of shoe polish.'

'Really? From nine months ago?'

'My wife…we never wore outdoor shoes around the house – it's always been slippers. I'd painted upstairs the week before she died, so the marks could only have been made since then.'

'I see.'

'If you want all the details, there's a police report,' he said dismissively. 'That's about as much as I can tell you.' He looked weary, his buttoned jacket rumpled with heavy folds at the front, like a teddy bear that's lost half its stuffing. He seemed to lose interest in talking to me after that so I got up to leave.

'I'm very sorry,' I said again, and thanked him.

He dragged himself to the hall to show me out and I glanced up at the staircase. It curved round at the top and the bottom with an extensive flight in between; it must have been a long tumble all the way down.

He was about to shut the door behind me when he said one final thing: 'She was holding a blank card when she died. She must have been about to send it to someone.'

'A card?'

'Yes. It was the last thing she'd touched, so I kept it. Silly, really.' He sighed, avoiding my eyes. 'It wasn't signed; there was nothing written on the envelope and it didn't have a stamp on it. Just a simple greetings card with a little dried flower on the front.'

My breath caught in my throat and I swallowed hard. I tried to think straight.

'You think Erica was going to send the card to someone...but could someone have sent it to the house, instead?'

He puffed out his bottom lip. 'The police didn't think so. The letterbox needs mending; there's a faulty spring on the inside that always leaves a dent in the mail. The envelope wasn't marked. In any case, why would anyone give Erica a *blank* card?'

He was starting to sound tetchy.

'Do you mind if I take a look at it?'

He sighed, but ambled down the hall and came back holding an envelope.

I knew what it would look like even before I opened it. My fingers were hot and trembling as I dragged the card into the light. A dried red rosebud and *Thank you* written in silver printed letters. Exactly the same as mine, except this one was blank inside.

I wanted it to be a coincidence, but I knew it couldn't be. It was too distinctive. I saw the design differently this time: the delicate flower in its prime, not captured forever, but flattened against its will, all the life squeezed out of it.

I handed it back. 'Keep this safe. Don't let it out of your sight. I think the police will want to speak to you again.'

I rang them as soon as I got to the gate, explaining about the identical card Rosie had sent me. I said I'd hand over the card she'd sent me within the hour. It was at work with all my other correspondence from patients, safe in my office at the back of a drawer.

All I could think of was Rosie. Unstable Rosie. Terrifying Rosie. One of life's lost souls. I felt sure now. Erica's death hadn't been an accident at all – and Rosie was the one who'd pushed her.

Chapter 43

Sam

I flagged down a cab and went straight to St Luke's, telling the driver to wait outside while I dashed in and out of my office.

With Rosie's identical card in my bag, I asked him to drive like a runaway train to the police station on Earl's Court Road. I had to wait ages before someone would see me, but by then I was piecing everything together.

Rosie must have returned to Erica's after her consultation. Mr Mandale said there were no spare keys...and yet...

Suddenly it hit me.

How could I have been so stupid? Rosie had been getting into *my* flat, too. It explained why, for a few weeks now, certain things weren't where I'd left them and others had gone missing altogether; it wasn't absent-mindedness, Rosie had *been* there.

I thought back: ironing folded away, dishes cleared, vases emptied. Rosie had been coming in and tidying up for me – how bizarre! And the missing bra, the belt, the comb, my boots, my pale-blue scarf? She must have pinched them, stolen my keys at some point when I wasn't looking and had them copied. Unbelievable!

After I'd handed over Rosie's card to the police officer, I explained all this and she suggested I get an emergency locksmith to change my locks. There was no concrete proof Rosie had been getting in, so that was all I could do, she told me. It didn't seem enough.

Levi, from 'Loxenkeys', wasn't as burly as I would have liked. With a crinkly round face and a few wisps of hair, he stood only an inch or so taller than me and gave the impression that he'd missed the boat to retirement some time ago. While he chipped away at the doorframe, I scoured every room. Given her past performance, I wouldn't have put it past Rosie to be already inside, hiding somewhere.

Even after Levi left and I had a shiny new set of keys in my hand, I still felt jumpy. I had a nagging feeling that keeping Rosie out of my home wouldn't be enough to end our connection. She was too persistent and I was convinced that she wasn't going to let things rest as they stood.

She'd fought the idea of ending our sessions and acted very strangely in the Lake District, but was I actually in danger? In any case, shouldn't the police be questioning her about Erica by now?

As I turned on the taps for a long soak in the bath, I silently urged the police to hurry up and find sufficient evidence to stop her. I'd made a terrible, terrible mistake letting her into my life. She was like a snake, wrapping herself, oh so tenderly, around my neck then slowly starting to squeeze.

I scattered a handful of expensive bath salts into the gushing water and watched the bathroom fill with sweet-smelling steam. Then I stripped off and sank into the water. I shut my eyes and willed my limbs to relax.

It was then I heard it. A soft patter like a book falling. I shot up, straining to listen, urging the rush of disturbed water to settle, but I couldn't hear anything above the loud thudding in my chest.

I stepped out of the bath and wrapped my bathrobe around me tightly, before creeping barefoot into the hall.

The door of the sitting room was wide open and nothing stirred inside. I dashed towards the coffee table and picked up my mobile, then turned to the bedroom. The door was slightly ajar, so I stood outside trying to listen. I could hear a tiny fluttering sound followed by louder slaps as if someone was checking through my wardrobe.

My jaw snapped shut. I'd gone into every room when Levi was here, even checked the shower cubicle, but he'd called me just after I'd looked under the bed and I'd been distracted. The wardrobe was the one place I hadn't checked. Rosie must have darted in there when she heard me approaching.

I gave the bedroom door a gentle shove and waited for it to swing inwards, my ears and eyes on full alert, my muscles crackling with anticipation. A movement made me jump; the curtains flapped against the wall, the sash window standing wide open. I jerked my head to the left; the wardrobe was open too, clothes dropped on the floor – but there was no one there. I checked under the bed again, but the chill in the room told me the window had been open for some time.

Rosie was long gone.

I leaned out of the window and looked down below. At ground level, a wheelie bin was on its side, wrappers and empty tins spilling onto the path. Rosie must have climbed down the drainpipe like a cat burglar, but which Rosie? The sweet, eager one, wanting to take care of me or the resentful one, keen to show me how much I'd hurt her?

My mind kept returning to those few awkward moments in the woods before the gamekeeper found us. What if…?

I ducked back inside and slid the window shut, flicking the flimsy catch at the top. Maybe it was time for a full security upgrade. I turned round, about to flop onto the bed with relief, then I froze. Instinctively, my fingers gripped the collar of my bathrobe pulling it up around my neck.

Rosie had left something.

Lying innocently across my pillow was a single red rose.

Chapter 44

Rosie

I'm meandering aimlessly across the Common near Sam's flat, not caring that it's started to rain.

Sam's keys are no use to me anymore. I hid for a while after she came back to the flat, but she had someone with her. When he started hammering and clattering away, it was obvious she was getting the locks changed. To double-check, I sneaked out of the wardrobe to take a peek and I was right. Oh, well. She must have realised I was coming in. Leaving the rose on her pillow just now would have told her that, anyway. It was only a matter of time. Now I need to think of another way to reach her.

A dog darts out of the bushes and yaps at a boy holding a ball and I think of Rupert, the dog I used to see at Erica's.

I can remember every detail of what happened when Erica died. I walk on and let the scenes roll, hoping they'll take my mind off how upset I am about Sam.

Erica's house in Chelsea was big and stately. I loved going there; it was like walking into *House & Home* magazine. My feet didn't make a sound on the carpet and all the furniture was plush and comfortable. She used to take me to a room at the top of the house; a small box room in the eaves. She insisted we had to traipse up there, even though her foot was sore after the operation and she found the stairs difficult. I don't know why we couldn't have chatted in the fancy drawing room downstairs instead.

Erica was kind enough, but she was a bit long in the tooth and I don't think she ever really understood me. I didn't feel that much of a connection with her. I *said* I did – to make her like me – but it wasn't true. She didn't have the same depth that Sam has. Sam seems able to see right inside me; although I've learned that's not always a positive thing.

The last time I saw Erica, she was cold and off with me. I didn't know what I'd done wrong and she didn't tell me. I think she'd decided I was too much trouble in the end and wanted rid of me. *Just like everybody else.* She had a long list of well-rehearsed excuses, of course – about how it might be good for me to see someone new, about how we hadn't made much progress recently. I started to boil. It wasn't fair. Why did people say one thing and mean another? Why did they claim they were interested when they bloody well weren't?

When the session was finally over – our *last* session, she'd decided – I didn't want to say a nice, friendly goodbye. She held the door open for me, ready for our sad little farewell – after eighteen months – but I stormed out without a word and didn't look back. I bet that gave her a shock.

I did go back, of course. She didn't know I'd copied her keys and had been popping in for regular visits.

Rupert, the little dog, didn't seem to mind me

turning up. He barked the first couple of times, but after that he knew who I was. He was old and spent most of the time curled up in his basket in the hall, anyway. He used to lift his head at the sound of the key in the lock, sniff the air and go back to sleep again. Her husband was never around during the day and Erica had got into a little routine of going to the library just after our session, every week. I'd watched her, followed her and knew how long she took.

So, shortly after that last time, I let myself back in to the house. Rupert didn't even look up. I wandered through all the rooms and sat down in every single chair. I sank into the cushions, handled her ornaments. I wanted to belong inside that house – for it never to forget me, even if *she* did. I smelt the flowers, took away the dead leaves, shifted a few items round here and there to leave my invisible mark.

I found her file of notes about me in the filing cabinet in the study and read through chunks of it. It upset me. Hateful words, critical, tearing my personality to shreds. She'd *never* liked me; it was all a farce. Nice little earner, taking money and not caring a jot. I thought she was my friend! I felt crushed and devastated; I ripped out sheet after sheet and stuffed them in my bag.

Next, I went into the bedroom. I'd used the shower in the ensuite before, but this time I thought I'd have a lie down instead. I could tell which side of the bed she slept in; her familiar tiger-striped reading glasses and a ladies' handkerchief were on the bedside table. I rolled back the duvet, took off my boots and got into bed. It was a mistake. I must have been tired. I didn't hear her come up the stairs, slowly, one at a time in her slippers.

'Rosie?!' She stooped over me, sounding cross. 'How the hell did *you* get in?'

I sat bolt upright, still half asleep, taking a moment to remember where I was.

'What are you doing? How *dare* you?!' she shouted at me. *Can you believe it?* She really shouted, like I was a common thug. Her true colours were shining through now, good and proper.

'Don't worry, I'm going…' I said, squashing my feet into my boots.

'Did you break in?' she asked sharply.

I held up the keys and dangled them in front of her face. 'Duh…' I said.

I was pissed off by then. She was totally overreacting. She knew exactly who I was and how harmless I'd be. We were friends, almost, for goodness' sake. I wasn't doing any harm. In fact, I'd been helping her out around the house for weeks, if only she'd put two and two together.

'I think you need to give me those keys and leave,' she barked, holding out her hand. 'This is totally unacceptable.'

'*Totally unacceptable*,' I mimicked, my hands on my hips. I jerked towards her suddenly to see what she'd do and she recoiled, dragging her bandaged foot, nearly losing her balance. She was scared.

I laughed.

'Silly cow! What do *you* know about never being properly loved through no fault of your own? How can *you* know what's it like to never belong?!'

She didn't have a clue and I despised her for it.

She started backing away from me, heading towards the phone. 'This is a matter for the police,' she huffed, snatching at the handset.

She was about to press numbers on it, so I went straight after her. She was forced to turn round to see her way to the stairs and lowered the phone, more concerned, now, about getting away from me.

Her chest was heaving under her lacy blouse and cashmere cardigan. I always hated her clothes; so old-fashioned. She got to the top of the stairs and held on to the newel post with her free hand, then she swung her good leg onto the top step and let it take her weight.

I was right behind her, but she was going so slowly, I decided to squeeze past and get to the front door first. I thought if I left without any further fuss and nothing was damaged or stolen, she wouldn't report me.

I barely touched her. In fact, it was an accident really, her foot got caught up with mine and my heel jammed against the skirting board for a second, before she let out a whimpering cry and tumbled forward.

By the way she landed near the bottom of the stairs I knew straight away that she was dead. Her limbs were kind of limp and floppy and the light had gone out of her eyes. Rupert down the hall didn't even stir from his basket.

I thought it would be better if I put the phone back, but she was lying on it, so I lifted her shoulder and rolled her over a fraction to find it. She bumped down another step when I let go of her; it gave me a hell of a fright.

I took the phone back upstairs, wiped my fingerprints off it and put it back on its cradle by the bed. Erica's eyes were open staring at the wallpaper as I came back down. I didn't want to touch her again, or take her pulse or anything. I just wanted to get away.

There was no point hanging around after that. Before I left, I opened my bag and slid out the pretty *Thank you* card I'd always kept tucked away, ready for the right time for me to give it to her.

I was going to leave it on the doormat, but I decided I might as well hand it over in person, so I left it in her hand, making sure I didn't have any contact with her lifeless fingers. I wasn't feeling particularly generous at that point, but it seemed only right, under the circumstances. I hadn't got around to signing it, but it hardly mattered now that she was dead.

On my way out, I called over to her. 'It's been a real pleasure, Erica. You taught me to stand up for myself, so I hope you'll see it's all been worthwhile.'

So, I suppose she got her proper goodbye after all.

Chapter 45

Sam

I plucked the rose from my pillow, not knowing what to do with it. It was just like the 'signature' rosebuds Rosie had dried and pressed on the cards she'd sent to Erica and me – only this rose had thorns. I carried it at arms' length into the kitchen and dropped it in a plastic bag, my jittery mind telling me I should keep it as evidence.

I went back to the bedroom to see if anything else was out of place, but there was nothing obvious. I got changed, pulled on the nearest clothes from the pile on the floor.

I didn't know what the 'gift' implied. Red roses are a symbol of love, but they're also traditionally tossed into a grave at a burial. Knowing how abruptly Rosie could swing from one emotional extreme to another, I could imagine her having both interpretations in mind.

Was she about to take things one step further, like she must have done with Erica when she'd ended their sessions?

I stood by the window Rosie had escaped from. So quick. So unpredictable. Would she be waiting for me out there somewhere, ready to nudge me off the platform as a train came in or push me into the path of a bus?

Would she?

I picked up my pillow and tugged off the pillow case in a bid to clear away any lingering trace of her.

Wretched woman! How dare she burst her way into my life like this?! How could I shake her off once and for all?

At that point, my thoughts swung to an image of Rosie's room in the Lakes and the book that lay open on her bed. Now I thought about it, it wasn't just the book about soulmates that unnerved me. There was something else.

I pictured the leaflet I'd noticed for a takeaway pizza place – she'd used it as a bookmark. There'd been a scribble on the logo, but not just any scribble, I realised.

It was a specific doodle.

A sketch of a little ladybird, in fact, and I knew exactly where it had come from. It was one of Miranda's tiny creatures. She was leaving a trail of them behind her wherever she went these days, on napkins, tube tickets, receipts, shopping lists. It meant only one thing. Rosie had been near Miranda. Too near for my liking.

Ah. The penny dropped. The anonymous note about the baby – now I knew who'd sent it.

They *knew* each other.

How much had Miranda told her? A shiver ran across my shoulders making my teeth chatter. Did Miranda know what Rosie was capable of?

I tried Miranda's number, but she wasn't answering. That in itself wasn't unusual. I braced myself to leave a message, but instead it rang and rang and finally cut off. Now *that* was unusual. I felt a queasy lurch inside my stomach and called again. This time the phone went straight to an automated message which said: 'It has not been possible to connect your call…'

What? I rang Con's number without a second's hesitation.

'Where are you? Is Miranda with you? Is she okay?'

'Whoa… hang on, slow down, Sam.'

'Where is she?'

'She's painting at her flat – she wants to get a canvas finished and needs to be on her own.'

'When did you last speak to her?'

A breath of silence. 'This morning sometime. What's going on?'

'She's not answering her phone. Her voicemail was switched off a minute ago, now I can't get through at all. That's really odd, don't you think?'

There was a huff of annoyance. 'I think you're overreacting. Miranda's been great lately, her new medication has really settled her. She doesn't want to be disturbed, that's all.'

'It's not *her* state of mind I'm worried about,' I said. 'Has she mentioned someone called Rosie to you?'

'Rosie? Not that I know of. What's this about?'

'Has she mentioned any new friends? Has anyone new been hanging around lately? A woman with red hair – no, a woman who looks a bit like me – actually, a *lot* like me? Dark straight hair, in a bob?'

'Doesn't ring a bell, but she meets lots of people at the Arts Project.'

'It's one of my patients, I think she might have taken a shine to Miranda, but she's not stable, she's…' I didn't know how to end the sentence. 'We should go round to Miranda's flat and make sure she's okay.'

'Sam, I've got a rehearsal in twenty minutes,' he said wearily. 'You'll have to go on your own.'

'I'm worried, Con. I'm serious. This woman might have…killed someone.'

He laughed. 'Might have? Did she or didn't she?'

'The police don't know yet. It's not a laughing matter.' I hurried into the hall for my coat. 'I'm going over to Camden myself, then,' I said and cut him off.

For once I really hoped Miranda would lay into me for disturbing her. At least then I could be sure she was alive and kicking.

There was a light on when I arrived at Miranda's flat, which was a good sign, but no one was answering the door. On the way over, I'd thought again about my conversation with Con and the way I'd started to describe Rosie. Gradually, over time, she hadn't just been altering her appearance, she'd been making herself look more and more like *me*. The busy ginger hair now straight and dark, the weight loss, the contact lenses, the stylish clothes. With someone else, I might have been flattered, but this made me freak me out even more.

My mind raced back to something Mrs Willow had said just after Christmas, as Rosie left my flat after an appointment. 'Is that your sister?' were her words, as she watched Rosie drift off down the stairs. I'd laughed it off at the time, putting it down to failing eye-sight, but Mrs Willow had been spot on. 'She looks just like you,' she'd said. Now I saw the significance, it was seriously creepy.

I pressed the bell five more times and heard it

trilling loudly inside the hollow recesses of the hallway. I ducked down and pushed open the letterbox to peer inside. I smelt a pungent mix of linseed and oil paint, but couldn't hear a sound. I pushed the door hard to see how much it budged. When Miranda was home, she only left the latch in place and the door shifted a fraction at the top and bottom. Under my weight it didn't move at all, which meant it had been bolted. She only ever did that when she went out.

There was one more test to try. I angled my head over to the left, so I could see the coat rack. Miranda's winter coat had gone, but what really freaked me out was the pale blue scarf that was hanging in its place. It was *mine*. The one I'd noticed was missing recently.

Rosie had been here.

I spun round, reeling in panic. Was Rosie with Miranda? Where had they gone? They could be anywhere.

It was a long shot, but I frantically pressed the buzzers for the flats either side to see if anyone else was around. There was no reply from one side, then I heard a sash window slide open above me. A man in a string vest shouted down.

'Bugger off,' he called out. 'I ain't buying nowt.'

'I'm not selling anything,' I shouted, standing back on the edge of the pavement so he could see I was empty-handed. 'I'm looking for Miranda Willerby from number three. Have you seen her today?'

He clucked as if I'd offended him and I thought he was going to slam the window shut. 'Artist lady?' he said unexpectedly.

'Yes. She's my sister.'

'You don't look nowt like her,' he said. 'She's blonde and cute and—'

I cut across him. 'Have you seen her?'

'Yeah, as it happens. She was with someone. They went out.'

'Man or woman – can you remember?'

'I dunno. Wore an anorak with the hood up, but they was shorter than her boyfriend, so it wasn't him. I've seen 'em before. Carrying paintings in and out.'

'Anything else? From the other times you saw them, maybe?'

'Na.' He folded his arms. 'Whoever it was wore black, that's all. Oh – and one of them was carrying a bag with cats and dogs on it, as they left. I remember that.'

Cats and dogs?

Of course.

I asked the million-dollar question. 'You don't know where they went, do you?'

He was right to laugh; it was stupid to ask. 'To the moon, honey. How would I know?'

I thanked him and raced off to the high street.

That's when a thought occurred to me that chilled me to the bone. Surely, the best way for Rosie to hurt *me* would be to target someone I cared about: Miranda.

Chapter 46

Rosie

We're sitting on the floor. I've got one arm around her neck and I'm playing with her short yellow hair. The colour is too fake for my liking and when I scrunch it with my fingers, it's stiff and spiky. Not like Sam's hair. Hers is soft and glossy. I've only managed to touch it once, when she hurt her ankle in the woods. She leant on me then. She needed me.

Miranda doesn't push me away. Her head is lolling forward and her arms are limp. She's like a worn-out puppy, all floppy and sleepy. Must be something to do with the sedatives I swapped for her tablets earlier.

I know she's got mental problems; that's what her tablets are for. She told me all about it one time over a coffee; she's touchy-feely and candid, like a lot of people with mental disturbance.

I've seen her in Camden a few times, 'accidentally' bumping into her in the café she likes and dropping by the Project, pretending to be interested in her paintings. She's my new 'friend'. She even invited me back to her flat to look at some pictures and that's when I saw the bottle of tablets. It was lying in her handbag; she'd left it open on the floor next to a grubby bean bag.

I'm jealous of her flat. The downstairs is one big open space where she paints, socialises and watches telly, all in one. There's a dark chunky dining table at one side and a settee that looks like it's been dragged out of a skip, in front of the fireplace. She doesn't seem to 'do' carpets – everywhere is just floorboards and she wanders around in her bare feet. The first time I was there, she got a splinter on the sole of her foot – it was the perfect excuse for me to pretend to take care of her. It fitted nicely into my plan.

This time, when she went to the kitchen to make me a coffee, it was the simplest thing ever to pretend to scratch my ankle and switch the bottles. She's either too trusting or plain stupid. Fancy leaving your bag open like that right under the nose of a virtual stranger?

She knows nothing about me. Nothing real, anyway. I've fed her a pack of lies so far. She's obviously completely taken in by my 'interest' in her work and because she's seeing pound signs she's bending over backwards to be nice to me, but I can see right through every sweet sigh.

She wants my money, that's all, she doesn't actually like *me*. She asks token questions about my life, but I can see from the way her eyes wander when I answer that she's not really listening. Not like Sam. Sam watches my face when I speak and her eyes reach into mine; she's genuine, warm. *She's* the one I'm really interested in.

I always wanted a sister. All those lonely days when I was growing up, stuck in a room with only my viola for company. I never learnt how to make friends. Never went to Brownies or Guides or after-school clubs. Everyone thought I was sickly and feeble, but it wasn't my fault. Mum and Dad made me stay at home when I was little, rather than let me get involved with other kids. Then, after I lost them, I was always dumped with the wrong families. No one ever really cared – not until Sam.

I let the sound of her name echo inside my head. She's the light of my life, although now she's pushed me away, I'm decidedly confused.

Miranda moans and tries to lift her head. I stroke her cheek and she's quiet again.

'So, what can you show me?' I said to her earlier, as she came back from the kitchen with hot drinks.

She busied herself spreading out canvases against the wall for me to see. They were all dreadful – I wanted to laugh, it was so embarrassing – but she looked genuinely proud. She really is off her trolley. It explains why Sam is patient and such a good listener, though, she's had to put up with Miranda's crazy behaviour ever since she was a kid, poor thing.

'I quite like these,' I said, pointing at two pictures under the spiral of her staircase. 'But they're…' I made her wait, then straightened up. 'Are there any more…?'

'Er…not here.'

'Ah…oh, well…' I clapped my hands together, making it look like I was ready to call it a day.

'I've got more at the Arts Project, though. I could show you, if you want to pop over there now?' She hooked a question in at the end, painfully eager.

I looked at my watch doubtfully, then nodded. 'If we go straight away,' I told her. 'I need to get to work for the late shift.' I wanted to get things moving, didn't want her snatching the chance to let anyone know where she was going.

That's when we legged it over to the building where she exhibits. Miranda talks a lot and it's so easy to get stuff out of her. The Project is a place for so-called artists, but they're all a bit sick in the head with issues like anorexia, abuse, psychosis and stuff. Not her words, obviously, but that's what she meant. This is their sanctuary; they come here to get therapy and to express themselves.

The classes have finished for the day, the café is empty and everything is closed up, but Miranda has a bunch of keys, which is handy. They don't give them out to everyone, she told me, but as she's regarded as 'reliable', she's allowed to work in the ground floor studio out of hours and leave unfinished work in the storeroom in the basement. That's where we are now.

It's cold down here and there are tiny high windows so it's gloomy, but there's no one else around. Even the cleaners have been and gone. Miranda's been drivelling on about why she paints what she does, telling me all kinds of yucky, personal stuff about her past that I don't want to know about, but I've been encouraging her so she'll talk about Sam. I only listen properly when she brings her sister into the conversation; it's like she's ushering Sam into the room with us.

I've been noticing the similarities and differences between the two of them. Miranda does this thing where she purses her lips, like she's looking down at you. She's more brash and outspoken than Sam. Sam's sweeter, gentler, and she's got sparkly grey eyes that change colour like quicksilver. Sam's stylish, she wears floaty, feminine clothes like a newsreader, but Miranda is more like a student; too much denim and cheap jewellery. Tarty, if you ask me. They're not at all like sisters, you'd never guess they were related.

Before she went all woozy on me, I probed Miranda with questions.

'Have you seen your sister lately?' I asked, making it sound like I was just trying to make small talk.

'Oh, not much,' she said, pulling canvases out of the taller stackers and leaning them against the wall. 'She interferes – tries to be my mother. I know it's because she cares, but it gets on my nerves.'

All I could think was how perfect that would be: a sister and mother rolled up into one! How could Miranda not appreciate that?!

'She's always on my case,' she added with whine in her voice. 'She hardly wants to let me out of her sight…'

Talk about ungrateful! That makes me really angry. It's perfectly clear that Miranda isn't worthy of her sister. Sam deserves wholehearted devotion, someone she can rely on. But that's where I come in. I'd appreciate Sam – I really would.

'Your sister is a very special person. You don't deserve her.' It came out before I could stop myself.

'You know my sister? How do you know Sam?'

'Oh, I *love* this one,' I said, ignoring her questions, standing back from an ugly mess in swirls of purples and greens. I hated all of them.

'Really?' she said, her voice rising with glee.

I made her wait as I thumbed my lip and tipped my head from side to side, pretending to mull it over. 'I'm trying to think whether this would work in the reception area...' I muttered. 'Have you got anything with a bit more blue in it?'

Miranda busied herself searching through more canvases, before she had to sit down on a small folding stool, suddenly weary as a wave of tiredness washed over her.

The sedative I'd given her earlier took a firm grip on her after that and the little she's said since has been slurred and incomprehensible; she sounds drunk.

We've stopped looking at the paintings and since she can't stay upright on the stool, we've been side by side on the dusty floor. It's cramped in here and no one's going to come in unless they've got a key and they're looking for a specific painting.

'Do you think we all have a soulmate?' I say. 'Not necessarily a lover, but someone who totally accepts us for who we are?'

'Mmmm.' Her breathing has slowed and her eyes are flickering shut.

I take hold of her hand. 'Well, that's Sam and me. I've known it almost from the moment we met. It was meant to be.'

Miranda groans a little and tries to sit up, but flops back against the wall.

'I've been bursting to tell Sam how I feel for weeks, but I've never had the courage. It's fate – don't you see? The crash was terrible, but it brought Sam and me together.'

'Crash...?' she mumbles.

I cradle her chin between my thumb and fingers and

she can't do much about it. She feels like plasticine. I can do anything I want with her. 'People wouldn't understand. If we tried to explain it, they wouldn't get it.'

She makes a funny noise that sounds a bit like. 'W-h-a-t?'

She's bleary-eyed now and tries to get up; she makes it onto all fours and sinks down again.

I carry on, ignoring her. 'Sam and I are going to make a pledge to each other.' Miranda responds with a half-hearted grunt. 'We're going to seal our relationship. I'm going to tell her exactly how I feel and we're going to make a pact to be together.'

She stops and fixes her eyes on mine, only they won't stay in one place and they slip up under her eyelids. 'We'll be soulmates, blood-sisters – whatever she wants.'

My fingers begin a swirling pattern on her neck. 'We'll take a blood oath together, then we'll share everything; we'll have no secrets from each other. We'll be like family.' I feel my mouth fall open in awe at the idea of it. '*Family* – just think. I know there's no one special in her life. That's because she's been waiting for me, she just didn't know it.'

'Help me…p-lease…' Miranda wriggles and tries to get up in a burst of animation. She pats her hand against the pockets of her jeans, then beside her on the floor.

'No phone, I'm afraid. I'm looking after that for you.'

My bag is out of her reach.

I look around the room. It stinks of turpentine and linseed oil. All rather flammable, I would have thought. I glance up at the ceiling.

'Good job there's a smoke alarm,' I tell her, 'with all these combustible substances around the place. Must be a bit of a fire risk.'

There's a fire extinguisher by the door, but no sprinklers, I notice. 'I'll check the alarm still works,' I tell her, hopping onto a box.

She's in no fit state to lift her head to watch me unclip the battery and slip it in my pocket.

We won't be needing that.

I squat down beside her on the floor. 'I don't think you've been a good sister,' I tell her. 'I reckon you've got a lot to answer for, personally.'

Chapter 47

Sam

I tried Con's phone again as I reached the main road, but it was switched off; rehearsals must have started. I was furious with him. Why hadn't he taken me seriously? He'd probably have a better idea of where Miranda had gone. He could be helping to track her down. If anything happened to Miranda because of this, I'd never forgive him.

As soon as her neighbour mentioned the canvas bag, snatches of conversation started clicking together in my head. A while ago, Miranda had said a woman from Battersea Dogs and Cats Home had bought one of her paintings. Could that have been Rosie, all those weeks ago, lying through her teeth to get close to my sister? What else had Miranda said about that woman? I wished I'd paid more attention.

There was no point in aimlessly wandering the streets of Camden hoping to come across the two of them, so I stepped inside the first wine bar I came to and sat on a barstool at the window with a small brandy.

I made myself think back to that conversation. Miranda certainly hadn't mentioned Rosie's name, but the coincidence was too great. Miranda hadn't been at my flat for ages, so how else could my blue scarf have ended up in her hall? It *must* be Rosie that Miranda's neighbour had seen.

I swirled my glass and took a sip, letting the brandy burn my throat. Then I went back to what Miranda had said on the phone. I remembered now. She'd said she was excited about the possibility of getting an agent…and something else…about the woman from Battersea Dogs and Cats Home wanting to 'see more'.

That was it. Suddenly, I had an inkling as to where they might be.

I abandoned the unfinished drink on the window ledge, pushed past a man reaching down to pick up a pound coin from the floor and dashed out into the street towards Camden Lock.

When I reached the gates of the Community Arts Project, it was all locked up. I shook the gates in frustration, but they didn't budge. Everything was dark and still inside, there were no lights on anywhere.

I bolted around the corner to the Urban Shack Café and asked everyone in a stripy red apron, if they'd seen Miranda.

'The Project closes at five,' said Shontal, 'unless there's a special event.' She sprayed disinfectant onto the table beside me and leant forward to wipe it. 'No one will be there at this time.'

'Is there any way to get inside after dark?' I asked, shouting against the loud off-beat thud of the Reggae music.

She shrugged, shaking her head. 'We don't have keys.'

Dezzie came over carrying a sausage roll for a

customer. 'You could try round the side, near the back of the café,' he said, his mouth right by my ear. 'Someone's left an old chest of drawers in the alleyway. I spotted it the other day. Climbing on that'll probably get you over the wall, but you won't get any further. The building's usually locked.'

With that I was on the run again, back to the Project. I followed the fence until it joined a brick wall at the side of the property; half way along there was a shadowy gap. I didn't like the look of it, nor the smell of it one bit, once I got there. The street light only lit up the first few feet and beyond that there were only jagged, undefined shapes.

As I edged forward, I came across a discarded tumble dryer, some soggy cardboard boxes, an abandoned kid's tricycle. Dezzie was right; piled on its side at the end was a sideboard without drawers. I clambered onto it and hoisted myself up so I was sitting on the wall. From there the only thing to do was jump.

It seemed an awfully long way down to the tarmac on the other side and there was nothing to break my fall. I was worried about hurting my sprained ankle, but with the image of Rosie with Miranda uppermost in my mind, I turned round, gritted my teeth and inelegantly half slid, half fell letting my right foot reach the ground first. I narrowly missed a pile of broken bricks and apart from a few scratches, I was fine.

A security light came on as I approached the back entrance, but there was no movement and, as Dezzie predicted, the door was bolted. I ran around the whole building trying every door, but the outcome was the same. I pressed my ear to the glass at the front, but there was nothing.

I'd got it wrong. They weren't here.

In my rush to find Miranda, I hadn't even thought about getting out again. I hurried back to the spot where I'd hit the ground, searching on the way for an industrial waste bin or something big to push against the wall.

Then, out of the corner of my eye, I saw it.

From a tiny narrow window at ground level – something bright was bobbing from side to side. Not a light, but something flickering – a flame!

The place was on fire.

Chapter 48

Sam

I called the fire brigade straight away, then grabbed a brick from the pile by the wall and bolted back to the building. Standing as close as I dared, I hurled it at one of the smaller windows on the ground floor, not thinking, or caring, about shielding my face from the shards of glass that flew back at me.

From there, I followed the smoke down the stairs to the basement.

When I burst into the storeroom, the heat hit me like a scalding tornado. Curling and swirling billows of smoke were everywhere, making me double over in a coughing fit.

'Miranda?!' I croaked, barely able to see through the choking clouds.

A figure came at me, her hands on me, shoving me back towards the doorway.

'Stop!' she screamed. 'You don't understand, you're spoiling everything. This is for *us*! This is so *we* can be together. Not *her*. Just you and me.'

Wild flames leapt across the ceiling, crackling and roaring.

'No! Not like this, Rosie. Where is she? Help me…'

Rosie looked confused and ducked down, disappearing into the swelling smoke. I reached out to grab her and caught hold of her jumper, but she pulled away. I wrenched the scarf from my neck, took a deep breath and wrapped it around my mouth. Then I dropped to my hands and feet and crawled after her.

I was so blinded by the smoke that I couldn't tell if my eyes were open or closed. I went headfirst into something – an easel or ladder – and changed course, flinging my hands out around me, feeling for Miranda. I found only empty frames and scorching tins of paint that burnt my gloves. I knew she was here. She had to be here.

By now the heat was phenomenal. It tried to scorch my eyebrows and stung through my clothes. I had to turn back, I had to get out – but I couldn't leave Miranda. This was all my fault. I should have realised sooner. I had to find her.

Orange lights flashed under my eyelids and everything hurt. My clothes stuck to me, cooking me, like tin foil. I used my last ounce of air to call Miranda's name, but it came out as a muffled wail through my thick scarf. It was no good – my lungs were bursting, I had to go back. I threw out my hand in one final attempt to find her and turned round.

Then I knelt on it. Miranda's foot. I felt the sole of her shoe, traced it up to her leg.

'No - No!' Rosie was pulling me away.

'I can't leave her!' I spluttered back at her. 'Do this for ME, Rosie!'

I tore away from her clutch and found Miranda's shoulder. I felt my sister's hair, touched flesh, an arm, her fingers, but the flames had already reached her, licking around my hands. I grabbed her as best I could and pulled, dragged, tugged her towards the door, the thick plumes like knives, slicing and cutting my chest with every snatched breath.

As I humped Miranda's body over the threshold, I ripped off my coat and flung it over her, patting and rolling her to smother the remaining flames that were trying to take hold.

Rosie was still inside. She seemed to be searching for something. It would have been so easy to reach out and slam the door, but I couldn't wash my hands of her completely. Once I'd left Miranda somewhere safe, I'd have to go back for Rosie.

I hauled Miranda to the foot of the stairs and carefully peeled away her coat. The remains of her clothes were full of huge holes where red, moist bulges of skin had burst through. As I tugged the scarf from my mouth a violent surge of nausea made me want to look away.

'I don't care about the baby, and you being with Con,' I shouted at her. 'I just want you back. I can't lose you…'

I rolled her gently onto her back and forced myself to look into her face. Her eyelashes were crisp, her lips cracked and split. She looked strangely peaceful. I knew in that moment that she was dead – I just knew it – she hadn't moved an inch of her own accord since I'd found her. I had merely pulled her away and put out the flames; I hadn't saved her.

In a last-ditch effort, I tried mouth to mouth, but as I knelt down and touched her cheek, a hand grabbed my hair from behind, and I heard a crack. A sharp pain in my neck made me crumple and my legs went from under me. Then the darkness wiped everything away.

Chapter 49

Sam

Rosie's sing-song voice came out of nowhere.

'Dad must have been really angry that day...when he saw the suitcase,' she said, the sound drifting towards me from far away.

'Rosie...?' I croaked. I was sitting on a tiled floor, leaning against something blissfully cold. The pedestal of a sink.

'That must have been the point Dad made the decision to do what he did. With the air rifle. Something inside him must have snapped, just like that.' She snapped her fingers.

'Miranda...where is she?' I murmured.

My head was still on fire, throbbing, fit to burst. I coughed and reached up to rub the back of my head where she'd hit me, but Rosie grabbed my hand, securing it in her own.

'Let's not talk about her,' she said. 'It's just you and me, now.' She spoke as if we were in the middle of a conversation, winding a clump of my hair around her finger with her other hand.

'The fire. Have they put it out? Where's the fire brigade?'

Rosie's face was blackened with soot. She stared blankly ahead towards the men's urinals, but in her mind she was obviously somewhere entirely different.

'Had Dad always planned to hurt my mum, do you think?' she said.

'I d-don't know,' I said. The air was still churning with wafts of smoke. Everything was spinning and I felt like I was going to throw up any second. 'Is the fire out, Rosie? What are we doing in here?'

'It's safe. Everything's fine,' she said, her tone offhand.

'We should get out,' I said, straining to lean forward.

She shoved me back against the wall and a wave of giddiness forced me to stay still.

'Not yet. This is important.' She stroked my fingers tenderly. 'Why, after he'd shot her once, did my dad carry on shooting her another fourteen times?'

Never-ending bloody questions. Would they ever stop?

'M-maybe he didn't really know what he was doing,' I replied vaguely.

'Mmm…' she said. 'I think he must have known she was dead after the first few pellets, don't you?' She followed a ridge of grouting around a tile with her finger, her other hand still held firmly over mine. 'Why didn't he shoot me?'

'Because he wasn't angry with you,' I said.

She stared straight ahead, taking a long while to process my response.

Rosie had always seemed fixated on her father, dismissing any attempts I made to remind her that from her own accounts it was clear that her mother truly loved her. As that young child, however, it was her father she'd been desperate to win over. His love seemed to matter more to her. Maybe, because he was harsh and cruel she thought his love was worth more.

'Do you ever have that feeling when something snaps inside, when your heart boils over and you don't know what you're going to do next?'

I hesitated. 'Once or twice, when I've been...very upset.'

'Yeah...me too.' She patted the floor, like a toddler in a sandpit. She turned to face me. 'Did you lie when you said you were fond of me?'

Dangerous territory. I kept hearing the name Erica inside my head, like a distant mantra.

'I *do* like you, Rosie.' I straightened slightly, trying to get my good foot into a position where I could lever myself upright. 'I haven't been lying to you.'

'The weird thing is – it feels real,' she said. 'The way you take an interest in me, listen to me, seem to understand about my life.'

Being with Rosie was like holding a harmless sheet of paper in your hand and realising it's cut your finger. I knew she was capable of turning from sweetness and light to downright aggressive within a single sentence. I was vulnerable after the crack on the back of my head. I needed to keep her stable, pull her back from any emotional extremes, any rash actions.

'It *is* real...' I assured her.

'So why didn't you get *me* out of the fire?'

'You didn't need my help!' I snapped. 'In any case I was *going* to come back and check, but you *hit* me...'

'You only pretended to like me because I'm a patient and I'm paying you, that's it, isn't it? For a while

I thought it was going to be real, but you're just like everyone else.' Her fingers were on my face, gently tracing the folds of my eyelids, before she trailed them down my cheek.

I cleared my throat, ducking away from her touch. 'I genuinely feel a great deal for you – as a patient I want to support.'

With every word I uttered, I was reinforcing all Rosie's worst fears. She'd put me on a pedestal and now I was coming crashing down. Was this what happened with Erica?

'Don't you like the way I've been helping you?' she asked.

'Helping me?'

'Dusting and cleaning your flat. I wanted to make it nice for you.'

'*Excuse me*?! You copied my keys,' I retorted. 'You were breaking in.'

'Only to help. Like a fairy godmother.'

'Were you ringing my landline, too, Rosie? Were you calling and not speaking when I picked up the phone?'

'Oh, that,' she said dismissively. 'I was just finding out if you were at home or not. I didn't want to barge in…you know…it was just to check, that's all.' She brushed her nose with the cuff of her sleeve. 'And I told you the truth about Miranda's baby. That was a nice thing to do, wasn't it?'

I shook my head. In her mind she had an innocent explanation for everything.

There was a rustle by my feet as she delved into a bulging canvas bag – the one Miranda's neighbour had said Rosie was carrying. That must have been what she was searching for in the storeroom earlier. The handles were scorched and it was covered in ash.

'By the way, I solved one of the mysteries,' she said, her hand inside it.

I waited for her to explain.

'The fortune that was "under the bridge", remember? Well, I was right to keep asking questions, I was just looking under the wrong sort of bridge. It wasn't a bridge on the landscape. It was much closer to home. Let me show you.'

She drew out a mass of splintered wood and twisted strings.

'Your viola?! Oh, Rosie, it's completely ruined.'

'I know. I got very cross when I found out.' She blew her fringe into the air with a heavy breath. 'But there's a silver lining to the story. You know the little arch that holds the strings up? It's called a "bridge"', she pointed it out. 'I should have realised. That's where the fortune had been hiding all along. Just here, look…' She showed me a tiny envelope taped to the back of a piece of broken wood.

'Open it,' she said.

I thought it was empty at first, but when I tipped it up a small scrap of paper fell out. An old black stamp.

'Who'd have thought it?' she went on, 'Hidden inside my worthless viola!'

'But how…how did..?'

'It was after Mick Blain gate-crashed our rehearsal in 2001. When I dashed off to get Max to fix my viola, he must have put it there.' She shook her head at the audacity of it. 'I mentioned his name to Dawn and she found out all about him from her colleagues at the auction house. It turned out Mick had lived a very colourful life fencing stolen instruments before he'd moved on to coins and stamps. The whole "wanting to play my viola" thing was all an act. He must have known exactly what he was doing. He staged that stunt purely to get hold of it as a hiding place.'

She showed me the small f-shaped hole Mick must have squeezed the envelope through, when he knew the police were on to him. It looked like it would have been an intricate procedure, but perhaps not if you'd done it before.

She held up a scrap of wood. 'The tiny envelope would have been invisible to everyone, even me, and we were so concerned about fixing the viola that no one spotted it. You remember Max said there was a label inside and I laughed at him? Well, it must have been this little envelope. I thought no more about it at the time, I was just glad my viola was back in one piece. Dawn told me a stamp in the same series sold last year for a million dollars.'

Rosie's lost viola. It was worth all her trouble in the end, although not in the way she expected. It had a hidden surprise for her.

'I knew I had to get my viola back. It was my friend, my voice, my place in the world even though I couldn't play like I used to. I was gutted when I found it smashed to pieces, but I didn't expect this bonus!' She guided the mess of strings and wood tenderly back inside the bag. 'This extra gift my viola had kept secret for me all this time.'

She stroked the bag, a dreamy look on her face.

'Richard's brother, Greg, caused the crash, by the way,' she added with a sigh. 'He was after Max's violin. He took my viola, too, because he thought it might be valuable, but of course, in itself, it wasn't. He didn't know about the hidden fortune.'

I was still trying to process what she was telling me when I felt something cold against my neck. I swallowed hard as she ran the point of a blade down to my throat.

'Rosie, stop…'

She must have had it in the bag.

'This is how we can be joined together, Sam,' she said. 'Just two little cuts – I've seen people do it in films – then we let our blood run together. It won't hurt – well, maybe just a bit.'

I lay still, frigid with fear.

'Rosie, don't, this is dangerous.'

'Lovely skin,' she cooed. 'Where do you think we should be joined, Sam? You choose.' She pressed the point into the skin behind my ear. 'Here?'

'Rosie, you're hurting…'

'Yes, I know. But love does hurt sometimes, doesn't it? Here?' She ran the blade flat across my cheek.

How many seconds before she broke the skin? Rosie was in a bubble of her own; deranged, capable of anything.

That's when I heard the sirens.

Chapter 50

Sam

Rosie scrabbled onto her knees in front of me, the knife under my chin – it trembled as she started to shake. She'd heard the sirens too.

I had to act quickly. *Think.*

I was no match for her physically with my damaged ankle and swimming vision and I'd only make things worse if I tried to fight back. Instead, I needed to call on all my experience with disturbed patients to forge my way out of this, before the sounds of rescuers in the building made her panic.

There had to be something; a clue tucked away in her childhood, on that day her life was turned upside down when she was seven, perhaps.

I took a chance. 'I need to ask you something,' I said, trying to keep my voice even.

'What?' The knife was tickling my throat.

'On that terrible day…your father could easily have turned the air rifle on you, like you said…'

'I know. Maybe he ran out of pellets.'

'No. I looked at the reports online and there were pellets left. The report said the rifle was capable of firing twenty shots, one after another.'

'So, there were five pellets left…'

'That's what it said.'

'Hmmm...' She was breathing into my face.

The sirens were suddenly deafening, then they stopped.

I had a sudden flash of inspiration. 'You said your father didn't love you, but did it ever occur to you that he loved you *too much* to take you with him?'

She drew her face away from mine. 'What do you mean?'

'Well, if he'd taken you with him, you would never have had the chance grow up or enjoy a life of your own. Taking you with him meant condemning you to everlasting darkness and he *didn't want that.*'

She examined my face, taking in what I'd just said.

'He had five shots left and he couldn't bring himself to rob you of your life,' I said. 'He couldn't take away your chance of happiness. He couldn't do it to you.'

'Because...because...'

'Because he *loved* you. Because he couldn't bear to make you suffer.'

'But...I thought it was because he didn't want me enough to take me with him.' She spoke slowly, examining her words as they came out.

'No. That's how a seven-year-old would understand it. You saw it as pure rejection back then, but in his own way, in the only way he knew – your father was protecting you.'

'So, you're saying he stopped firing because he wanted to save me?'

'Exactly.'

Her face quivered with doubt while she considered it.

In the next moment something lit up behind her

eyes. Suddenly the whole world wasn't the way she'd thought it was.

She stifled a sob. Then she gave herself up to it, letting everything out with an ear-splitting howl, like an animal. Her body shook in spasms as she clung to me, wailing helplessly.

'It's okay,' I whispered as I wrapped my arms around her. The knife was still in her grasp. I could hear the thuds and shouts in the corridors getting closer.

'So, he *loved* me...' she gasped. 'That's what you're saying, isn't it?'

'Yes, he *did* love you in his own way. And he couldn't bear to pull the trigger to end your life.'

'Oh, God – I never realised...'

Sometimes therapy was like that. Life-changing breakthroughs could burst out into the light in the blink of an eye, smashing open lifelong misconceptions.

Rosie wept again, grieving for all that could have been, drowning in the realisation that for years she'd seen every memory of her childhood through a distorted mirror.

I closed my eyes, worn down and weary, contemplating the hours she'd spent feeling hurt as a result of the far-reaching damage her father's actions had caused.

As she finally relaxed, still leaning against me, the knife slithered to the floor. I kicked it under the waste basket and waited for the door to open.

Outside, I pulled away from the paramedic as she tried to wrap me in a blanket and make me sit down.

Miranda's charred body was being trundled away on a trolley and I needed to be by her side. There was a mask over her mouth and a paramedic was taking her pulse.

'But she's…she's…' I said.

I needed to tell them they were wasting their time. I wanted them to leave her in peace.

'We're doing all we can,' said one of medics, with a sympathetic smile.

'I know…but it's too late…' I gripped the edge of the stretcher as they lifted her up into the ambulance. Miranda was just a shell now, her eyes were closed, her body having shut out the rest of the world forever.

'Please…leave her alone…she's gone…let her be.'

I wanted to drag her body into my arms, but I had no strength left. They would take her away and from this moment on, for the rest of my life, I'd be without her.

It seemed impossible. Not my sister. Not after all she'd been through. All that sparky, crazy, adorable spirit that made Miranda such a huge part of my life.

I grabbed hold of the door to the ambulance. It was all I could do not to sink to the ground in a crumpled heap.

Then came the most miraculous words I'd ever heard.

'Stand back. Her pulse is weak, but she's alive.'

'What?!' I stared in amazement, flooded with disbelief and elation at what I'd thought was my sister's lifeless face. 'But she…she wasn't…'

'Come on…climb in,' the woman said, giving me a hand up. 'She was so heavily sedated that she probably couldn't respond when you found her.'

My hand was over my mouth. I couldn't utter a word. Beside her in the ambulance, I cried my heart out. I really thought I'd lost her.

As Miranda was wheeled away to begin her recovery, I was being checked over in A&E. I didn't have concussion, just a throbbing bruise on the back of my head, a few cuts on my face from the broken window and a nasty cough from the fumes, for a few days.

Over the next few days, Con and I took turns to sit by Miranda's bedside in intensive care. We watched her damaged body writhe and squirm as the sores and blisters raged under their dressings. Her eyes stayed shut, while machines helped her breathe. There were problems with her respiratory system, thermal damage and pulmonary irritation, but the doctors were optimistic about her recovery.

During those hours, my hurt pride and resentment about my sister being with Con melted away for good. What really mattered was that Miranda had the chance to live her life to the full and be happy – and I was grateful beyond belief that I had her back. It was clear Con really cared about her and I had to admit they appeared to share more of a connection than he and I ever did.

She didn't stir for hours at a time. Then, on the third day, she suddenly let out a faraway moan. After that she muttered in her sleep, whispering funny little phrases such as 'sequin feathers' and 'fountain lady'. She was coming back.

Part of me wanted her to stay where she was, in some dreamy promised land. I knew that as soon as she woke up she'd feel terrible pain. All the same, I felt blessed that I was there when she opened her eyes. She asked me what time it was, then said, 'I could murder a sausage roll.'

Chapter 51

Sam

I'll never know how it happened, but when the fire officer had finally helped me up from the floor of the gents' toilet at the Arts Project, Rosie was nowhere in sight. Only the cats and dogs canvas bag was left lying on the floor. She'd managed to slip away from the scene of the crime once again.

The police had called me in that same day. They'd assured me Rosie's time was up. They were convinced that the new evidence put her well and truly in the frame for Erica's death. The scuffs on the stairs matched damage to a pair of Rosie's boots and a local window cleaner had come forward to say he'd thought Rosie was Erica's home help, as he'd seen her let herself into the house more than once. It was all there, it just needed piecing together.

The police assured me Rosie couldn't go far. In her rush to get away, she'd left her credit cards, her phone and another mobile I recognised as Miranda's in the canvas bag. Rosie only had what she was carrying in her pockets. They'd launched a 'manhunt', confident she'd be in custody in a matter of hours. They promised to ring me the moment they brought her in.

If Rosie went back to her flat in Streatham the police would stop her, they said. She didn't even have the keys to get in – they were also in the bag, next to a set of my old ones.

Still inside the bag, too, was the smashed viola and the rare stamp. She hadn't even taken those precious things with her.

I couldn't work out whether Rosie had left the bag with me for safekeeping or abandoned it for good. She must have known the police would be closing in on her. They were now keen to question her about Greg's death, too. It was the end of the line for her.

Nevertheless hours turned into days and still I didn't get the call.

If I'd learnt anything from this experience, it was that sometimes, with the best will in the world, you can't save everyone. Likewise, even the best psychologist in the world can't always predict what people will do.

I finally needed come to terms with this where Joanne was concerned, as well as with Rosie. I wasn't a mind-reader and could only do what I thought was right in any given circumstances. Perhaps, too, I had to learn this same lesson on a deeper level with Miranda.

One thing was certain, I needed to be kinder to myself. Grant myself some slack. I had to grasp that sometimes my best would never be enough.

Once Miranda was discharged from hospital, I returned to my flat feeling like I was coming home from a gruelling expedition through the desert. My bones ached; I was knackered from spending hours in a plastic hospital chair, propping my eyelids open at Miranda's bedside, and I was emotionally wrung out.

I thought I'd lost my sister.

With indentations still visible on my neck from Rosie's knife, I'd been lucky to get out in one piece, myself.

When I let myself in, I stood with the door ajar and listened. Rosie had only ever had my old keys, so she couldn't possibly be inside, but even so, with Rosie, you could never be entirely certain.

I waited a while, heard nothing, then shut the door. I dropped my bag on the sofa and went straight to bed. I crawled the duvet without undressing, but sleep didn't come. Instead, I lay staring at the map of cracks on the ceiling, mulling over the pieces of the puzzle that had snapped into place, following my interview with the police.

I'd told them what I knew about the stamp and the smashed viola Rosie had left behind and it linked up to their interview with Karl Hinds after the crash. They told me that when the police raided the Hinds' property in 2001 and Mick Blain had made a run for it, Karl was the first one to get to him on the forecourt after he fell from the drainpipe. In his dying breath, Mick had muttered something about Rosie and a 'fortune under the bridge'. Karl didn't have a clue what it meant at the time, but during the quartet's second visit, something must have clicked.

It made sense. During one of my sessions with Rosie, I remembered that she'd mentioned Karl asking the quartet if they were each playing the same instruments, during the second visit, as they'd had in 2001. He wanted to make sure Rosie had the same viola.

Karl also admitted to the police that he'd made a call

to one of his associates about Rosie's 'fortune'. That must have been the phone conversation Rosie remembered hearing the day of the crash. It was the stamp Karl was after when he followed the van, that afternoon. Only it plunged into the lake before he could get his hands on it.

I pulled the duvet up tightly under my chin and followed one of the cracks from the light fitting all the way to the wall, trying to figure out where Rosie might be and what she was up to.

Who would she turn to? How long would it be before the police caught up with her?

Chapter 52

Rosie

Dear Sam

I'm at London Bridge Tube station, near St Luke's Hospital, because I have a journey to make. I had to come here. It's the only station that has any proper connection to you. I need to write this letter, then I'll leave you alone, I promise.

Memories are fickle, don't you think? Greg accused me of being in on the plan to crash the van from the start, so he could get his hands on the violin amidst the mayhem, but hand on heart, I can't remember any plan. He had a map in my handwriting, but I could have drawn it afterwards. I can't believe I had a hand in it. I'd never have risked all our lives, never have risked losing my viola in order to steal Max's violin. Besides, I would never have come to you – to get my memories back, would I – if I'd been involved?

Although, I hate to admit it, but his story kind of makes sense. I won't believe a word of it, though, unless I get those memories back – the ones of the conversations I'm supposed to have had with Greg. Only you're not there to help me with that, are you? So I don't see how I'll ever really know.

Anyway, Greg paid the ultimate price. You might have heard he was stabbed and I'm afraid to say I was the one who did it. I know it wasn't my place to pay him back, but he really did ask for it. You wouldn't have liked him.

The police have stopped looking for Richard now. I meant to tell you. I think he's lost forever. Strange, isn't it?

Now, to the real reason I'm writing to you.

I tried very hard to be the sort of person I thought you'd like, Sam - the kind of person you'd want as a sister or best friend, but I can see it wasn't enough. You don't feel the same way. I know that now. To you, I was only ever a patient. I wanted so much for us to be together, for you to be my soul-sister, and now I know that isn't going to happen.

I'm sorry for the way things ended. I didn't mean to frighten you – but everything was going so wrong. Erica once said I was like two sides of a coin; I could flip between loving a person to hating them in no time at all. I think I know what she means – I'm a bit like my dad, don't you think? What happened to Erica was a terrible shame – she caught me unawares and I'm afraid I panicked. It was unfortunate, I admit, but I wasn't attached to her like I am to you. I'm sorry I had to keep it from you. I wanted to tell you about it, but I knew it would only have come between us.

Sorry for the other things too. I didn't set out to hurt Miranda, I just wanted her out of the picture so we could be together.

When you revealed the truth to me about my dad, you gave me the BEST gift I've ever had in my life. Did you know that? What you said about him makes the world of difference. It means I can forgive you, in the end, for not wanting to be my friend. It means I can forgive my dad and let go of all the rage and hurt I've felt, thinking he didn't want me.

Knowing my father actually LOVED me, after all – it changes everything. I thought he didn't love me enough to take me with him when he died but, like you said, he loved me TOO MUCH to want to end my life. Wow – what a revelation! I didn't know therapy could be so powerful. I can never thank you enough for that.

Anyway, my gift to you is inside the canvas bag. Who would have thought there were two mysteries to solve at the Lakes – the violin Greg stole and the stamp Mick Blain would have come back for, if he hadn't fallen to his death? You can sell the stamp, keep it or give it to the police – whatever you like. I don't mind. It's yours.

I've thought about what to do next, long and hard. My first thought was to go and find Mum and Dad. That's why I came to the station. I was going to wait for a train so I could make that special, final journey to see if they'd have me – second time around. To see if we could start again.

But I've changed my mind. I'm going to do the right thing, instead, and hand myself in to the police. I've told them I'm on my way.

That's where you come in.

I've told them you'll vouch for me. I think once they know the whole story, they'll understand. I didn't set out to hurt anyone, after all. You know that, don't you?

The police will want to be in touch with you soon, no doubt, so you can explain everything. I know you'll do your best to make them see that I'm a good person.

I know I can count on you, Sam.
I will love you always.
Rosie XX

~

Coming soon from AJ Waines

Perfect Bones

(Dr Samantha Willerby Series – Book 3)

When art student, Hayden Blake, witnesses a murder on a London towpath, the police need him to identify the killer without delay. But there's one problem: refusing to leave his canal boat and traumatised by the shock, Hayden has been rendered mute by the horror of the event and can't speak to anyone.

In a desperate bid to gain vital information before Hayden's memories fade, The Met call in trauma expert and Clinical Psychologist, Dr Samantha Willerby.

When Hayden finally starts to communicate through his art, the images he produces are not what anyone expected and before Sam can make sense of them, another murder takes place. With her professional skills stretched to the limit, Sam strives to track down a killer who is as clever as she is – someone who always manages to stay one step ahead.

The third book in the Dr Samantha Willerby series, *Perfect Bones* is a tense and creepy Psychological Thriller that will send your pulse racing.

For updates, join the Newsletter:
http://eepurl.com/bamGuL

Printed in Great Britain
by Amazon